BROKEN TRAILS

D JORDAN REDHAWK

BELLA
BOOKS
2013

Bella Books, Inc.
P.O. Box 10543
Tallahassee, FL 32302

Printed in the United States of America on acid-free paper
First published 2013

Editor: Medora MacDougall
Cover Designer: Stephanie Solomon

ISBN 13: 978-1-59493-389-9

PUBLISHER'S NOTE

Other Bella Books by D Jordan Redhawk

Sanguire Series
The Strange Path
Beloved Lady Mistress
Inner Sanctuary
Lady Dragon

Orphan Maker
Darkstone
Alaskan Bride
Freya's Tears
Lichii Ba'Cho
Pixie
Tiopa Ki Lakota

Acknowledgment

First, my apologies to the good people of Talkeetna in particular and Alaska in general. I plopped a fully fictitious dog racing kennel into a town and state that I've never had the fortune of visiting. With no basis in reality, I've taken the liberty of creating an Alaska that I've read about in several books over the years rather than portray the true one. Perhaps some day I'll be able to enjoy the bounty of natural wonders available to you on a daily basis.

Many thanks to the following people who spent time and effort reading the original chapters as they came hot off the word processor and into their email boxes: Anita Pawloski, Teresa L. Crittendon, Karen Speers, Jean Rosestar, Jeri Tallee-Dawson, and Linnet. Their comments and suggestions turned this debacle into a cohesive tale that I'm proud to have written.

Additional thanks go to Shawn Cady, for those moments when sparks should fly; Blayne Cooper for opportune suggestions, soulmate discussions and visions of pork chops; Kim Watson for an Alaskan reality check and the truth about life on the trail; and Ann Campbell for those niggling little details that I really needed to know.

In keeping with one of the characters of this book, I wanted to mention that Alcoholics Anonymous has been a wonderful support group to more people than I can count in dealing with their addictions. Look them up if you have any questions.

Dedication

This book is dedicated first to my wife, Anna Trinity Redhawk, who has supported me with proper encouragement when needed, ego flattening reality when appropriate, and sitting glazed-eyed through many one-sided discussions of a wintry race.

Secondly, it's dedicated to all the men and women involved in the Iditarod—The World's Greatest Race. Without your firm commitment to the sport of dog sledding, this novel would never have been written.

About the Author

D Jordan Redhawk lives in Portland, Oregon where she works in the hospitality industry. (But don't make the mistake of thinking she's hospitable.) Her household consists of her wife of twenty-four years, two aging black cats that provide no luck whatsoever, and a white buffalo Beanie Buddy named Roam.

For more information on D Jordan Redhawk, visit her website: *http://www.djordanredhawk.com*

CHAPTER ONE

March

"No!" Lainey Hughes closed her eyes; her voice took on a lecturing quality. "It's fucking cold, with huge glaciers, frozen lakes and hibernating bears. I don't do cold. The only ice I want to see is floating in my scotch, you follow?"

"I need you, Lainey." His voice sounded tinny through the ancient pay phone.

She leaned her forehead against the wall, the plaster cool against her forehead. "Why should I do this?"

"Because you love me?"

Her lips thinned as she did a passable impression of Marge Simpson's growl.

"Look, Lainey, it's not like Henry planned to slip off that bluff. The piece isn't done. I need coverage at the awards banquet on Sunday night."

"That doesn't answer my question."

"All right, you want the truth?"

Lainey fought the desire to wince at his grim tone. When he asked in such a manner, it was typically best not to hear the answer. Still, she rejected the thought of making it easy for him. She was free*lance*, not free labor. "Yeah."

"One, I need someone of the same caliber as Henry. Two, you're the best in the business. Three, you've just finished up a piece and are already in transit, making your travel plans easy to alter. Four, it's only for two days, and you know I'll compensate you damned well for your trouble. And five—"

She flinched in anticipation, knowing what he was going to say before the words left his lips a half a world away.

"—you owe me."

She thumped her head lightly against the wall. It had to be a pretty important layout for him to pull out that particular reminder. Hearing the motor of an approaching bus, Lainey glanced over her shoulder. Only one was due in today. If she missed it, she would be stuck in the African bush for another week.

"Lainey?"

She sighed in resignation. "Don't ever try to play that card again."

"I promise. I didn't want to use it at all." His voice lightened. "What's your itinerary?"

"Providing things go well, I plan on leaving out of Nairobi tomorrow, arriving at London International the following day, and then on to New York." She looked over her shoulder again to see the tattered bus idling on the dirt road. Most of those who had been waiting were already outside the Customs building, passing their bags and parcels up to several men precariously balanced on top.

"Fly into London. I'll leave a ticket to Anchorage at the British Airways desk. You can find a connecting flight into Nome when you get there."

Lainey scrabbled for a pencil and pad and jotted down the details.

"Henry's at the hospital in Anchorage. I've made arrangements for you to take over his room in Nome. When you get there, just go to the Polaris Hotel and tell them you're with the magazine."

"I'll be there." She stashed the pad and grabbed her gear.

"Thank you, Lainey. I swear I'll make it worth your while."

The last of the passengers had boarded the bus. The customs agent at the counter glared pointedly in her direction.

"Yeah? Next time I pitch an idea, buy it without bitching and we'll call it even." She didn't wait to hear his response before she hung up the phone. Checking that her camera bag still hung securely across her shoulder, she grabbed her duffel and ran into the hot Ugandan sun.

Relegated by her late arrival to a spot on the front floor of the bus, Lainey sat on the duffel and cradled her precious camera bag. The arm of the door mechanism periodically brushed the top of her head, but she counted herself lucky. At least she wasn't riding on the roof with some of the others. Elbows on her knees, she rested her head on her folded arms. Despite the constant sway of the transport and the swirl of native conversation, she was able to focus her thoughts on the phone call with her editor, Benjamin Strauss.

She'd only wanted him to know she had finished her current assignment, not that she was available for another. His goading her into the job meant he was under a lot of pressure. He probably didn't have anything to take the place of that article in time to make the next issue of *Cognizance* before it went to press. Lainey owed him her life. The least she could do was brave arctic weather for him. He had braved far worse dangers to return her to the living.

When she arrived in London, she would call her mother in Jersey and let her know their visit would be delayed. She would miss her lunch date with Carol, too. *Damn*. Lainey had so wanted to get laid and drunk. Living in the African bush while hunting small colorful birds for an upcoming spread left little opportunity for such considerations. The only things they grew in Alaska were sled dogs and polar bears; the women had to be beyond butch to survive the wilds and weather. Lainey preferred that her women look like women, not truck drivers.

Grumpily, she pondered what exciting and very tropical idea to pitch when she next met with Strauss.

* * *

Lainey stamped her feet in a futile effort to get warm, consciously ignoring the vague ache in her side. Her snowsuit—rated for a temperature of forty below—didn't work as well as advertised. She toyed with the idea of writing a letter of complaint to the manufacturer. They'd probably just send her another like it, the last thing she needed. She didn't plan to return to this dump.

Truth be told, she didn't actually have to be out there on the sidelines freezing her ass off. Her deal with Strauss was banquet coverage, nothing more. It seemed somehow defeatist to her to miss the finish, though. She was already there, she had the time and she had the gear. She might as well give the appearance that this was her gig.

A slight gust of wind riffled the edges of the fake fur ruff about her face, the frigid temperature at odds with the brilliant sunlight reflecting off snow. It felt weird—needing sunglasses at the same time she needed long johns. As she suffered, she entertained herself with thoughts of demanding a year-long assignment in the Mexican

Caribbean. She burrowed her hands deeper in her pockets. Why the hell did people want to live in places like this?

An air raid siren went off in the distance, the second blast in the last ten minutes, diverting her attention to the far end of Front Street where an incoming racer would soon make an appearance. As she watched, the sleepy street began to fill, doors opening to spill out people excitedly awaiting the new arrivals. When not outside to cheer on the mushers, the spectators sat around in the bars and restaurants, visiting. It was one big, happy party—a town-wide celebration that lasted a week or more.

Lainey reluctantly removed her hands from her pockets and took off the thick Gore-Tex mittens. Adjusting her camera for the upcoming shot, she ignored stabs of pain as her fingers began to freeze. She consoled herself with visions of a shimmering white sand beach, half-naked women and fruity drinks with little umbrellas sticking out of coconuts. Glancing through the viewfinder, she saw the flashing lights of the police escort nearing her position. Rather than lose her appendages to frostbite, she thrust her hands back into her pockets until she could get a decent shot. The gathering crowd began cheering the new arrival.

The excited swell of sound was louder than Lainey's rudimentary experience deemed typical. Abandoning the viewfinder to actually look at the approaching sled, she realized that two dog sleds were barreling down the fenced-in run, both drivers shouting encouragement at their animals for all they were worth. In a race that lasted two weeks or more, seeing more than one musher headed for the finish line at the same time was unexpected. The police car stopped where the fence began, so as not to impede the racers who dashed toward the finish. Lainey zoomed in on the dogs, her irritability overshadowed by her pleasure at being in the right place at the right time. Though she couldn't hear above the noise of the spectators, the animals barked and grinned as they ran, tongues lolling out in excitement. They looked pretty good for having run a thousand miles. She took a series of photos, pulling back her focus as the sleds neared and passed. For variety, she turned her camera on the audience across the way to capture their emotions.

As quickly as that, it was over. The teams reached the finish line, a carved wooden arch spanning the street, and several volunteers grabbed the dogs to halt them. The announcer called the names and times of the two mushers and reminded everyone that the awards banquet was that evening. Then the crowd melted away, returning to the warmth of houses, bars and hotel rooms until the call of the siren urged them into the street once more. Only a few remained outside to enjoy the bright, insubstantial sunlight.

Lainey knew from race reports that the next mushers weren't due for three or four hours. Her elation fading, the bad temper reasserted itself. With chattering teeth and numb fingers, she collected her gear. She stashed her camera inside her jacket to better protect it from the elements. There was a hot tub in her hotel. She planned on making full use of it before the awards ceremony. Hopefully that would soak the ache out of her ribs. Tomorrow she would be on her way to New York, affording Strauss the opportunity to show his thanks by buying her a bottle of Glenlivet and dinner at the most expensive restaurant in town.

Lainey slung her empty camera bag over her shoulder, musing over the shots she'd gotten. Hands deep in her pockets, she trundled off toward her hotel. She had a lot to do—upload the digital data to her laptop, fine-tune the photos, research the Iditarod public relations folder for the names of the recent arrivals, write a proper blurb and email it to Strauss. That all had to be completed before she could indulge in her ultimate destination—the hot tub.

Pondering her to-do list, Lainey didn't watch her step. One minute she was walking on slush created by the salt and sand used to aid traction, the next her foot hit a patch of solid ice. She yanked her hands from her pockets as she slid about, making a comedic attempt to remain upright, flailing her arms to keep balance. Gravity won the battle. She barely had time to clutch her camera to her chest before landing on her rump. She grunted, ribs jarring with the impact.

"Whoa! You okay?"

"I'm fine!" Lainey snapped. Performing the perfect pratfall was never enjoyable; having witnesses made matters worse. She tried to stand, only to return to the ice with a thump and another grimace. Hands grasped her upper arms, and she was hauled up like a sack of potatoes.

"Those shoes aren't made for this terrain."

Exasperated, Lainey lashed out. "Well, thank you for that shrewd observation." She pulled away from the hands still holding her, double-checking the camera through her jacket. Belatedly, she looked up at the person standing before her, and her mind stuttered to a halt.

The woman wasn't that old, maybe a handful of years younger than Lainey. Taller by about four inches, her build was hidden beneath a blue bulky pullover parka that matched her eyes. The fur-lined hood had been pushed back, revealing a rust-brown baseball cap and tawny golden curls. Her ruddy, weathered skin seemed an incongruity to Lainey, who assumed women in the North would have pasty complexions from being inside all winter. Something about her stance intrigued Lainey, radiating subtle confidence most women her age didn't possess.

The friendly smile was already fading in light of Lainey's acerbic attitude.

"I'm...I'm sorry." Lainey wished she had developed the habit of thinking before opening her mouth. "Thank you for the help."

The woman seemed mollified, but the smile didn't return. She nodded politely and stepped away, returning to whatever errand she had been on prior to running into a klutzy photojournalist with bad manners. Only then did Lainey realize the woman wasn't alone. A teenager with a hint of peach fuzz on his upper lip gave her an apologetic shrug and followed his friend. Not knowing what else to say, Lainey watched them walk away.

She shivered, the ache in her ribs reminding her that she was in Alaska—where the men were tough and the women even tougher. As she trudged toward the hotel, she wondered why God would be so cruel as to taunt her admittedly overactive libido with a gorgeous woman like that.

CHAPTER TWO

Lainey sipped a club soda at one of the press tables at the awards banquet. She wanted scotch, but she made it a habit to never drink in the field. There would be plenty of time for that when she returned to civilization. She had struck up a rudimentary friendship with the other journalists at her table, pleased that no one recognized her name. Unlike her, they were enthusiastic supporters of the Iditarod, inclined to focus more on local or sporting news than global or environmental issues. Many came out here every year to slog through snow and blizzards to distant checkpoints and that elusive interview. Most were newspaper reporters with steady jobs in the northern states or Canada. It didn't make for much common ground between them and her.

There was a natural level of animosity between the regular joes and the freelancers, so Lainey had expected the gentle cold shoulder she had received. She supposed it would have been more rabid had this not been Alaska. One thing she'd noticed was how they all watched out for one another. It gave rise to a small town ambiance, even though several thousand people lived in Nome. The only other freelancers following the race were a pair from Norway and a half dozen Japanese seated at other tables. In both cases, the language barriers and the level of interest in their subject were reasons enough to keep them apart.

She was able to breathe easier after her long soak, but her attitude hadn't changed much from the afternoon. Her decided lack of enthusiasm clouded the air around her, yet another reason for her peers to keep their distance. She placated herself with the weather report she had received from the front desk. Tomorrow was going to be bright and sunny, meaning that her plane would be leaving out of the airport on time in the morning. That would be followed by the drunken binge she had planned for herself when this gig was complete. She silently toasted her good fortune with the last of her soda and ordered another from a passing waitress.

The other reason for her attitude was the woman she had met on the street. Lainey had tried everything she could think of to shake the memory, but the beauty helping her to her feet remained firmly lodged in her brain. Unable to pry loose the thoughts of her, Lainey had chalked it up to her dormant sex life. She couldn't wait to get back to New York to relieve the itch with her friend Carol.

Things picked up onstage. In response, the spectators quieted and the reporters became more active. Lainey gave her camera a final once-over. A handful of photographers jockeyed for position on the dance floor in front of the podium. Rather than fight for the prime real estate, she moved to one side, giving her a clear shot of the audience and a three-quarter profile of the current Iditarod president as he began his speech. She had a fifty-fifty chance of catching the award winners as they came past her to the stage. If they chose to enter from the other side, she would get a full frontal shot as they approached the dais. Later, there would be a posed photo shoot while the scheduled dancing began.

The winner of this year's race, a ramshackle man with a droopy blond mustache, chose to head to the opposite side, pleasing Lainey. No doubt many others would follow his lead. This afforded her an advantageous position, and she used it well.

Using her small photo notebook, she jotted down the names and awards as the mushers passed by. The big winner won the grand prize—a check for sixty-nine thousand dollars and a new diesel truck from a local dealership. Rather than bore her editor and his readers with all the prize details, Lainey stopped photographing after the fifth-place winner accepted his prize. She checked her digital readouts and readjusted for the upcoming round of special prizes.

"Tenth place...Scotch Fuller of Fuller Kennels! Twenty-eight thousand dollars!"

Scotch? Who'd name their kid Scotch? Intrigued, Lainey searched the audience for the owner of such a moniker. A table burst into rowdy cheering at the announcement, several members of the party seated there standing as they clapped the mysterious Scotch on the back. Lainey half expected the man to be as drunk as his friends appeared to be. It was a couple of moments before she realized the tenth-place winner was a woman, and she wasn't drunk. When the prizewinner got to the base of the stairs and into the lights of the stage wash, Lainey's mouth dropped open. It was the woman who had helped her to her feet that afternoon, the one who stubbornly refused to leave her thoughts.

Without the parka, she looked even better. Jeans and a rose-colored turtleneck sweater revealed a lanky form that held more than a hint of femininity. Her hair was short and curly, like Lainey's, but the stage wash sparked it into golden fire. She had a brilliant smile on her face as she accepted her winnings, along with a handshake from the Iditarod president. Then she spoke into the microphone, thanking her family and sponsors.

With a start, Lainey aimed and shot, allowing the automatic shutter to keep collecting data as Scotch finished her speech. Lainey, completely enamored, didn't return her focus to her surroundings until the digital camera ceased operating. With a curse, she examined the readout to discover she'd used up the entire data storage disk. She fumbled another from her pocket but didn't replace it quickly enough to get a close up of Scotch leaving the stage.

The rest of the night passed in a blur of photo ops and reveling. Knowing the job came first, Lainey got the required interviews with the top three placers. It didn't help that they all reminded her of second graders. *Can anyone out here speak proper English?* Her mind simply wouldn't allow her to focus, constantly dragging her attention to one particular table.

Disgusted at both her lack of control and her inability to get more photos of the intriguing Scotch, Lainey was almost relieved when she saw the Fuller celebrants leaving the banquet. At the same time, she had an abrupt urge to follow them, properly introduce herself and thank Scotch again for her assistance that afternoon. Instead she scowled and downed her soda, yearning for the burn of alcohol in her throat.

* * *

Late that night, after her final installment had been sent to Strauss, Lainey sat in the dark of her hotel room. The only illumination was her laptop display. She had taken the consecutive photos of Scotch Fuller and strung them together to create a rudimentary movie. She sat at the desk, chin in her hands as the impromptu collage played in a continuous loop.

What kind of person was she? Was her name real or a nickname? Did she have a boyfriend? A husband? She had to be a strong person. Winning tenth place in a thousand-mile dog sled race wasn't something to sneeze at. She was the highest-placing woman this year too.

An Internet search had turned up some interesting facts. Scotch was twenty-three, and this was her third Iditarod and her best time overall. This year she had also won the Leonhard Seppala Humanitarian Award for the care she had given her dogs during the race. Would she make another Iditarod attempt next year? Did she have what it took to win? And why the hell would a beautiful woman want to torture herself by racing dogs?

Most intriguingly, where had she acquired such self-assurance and poise? She was a kid who was born and raised in the boonies, yet she carried herself with a level of confidence Lainey had only seen in ancient matriarchs of a variety of cultures around the world. Since the advent of the women's liberation movement, a lot of women in America held themselves in a similar way. If feminism had made such great strides in the Alaskan brush, however, why did the front desk clerk routinely refer to Lainey as "little missy"? Scotch seemed to carry a lot of weight with the men around her, more an equal than a "woman." It was only natural that Lainey would find the subtle authority exciting.

She closed her eyes, the light of the display flickering against her lids. Despite her blindness, she still saw Scotch sharing a smile with her. Her thoughts took her to other, more intimate questions as her fingers began to stray along her body.

What does she taste like?

* * *

"You're kidding." Lainey stared at the man seated across from her.

Benjamin Strauss' incongruous tan contrasted with his business suit and well-trimmed salt and pepper hair. It proclaimed him an outdoorsman, though his clothes and demeanor screamed "corporate executive." Having spent several years in multiple countries on shoots with him, Lainey knew him to be more the former.

"Nope. Dead serious." His iced tea and half-eaten plate of linguine had been shoved aside in favor of a manila folder. Spread open on the table, it disclosed the final proofs of the article she had assisted with in Alaska. He looked up from the paperwork. "This could be a killer series, and you're the best. I think it could net us both a lot of money."

Lainey shook her head, more in annoyed confusion than to turn down the offer. Ben was much more than an editor with whom she negotiated gigs and pay. They had become fast friends since their early days, the intervening years tightening their bond. The only drawback was his recent conversion. For some God-awful reason, he had convinced himself he was an alcoholic. And he had been harping on her to attend AA meetings with him ever since. For the moment, he had ceased expounding on that particular subject, hardly batting an eye at the glass of scotch at her elbow—her third.

"You don't think so?"

"You're publishing an Iditarod article this month and you want to do a series piece on it now? You'll saturate the market and lose money, Ben."

He tapped a finger on the layout between them. "No. This is a three-page spread on this year's race, more a visual tidbit than informational. I'm proposing that you follow a musher from sign-up in June, through training and preparation, and on the race itself. It could be pulled off as an in-depth portrayal of an up-and-comer. It'll be published in quarterly installments, beginning this summer. I've already got the backing of my senior editor."

Lainey frowned at him, gauging his enthusiasm. He seemed determined. He probably had some marketing information to which she wasn't privy. *What do I know? I'm just the grunt.* She sipped her drink, sighing in contentment as it burned its way down her throat. "Look, I went there to help you out but I'm not looking for a repeat performance. Especially for...what? Nine freaking months? Find somebody else."

"What if I hire you as a temporary employee of the magazine? That'll put you on the payroll with a monthly salary."

Lainey squinted at him. "What?"

"I can have a contract drawn up this afternoon. You'd have a solid gig for a year—steady salary, medical benefits. Best of all, you get the next two months off."

A monthly salary was a luxury every freelancer lived without. To have a year of guaranteed income meant a year's rent paid on her tiny flat in Jersey, bills from her recent trip to Africa paid off and future expenses covered without having to finagle money out of her contract holder. Two months of hard partying wasn't a bad incentive, either.

She shook her head. *I am not considering this ridiculous idea.* She opened her mouth to say no, but what came out was, "Which up-and-comer?" *What the hell did I just say?* Strauss' satisfied grin made her scowl at her glass.

"You tell me." He leaned closer. "You got an up close and personal look at these fellas. Any of them catch your eye?"

The image that popped into her head was of a blonde woman, smiling graciously at the audience as she accepted her tenth-place winnings. Lainey casually relaxed in an effort to disguise her sudden interest. "I don't know. Scotch Fuller comes to mind."

"What makes him so special?" Strauss shuffled through the folder for a list of final standings.

"The fact that she's a woman, for one—young, photogenic. This was her third Iditarod, and she's improving consistently with each experience. Talk is that she's got a good shot at winning next year, all things being equal."

"A woman?"

Lainey felt her hackles rise at his tone. Not that he didn't have cause for his suspicions, considering why she had introduced Fuller's name into the discussion. *You aren't going to take this gig anyway*, she reminded herself. *Nine freaking months!*

When she didn't answer, he continued. "A good looker, no doubt."

"She's not bad on the eyes," Lainey granted. Before he could take his insinuation further, she sat up and thrust out her chin. "It's not about that."

Strauss feigned innocence. "About what, exactly?"

Scoffing, she said, "It's not about a roll in the hay. I really think there's a story there." *Wait a minute… What am I doing?*

While she puzzled out which side of this debate she was supposed to be on, he said, "What about the cold? I know how it messes with your ribs. You're not going to do either of us any good if you're too wracked with pain to get out in the field."

At the reminder of the legacy of her injury, she forgot her intentions and gave him a scornful expression. "Come on. It's been years since I've been anywhere that was below forty-five degrees. I admit I ached some on this trip, but it wasn't as bad as I'd expected."

His examination remained focused upon her, as if he sensed the falsehood.

"Oh, please. No piece of ass is worth that amount of aggravation. She's straight."

That seemed to pacify him, his wary expression fading. "All right. What about copyright?" Ever the journalist despite being an editor for a magazine, he pulled a small leather notebook from his breast pocket and began scribbling.

"Stays with me." Her answer was automatic, distracting her from the voice in her head reminding her she wasn't interested in this gig.

He looked at her from beneath his brows. "As much as I understand your end of the business, Lainey, we both know my bosses aren't going to let that fly."

She stared out at the street in thought. The rain had stopped, though the sun remained muted by the clouds overhead. *Still early enough to get a head start on that two months of paid vacation. Holy shit, am I going to do this?* "Okay, you retain copyright of what I send you. But I reserve the right to not send everything. The salary pays for three full pictorial and written articles and nothing else."

Strauss pursed his lips. "Sounds fair. I know you won't stint on the articles." He wrote down the specifics. "Let's get back to my office and have the Legal Department draw up a contract. As of this afternoon, you'll be an official employee of *Cognizance*."

As he gathered up the paperwork, Lainey felt numb. *I guess I'm doing this.* She downed her whiskey. Its fire lit her gut as she stood to don her jacket. *I'm really doing this.*

* * *

Lainey peeked back into the room as she eased the bedroom door shut. Her friend Carol was splayed naked across the bed, snoring. When the door blocked her view, Lainey turned the handle to close it without noise. Once safe from waking her evening's entertainment, Lainey inhaled and stretched with lazy abandon. Nude, she padded into Carol's living room. She ignored the open curtains, not giving a damn if anyone in the building across the way saw her. She'd be gone to her flat in the morning. Besides, anyone finding her attractive had to be a freak, and there weren't many of those who could afford this neighborhood.

"Now, what the hell was I going to do?" She surveyed the room, hands on her hips. Bottles of beer, scotch and champagne littered every surface, evidence of her welcome home party. Her clothes had been discarded with reckless lack of constraint, as had Carol's. Lainey half expected to see a bra hanging from the ceiling fan, since the place looked like the aftermath of a frat party. All she needed to complete the picture was a jock passed out in the corner.

She spied her luggage near the door, and her focus sharpened on a white legal-sized envelope sticking out of her camera bag. Snagging it, she flopped onto the couch to study the contract. A year. She'd signed on with a magazine for a goddamned year. At the rate she was going, she might remain gainfully employed for the rest of her career.

She snorted. *Like that's going to happen! You'll always be a freelancer.* Sobering, she reached for the nearest bottle. She swallowed champagne and grumbled at the unexpected bubbles. They didn't stop her from taking another swig.

As soon as Strauss had cut her a check for the African and Alaskan gigs, she had bailed his office in search of Carol. Now that she had covered both getting drunk and getting laid, it was time to consider what she had done. *A year. Nine freaking months in Alaska! What the hell was I thinking? Christ!*

She saw Scotch Fuller in her mind. *That's what I was thinking.* Lainey tossed the contract aside and let her head drop back onto the couch. For several moments, she daydreamed about spending nine glorious months getting to know Scotch better—much better. When her fingers brushed against the sensitive scar tissue along her ribs and abdomen, her fantasy bubble burst. "You're going to Alaska to spend— at minimum—six months in the frigid cold to watch a beautiful straight woman train and compete in a thousand-mile dog sled race."

Amorous thoughts put firmly in place, she considered the gig with fresh eyes. Of course, no one had contacted Scotch Fuller to ask whether she was interested in having a nosy reporter hanging about. That was Lainey's task since the gig was hers. If Scotch turned her down, the whole thing could fall apart before it started. The last thing Lainey wanted to do was sacrifice a year of her life to hang out with some smelly mountain man.

Lainey stood, setting the champagne bottle on the coffee table. It took a few minutes before she found her pants, then her cell phone. Returning to the couch, she calculated the time difference between Alaska and New York. As she dialed Information, she wondered whether Scotch Fuller even had a phone. A half hour later, she had learned that Scotch didn't have a phone, listed or otherwise. There was one for the Fuller Kennels in Talkeetna and another for a veterinarian's office in the same town. She scribbled both numbers on the white envelope and stared at them a moment.

It had been a couple of days since the awards banquet. Would Scotch have arrived home yet? Where was Talkeetna in relation to Nome? Scotch had come in tenth place this year, so she'd have had time to recuperate from the days on the trail before the dinner. Lainey stared at the phone numbers. Her gut told her it was too soon. She would wait a couple of days, give Scotch time to get back home and rest up.

"Speaking of scotch…" Lainey reached for a half-full bottle.

CHAPTER THREE

April

Lainey hung up the phone. It took three attempts, but her hangover-fogged reflexes eventually allowed her to find the cradle. Strauss' angry tone still buzzed in her ear, jangling tender nerves. She couldn't blame him for being pissed off. It had been three weeks since she had signed that damned contract. He had a right to a progress report. It was her misfortune that she had been on a bender since her return to civilization.

"Ugh." She rolled over, almost falling off the couch. *Christ. I didn't even make it to the bed last night?* An attempt to sit up brought on a round of vertigo. She decided to forego any unnecessary movement for the immediate future. As she waited for the room to cease its spinning, she closed her eyes.

Several hours later, she woke from her nap, better equipped to deal with the logistics of standing. It took two tries before she made it off the couch. She staggered toward the bathroom and a shower, stopping once to grab a shot of alcohol to fortify her.

When she came out of the bathroom, she wrinkled her nose at the musty, sweaty aroma of her flat. She threw open a window, shivering as the chill night breeze washed over her. The added ventilation didn't do much to dispel the odor, but at least she'd made an effort. She spent the next several minutes tidying. Finally, her stalling tactics exhausted, she stood in the center of the living room, staring at the phone. The envelope with the scribbled phone numbers sat beside it, a constant reminder for her to get a move on. It had been much easier to reach for the whiskey bottle.

"It's just a fucking phone call." Reaching for the receiver, she quickly dialed the first number on the envelope. Only after the phone was ringing did she think to consider the time difference. Slightly panicked, she checked the clock on the DVD player and did the math. *Eleven eighteen. So…five hours, a little after seven their time. Should be okay, right?*

"Hello?" a gruff male voice asked.

Great. Not Scotch, that's for sure. "Hi. I'm looking for Scotch Fuller. Do I have the right number?" Lainey leaned against the arm of the couch.

"I don't recognize the voice. Who is this?"

Lainey frowned. It was an odd question for a wrong number, so she must be calling the correct place. "My name is Lainey Hughes, sir. I work for *Cognizance* magazine. And you are?"

"Oh!" There were muffled voices on the other end. "Sorry, didn't mean to be rude. I'm Thom Fuller, chairman of Fuller Kennels. Scotch has already gone off to bed."

At seven o'clock? Lainey couldn't fathom the idea of a twenty-three-year-old American woman going off to sleep at this hour on a Saturday night, no matter where she lived. Still, Lainey didn't want to struggle through another bout of nerves to call back in the morning. Latching on to Fuller's-puffed up title, she said, "Chairman, huh? Is Scotch an employee of yours, so to speak?"

"Board member."

Lainey grinned. *Board member. There's a laugh.* "Ah." She relaxed into the conversation. "Then I guess I can speak to you, since she's not available. My magazine would like to do a three-issue article on Scotch, beginning this summer. We'd like to follow a musher from sign-up in June, through training and qualification and on through the Iditarod. Do you think this is something she'd be interested in?"

Again he spoke with someone nearby. "Sorry, do you mind if I put you on speaker phone?"

"Please do."

The voice on the phone became thinner. "So, you want to follow Scotch through the entire training season and race?"

"Yes, that's the plan." Lainey wondered who else was listening to the conversation. "The magazine has authorized me to pay ten thousand dollars in room and board for the season, and I'd want to work as a handler."

"Ten grand?" He seemed impressed. When he spoke again, it was to whomever was with him more than to Lainey. "That'd pay her entry fee this year."

"Excuse me, Ms. Hughes, is it?"

This was a woman's voice. "Yes, ma'am. Please call me Lainey." Dear old Mom? *Wonder if she's a board member too.*

"Lainey, it's a pleasure to meet you. I'm Helen Fuller, Scotch's mother."

Bingo.

"Scotch doesn't usually race the Iditarod in consecutive years," Helen continued. "I have to admit that's primarily due to finances. We'd have to run this by her and get her input before we could say yes or no."

"I completely understand, Mrs. Fuller. I'm just getting the ball rolling here to see if there's a possibility of our working together."

"Have you talked with any other mushers?" This from Thom.

"No, sir. This is my first phone call." *And hopefully my only phone call.* "Scotch has an impressive record for her youth and experience. I'm actually hoping to catch a first-place winner next March." She grinned at their pleased chuckles. "I have to get back to my editor about this by the end of the week, however."

"Not a problem," Thom said. "We'll see Scotch in the morning and have a board meeting. You'll have your answer by the afternoon."

"Great! Let me give you my number." Lainey finalized the arrangements for the return call and hung up the phone. "I think that deserves a drink." Strutting into the kitchen, she grabbed a fresh bottle of her favorite liquid and cracked it open.

CHAPTER FOUR

Scotch Fuller doled the last of breakfast into Idduna's bowl. Ignoring the food, the dog gazed at her with adoration. Dropping the feed pail, Scotch lavished a thorough scratching on her teammate. Only then would Idduna attend to her meal—a mixture of dog chow, rice and hot water.

Around Scotch, the rest of the kennel ate with healthy greed. Her brother and sister had finished feeding their sections and were threading through the canine population toward the dog kitchen. She joined them there. Engrained by years of habit, they didn't speak as they continued their daily ritual. Nine-year-old Irish collected feed pails to rinse out and store inside the barn. Scotch and her brother Rye pulled the fifty-five gallon drum off of the barrel stove where it doubled as a huge pot. Rye rolled it outside the kitchen area for cleaning. Scotch hung the stir "spoon"—a snow shovel—on a hook. She threw sand across the floor to soak up spills before sweeping the concrete floor clean.

As she worked, her thoughts remained occupied with Idduna. The dog had gone into heat a week into the Iditarod. It had been a considerable distraction to the team and had cost them a higher finish in the race. Using a lot of creative management, Scotch had succeeded in keeping Idduna separated from the eager boys. When the race was over, she had allowed Sukita, one of her leaders, to breed Idduna. Scotch expected her to give birth by mid-May and was already contemplating the potential of the pups. Idduna was a solid dog on her team and Sukita one of the smartest leaders. He could sense a blown-out trail where most dogs would get lost. Scotch hoped the pups would inherit their sire's gift.

After Scotch finished sweeping, she and Rye returned the pot to the stove in preparation for the afternoon feeding. Irish gave the two large free-run kennels a cursory inspection. They apparently met with her approval, and she began transferring five dogs into each one for some playtime. Ten more would have an opportunity to frisk together that afternoon.

"Kids!"

Turning back to the cabin, Scotch saw her mother leaning out the back door.

"We've got a board meeting after breakfast today."

Rye waved acknowledgement. "Okay, Mom."

"Wonder what that's about." Scotch pulled two shovels from their storage pegs and followed Rye, who lugged a plastic trash barrel out to the dog yard.

"Got me. I didn't expect a board meeting until the first of May."

"Me neither." They scooped excrement from around the yard, a nasty yet entertaining occupation as the canines did their level best to distract them. As usual, the dogs succeeded to some degree, receiving scratches and pats as the siblings worked their way through the crap left by ninety-five animals. Luckily, breakup hadn't yet occurred, making the chore less filthy than it would be with melt off and mud on the ground. That would happen within the next month.

"Maybe it's your adoring public." Rye grinned as he wiped sweat from his forehead with one arm.

A smile on her face, Scotch snorted and kept shoveling. "If my 'adoring public' will bring in money to sponsor me for next year, I'm for it."

"I hear you."

After the job was completed, they put things away and headed into the main house. Standing in even the minimal heat of the entry, Scotch felt the itching of sweat. She divested herself of boots, work gloves and jacket. Inside, the aroma of bacon and eggs filled the cabin. She shed further layers of clothing. After washing up, the family sat down to a big Sunday breakfast.

CHAPTER FIVE

Leaning back in his chair, Rye patted his belly in contentment. "That was wonderful."

Helen Fuller, clad in a pale blue bathrobe and worn slippers, put dishes in the sink for later washing. She wiped her hands on a towel. "Thank you."

Scotch passed, pausing to kiss her mother's cheek. Dodging two-year-old Bon who precariously balanced his silverware on his plate, Scotch divested herself of her dishes before scooping him into her arms.

"Sco'sh help!" Bon exclaimed as his older sister lifted him high enough to put his brightly colored plastic plate with the rest.

"Bon help." Scotch planted him on her hip, reaching for a washcloth to remove the sticky residue of syrup from his grinning face.

"So, what's up with a board meeting?" Rye added his plates to the others and ruffled Bon's white blond hair. "Is this about the phone call you got last night?"

Scotch returned to her chair. For the moment, Bon contented himself with remaining in her lap. "What phone call?"

"It came after you'd gone back to your cabin." Helen sat down, tucking a strand of graying auburn hair behind her ear. She retrieved a notepad and pen from the armoire behind her. "Shall we begin?"

Thomas Fuller nodded. He wiped his red mustache and beard with a napkin. "The Fuller Kennel Board of Directors is called to order. All members present and accounted for."

Scotch smiled. She had been a member of the board since she was Bon's age, when the kennel had come into existence. Her parents had legally incorporated it and, at the birth of each child, officially added a new member.

"Last night we got a call from a reporter for *Cognizance* magazine."

"They've just published an article about the Iditarod," Helen chimed in.

Both Rye and Irish looked at their sister. Scotch felt her face heat up.

"They want to do an in-depth piece on Scotch for next year."

Irish whooped, clapping her hands. Enjoying the enthusiastic atmosphere, Bon followed suit.

"That's fantastic!" Rye said when the celebration died down. "So, why the meeting? What's this got to do with the kennel?"

Thomas leaned back in his chair. "The reporter has requested to live and work here from sign-up until the race next year."

Scotch's innards swooped low. It was one thing to get decent publicity, opening avenues to sponsors to help defray the costs of the kennel and racing itself. *But to have a stranger living here? What kind of creep wants to keep me under constant surveillance?*

"Live here?" Irish wrinkled her freckled nose. "I'm not giving up my room."

"You won't have to."

Rye's eyebrows rose in anticipation. "I get to move into my cabin?" The property was large enough that several cabins and outbuildings had been erected over the years. As had been done for his sister before him, one was being built for his eighteenth birthday and official adulthood.

"Not at sixteen, mister." Helen's voice and eyes held a note of warning. Rye's face fell.

"Well, providing we vote to accept him, where's he going to sleep?" Scotch asked.

Her father answered. "He is actually a she, and your mom and I were thinking there's room at your place."

"What? My place?" *This is beyond creepy.* A tight band wrapped around Scotch's chest, constricting her ability to breathe. *I do not want a…roommate.* "Why my place?"

"She'll be here to do an article on you, honey," Helen said. "What better place for her?"

Unable to argue the logic, Scotch held her tongue.

"This reporter, Miss Hughes, she says the magazine will do a series of articles leading up to the Iditarod and through to the end of the race." Thomas rested his elbows on the table. "You know how tight money is. The magazine is willing to pay ten grand for room and board, and the reporter will work at the kennel on top of it. With this exposure, Scotch, you could get national sponsorship. Hell!" He slapped the table, causing the detritus of their meal to rattle and Scotch to jump. "You might even get the magazine to sponsor you!"

Scotch swallowed her dismay and considered her father's statement. Being intimately acquainted with kennel finances, she knew the truth of his words. The Fullers were well enough off to afford nice things, but that was in large part due to Fuller Construction, Thomas' business, and Helen's veterinary practice. Money from the kennel's earnings paid for racing fees, and they spent summers running tours and weekend adventures to bring in additional money to cover costs.

She weighed the absence of financial problems against the idea of some stranger living in her cabin with her. For months. It had been two years since she had shared living space with anyone. Did she want to repeat that disaster? Her recent meal sat in a lump in her belly. Bon squirmed in her grip, and Scotch realized how tightly she was clinging to him. Realizing that everyone was looking to her for a cue, she blushed, covering her embarrassment by jostling her baby brother. "What did she sound like?" She hated the pathetic tone in her voice.

Her father understood the true question. "She sounds like a professional young woman. She's excited about the idea. Apparently she was at the awards banquet, and that's where she came up with it." He gave his oldest daughter a serious look. "I think she's done her research and really wants to make this work."

"Regardless of the vote, you are the most affected," Helen said. "If you don't want to go through with it, Scotch, that's that. We can always shuffle people around inside the house here, if things get too bad."

Scotch scanned her family, chewing her lower lip. Understanding her reticence, her parents remained carefully neutral. In her arms, Bon clapped twice at the expectant feeling in the air. He made a dive for a slice of bacon still on the platter. She retrieved it for him and he nibbled the treat. Irish watched with wide blue eyes, twirling a lock of strawberry hair with one hand. They were both children, neither of them aware of the emotional turmoil Scotch was suffering at the thought of anyone living cheek by jowl with her again.

Rye understood. He had been there when…His eyes somber in remembrance, his facial expression all but yelled at her to accept the proposal. Not yet old enough to run the Iditarod, he had placed well in the Junior Iditarod the previous two years. Any national exposure for his sister would naturally shine on him as well.

The reporter would only be there a few months. Scotch would be so busy training through winter, she probably wouldn't even notice the woman's existence. The payoff would mean an easy season free from financial concerns, another run in the race without waiting a year to save up the money and the possibility of more income in the future. And if the roommate aspect didn't work out, the woman could bunk here at the house.

"All right. Let's vote."

"Those in favor of accepting Miss Hughes' offer?" Thomas asked.

Everyone around the table raised their hands except Bon. Seeing the movement, he grinned and waved his half-eaten bacon, almost swatting Scotch in the head.

"Whoa there!" Scotch forced a laugh and ducked out of the way. "You'd better put that thing away before you poke an eye out."

"Poke, poke!" Bon crowed at the attention.

"Meeting adjourned." Thomas stood. "I'm going to call that reporter and give her the good news."

Scotch watched him leave. Bon demanded down and slid out of her lap. Everyone else took her father's lead. Chores needed doing, even on a fine Sunday morning. She helped finish clearing the table.

Her mother leaned close, voice low. "I'm proud of you, honey. I know this decision wasn't easy for you."

"Thanks, Mom. It'll work out fine." Scotch heartily hoped for such an outcome.

Helen gave her a bracing hug, then moved away to the sink.

As soon as their mother was out of earshot, Rye said, "You won't regret it, Sis. This is a hell of an opportunity for you."

She risked a glance at Helen when he cursed. "Mind your tongue, or Mom's going to cut it off." He gave her an impish grin and sauntered away with a handful of plates.

Watching him, she hoped he was right.

CHAPTER SIX

May

Despite a hot shower and the requisite hair of the dog, Lainey still felt like warmed-over shit. A perpetual scowl creased her forehead, and the overhead lights seemed determined to pierce her eyes. The warm, welcoming ambience of the coffee shop left much to be desired with her brain leaking out her ears. She struggled with her umbrella in the doorway, shaking off drops of spring rain before folding it into its accordion-like form. It stubbornly refused to close, and she cursed, redoubling her efforts. She had about reached the point of throwing it out onto the sidewalk when it yielded to her superior will.

Lainey took a few steps into the coffee shop, scowling through her sunglasses. Ben Strauss stood and waved at her from a corner table. She gave a half-hearted gesture of acknowledgment in return. He looked far too cheerful for this hour of the morning. Grumbling, she went to the barista and ordered a weak peppermint tea. Her stomach wouldn't be able to handle much else. The clock behind the counter showed it was a little after ten. Good. *At least I'm not too late.* She couldn't imagine why Strauss would want to meet with her—she'd made the proper arrangements with the Fullers and had spent hours in telephone conversations with Thomas to get a better idea of what clothes to bring or buy. When not purchasing cold weather gear, writing packing lists or preparing to divorce herself from her life for the better part of a year, she had partied with a long succession of women. She had updated Strauss on every professional move. What more did he want?

Tea in hand, she took a deep breath and headed for his table. It took a moment for her dry, gritty eyes to notice a second man sitting at the table. Her frown deepened, though she recognized him.

"Lainey!" Strauss stood at her arrival, the other man doing the same. "Thanks for coming. You remember Don Howry?"

She set her cup down, shaking Howry's outstretched hand. "I do. It's been a while, though. How've you been, Don?"

He grinned. "Pretty good. Yourself?"

Lainey shrugged, forcing congeniality. "Not bad. Talk softly, though." She rubbed her temple, smiling as he laughed. They'd been on a few benders together in the past; he would understand the joke.

Strauss didn't seem to appreciate the humor but didn't comment as he gestured toward their seats.

When everyone was comfortably ensconced, Lainey eased her sunglasses off, subduing a wince. She hoped the eyedrops had done a decent job. When neither man recoiled in horror, she figured she had things in hand. "So, what's this about?" *Why couldn't you have called me on the phone or scheduled this at a decent hour? Like…midnight.*

Howry leaned back, turning his attention to Strauss with an air of expectancy. He, it seemed, had been informed of the meeting's topic. Lainey's eyebrows dropped into an anticipatory frown. Warning bells resounded in her already ringing head, an unpleasant sensation all around.

Strauss retrieved some files from his briefcase and opened them on the table. "My senior editor had a brainstorm about these articles this weekend. Things have…changed."

Lainey pursed her lips. Senior editors mucking things up. She sipped her tea, the hot liquid doing nothing for the acid bubbling in her stomach. "Define 'changed.' Why has Don been called in?"

"Liz wants a different focus for the main article." Strauss tapped one of the files. "Don's been hired to do a series of fluff photography pieces to back up your articles. Plus, we'll be using his stuff for television and print advertisements for the issues."

"So why call a meeting? You could have told me that over the phone, Ben." When he didn't immediately respond, her frown became a glare. "What's the new focus on the main article?"

Strauss sighed. "She wants the main article to be written from the point of view of a rookie training for and running the Iditarod rather than concentrating on Scotch Fuller."

Lainey's sluggish brain chewed through his words, trying to see the relevance. "So…what? I have to cancel the deal with the Fullers and find myself a rookie to follow?" A slow anger blossomed in her already burning stomach. She had only signed on for this job because she had talked him into using Scotch Fuller.

Before she could work up a full head of steam, Strauss held up his hands. "No! That's not it at all." She stared at him, one eyebrow raised.

"You're the rookie, Lainey. The magazine will provide an additional twenty grand to the Fullers, for a total of thirty thousand dollars room and board for you and Don, plus the fee for training you and letting you use their equipment. We'll toss in sponsorship money for you and Scotch and cover your placement and Iditarod fees."

Her stare became one of astonishment, both eyebrows meeting her hairline. "You have got to be kidding me." She slumped back in her chair, heart pounding.

"Nope." Strauss opened the manila folder, which turned out to be a dossier on Scotch Fuller. "We've done some research. You were right when you said she has a shot at winning the next Iditarod. Liz wants to center both articles on women. A professional woman musher with a shot at reaching the finish line first and a companion piece on a rookie woman musher on her first attempt." He spread the sheets of paper out in front of him, giving them his eager attention. "It would make for a killer series, especially if Fuller can pull off first place."

Lainey glanced wildly around the room, catching Howry's gaze. He gave her a faint shrug, and she almost heard his thoughts. *"Sucks to be you."* She grimaced at him. "What if I say no?"

Strauss deflated. He looked at her, an expression of resigned acceptance on his face. "I wouldn't blame you if you did. I'll admit that I railroaded you into this gig." He pulled another folder from his briefcase and handed it to her. "This is your contract with *Cognizance*. You can destroy it if you wish, no hard feelings. I'll see about digging up another gig for you, something a little less…involved."

She took the paperwork, mouth open. Her hangover-fuzzed mind had bolted to top speed and was furiously working through her options. She had spent nearly two months planning this fiasco—making the phone calls, buying the gear—and now he wanted to show her the door? *No. If that were true, he'd have canceled my contract outright. He's giving me an out.* She didn't like that any better. That meant

Strauss didn't think she could hack it, couldn't take the physical aspect of the gig, couldn't lay off the booze long enough.

He's got you there. Lainey stubbornly throttled the thought. She had been dreading the fact she would be nine months sober while doing this gig. It had been years since she'd been on that long of a stretch without alcohol. Strauss kept asking to her his AA meetings— he thought she was an alcoholic like himself. *Well,* fuck *that. I can quit any time. I'm not a drunk.*

"You're not getting rid of me that easily. I'm still in." Lainey held the contract out toward him, chin thrust forward.

Strauss didn't take it. "Are you sure? The magazine can't afford to send you there only to have you change your mind."

She dropped the folder in front of him. "I won't change my mind. I can do this standing on my head. All of it," she said, knowing he would understand the inflection.

A smile crossed his face. "Great! Glad to still have you on board."

CHAPTER SEVEN

June

"So, when's that fancy New York reporter supposed to get here?"

Scotch looked up from her perusal of the dairy cooler to see the store's owner, old Jamison Drew, peering at her with his fading eyesight. He held a price gun in one hand, and she saw the case of cereal boxes he had been tagging when she'd passed by him.

Turning away, she opened the cooler and reached for a gallon of whole milk. "Photojournalist. She'll be here sometime next week. Cliff Roberts is flying her in."

"Flying her in?" Jamison clicked his tongue. "Anchorage ain't all that far. Why ain't she driving?"

She put the milk in the rickety shopping cart. "I expect she'll have a lot of gear with her. If she rented a car to haul it here, she'd just have to drive it back to the rental place."

His weathered face screwed into an expression of grudging acceptance. "I guess you're right."

"Jamison!"

He frowned, rolling his eyes at Scotch before turning to the approaching woman. "Yes, dear?"

A heavyset woman with thinning gray hair came to a halt beside the cereal section, hands perched on her hips. "Quit bothering Scotch!

She's got lots better things to do than stand about jaw-jacking with you."

"It's okay, Mrs. Drew." Scotch patted Jamison's shoulder. "We were just catching up on the news." She could almost see Florence Drew's ears grow longer.

"News?" Florence stepped closer. "What news?"

"Well, I'd know by now if you'd let me finish talking," Jamison grumbled under his breath.

Scotch rubbed at her face to hide the grin.

Florence either didn't hear her husband's remark or ignored it. "Is it about that fancy New York City reporter?"

Why did everyone assume Lainey Hughes was "fancy"? Scotch knew better than to argue with her elders and let her moment of irritation pass. "Yes, Mr. Drew was just asking when she'd arrive."

"Oh!" Florence leaned closer. "When will that be?"

Scotch wasn't about to give out details, not here. Rumor Central of Talkeetna began at Florence's door. If Scotch mentioned the specific date and time the reporter was due to arrive, it would be all over the village before she reached home. "She'll be flying in sometime next week."

"Flying?" She sniffed disdainfully. "She's not even here, and she's putting on airs?"

Jamison shook his head with a grimace. He gave Scotch a wink and trundled back to his task.

Scotch spent the rest of her shopping trip defusing Florence's wounded sense of propriety. She didn't need any animosity toward her future roommate by friends and acquaintances, not if she wanted her living situation to occur with a modicum of peace. An hour later, she placed her purchases behind the seat of her truck, hoping she had alleviated any hard feelings toward the newcomer.

The questions, coming from all directions, had been getting more and more pointed. Not more than a week after agreeing to the articles, Scotch had attended an elementary school rally to discuss her last race. One of the first questions asked was about the mysterious reporter that would arrive in June. Her sister, Irish, sat in the audience, face blazing. The gossip had snowballed from there. Scotch couldn't go anywhere in the village or surrounding area without fending off questions.

She waved to the gas station attendant as she passed, honked her horn at the mayor as he walked his dog and hollered out her window at a teenager she knew through Rye, all the while wishing she could just be alone. Preferably for the next nine months.

Her father had been the point of contact for the reporter. Lainey Hughes called the house with regularity to ask questions about her arrival, what to wear and the type of gear in which she should invest. Scotch knew she would be less antsy about the matter if she had talked to Lainey herself, but she'd refused to get involved. She knew her petulant refusal disappointed her parents, but she wasn't ready. Delaying their initial introduction, whether it be by phone or in person, gave her at least some control over the situation.

Idiot. You have control. You can still cancel the deal, send her packing and save money for the year after next. Scotch shook her head as she pulled out of Talkeetna.

She had done some research on the photojournalist in a failed attempt to alleviate her fears. Lainey Hughes' original career began in Rwanda, covering their civil war. Her photos of the atrocities between the Hutu and Tutsi people helped convict the prime minister of war crimes, making her a household name by the time she was Scotch's age. From there, Lainey wandered the globe, following wars and military coup d'etats. The photos she took revealed to the world the true brutality of war, simultaneously highlighting the humanity of the people embroiled in conflict. Scotch's favorite picture was of a Middle Eastern boy—maybe five or six years old—playing in the dusty street, the rubble of a bombed-out building still smoking behind him.

Lainey's luck eventually ran out, and she was wounded in Kosovo in 1998. For a year the reporter dropped off the face of the earth. When she returned to work, she focused her lens on nature, predominantly rare animals or plants in the wild. She still traveled extensively but avoided the political hot spots of the world.

This idea to follow Scotch through the process of the Iditarod was yet another departure for Lainey. Four years as a war correspondent followed by four more as a nature observer were nothing like the planned magazine series. When Lainey focused on the human condition, it was within a framework of violence, not sport. Plus her experience since her first career deviation had been entirely in tropical or sub-tropical climates. From the scant personal information Scotch could gather, Lainey Hughes rarely strayed farther north than her home state of New York.

Scotch turned left onto a wide gravel road. She pulled over long enough to roll down the passenger window before continuing. The breeze was brisk but soothing, mixed with pine scent and the slight chill of remaining snow. Breakup had occurred a little early this year, but there were still patches of ice that had yet to succumb to the warmer temperatures. She let the familiar scents and sensations wash over her as she drove, her mind returning to the problem of her upcoming "guest."

Seasonal Affective Disorder was a real danger for *chechakos*. Those unused to the lack of sunlight had a tendency to go into depression come winter, a fatal occurrence on occasion. Scotch shivered as an icy chill trickled down her spine. From what she had gathered, Lainey Hughes hadn't lived in any place that received less than ten hours of sunlight a day in years. *Will she be able to hack darkness for weeks on end? What happens if she can't?*

The dread Scotch had held at bay since she had agreed to this arrangement threatened to overwhelm her. She fought it back, almost missing her family's driveway. The dogs howled and barked at her approach, their joyous welcome drowning out her fears. *I'll talk to Dad, maybe pick up a couple of those light panels people use. Just in case.*

* * *

Scotch stared nervously at the airstrip, tapping a staccato on the steering wheel in time with a bluegrass tune on the radio. The June morning had dawned beautifully, the temperature sitting at a balmy fifty-eight degrees. It was expected to reach sixty-five before the day was through, a perfect day to welcome a pair of newcomers.

It wasn't clear why there would be two of them. There had been a last minute change a week ago. Thom Fuller had been somewhat vague on the matter, possibly because he didn't know either. Another bunk had been added to the handler's cabin where Miguel Sanchez, the kennel's sole employee, resided. Once Scotch discovered the other photojournalist was a man, she felt a measure of relief. Perhaps the two were engaged or something. At least it would distract them from her to some degree.

Her ears picked up the sound of an engine. She turned off the radio and leaned forward to peer out the windshield, locating the airplane. It cut into sight, emerging from the tree line on her left. The tiny plane swung around, lining up with the runway as it approached. There was just enough clearance for it to land, leaving little room to taxi. The plane halted no more than fifteen feet away. As the motor shut down, Scotch got out of the truck and leaned one hip against the front side panel.

The door popped open and a stool plunked beneath it to accommodate a gruff man in coveralls. He clambered out of the plane, spying her. With an exuberant wave, he marched forward. "Scotch! How the hell are you?"

Grinning, she met the pilot halfway, giving him a hug. "I'm doing great, Cliff. You?"

"Been better," he confided. "These old bones are acting up. And Delores is threatening to quit on me."

He said the same thing every time she saw him. "No way! Delores loves you. It'll be a long time before her wings are clipped."

He eyeballed the small charter plane. The only section of its hull not banged or scraped up was a carefully painted pin-up girl by the pilot's seat. She wore a skimpy red dress and smiled coyly at her admirers. "You think so?"

"Guaranteed."

Cheered, Cliff shifted his gaze to the two people unloading luggage and gear. "That little girl there says she's doing a big magazine article on you this year. That true?"

Scotch blushed. "It's true. We're hoping to get a national sponsorship out of the publicity."

He nodded in agreeable contemplation. "Sounds like a plan. Hope it works out for you."

His tone rang with uncertainty, catching Scotch's attention. "You think it won't?" she asked, lowering her voice.

Sucking his teeth, Cliff said, "I think it can go either way. She seems a bit high maintenance to me." He chuckled, nudging a worried Scotch with his shoulder. "But don't mind me, I could be wrong. If I could judge women as well as airplanes, I'd be married six times over by now."

She laughed with him, stowing his reservations for later perusal. The reporters had finished unloading the plane, and she stepped forward to introduce herself. "Hi, I'm Scotch Fuller. Welcome to Alaska."

"It's nice to finally meet you." The woman offered her hand. She stood a few inches shorter, her short, curly dark hair shot through with threads of silver. "I'm Lainey Hughes, and this is my associate, Don Howry."

"Pleasure to meet you, Ms. Fuller."

Associate? Scotch found the introduction lacking. If these two were romantically involved, they certainly covered their relationship well. She had the weirdest sensation she had met Lainey before. Her father had said that the photojournalist had covered the previous race, so maybe she'd seen her then. "Call me Scotch." She led the way to the truck. "Since you'll be with us a while, no reason to not to be on a first name basis."

With Cliff's help, they loaded the bags into the back of the truck. He declined an invitation to the kennel for coffee but gratefully swapped his thermos with Scotch's. Soon he was back in his plane, cranking it up for the trip back to Anchorage. They watched as he turned Delores around and took off, the landing gears just barely clearing the tops of the trees at the other end of the airstrip.

Left alone with the strangers, Scotch sighed. She had plenty of experience with public speaking and the local media and reached for that knowledge. She forced a smile. "Let's get you back to the kennel and settled in." Opening the truck, she folded the driver's seat back. "I've only got jump seats here. It's kind of small, so maybe Lainey should take the back."

"That sounds fine." Lainey smiled and stepped forward. Howry went around to the passenger door.

Still holding the seat out of the way, Scotch leaned back against the door hinge to give Lainey room to maneuver. She couldn't help but enjoy the curve of the snugly fitting designer jeans and the faint scent of perfume. Lainey folded down the small seat behind Howry and settled into the cramped space.

Soon they were traveling on a paved rural road, heading into Talkeetna. The silence unnerved Scotch. Within her peripheral vision, she saw Howry avidly soaking up the sights of small town Alaska but felt like she was being watched. A quick glance proved her instincts correct as Lainey looked away. Somewhat out of her element, Scotch reddened at the intensity of Lainey's expression and gripped the steering wheel tighter.

Lainey cleared her throat. "So, how long have you been driving dogs?"

Scotch grinned, welcoming the distraction of dog talk. "About twenty years." At the abrupt quiet, she regarded her passengers, noting Howry's puzzled look and Lainey's expression of disbelief. "My parents started the kennel when I was two. As soon as I could stand and hang on alone, I was on a sled."

"Wow." Howry turned toward her in his seat. "Sledding as long as you've been walking. That's cool."

Scotch navigated her way through the small town, waving to the sudden multitude on the streets that the appearance of Cliff's plane had summoned. Considering the abrupt population increase, she thought the entire village's friends and family had been invited to visit today. "I only had one dog for a team, but it was a beginning. My brother and sister started the same way."

"That would be…Irish and Rye?"

Scotch nodded at Lainey's question, turning off the road and onto a hard-packed gravel lane. "Irish is nine; she's running up to ten dogs now. Rye runs a full load."

"Interesting names." Howry's tone hinted for more information.

Chuckling, Scotch shook her head. "Talk to my dad about that. He loves telling the story."

"I will," Lainey responded, her voice soft.

Scotch glanced sharply over her shoulder, not certain what she expected to see. Lainey smiled back at her. Unsettled, Scotch turned back to her driving.

CHAPTER EIGHT

Deep in her thoughts, Scotch didn't catch Howry giving Lainey a raised eyebrow. She returned a warning look, not quite sticking her tongue out at him, though she did give his seat a slight nudge. He slid his eyes back to the scenery.

As Lainey watched Scotch's profile, her libido kicked into overdrive; her masturbatory fantasy for the last three months sat inches away. *Good God, how am I going to survive this? Whatever possessed me to take this gig?* Lainey's sudden rush of nerves unsettled her. *Damn, I could use a drink.* She pushed the yearning away as she imagined Strauss' response. The last thing she wanted to do was make him think she had an alcohol problem. He'd gloat forever. Rather than allow her editor to sour her elation, she returned her attention to Scotch.

Scotch exhibited an unconscious beauty. She needed no makeup and apparently didn't wear any. Her nose was slightly crooked. Lainey wondered whether it was natural or the result of a healed break. Otherwise, her features were flawless. Her skin was tanned, with a light brushing of freckles across her nose and cheeks, not as weathered as when Lainey had first seen her. Tawny golden curls stuck out haphazardly from beneath a cream-colored baseball cap, curling at the nape of her neck. Lainey was hard pressed to not reach over and finger the tresses.

A growing cacophony of sound interrupted her assessment, distracting both her and Howry. Scotch turned down a driveway, past a sign welcoming them to Fuller Kennels. Hours of operation were posted there, and Lainey wondered why. She made a mental note to get a picture of the sign as she focused her attention on the nearing buildings.

The drive was a large loop. A central circle held a smattering of wooden chairs and a stone barbecue. A station wagon with Virginia license plates sat in a rudimentary parking area to the left, the back piled high with camping gear. Two log buildings stood central to the drive, one with a rustic wooden sign proclaiming the Fuller Veterinary Hospital. That would be why there were hours of operation, of course.

Lainey identified the noise as several dogs barking in excited welcome.

Scotch grinned as she parked in front of the second cabin. "Don't worry. The dogs only make that kind of racket for our trucks. They won't wake you up for everything on wheels that passes by."

"That's a relief." Howry opened his door. "I need my beauty sleep."

"I'll say." Lainey grinned, unrepentant at her dig.

The canine enthusiasm seemed contagious. Lainey took Scotch's hand to steady herself as she climbed out of the truck. A shock traveled up her arm at the touch, and she quickly drew away before she could be tempted to follow her body's natural instincts. She promptly fished for the luggage in the truck bed, receiving another questioning look from Howry. She ignored him. Now wasn't the time to get into a discussion of what was going on with her. It was bad enough the senior editor at *Cognizance* had altered the gig, thereby ensuring she'd have a colleague to witness her foolishness. She didn't need to give him any more ammunition than was absolutely unavoidable.

"We'll wait until after lunch to get you settled in." Scotch hefted a duffel bag with ease and clambered up the steps of the cabin, setting it near the front door. "In the meantime, let's leave your stuff here and I'll take you on the ten-dollar tour."

"Tour, huh?" Howry dropped a suitcase on the porch. "Sounds like you do it regularly."

"We do." Scotch relieved Lainey of a full-sized backpack, an expression of surprise flickering on her face as she noted its weight. "Two tours a day, Monday through Friday. We also arrange day trips, overnight campouts with the dogs, weekend excursions and sled rides or lessons."

"Impressive." Lainey pointed at the building they had passed as they swung into the drive. "Plus an animal hospital?"

Scotch grinned. "Yeah. That's my mom's. She takes care of all the dogs here and is a volunteer vet for the Iditarod."

Howry, his camera already in hand, fiddled with a lens as he eyed Lainey with a cocked eyebrow.

Realizing she was staring at Scotch with more than general interest, Lainey quickly dissembled. She rummaged among the bags for her camera. The cabin's screen door burst open—a distraction Lainey welcomed—and two bundles of energy rolled out, one human and one canine.

"Dey here! Dey here!"

Scotch scooped both of them up in an effort to avert potential disaster. Only then were they still enough for Lainey to register what they looked like. "I'd like to introduce you to Bon, my youngest brother." Turning slightly to indicate the puppy, she continued. "And this is Aphrodite."

Lainey reached out and shook Bon's hand. "It's a pleasure to meet you." The boy gave her a bashful smile and clung to his sister. There was no doubt they were related; both had wavy golden hair, though his coloring was much lighter. Hearing a shutter click, she saw Howry taking a picture.

"Oh, watch out," Scotch warned, setting her burdens down. "He's a major ham."

Bon laughed and bustled to the screen door, throwing it open. "C'mon, Aph'dite!" Tail wagging eagerly, the pup gamboled forward and they disappeared inside.

Chuckling, Scotch looked after them as she removed her ball cap to run her hand through her hair.

Lainey wondered if it felt as wonderful as it looked, mesmerized until Howry bumped her from behind. She gave him a quick glare, knowing she'd have a lot to refute the next time they were alone. Breaking the silence, she smiled brightly and said, "Well! How about that tour?"

Howry snorted at her but followed as Scotch obligingly led them down the steps that led to the path around the cabin.

Lainey reflected ruefully on the expression, "Absence makes the heart grow fonder." She didn't know if she had grown more interested in Scotch over the last few months as she planned this assignment, but her attraction seemed every bit as strong as it had been the minute she'd first laid eyes on the Alaskan. At least in New York she could fool herself into believing this was a strictly legitimate gig with a little eye candy to stimulate the senses. Here in Scotch's presence, everything changed. She dearly hoped constant contact would cure her of this infatuation.

"Lainey? You coming?"

Startled from her musing, she waved at Scotch, noting the guarded expression in her eyes. *Small wonder. You're acting bizarre, even in her estimation.* She trotted down the steps to join them.

* * *

A gravel path led them around the side of the cabin. Instead of a traditional backyard complete with manicured grass and rose bushes, the bed of rock opened up before them, encompassing most of the available clearing. The cabin sported a raised deck, where Bon played with his canine goddess and two other puppies. A handful of outbuildings and what appeared to be a carport peppered the edges of the expanse, though the covered concrete section didn't seem accessible to a vehicle, given the clutter of equipment there. Two large kennels held a handful of dogs receiving cautious attention from a family of four.

Beyond all this, Lainey saw the dog yard. The sheer number of animals amazed her. She had never seen so many at once. She immediately corrected herself. There had been many more during the race in March. What she hadn't been prepared for were the neat rows of wooden houses, each with a dog chained nearby. Lainey immediately wondered how this could be healthy for the animals. She noted some sleeping in the sun, others playing enthusiastically with toys or bones or standing atop their homes, tails wagging as they yipped for attention from the people in the yard. They hardly looked abused.

"Scotch!"

A young man waved from the group at the kennel. Lainey recognized him from the time she had fallen on the sidewalk in Nome. He was the boy who had been with Scotch. "C'mere!" he called.

Scotch waved at him. "I'll be back after I help Rye. Go ahead and poke around some. Don't worry. All the dogs are friendly."

Howry gave a noncommittal murmur of agreement. Scotch trotted toward the kennels and, presumably, her fans.

"So. Is this attraction fatal or just a minor infatuation?"

Lainey scowled at him. She glanced around to see if anyone could overhear. "It's not like that."

"Oh?" He raised an eyebrow. "She's cute, in an athletic sort of way. I mean, if you're attracted to that type—and I know you are." He busied himself with taking a picture of the subject of their conversation as she shook hands with the visitors.

"That's not why we're here."

He turned his lens toward her, adjusting the focus. "You can't lie to the camera, Lainey." *Click.*

Her face hot, she placed her hand on the lens to avert further photos. She didn't need photographic evidence of her folly. "All right." She rolled her eyes. "I saw her last March. There's something about her that won't leave me alone."

Howry dropped the camera, giving her his undivided attention. She looked away, feeling the blush deepen on her cheeks and neck. "I thought if I could spend some time with her, I'd get over whatever this is." She glared at him. "It's a good idea, even if Ben railroaded me into it in the first place."

"Must have been a hell of a wrinkle when his boss added me to the equation."

She perceived no sarcasm in his expression. "Somewhat."

Howry tilted his head at the gathering by the kennel. "What did they say when you told them?"

Lainey watched as Scotch knelt down to be on a level with a small boy, patient and smiling as she explained something to him. Her chest went tight with an unidentifiable emotion, and she resisted an urge to approach the group. "I haven't told them yet."

Howry stood silent a moment before whooping in laughter. Irritated, she turned her back on him as he bent nearly double in his mirth. Lainey plastered on an apologetic smile as the others regarded them curiously. "It's not that funny," she said from between clenched teeth.

It took a few moments before he regained control, straightening and wiping his eyes. "It is from where I'm standing."

"Are you the reporters?"

Lainey looked up to see a girl hanging over the railing of the deck. She promptly put on her best diplomatic face. "Yes, we are. I'm Lainey Hughes and this is Don Howry."

The girl smiled, and Lainey saw an echo of Scotch in the girl's face. She had to admit that their parents certainly threw good-looking offspring.

"I'm Irish Fuller." She gave them the onceover, tucking a length of strawberry blonde hair behind her ear. "I heard the truck drive up, so I made coffee. Where's your stuff?"

"On the front porch. Scotch was going to give us the ten-dollar tour, but she got sidetracked."

Irish screwed up her face in thought, spying her older sister leading the family of visitors toward the carport structure. "They're just getting started. I can't leave Bon alone, or I'd take you."

Howry waved his camera. "That's okay. We can manage on our own."

"Why don't you come up? I can bring you coffee while you wait for her to finish." Irish opened a child- and puppy-proof gate, deftly intercepting a dog with her foot as it made a bumbling lurch toward freedom.

Lainey took a step backward in mild protest. "Oh, no. We don't want to put you out."

Irish's expression cooled, a flash of displeasure quickly replaced with comprehension. "Mom said you wouldn't understand." Her voice taking on a slight sermonizing tone, she continued, "It's rude to not offer guests something to drink when they arrive. It's kind of like Alaskan etiquette."

Lainey realized that, by extension, it would be considered impolite to refuse such an offer as well.

Her companion also caught the hint and slung his camera over his shoulder. "We'd be grateful for some coffee."

Irish smiled and gestured for them to come up the steps.

At least on the deck, Lainey had a better view of Scotch's activities. Sitting on a patio chair, she leaned against the railing and watched the woman explain the operations of the kennel to her audience, her voice not quite carrying. Rye went into the building by the carport and pulled out a racing sled. The group drifted toward it and Scotch pointed out the various parts of the vehicle.

Lainey saw movement in the dog area. A Hispanic man in jeans released a chained animal and brought it to a four-wheel ATV with an odd contraption attached to the front. It looked like a roller coaster car made of wood and painted with the logo she had seen on the sign out front. As the man moved through the yard, the dogs barked joyfully, jumping about to gain his attention. When Irish returned from inside, Lainey asked her, "Who's that?"

After setting a tray of refreshments on a table, the girl skillfully stopped Bon's attempt to climb into Howry's lap. Keeping her little brother wrapped in her arms, she looked where Lainey was pointing. "That's Miguel. He's our handler."

Howry stood to get a better angle, looking through his camera. "What's he doing?"

Irish set down the squirming Bon, who immediately wrapped himself about Howry's leg. "He's hooking the dogs up to the ATV. Those people have paid for a tour. They get a dog ride too." She shrugged, a slight grin on her face. "It's not a sled, but it does the trick when there's no snow."

Lainey split her attention between her lust object and the handler. No dog was ignored as Miguel filtered among the dogs, though he only picked half a dozen to lead to the vehicle. Meanwhile, Scotch whistled, and a single unchained dog trotted over to her, tail wagging. She demonstrated how the canines were attached to the sled with the help of the boy who beamed proudly at his father.

"Why is that dog running loose?"

At the same time, Howry asked, "How does he choose which dogs to use?"

Irish looked between them, uncertain who to answer first.

Bon had no problem. "Rock big dog!"

Grinning, Irish nodded. "Yeah, Rock is the Big Dog today. Every day, one dog is allowed to run free. It's usually done on a rotation except for race days or when the girls are in heat."

Her question answered, Lainey watched as Scotch finished the lesson, barely hearing Irish's response to Howry.

"The rides are on a rotation schedule too, at least during the tourist season. Once race training starts, at least half of them are dropped from the list. Those dogs that aren't going to be racing take up the slack." She set a steaming coffee cup in front of Lainey. "Any tourists wanting a real sled ride won't know the difference between first- or second-string teams."

Miguel had finished his task. He climbed onto the ATV and called out a command to the dogs. Lainey smiled at the enthusiastic barks as the team leapt forward. It reminded her of the photos she had taken in Nome—the eager animals barking as they made their way to the finish line.

Miguel directed the animals to circle the dog yard, sending up a round of excited howls from those left behind. The clamor distracted the visitors from their crash course in sled specifications, and they watched wide-eyed as he expertly drove the team toward them, pulling to a halt nearby. It amazed her that there were no reins, no method of control other than verbal commands. Sure, the ATV could be steered, but the dogs followed spoken commands rather than each trying to go a different way. Scotch made a show of greeting each dog, urging the children to do the same. Then she helped everyone aboard the cart, standing back as her brother joined them.

Lainey stared as sun dappled through the trees, illuminating the golden highlights in Scotch's hair. A trickle of desire eased along her spine, exploding to mild warmth when the musher turned and smiled at her.

"Interesting."

She tore her attention away to give Howry a glare. He ignored her, reaching for a cookie from the tray before resuming his seat.

"This cabin doesn't look all that big," he observed. "Where are we going to bed down?"

"There's an extra bunk in with Miguel for you, Mr. Howry. Miss Hughes will be sleeping with Scotch." Irish watched her brother as his gaze fell on the cookie in the man's hand. Fortunately, Irish zeroed in on Bon, scooping him out of reach of the cookies he made a dive for.

"Out of the mouths of babes," Howry murmured, grinning.

Lainey almost choked on her coffee. Her attention darted to the girl, praying she hadn't heard him. Apparently undetected for the moment, Lainey whispered, "Shut up!"

Scotch climbed the steps and opened the gate. "Is everything okay?"

Howry, his expression impudent, eyes never leaving Lainey's, nodded. "Everything's fine. I hear Lainey's sleeping with you."

Lainey seriously wondered how much of this she could stand. Surely there was some way to arrange an accident for her associate, something that would result in extreme pain for an extended amount of time.

Guileless, Scotch looked from Howry's glee to Lainey's irritation. "If that's not a problem." She appeared uncertain. "Unless you'd rather bunk alone. I guess I could move back in with Irish."

The expressions of both Fullers indicated their distaste for such an arrangement, and Lainey hastened to relieve them. "No! This is fine. I'm just...I tend to be a loner sometimes, that's all." She wished she were close enough to kick Howry's shin and wipe that smarmy grin from his face.

Scotch relaxed. "I can understand that. I'm a loner too."

The gentle smile on her lips washed away Lainey's anger at Howry's teasing. She smiled back, lifting her cup in salute, not caring if her intentions were transparent to him.

CHAPTER NINE

The promised tour eventually took place. Lainey learned that the carport was referred to as a dog kitchen, and the building attached to it was the dog barn. Like any standard barn, the loft held straw. Scotch explained that it was used for bedding during the winter. The lower floor had nine fenced animal runs, all empty. These were used during winter for injured dogs or new mothers and their pups. Two chest freezers hulked in one corner, with the remainder of the room relegated to storage—five sleds of varying styles, large locked bins of dry dog chow and rice, assorted tack lines and cables, shelves of vitamin supplements and cabinets filled with doggie blankets and booties. Several clipboards hung near the door, each clearly labeled. Lainey read "Big Dog" on one and scanned down to see Rock had a grease pencil checkmark beside his name. Others proclaimed "Kennel Rotation," "Vaccinations" and "Rides."

As the visiting family returned from their outing, the barking of dogs interrupted the tour, causing those dogs left behind to give enthusiastic greetings to their companions. Miguel brought the team to a halt just outside the barn, and the dogs grinned at Lainey, panting from their exertions. While Scotch and her brother helped the family out of the cart, their handler tied the team to a post. He gave Lainey and Howry a nod of greeting as he passed them, emerging a few moments later with chunks of frozen treats that he fed the dogs.

"I'm going to see these folks off. You'll be okay for a minute?"

Howry waggled his camera at Scotch, indicating he had plenty to keep him entertained. "Yeah, we'll be fine."

Lainey smiled in agreement, unable to contain the slight quickening of her breathing as she received a smile in return. *This is such a bad idea.* As Scotch escorted the tourists away, Lainey swallowed hard as she watched the slight sway of her hips.

"So, what are you feeding them?" Howry asked Miguel.

Steeling herself, Lainey remembered why she'd come. This obsession would fade. Scotch was young, probably stubborn, uneducated out here in the wild and smelled of dog crap. *She's also athletic, vibrant, possesses an extraordinary confidence and is a hot little number.* With an inner groan, Lainey forced her attention to the nearby conversation.

Miguel had started with the leaders, working his way backward as he heaped praise and caresses upon each animal. "Frozen whitefish." His tenor voice held little in the way of an accent. "Sometimes frozen salmon or chunks of liver. It helps them cool off from a run and rewards them for a job well done. Isn't that right, girl?" He petted the next in line.

Laincy made an attempt at professionalism. "How long have you been working here?"

"Since the beginning." Miguel returned to the front of the line, closely inspecting each dog. He massaged shoulders, hips and spines before checking feet and wrists. "I worked for Thom on a couple of construction sites. When he conned Helen into starting a kennel, I volunteered to help build the vet hospital and this barn." He shrugged. "Ended up hiring on permanently."

They watched his thorough examination of each animal in silence. When he finished, he stood and stretched, arching his back. "So, you're the reporters, right?"

Lainey smacked her forehead lightly. "Whoops, sorry! Yes. I'm Lainey Hughes and this is Don Howry."

Miguel wiped his hand on his jeans before offering it to them. "Miguel Sanchez, handler."

Introductions over, Lainey now smelled of dog, and she fought the urge to rub her palm on her shirt. She was always fastidious upon first contact, an ingrained habit of cleanliness that would dissipate as she immersed herself in a new situation. Smelling of dog was better than some odors she'd been forced to endure during her career. The handler appeared amused, and she wondered if she had given something away in her expression. As she worried the question, he continued speaking.

"You'll be sleeping in my cabin," he told Howry. "It's kind of dormitory style, but all right. It's just over there along that path." He pointed out the trail, a cabin barely visible among the trees. "We even have running water."

Alarm bells went off in Lainey's head. With a feigned casualness, she inquired, "No electricity?"

"Not yet." Miguel chuckled. "I've been meaning to get a generator set up out there. Haven't had the time."

Howry digested this information admirably. "So, propane lanterns are the rule rather than the exception?"

"For the most part," Miguel gave the man's camera a significant look. "The main house, the clinic and the barn here all have power, though. If you need to recharge batteries and the like, I'm sure we can accommodate you." He waved at the cabin where Bon played under the watchful eyes of Irish. "They even have an Internet connection."

Lainey stared out over the dog yard, imagining a bleak winter without even the simple amenity of electricity. Certainly she had been in places as rustic as this—war-torn cities in the Middle East or tramping through the bush of innumerable countries. *But this is America, for crissakes! I expected a certain level of civilization.* Another thought occurred to her. No electricity meant no water heater. *Good Lord, what has my libido gotten me into?*

"Where's Scotch's cabin from here?"

Lainey's gaze followed where Miguel pointed, seeing a path winding through the trees. She couldn't see the dwelling at all. "Is it far?"

"Yeah, a bit. It's actually tucked back behind a small hill." He sucked at his teeth. "Scotch likes her privacy."

The unspoken warning brought Lainey's gaze around. Her subject was a private person who not only agreed to be constantly followed about by strangers wielding cameras but was allowing one of them to move into her sacred space for nine months. Lainey's job was typically a solitary pursuit; she understood the sacrifice Scotch was making in exchange for the publicity. She resolved to tread lightly around Scotch. Regardless of her idiotic reasons for becoming involved in this assignment, she couldn't let the gig disrupt her subject's equilibrium. *Yeah. Scotch is merely a subject, just like so many others over the years.* Lainey vowed to keep a proper perspective.

Scotch rounded the corner of the cabin, her brother beside her, and Lainey felt her proper perspective drift away, a helium balloon lazily dancing into the distance.

* * *

Relaxed in spite of the reporters at the table, Scotch nursed her after-dinner coffee as Howry regaled her family with an anecdote from one of his assignments in the Amazon. His voice became quieter as he described being in a canoe, evading another people's war party and trusting his native guides to keep him alive. His audience collectively leaned forward in anticipation. Even Lainey appeared engrossed in his tale about the indigenous people he had come into contact with. Scotch used the opportunity to study her.

Lainey seemed a contradiction. She carried a watertight air of professionalism, yet Scotch had seen her blush and stammer like a schoolgirl over the smallest thing several times over the course of the afternoon. Was that because she usually worked with nature instead of people? Maybe she was uncomfortable around strangers. Considering the things Lainey had seen throughout the first half of her career, that didn't ring true, but Scotch couldn't think of any other reason for her behavior. Her features were more careworn than Scotch had expected. Laincy had six years on Scotch, but the wrinkles about her mouth and the silver threading through her dark hair made her look older. Scotch supposed that made sense. Lainey had seen several military actions and been wounded in a firefight. She decided that she liked Lainey's appearance.

The pesky déjà vu wouldn't go away. *Where have I seen her before? I didn't meet her at the banquet function. I would have remembered.*

She snuck clandestine glimpses of Lainey's slight body, noting the maroon plaid flannel shirt neatly tucked into her waistband. Worn hiking boots stood out at odds with the designer label on the hip pocket of those jeans. Where had Lainey been shot? There weren't any obvious scars, and she didn't limp. She had rolled up her sleeves during the day, revealing forearms as tanned as her face and neck. Lainey had told Irish that she had finished working in Africa earlier this year. *Seeing all those exotic places must be exciting.* Calluses on her hands showed she wasn't a stranger to hard work, a plus in Scotch's book. The faint hearted didn't survive hard Alaskan winters. Scotch had more than her fair share of experience with that particular truism.

Her gaze returned to Lainey's face. Hazel eyes regarded her, an eyebrow raised in question. Caught in her visual perusal, Scotch hid her embarrassment as best she could. She smoothly brought her attention back to Howry and took a sip of her coffee, knowing her blush belied her outward indifference.

Howry wrapped up his story and there was a lull in the conversation. "Well, now that I've told you one of mine, Thom, maybe you could answer my question."

Scotch's father leaned back in his chair, Bon sleepily resting in his lap. On his face was a knowing grin. "Who named my kids?"

Helen tsked good-naturedly, feigning irritation. Scotch grinned and winked at her equally amused brother. Irish rolled her eyes.

Lainey chuckled. "I'm betting you did. I think the question is why the names you chose."

Thom considered carefully before answering, though it was an obvious ploy. Scotch had seen this every time she had heard the story. Her father enjoyed the telling of it and was a natural entertainer.

"When I got married to this pretty little woman here," he said, ignoring Helen's snort, "we made a bet: whoever guessed the gender right could name the kid."

"Mom's shooting blanks in maternal instinct." Rye shook his head.

Thom defended his wife. "She does well enough in the motherly things."

Helen waved him on. "Finish it, Thom. Don't get distracted."

He gave his wife an air kiss and looked back to his guests. "Anyway, when Scotch arrived, I told Helen what I wanted to name her. She about had a fit."

Lainey glanced at Scotch, amused puzzlement on her face. Scotch smiled widely, ignoring the silent request for enlightenment.

"Tell them what it was."

"I'll let Scotch tell them," he said magnanimously.

Scotch set her coffee cup down, waiting for the precise moment for the punch line. "Scottish, as in Scottish Terrier."

"You're kidding!" Unable to believe what she'd heard, Lainey let her gaze travel around the table seeking confirmation.

"Oh, no," Helen said. "He was quite serious."

"You were going to name your children after dog breeds?" Howry demanded, flabbergasted.

Rye chuckled. "Oh, yeah. Dad loves his dogs."

Scotch enjoyed the befuddlement on Lainey's face as it turned to humor. She gave her a private little shrug, pleased to see her snort in burgeoning laughter.

"So, why the change?"

Thom shrugged, disappointed. "Well, you know women." He dropped his voice as if speaking conspiratorially, though they all heard him clearly. "Can't live with 'em, can't live with 'em." He yelped when Irish slapped his shoulder, and then he laughed. "She told me there was no way she'd let me call my kids after dogs. But we still had an agreement."

"Dad loves his dogs, but he also loves his whiskey," Scotch said.

"And you let him get away with that?" Lainey asked Helen.

She smiled. "It was better than a son named Labrador."

Rye groaned and covered his face with his hands as the rest laughed.

When the amusement died down, Howry spoke again. "Okay, I can see Scotch, Rye, and Irish. But Bon? I'm a newsman, and we have livers of iron. I've never heard of a whiskey by that name. Did Helen finally win a bet?"

Bon, who lounged half asleep in his father's arms, barely roused at the mention of his name.

Scotch leaned forward to set her cup down on the table. "Actually, that's his nickname. His given name is Bourbon."

Howry threw his hands up in the air. "Of course!"

Scotch's eyes met Lainey's. She felt an odd connection forming between them, a simple joy of sharing something good. While a part of her relaxed into it, a sense of unease undermined the sensation. It had been too long since she'd had a close friend. Lainey Hughes might be pleasant and funny, but that didn't mean she'd be Scotch's confidant. Scotch couldn't allow herself to get too close. *Even if Lainey survives the winter without... Well, she'll be gone after the next Iditarod, anyway.*

Miguel had mentioned Lainey had acted surprised when she'd learned there was no electricity at the cabin. The bush pilot, Cliff, had said the reporter had seemed high maintenance. What with all the talk around the village about the "fancy reporter from New York," Scotch wondered if there wasn't some validity to the rumors. She had never set foot outside Alaska except to run the Yukon Quest in Canada and had no earthly idea what her humble cabin would look like to the well-traveled Lainey Hughes.

Will I survive nine months with her?

Her family began their nightly ritual of cleaning up, distracting Scotch from her meanderings. She helped clear the table. It was her turn to do dishes, so she filled the sink with hot soapy water. When Lainey offered to help, she fought against the sense of contentment that washed through her.

CHAPTER TEN

Lainey picked her way along the worn trail. Her laden backpack sat comfortably upon her shoulders and hips, and her waterproof camera bag swung in one hand. Ahead of her, Scotch led the way to her home-away-from-home. Fortunately for Lainey's dignity, the uneven trail required her full attention, otherwise she would be staring at the well-shaped ass in front of her. Not surprisingly, lecherous ogling of the subject was frowned upon in most photography circles.

The sun still hung low in the sky, confusing Lainey's sense of time. By now it would be dark in New York. Here the dappled light combined with the cooler temperature mistakenly informed her it was early morning instead of ten o'clock on a midsummer night. It reminded her of youthful family camping trips in New England, breakfasts of flapjacks, the sun warming the lake. Lainey smiled. It had been years since she had thought of those times. *I wonder why I'd forgotten that. I used to love those trips.*

"Almost there." Scotch glanced over her shoulder. She carried Lainey's laptop and another suitcase.

"I'm right behind you." Lainey's pleasant grin slid into a leer as Scotch's attention returned to the trail. *Oh, I'm right behind you, all right.*

Rounding a bend in the path, Lainey got her first glimpse of the cabin. It stood about one level tall, with a neat little covered porch in front of the door. She cocked her head. From her angle, the windows sat higher than one would expect. The place also looked cramped, like it had been squashed down by a passing giant. She shivered, an edge of claustrophobia circling her vision as she followed Scotch up three steps. A swinging bench hung from the porch rafters.

Scotch opened the door and set the luggage just inside. "Come on in, and watch your step." She gestured for Lainey to enter.

Mindful of her feet, Lainey found herself on a landing with steps leading down. She carefully followed them, apprehension fading.

Scotch closed the door. "Set your stuff in the corner and I'll show you around."

On the lower level, Lainey dropped her gear. She touched the natural stone wall. It stood seven feet high, capped by the logs she'd seen from outside. "Are we below ground here, or did you build into the hill?"

"Both, actually. Out here we had to dig down, but in the back, it's the depth of the hill."

Lainey nodded absently. The space was small, maybe four hundred square feet, the wood floor covered with throw rugs. Central to the room stood a large fireplace of the same stone as the walls around her. A sofa and chair squatted before the hearth, bracketed by a couple of sturdy tables. An old-style dining table with chrome legs and green laminate top sat nearby, keeping company with three padded chairs in need of new vinyl. The fireplace divided the living and kitchen areas. Continuing around it, Lainey noted a small metal stove butted up against the back of the fireplace. Several pots and pans hung from the stonework above. An untidy stack of wood filled a nearby metal box. Storage cabinets and counters ran the length of the exterior wall. Surprisingly, a large metal sink with an old-fashioned water pump stood there. Remembering Miguel's statement earlier in the day, she glanced at Scotch. "Running water?"

Scotch, who'd had her hands firmly planted in the back pockets of her jeans, reached up to pull off her baseball cap and run a hand through her hair. "Yeah, with a little elbow grease."

She seemed embarrassed. Lainey hastened to show her appreciation with a smile. "It's really nice. Did you do a lot of the work yourself?"

Flushing, Scotch reset her cap and dug her hands back into her pockets. "We had to get a backhoe in here to dig the pit, and the guys helped me set the logs, roof and windows." She waved at the stonework. "I laid the rock and built the fireplace, put in the flooring and porch."

"Wow, that's a lot of work." Lainey gave the room another look, seeing it with new eyes. *Talk about focus. I couldn't do this if I had a hundred years.* "So, where do we sleep?"

"Upstairs."

Lainey realized the kitchen had a lower ceiling than the main room. She followed Scotch back upstairs, seeing that the entry landing was the same level as a sleeping loft. Sturdy pine railings jutted out from either side of the chimney. The windows here let in sunlight, bathing the natural stone and wood with warmth. They passed a double bed with a large dresser at its foot and a nightstand beside it.

"This is mine," Scotch opened a long curtain dividing the room and gestured Lainey forward, "and this one is yours. Unless you want to swap."

The same layout only in reverse. The bed frame was rough-hewn pine, just like the railing. The pungent smell of the wood told Lainey that it was new and probably built just for her. A thick, inviting quilt and several pillows decorated the bed. Beneath her feet, a rag rug warmed the floorboards. The dresser and nightstand were well cared for, if a bit worn. An oil lamp perched on the nightstand.

Scotch lit the lamp with a wooden match and closed the heavy curtains across the window. "Is it okay? If you want to swap or move into the main cabin, I'd understand."

Lainey grinned reassurance. "No! This is really great. Better than a lot of places I've stayed in over the years." She sat on the bed, testing the box springs. "You've put a lot of work into setting this up for me, I can tell. Thank you."

"You're welcome." Scotch reddened and glanced away.

Lainey thought the uncertainty endearing. Licking her lips, she wondered whether her infatuation would pass. *God, I can almost taste her!* A mild swell of lust set her heart thumping.

Scotch's moment of hesitancy disappeared. Her hands returned to her back pockets. "Well, I guess we should get your stuff up here so you can settle in. We get up pretty early in the morning, so it's best if we hit the sack soon."

She heartily agreed with the idea of getting into bed with Scotch. Lainey scolded herself. "Sounds like a plan. I'm looking forward to my first board meeting."

Back on secure territory, Scotch chuckled. "Chores come before breakfast or meetings." She left the sleeping loft for the door. "I doubt you'll be looking forward to that when you understand what needs to be done."

Intrigued with the woman muscling her luggage into the room, Lainey didn't answer.

* * *

Twilight filtered from around the curtains in the loft. Scotch's body lay in a languid stupor, unmoving. Her mind refused to release her to sleep, preferring instead to play back the entire day's activities.

Not surprisingly, neither of the journalists were what she had anticipated. Since March, she'd spoken with several of the more prominent mushers, trying to get an idea of what to expect. Few had had anything like this experience; the closest was a fellow whose major sponsor was an outdoor clothing company. They had put up an extensive website about his training methods, but he had written most of the copy himself. The only other reporters Scotch had ever dealt with were those who routinely followed the racing.

Lainey and Howry weren't fans of the sport. She enjoyed their refreshing ignorance. When questioned, Lainey said she hadn't arrived for the last Iditarod until it was half completed, covering for a colleague who had injured himself. Whatever the reason, she must have been bitten by the dog racing bug. Why else would she return so soon after the last time?

Scotch had envisioned hosting sports reporters, people who knew their way around a kennel and sled, someone who understood the intricacies of racing, the specialized training and language. It didn't matter that she had done her homework on Lainey Hughes and knew the woman had never been involved in sports reporting. For some naive reason, Scotch's mind simply hadn't made the connection.

In her opinion, their lack of knowledge would work to the kennel's benefit. Without prior experience, neither reporter could confuse things. Kennels trained their animals in different ways. Each racer trained in their own style—some less scrupulous in caring for their dogs, some more interested in the process than the results. At least Scotch didn't have to worry about defending her methods compared to others. Sure, she had hopes of getting to Nome first someday but not at the expense of her team.

She sighed and rolled over. From the other side of the curtain, she heard the steady breathing of her new roommate. It had been two years since she had shared her cabin with anyone. She reckoned that was the cause of her inability to sleep. Her ears picked up noises that shouldn't be there—the occasional squeak of bedsprings, the rustle of sheets as Lainey shifted, a gentle murmur when she spoke in her sleep.

She had helped Lainey unpack, avidly curious. Why the backpack? Some of the gear, like her hiking boots, was worn with use; other pieces were obviously new. Why had she brought an arctic sleeping bag? Usually magazines and newspapers lined up hotels in Anchorage and Nome for their reporters. Did that mean that Lainey planned to follow the trail with the other hardcore journalists? The thought comforted Scotch, the possibility of seeing a familiar and friendly face at each checkpoint a gratifying idea. The suitcase had held toiletries, assorted woolen pants, flannel shirts, jeans and thick socks. There were even two sets of thermal and silk underwear.

As they unpacked, they discussed inconsequential things, becoming acquainted with one another. It felt vaguely familiar to Scotch. Now, lying in the dark, she studied the sensation. Smiling, she remembered a similar sense of camaraderie during sleepovers at friends' homes, something she hadn't done since she was fourteen. Those rare moments of sleeping over at a friend's house had been new and exciting. The feelings were no different now. She felt almost giddy at Lainey's presence.

Despite her tired eyes, Scotch couldn't sleep. She flopped onto her back. Regardless of the new arrivals, tomorrow was another day—another round of visitors, another batch of chores. She had to go into town to pick up a tour group of retirees for a day trip. She might even be able to wangle a donation or two out of them if she played her cards right. Normally the knowledge of a planned day trip lightened her spirits. Tonight she regretted the fact that Lainey would remain behind, beginning to learn the ropes of kennel life. The reservation for the day trip called for ten people. That would fill up two carts, leaving no room for anyone but her and Rye to guide them.

Her thoughts aimlessly shifting between plans for tomorrow, Lainey's smile, the sight of designer jeans and the incongruous sound of creaking rope, Scotch finally drifted off to sleep.

* * *

The Big Ben alarm clock on her nightstand jangled Scotch awake. She slapped at it until it went silent. Eyes still closed, she sat up in bed. The coolness of morning against her sleep-heated skin felt nice. Still, she shivered as she stretched and yawned. *Why am I so tired this morning?*

On the other side of the curtain, she heard a mumbled protest and squeaking bedsprings. *Oh, yeah.* Sleep-encrusted eyes opened in remembrance. Her mind wouldn't shut up last night. She debated about checking on Lainey. From the sound of things, she had probably rolled over to return to her dreams. Scotch heard no further movement. She decided to give Lainey a chance to waken on her own.

Scotch climbed out of bed and shoved her feet into her boots, not lacing them. She paused long enough to stretch to her full height with a slight groan. At the door, she grabbed a lightweight jacket from a peg and stepped outside. She trembled as a light breeze caressed her bare legs. Stepping off the porch, she made her way to the outhouse, the path familiar after years of travel.

Back inside, she stood silent on the landing, listening. It didn't sound like Lainey had risen. She wondered if she should venture into the woman's space to roust her. She hung up her jacket and continued down the steps. She'd wait until she had brewed coffee. If Lainey were a morning sourpuss, it would be better to have an offering to assuage her ill humor.

Having laid wood in the stove the night before, Scotch lit the scraps of paper and kindling with a match, watching until the wood caught flame. While the stove heated up, she measured coffee into the basket of the percolator. She worked the hand pump until water spouted from it into the coffee pot. Once it was full, she continued pumping to fill a couple of water pails, one of which she emptied into a large pan. She set both the pan and the percolator on the stove to heat.

The kitchen became warmer, and Scotch felt her drowsiness return. She scrubbed at her face. Testing the pan of water, she found that it was just hot enough for her purposes. She cast a glance at the ceiling, assessing her chances. It didn't appear that her visitor had awakened. Decided, she transferred half of the heated water into a large bowl, returning the pan to the back of the stove so it would retain its heat rather than boil. She pulled a washcloth and towel from a cabinet and grabbed the soap from the sink. A quick sponge bath would wake her right up.

CHAPTER ELEVEN

Lainey drowsed, half awake. She heard movement below and vaguely puzzled over what Scotch was up to. Her curiosity wasn't strong enough to entice her to rise. Instead, she wandered the halls of her mind, memories and fancies mixing and melding with the sounds and smells from the kitchen: Scotch laughing at a joke, her face lighting up until she glowed like copper, her lips curled in invitation, her eyes beckoning Lainey to circle the kitchen table, the other people there disappearing. Lainey, free to experience what she desired, stood and leaned across the green laminate table, their lips moving close, breath mingling, the warm smell of alcohol blanketing her. But it wasn't scotch. *What's that smell?*

The dream dissipated, consciousness intrigued by what her nose told her. *Coffee. Definitely coffee. And something else.* She rolled onto her back and inhaled deeply to identify the second scent. *Soap. Yeah, that's it.* Pleased with her deductive abilities, she drifted.

A frown crossed her face as her body reminded her how much coffee she had imbibed the night before. There was an outhouse somewhere around, according to Scotch. Groaning, Lainey rolled into a ball and covered her head with a pillow. The sun teased from behind the curtain, but she didn't feel rested. She didn't want to get out of her toasty bed.

Lainey uncovered her head. *Is it early or late? It has to be late, why else is Scotch making coffee?* She thought she'd heard an alarm clock. *Or was that part of a dream?* Her bladder became insistent, shoving away any other considerations. Lainey tossed off her quilt and jumped to her feet. She rubbed her bare upper arms as she jammed her feet into her boots, resolving in future to sleep in long johns instead of a T-shirt and shorts. She barely registered Scotch's empty bed as she passed through, intent on relieving the demand of her bodily functions.

Once outside, Lainey realized that she had forgotten to grab a sweatshirt, and cursed at the day's coolness. Shivering almost caused her bladder to release while she glanced wildly about the clearing. She stumbled a few steps farther from the door, relieved to see a small wooden building nearby. *Thank God!* She hastened toward it, the door of the outhouse slamming loudly.

If the day had been warmer, Lainey might have drifted off again. Her body returned to its lethargic state as she sat on the cold plastic toilet seat, her eyelids drooping, heavy despite the chill. A twinge in her side reminded her of where she was, and she finished her task. Outside, she inhaled a bit of fresh air, wrinkling her nose as it chased away the general fetidness. Outhouses smelled the same worldwide. She hurried back to the cabin, pausing on the porch to look back. Despite the gentle ache in her ribs, it was kind of nice out. She hugged herself, her fingers finding the familiar thick scar tissue beneath the thin cotton of her T-shirt. Grimacing, she released her grasp and went inside.

Standing on the landing, Lainey shivered violently in the welcome heat. She heard movement, saw a shadow as Scotch moved about the kitchen. The smell of coffee beckoned, and she followed her nose.

Scotch leaned against a counter, cradling a cup, eyes closed as she inhaled the steam rising from its contents. Her tawny curls fringed in dampness, she smelled heavily of the soap that had roused Lainey. She wore flannel shorts and a baggy, sleeveless T-shirt. Her feet were encased in unlaced boots. Lainey didn't know which made her mouth water more—the coffee cup's contents or the sleep-tousled look of her roommate. She swallowed. "Good morning."

Scotch smiled at the sound of her voice. "Good morning." She opened her eyes. "Coffee cups are in that cabinet. Cream and sugar containers are over there."

"Thanks." Lainey busied herself with obtaining caffeine, trying to ignore the fact that the armholes of Scotch's T-shirt hung almost to her elbows. If she moved her arms, Lainey would have a delightful view of some compelling anatomy.

"Sleep well?"

Lainey basked in the heat from the stove, using a dishtowel as a pot holder. "Like a rock." She poured coffee and inhaled deeply of its aroma. This was one thing she never took for granted. Not every culture had coffee, and she sorely missed it when she was out of country. She sipped, pleased to note Scotch brewed it strong. Turning, she blinked. *Was she just checking out my legs?*

"That's good. Sometimes newcomers have trouble sleeping with the constant sunlight."

Lainey moved to copy Scotch's stance, leaning against the counter beside her to worship her coffee. "So, what are we doing up so late?"

Scotch chuckled. "This ain't late."

Lainey liked the sound of her laugh. "What time is it?"

"About five thirty."

"Ugh." She stuck her tongue out, eliciting another warm laugh.

"We meet up with Rye and Irish in the dog kitchen at six. The dogs have to be fed."

"And then we nap?" This time she got a nudge with a shoulder. Lainey grinned like an idiot. *God, I've got it bad! Surely Scotch has some horribly bad habit—nose picking, uncontrollable urges to spit, foul temper... Something!*

"No. Then we clean the dog kitchen and barn, do pooper scooper duty, transfer the kennel dogs, let the Big Dog out, clean up and eat breakfast."

Lainey feigned horror. "All that before breakfast?" Her voice became faint, her accent thickening into that of a Southern belle. "I think I have a case of the vapors." She batted her eyes at Scotch and received a smirk.

"No problem. Smelling salts ain't got nothing on dog crap."

"Hey!" She bumped her hip against Scotch's. Scotch laughed and drained her cup, distracting Lainey with the unexpected revelation of skin.

"There's hot water on the stove, if you want to clean up some. I put out a towel and washcloth for you." Scotch moved away to set the cup in the sink. "I'll go up and change, give you some privacy. Let me know when you're done."

Lainey lifted her cup in thanks, watching until Scotch had disappeared around the fireplace. She heard the tread of boots on steps, the light creak above her head as Scotch reached her room and began changing clothes.

She stared at the wood stove, her mind's eye upstairs. Separated by mere inches of wood, her lust object was getting naked, that beautiful body revealed as she shucked boots and sleep clothes. Sighing, Lainey forced away the brewing lust. *She's straight. Remember that.*

* * *

As promised, Lainey learned more about the care and feeding of dogs that morning than she had ever imagined possible. The sheer amount of time involved shouldn't have amazed her—what with ninety-five dogs to feed—but it did. She and Howry watched as the Fullers carefully measured out sixteen gallons of water and poured it into a metal drum. While Rye lit the propane, Lainey helped Scotch collect fifteen frozen salmon from the freezer. They went into the drum, heads and all. Lainey grimaced in disgust at the idea, glad that breakfast wasn't served until after morning chores. It might give her stomach a chance to settle.

With someone always stirring it, the fishy mixture came to a boil then was allowed to cool. The crew went over the lists posted by the door in the barn. These indicated which animals had specific dietary care instructions and what additional supplements the kennel as a whole required. Howry turned up the propane, and the dog stew attained a second boil. When it had cooled, Scotch climbed up on a stepladder to reach inside the pot and chop the now pliable salmon into chunks. A third boil came and went, this time with Irish using a large empty coffee can to measure rice into the stew. Lainey watched in dismay as yet a fourth boil was achieved. At this rate, the dogs wouldn't eat until noon. Rye turned the propane off and covered the pot. Lainey and Howry added measures of vitamin supplements, bone meal and dry chow to the cooling result. Then they took pails to fill.

This was Lainey's first foray among the dogs. Fortunately they seemed far more interested in the contents of her bucket than in her, though one or two turned a suspicious eye on her. She noted the Fullers giving each animal a little undivided attention and copied them. Before she completed her assigned section, she had stepped in three piles of crap, dog hair layered her sturdy work jeans, and saliva slathered her hands. She returned to the kitchen with a stupid grin on her face, the canine enthusiasm having rubbed off on her as thickly as their shedding spring coats.

More water was poured into the leftovers and a second trip made through the pens. Then followed a round of scooping excrement. While Howry, Rye and Scotch cleaned the dog kitchen, Lainey assisted Irish with putting the correct animals into the two runs. Lainey let the Big Dog for the day off her chain. She placed a grease pencil checkmark beside Heldig's name—wondering where the Fullers came up with the names and how they kept them all straight.

Bone tired though she had only been up for two hours, Lainey stumbled into the main house. It had been a while since she'd had that much of a workout. She eyed the family with new respect. Doing this day in and day out from childhood had to give them a hardiness that few their age acquired. She recalled Scotch's bare arms that morning and the play of muscle beneath the pale skin.

After a large country breakfast, the family remained around the table. Lainey realized this was standard practice. All meetings took place here. Helen, dressed in sweater and jeans, had a notepad and pen. Her husband, Thom, was dressed in a long-sleeved flannel shirt, the collar undone and a white T-shirt visible beneath.

He cleared his throat. "The Fuller Kennel Board of Directors is called to order. All members present and accounted for."

Lainey blinked at the formality, glancing at Bon who played under the table with an empty shoebox.

Rye smiled. "Yeah, he's a board member too. We all are."

"Interesting." Howry scribbled a note.

"We're here to finalize some things with Ms. Hughes and Mr. Howry, at their request."

Everyone, including Howry, looked expectantly at Lainey, and all those blue eyes, patient in their regard, unnerved her slightly. What would they look like when she explained the changes the magazine was insisting on? Lainey focused on Scotch, wondering whether she'd agree to the new deal. "As you know, I made last minute arrangements with you for Don to come with me on this adventure. The senior editors at *Cognizance* decided they wanted something a little different for the article. Don will have the primary responsibility for the article and photos of Scotch."

Scotch glanced at Howry with a frown. "What'll you be doing?"

Lainey didn't answer the question but continued speaking. "We realize that this might be a deal breaker. If you don't agree to these new stipulations, we will certainly understand."

Helen, her expression a mirror image of her eldest daughter's, cocked her head. "What sort of changes, dear? You must have some purpose for being here."

Lainey steered her gaze away from Scotch's sudden wary expression. *What does she think I'll say?* "I originally contracted with *Cognizance* to do a series on Scotch's next run for the Iditarod. However, my editor's bosses have decided to do another piece, as well. While Don is focused on Scotch, they have asked me to run the Iditarod."

CHAPTER TWELVE

"You mean like enter the race on your own?" Irish asked.

"That's the idea."

"What?" Rye snorted. "You don't know the first thing about mushing."

"Regrettably true." Lainey avoided Scotch's eyes, not wanting to see her response to the news. "The magazine's done some research into the cost of such a venture. They have authorized me to offer you thirty thousand dollars to train me and to allow me the use of a team and equipment for the upcoming Iditarod."

Thom whistled at the amount. "You know some kennels would ask for more."

Lainey met his gaze squarely. "I know. In addition, you'll still receive the monthly amount we agreed on to pay for our room and board. That ultimately works out to more than what you would get for a simple training contract. Besides, Don and I will both continue working, so there's also the added man-hours you won't be required to pay for."

"What if I refuse?"

Lainey's heart thumped at the seriousness in Scotch's voice, and she finally looked at her. Regardless of the position the Fullers now found themselves in, Scotch emanated the same confidence that had first drawn Lainey. And no doubt her family would back whatever Scotch decided. Laincy wondered whether this was the source of Scotch's self-assurance, and she felt a little let down. Surely it wasn't as simple as having a loving family. A lot of people had that. "Then I leave. Don will remain behind to do an original piece about your training. I've been instructed to approach two other kennels with the training offer."

Scotch's ears almost perked up. She leaned forward, elbows on her knees. "Which kennels?"

The sudden interest confused Lainey. Howry answered when she didn't. "Either the Larsens' or Mythic Spirit Kennels."

At the second name, Scotch scoffed, sitting upright. "The Thorpes?" she demanded. "They barely know how to point their dogs in the right direction!"

"You'd be lucky if they gave you a team worth the effort of training." Rye shook his head, a frown on his face.

"Be lucky if she didn't have to scratch the first day," Scotch told her brother.

"Don't they still bite their dogs' ears?" Helen received a round of disgusted agreement from her family.

Lainey wondered if they were yanking her chain. Her face contorted at the thought of putting a furry ear in her mouth. "Biting ears?"

Scotch's demeanor lightened at her expression. She smiled. "Yeah. It's a method of control some people still use to keep their teams in line."

"Uck." Lainey shook herself. "Okay, maybe not Mythic Spirit Kennels."

As the laughter died away, everyone's attention was riveted on Scotch, who rubbed her jaw in thought. From beneath the table, even Bon stared at her. Lainey found his highly tuned familial instinct intriguing. It had been a long time since she had experienced a family dynamic. Had she missed seeing the subtle wordless play in others, or were the Fullers unnaturally receptive to one another?

"I can't say that I like it," Scotch finally said. "I need to concentrate on my own team when I'm training for the race. I can't allow any distractions."

Lainey felt her spirits plunge. The other kennels were located across the state. She wondered if she could break the contract with

Strauss without damaging her credibility or reputation. *Damn, I need a drink.*

"Why'd they pick you?" Rye asked.

Drawn from her disappointment and her yearnings, Lainey looked at him. "Excuse me?"

"Why you? Why not Don?"

She considered the question. "Because the initial gig was mine, I guess. That, and the original premise focused on a woman musher." She shrugged. "They wanted a companion piece to a professional woman racer, hence, a rookie woman racer."

Thom cleared his throat. "So, if we don't go through with training you, Scotch still gets the national coverage?"

"Oh, yes." Howry hastened to ease their minds. "That plan remains the same. It's just that I'll be doing the piece instead of Lainey."

"Larsen's good," Scotch admitted, "but his kennel isn't that large. His second string would be pretty poor. And he doesn't have the extra time to train anyone, either." She snorted. "I'm not even going to get into the pros and cons of the Thorpes."

Lainey noted that Scotch was studying her with an odd intensity. Her body responded to the scrutiny. Fortunately she had worn a heavy sweater that hid her hardening nipples. *God, those eyes are penetrating.* Whatever Scotch was searching for, she seemed to find it.

"All right. Let's do it."

Ears buzzing faintly, Lainey wondered whether she was going to pass out from the shock of relief flooding her system.

"You sure?" Thom asked.

"Yeah." Scotch nodded, sitting back with a speculative demeanor. "Rye and Irish can help train her on the basics. I can give her the specifics she'll need for the Iditarod itself."

"Sure." Rye grinned at Lainey. "Besides, you'll place higher with one of our teams. There's a better selection of dogs to choose from."

Lainey cleared her throat. "You don't need to vote?"

Thom smiled. "Well, I suppose, just to make it official. All those for accepting a trainee for the Iditarod?" Every Fuller raised their hand, even Bon, who laughed and raised both. "Well, there you go." Thom glanced at a clock. "Holy smokes, I've got to get going or I'll be late. Meeting adjourned."

That was the catalyst. Thom headed out the door, grabbing a construction helmet on the way. Helen chased after to give him a good-bye kiss. When she returned to the table, she gave Lainey a hug. "Welcome to the family, dear. You too, Don. I'll see everyone at lunch." With that, she scooped Bon from beneath the table and carted him out the door.

Scotch placed her plate in the sink. "I'll be back in half an hour."

Lainey wondered if Scotch was acting a bit more wary. She had hoped to spend time with her after the bombshell to assess the potential damage to their non-existent working relationship. "Where are you going?"

"We have a day trip scheduled for some tourists. I've got to pick them up in town. You'll be on your own today."

"You can hang with me." Irish finished clearing the table and began wiping it down with a washrag.

"What are the chances of joining the day trip?" Howry asked.

Rye filled the sink with water in preparation for doing dishes. "Not good. The carts hold five people each and the reservation is for ten, so there will only be room if there's a cancellation."

"I've got to scoot." Scotch strode out of the kitchen.

Lainey almost followed her. Was Scotch's attitude a tad cooler than earlier? Lainey didn't know whether to laugh at the ridiculous concern or cry that it could be true. *What the fuck is wrong with me?* In response, a wave of need washed through her, so strong she reached out for a chair to remain standing. Her desire for a drink was strong, much more so than she had experienced in the past. Was Strauss right? She brutally smothered the small voice. *Bullshit! I'm not an alcoholic.* She debated the wisdom of backing out—finding a lawyer to annul her contract with *Cognizance* and taking the next flight to Peru to photograph monasteries. *When the hell did life get so damned complicated? Christ, I need a drink!* The thought dashed cold water on her jitters.

"Hey, you okay?"

Lainey stared at Howry a long moment before forcing a smile. "I'm fine. Must be jet lag."

He cocked his head, eyes narrowed. With a nod, he released her arm and went to the sink to help Rye with the dishes.

After a bracing breath, Lainey turned to Irish. "I'd love to hang with you today. You can show me the ropes about sleds and give me a personal introduction to the dogs."

Her reward was a brilliant smile, so like Scotch's that it took Lainey's breath away. Irish grabbed Lainey's hand and tugged her toward the door. "Cool! Come on!"

Lainey gave Howry a wave, receiving a wink in return before she was dragged out the door.

* * *

Scotch had a difficult time keeping her attention on their visitors. They were a group of retirees living out of their motor homes, the youngest an energetic fifty-four years of age. It helped that Scotch spent a good deal of their trip concentrating on the dogs. Ahead of her, Rye had a full load as well. They pulled into Lafferty's fish camp, a regular stop on this run. The Fullers notified Ray Lafferty by radio whenever they scheduled an overnight or day trip. In return for a percentage of the fee the kennel charged, he gave the tourists a fun "mountain man experience" and fed them a rustic lunch.

"Fuller!" he bellowed as the vehicle engines died down. "How the hell are you?"

Scotch grinned, seeing a couple of the tourists shrink away from his larger-than-life persona. "Pretty good, Ray." She disappeared into a bear hug. They stood about the same height, and his thick beard scratched her cheek. Pulling away, she gestured at her charges. "Let me introduce you to our guests."

Lafferty personally welcomed everyone with a warm handshake and an equally warm smile, relaxing even the most aloof of the visitors. As he distracted them, she and Rye snacked their teams on chunks of moose liver. Half of the tourists went with Lafferty as he showed them around his camp. The rest watched as Scotch and her brother saw to the dogs. She relaxed into teaching mode, explaining as she massaged each dog that she was searching for slight injuries as well as keeping the animals used to intimate handling.

Eventually the smell of frying fish drew their admirers away. Scotch went to the river to collect water for her team as Lafferty regaled his audience with tall tales of life on the frontier.

"So what do you think about this training business?"

She looked over at Rye, squatting beside her on the same errand. "I don't know. It makes sense, I guess. I just wasn't expecting it."

"Yeah." They filled their water jugs in silence. "What's she like?"

A well of emotion surged as Scotch tried to formulate an answer. "She's nice," she finally stated, painfully aware of how little that conveyed. "I just hope she can weather the winter."

"Not everyone's like Tanya."

Scotch shot her brother a sharp look. He didn't look at her as he stood, turning to lug the water to his dogs. Grim at his reminder, she collected her jugs and started after him. Spartacus and Cleatis were posturing, looking to squabble. They worked well together but, given an opportunity, would brawl like overgrown puppies. She welcomed the distraction, pulling Cleatis from the line to tie him off to a sturdy tree nearby. Once she had watered her team, she settled down in the shade to think. Her brother joined the party at the fire, running interference with their guests to give her time alone.

How the hell am I going to train Lainey to run the Iditarod? Why did I agree to this? She had a tough enough time ahead training her first-string dogs to do the job. She had never tried teaching someone else to do what she did. To be honest, Irish and Rye didn't have time to instruct Lainey either. When the snow flew, all three of them would be on their sleds, preparing for the races. This winter, Irish had her eye on winning a handful of sprints sponsored by local businesses. Rye wanted to run the Junior Iditarod for his third year and hit the Junior Yukon Quest if the kennel could afford the entry fees. Scotch aimed for the Copper Basin, a handful of adult sprints and the Iditarod itself. They had little time to devote to a rookie.

Her team settled down for a nap. She sighed and looked up into the overhead leaves. She'd had the perfect opportunity to get rid of her new roommate. With Howry writing the magazine article, Scotch would be left alone in her cabin—no stranger on the other side of the room, no emotional upheaval, no dread. *Why didn't I take it?*

She recalled Lainey's uncertain expression as she conveyed her news. At the time, Scotch only wanted to ease her obvious trepidation. She liked Lainey, had enjoyed the previous evening getting to know her. Despite her concerns with Lainey's emotional ability to handle Alaskan winters, she thought they could be great friends. More than friends. She pushed the thought away. No. Never that.

At some point in her life, Lainey had faced the business end of a gun and survived. But the Iditarod was an endurance run that could last anywhere from nine days to three weeks, depending on the weather and the trail. If Lainey got into a life-or-death situation, there would be places along the trail she would be utterly alone. Was she tough enough to withstand that type of test?

The inclusion of arctic gear among Lainey's things made sense now. Most of it was new, indicating that Scotch's assessment about Lainey's experience with severe cold was right on the money. Would Scotch be able to impart the important elements of how to deal with the extremes? The ability to gauge the climate was a learned ability. Would she be able to prepare Lainey well enough to keep her from frostbite and hypothermia? *Which is worse—becoming so depressed from light deprivation that you take matters into your own hands or dying on the trail from lack of knowledge?*

Scotch's stomach grumbled, reminding her it had been a while since breakfast. The strong smell of grilling fish drew her attention back to her surroundings. She saw most of her tour group filling up on Lafferty's lunch buffet. She had already agreed to teach Lainey. *Nothing to be done about it now except follow it through.* She would have plenty of time to worry it to death. Standing, she dusted off the butt of her pants and joined the group at the fire.

CHAPTER THIRTEEN

July

Intent on the packet of papers in her lap, Lainey hardly noticed the road. "The undersigned hereby elects to voluntarily enter the Race, knowing that it may be a hazardous and dangerous activity. The undersigned hereby voluntarily assumes all risks of loss, damage or injury, including death!" she quoted. She looked at the driver. "Death?"

Scotch grinned. "Don't worry. The trail is watched around the clock. If it looks like there's a problem or a musher is lost, snow machines are sent out from the checkpoints to find him. The worst you'll have to worry about is frostbite or hypothermia." She glanced at her passenger. "Didn't you read that when you got it notarized this morning?"

"Well, yeah. Sort of." She allowed herself to be distracted, not wanting to dwell on the issue of frostbite. "I guess I got a little overwhelmed by the number of forms required."

"Read it carefully before you sign up this morning. You'll lose a portion of your entry fee if you pull out before the race starts."

Though she knew she didn't really have the option to back out of her agreement, Lainey nodded as she returned her attention to the stack of forms the Fullers had given her the previous night. Having done her research as soon as Strauss had tossed down his creative gauntlet, she had already familiarized herself with the rules and regulations. Now she had a race application, a housing request for after her eventual arrival at the finish line in Nome, forms to list her sponsors and request banquet tickets, a questionnaire about her possible needs that included everything from dog booties to horse meat, a membership application for the Iditarod Trail Committee and a list of smaller races that she could run in to qualify for the real thing. "I never figured there'd be such a paper trail."

"You ain't seen nothing yet." Scotch turned off the main road with familiar ease. "There's also the dog care agreement, a local contact list, a vet form and a vet check form for every dog on your training team, whether they make the final cut or not. You'll get those when you sign in."

"And you do this every year?"

"When we can afford it. I usually run one year on, one year off. This will be the first time I've run two years in a row, thanks to you." She pulled into a busy parking lot. "We're here."

Lainey looked at the crowd milling outside Iditarod headquarters, close to fifty or sixty people. She recognized several veteran mushers from the previous year's press packet. An awning near the building sheltered an impromptu area for the sign-up. A few feet away, smoke from a barbecue streamed into the air. "Are all of these people signing up?"

Scotch chuckled. "No. Maybe a handful are proxy—holding places for someone else who can't make it today." She turned off the engine and leaned on the steering wheel to assess the gathering. "Looks like maybe thirty or so mushers are here. Don't know about rookies, though. A lot of them come from established kennels or from out of state. For all I know, half the family members here are rookies looking to sign up."

The woman's profile captured Lainey's attention. She stared at the motion of light and shadow from sun shining through trees, playing on Scotch's golden skin. Today she wore the rust-brown cap, the same one Lainey had first seen her wearing in Nome. It seemed appropriate.

Seemingly aware of her intense scrutiny, Scotch turned with a curious smile on her face. "What?"

"I see Rye and Don." Lainey pointed to another parked dog truck, the photographer comfortably seated on the hood and the teenager leaning against the front wheel well. She smothered a sigh of relief as Scotch looked away, distracted from pursuing whatever she thought Lainey was thinking.

"Come on." Scotch opened her door. "Let's go see where we stand." She scooped up a folder from the seat.

Lainey climbed out of the truck but remained behind to dig her camera out of the bag on the floorboard. She watched Scotch casually wave greetings to people she knew, amazed again at the way she carried herself. Over the last couple of days, she had witnessed quite a dichotomy within the young woman. There were times she exhibited the easy assurance she had shown at the awards banquet in Nome. Then it would disappear, revealing a sweet uncertainty, perhaps even a pensive quality. Maybe the sense of community fueled Scotch's confidence. It seemed she knew almost everyone there. What was it like to grow up in one place, never moving, never having to make new friends?

Satisfied with the condition of her equipment, Lainey hung one camera from her neck and another from her shoulder. She retrieved her paperwork and closed the truck door.

"Welcome to Iditarod headquarters." Howry hopped down from the hood. "Scotch is number twenty-seven and you're number twenty-eight."

"Geez, and you got here early?"

"Yeah." Rye chuckled. "Some of these guys actually came out last night and made a party of it." Someone called his name and he excused himself.

"You ready for this?"

Lainey gave her colleague a rueful grin. "Not really. I don't have much choice, though."

"Sure you do. You can always call Ben, tell him the deal's off. He'd understand."

The mention of backing out raised Lainey's hackles. Strauss would think she'd dropped out because she couldn't handle the prohibition against booze. *Damned if I'll go back and prove him right.* Besides, Scotch Fuller became more intriguing the longer she stayed. She had barely scratched the surface of what made Scotch tick and Lainey wasn't willing to jeopardize that. If she reneged on the contract, Scotch would probably find it impossible to raise the fees and kennel costs for an Iditarod run this year. The Fullers had taken a major financial chance in agreeing to this article. "Nope. Not an option."

Howry shrugged. "Hope it's worth the hassle."

Lainey's anger stabbed ice through her veins. She leaned closer, her voice lowered to avoid projecting. "Get this straight: this is not for a lay, not for a seduction. I don't want to hear any more innuendo in that area. Understood?"

Howry's face blanched, his tan fading, followed immediately by a flush. She hadn't seen him furious in a long time, almost failing to recognize the signals as his anger also blossomed. She took an automatic step back.

He followed her, responding in the same low tone. "The hassle I was referring to was the potential injury you're facing for a stupid magazine spread, not of getting into her pants."

"I'm sorry. I'm an idiot."

Mollified, he still glared at her. "If we're going to work together, you need to get over this hypersensitivity. We both have a good idea why you went with this, but if I thought for a minute that was the only reason for this gambit, I'd bail in a heartbeat. Give me a little credit."

She blushed and dropped her gaze. "I know. I'm sorry. I just...I haven't figured out her draw, and it's driving me batty."

"Lainey."

Forcing herself to face him, she saw his expression had changed.

"I wasn't forced here, okay? It's a damn good idea, regardless of who came up with it. I think it'll sell magazines. If we're lucky, it'll also win us a couple of awards." He grinned and winked, the familiar devil-may-care attitude returning full force. "If we both get laid, all the better."

Lainey wondered if she should laugh or smack him. She did neither, hearing Scotch call her name. Squeezing Howry's arm, she released him and turned.

* * *

Scotch lounged in a plastic chair, legs crossed at the ankles and hands laced over her belly, a bottle of beer within easy reach. She had tipped the bill of her cap over her sunglasses and appeared to be napping. In reality, she was watching the comings and goings at the sign-up tent as the sun slipped farther west. Rye spoke with friends from the Junior Alaskan Sled Dog and Racing Association. Howry wandered about with a hamburger in one hand and a camera in the other, getting what he called "flavor" for the first article. He had already taken photos of her and Lainey signing up for the race, as well as shots of a handful of the better-known mushers. Her father had exercised his right as owner of Fuller Construction to take the afternoon off. Thom hung out under the sign-up tent, swapping tales with the older men there. Not many entrants went home after signing in, and the party was in full swing. Scotch figured Irish would be by when their mother and Miguel finished at the kennels. Right now, her roommate was attracting most of her attention.

Lainey lay in a patch of sunlight, leaning on her elbows as she soaked up the rays. She appeared to be enjoying herself, and Scotch took pleasure in watching. She mused on the color of Lainey's skin tones, envying Lainey's darker complexion. No matter how hard Scotch tried, she never got more than a light golden tan during summer. She bet Lainey turned almost bronze, given the proper amount of exposure. Scotch looked forward to seeing it happen. Her veiled gaze idly roamed the slim body. She'd had the opportunity to see Lainey wearing the shorts and T-shirt in which she slept. There had been no evidence of a gunshot wound on her arms and legs. That meant it had to be a torso or head wound. If Lainey had been wounded in the head, it would have had to have been a minor injury. *Otherwise, she'd be dead, right?*

Scotch frowned at the thought of how a gunshot wound scarred. She knew a boy who had shot himself with his father's pistol; it wasn't pretty. Did Lainey feel self-conscious? Did she have reconstructive surgery during that year off?

Did she have a boyfriend?

The thought startled her. She searched her memory. After their arrival, Scotch had realized that Howry and Lainey weren't romantically involved. Lainey hadn't mentioned anyone special in her life. Scotch hadn't seen a ring. Would a strange man show up at some point to visit Lainey? Her nose wrinkled in distaste. It suddenly became very important that she know. "Do you have a boyfriend?"

Lainey opened her eyes, shifting to one elbow as she brought her other hand up to shade her face. Her movement revealed a nice bit of cleavage. "No."

Scotch felt a wave of relief followed by disgruntlement. *It doesn't matter. Don't get close. It's too dangerous.* It made no difference whether or not Lainey had someone. After next March, she'd be gone.

A smile curled Lainey's lips. "Do you?"

Scotch laughed, relaxing into the increasingly familiar friendship developing between them. "Nope. Most of the men I know aren't what I'd consider dating material."

Nervous under Lainey's examination, Scotch picked up her bottle. "You want a beer?"

Lainey paused a fraction too long. "I don't drink."

There seemed to be a wealth of meaning in the simple phrase. Scotch hesitated in the process of standing. "Ever?"

Lainey's smile held a tinge of wistfulness. "Not on a gig."

Scotch stared at her a moment. "All right then." She finished rising. "Want a soda instead?"

"Yeah. That'd be nice."

"One soda coming up." Scotch poured the dregs out of her beer bottle as she headed for the coolers located near the barbecue. There she retrieved two cans of soda, wondering why. The smile she received from Lainey upon her return didn't answer the question, but it definitely gave her cause to do whatever she could to see it more often.

CHAPTER FOURTEEN

Under Scotch's watchful eye, Lainey carefully attached the tug line to Jonah's harness. She completed the connection by attaching a short neck line from the main tow line to the dog's collar. Laughing, she fended off the exuberant licking of her new friend and stood up to examine her work.

Jonah was the largest of the six dogs given the dubious honor of being on Lainey's team. As soon as she stepped away, he pulled, trying to get the ATV to move. With all the effort he put into it, she almost expected the vehicle to pop its brakes and take off without her. "He certainly seems...eager."

"Oh yeah." Scotch leaned against the second ATV, her team already hitched and clamoring to get on the trail. Her arms crossed, she regarded Jonah with indulgent pride. "He's run all three Iditarods with me. The boy's a go-getter, a powerhouse."

Lainey wondered why Scotch was allowing her the use of dogs from her previous races. Surely she would want the more experienced animals on her own team. Maybe Lainey had misunderstood when Scotch officially introduced her to her team that morning at breakfast. Perhaps Lainey would train them, but then Scotch would take them on the Iditarod.

"Who's next?"

"Aegis." Lainey grinned as she gave the correct answer. Scotch waved her off to retrieve the dog.

Shy and sweet, Aegis had an attitude that was at odds with her size. She too was a heavy animal. Lainey remembered from her lecture that the four-year-old was close to eighty pounds. Both Aegis and Jonah ran in the wheel positions, which required the extra weight and power. Their job was to turn a sled that weighed upwards of five or six hundred pounds.

Once Aegis stood in position, Lainey went back to get the next. She stopped at an off-white dog called Kaara. Before she released the dog, Scotch called to her.

"That's a mistake, believe me."

Lainey frowned, ignoring the smiling animal at her feet. "She's on my team, right?"

"That she is." Scotch smothered a grin. "But who's her partner in crime?"

"Bonaparte!" Lainey turned to see a black and white male standing majestic atop his doghouse, nose held in the air with disdain for his canine comrades. Bonaparte was small and as snooty as his namesake. Lainey had been warned that if he felt slighted in any way, he would refuse to run. She detached his chain and got a firm grip on his collar in anticipation of his lunge, only to have him stalk regally toward the ATV. Lainey bit back a chuckle, feeling more like a courtesan than a dog handler.

"Whew!" Scotch wiped feigned sweat from her brow. "That could have been a disaster."

"Oh, come on. He's a dog. In a week he wouldn't remember that it was me who flubbed up." Lainey attached the neck and tug lines.

Scotch shrugged. "You'd think so, wouldn't you?" She didn't offer more.

Lainey wondered if this was a set up for a joke. "Now Kaara."

"Yup. She's the only one that can work with him. I think it's true love."

"Is that so, Kaara? Are you in love with Bonaparte?" Kaara squirmed as she wagged her entire body in response. Lainey gave her a good scratching before leading her away from her house. "Well, far be it for me to interfere with Cupid's arrows."

Bonaparte and Kaara were swing dogs. Their purpose was to not only play follow-the-leader, but to keep the team in line during turns. They heard the commands from the driver, but heeded the lead dogs in front of them. As Scotch had explained things, if she called out "Gee!" and every dog immediately obeyed, the entire team would take a right turn at the same time. Instead, the swing dogs kept the team moving forward until they arrived at the turn.

Next came the lead dogs. Lainey had been given two. Sholo was an all-black male with liquid brown eyes. He had never run a long-distance endurance race, though he had experience leading in shorter contests. In particular, he had been with Rye during the previous Junior Yukon Quest, which gave Lainey an edge on the next Yukon 250. She would have to run it to qualify for the Iditarod, and Sholo knew the trail from firsthand encounter.

Trace was Sholo's opposite in appearance, all white with bright blue eyes. If Lainey kept him on her team, he would be worth his weight in gold. He had run the Iditarod with Scotch for two of her three races, finishing both times. Only a training injury had kept him at the kennel for her most recent run.

Lainey hooked Trace's and Sholo's collars together and stood to regard her handiwork. Six sets of canine eyes looked back at her.

"Who's the lead dog?" Scotch climbed aboard her ATV.

"I am." Lainey felt anticipation skitter down her spine as she walked down the line of dogs to her vehicle.

Though the brakes were still on, Scotch's team tried to pull as soon as she started the engine. "These guys are used to a more knowledgeable driver. They'll mind their Ps and Qs for a day or two. Expect some acting out after that."

Lainey clambered onto her four-wheel vehicle. "Yes, ma'am," she called over the sounds of engines and anxious barking, sending an impish grin to her mentor. Directly in front of her, Jonah redoubled his efforts, standing on two legs in his harness as he tried to get them moving.

Shaking her head, Scotch returned the smile. "Follow me and don't let your dogs get too close to us. Remember your commands."

"Are we talking or are we driving?"

Scotch's expression changed to amused warning at the challenge. Rather than speak, she called out, "Ready!" Her team tightened any remaining slack on the mainline in anticipation. "Let's go!" She released the brake and jerked forward as the dogs did what they loved to do.

Lainey watched them go, her team barking in demand to go after them. Sudden anxiety hit her and she swallowed. *What if I can't control them?* For a moment she ached for the burn of alcohol, a little fortification.

Sholo and Trace stared over their shoulders at her. Brown and blue eyes begged. She almost heard their thoughts: *Why suit us up for the big game if we're stuck sitting on the bench? Let's go!*

I do not need a drink! Her hands shook, belying the falseness of her determined thoughts. "Ready!" she called, her voice holding more confidence than she felt. Her leaders swung their heads around in preparation. She popped the brake. "Let's go!"

Her head snapped back as the team surged forward. She clutched at the handles to retain her seat. The dogs barked happily and frolicked on their run, kicking up their feet, tails wagging madly as they towed her along. Her thoughts of acquiring a neck brace in the near future flew away along the wind that caressed her face.

The team followed Scotch's out of the dog yard and along a wide path. Trees whipped past. Lainey eyed the speedometer with amazement as it hit eleven miles per hour. She grinned in delight, focusing on the journey. Up ahead, Scotch's team turned right, leaving the main trail. Lainey glanced quickly at her right hand where she'd scrawled a large "G" in blue marker. On her left hand, an "H" reminded her of the word "haw." When Sholo and Trace arrived at the turn, she hollered, "Gee!" Her smile widened as the leaders made the easy turn onto the new trail. The rest of the team followed smoothly and she steered the ATV after them.

Heeding Scotch's warning, Lainey used the brakes to keep the vehicles apart by two car lengths. The smaller path was rougher than the previous one. Lainey realized she might have saddle sores before the summer was out. Needing little encouragement from her, the dogs joyfully chased after Scotch. Sun flickered between the trees, splashing across Lainey's face.

After too short a time, Scotch raised her hand to signal a stop. The mood of her dogs contagious, Lainey frowned. It was too early; they had hardly gotten started. Despite her disaffection, she called out, "Whoa!" With steady pressure, she applied the brake, bringing her team to a halt behind Scotch's. The woman had parked and shut down her ATV. She now stood beside it, rummaging in her backpack for treats.

Lainey parked, as well, and climbed down. "Is that it?" Disappointment was clear in her voice.

Scotch looked up at her, pleased surprise on her face. "Not enough for you?"

Refusing to be drawn in, feeling a need to be petulant, Lainey crossed her arms. "No. Not for them either." She nodded at her eager team.

Laughing, Scotch untied a gallon water jug from the ATV. "Boy, do I understand that. But it's way too hot to give these guys a decent workout. It'll be better when it snows."

Lainey narrowed her eyes. The sun filled the small clearing. She felt a haze of sweat on her face, even though she hadn't done anything. She looked at her team, noting the thick coats and panting tongues. If she was hot, she could only imagine how they felt; they had done all the work. Grudgingly, she agreed to the wisdom of stopping.

"You'd better snack them or you'll have a riot on your hands."

She became aware of the six canines staring at her. Lainey blushed under their scrutiny. "Sorry, guys. Lost my head for a moment." She removed her daypack and pulled a large food storage bag from within. Starting with Sholo and Trace, she gave each dog praise, petting, and a healthy chunk of frozen whitefish. Kaara waited politely while Lainey served Bonaparte first. As a reward for her patience, Lainey gave Kaara an extra bit. Jonah was as exuberant in his snacking as he was in pulling, standing in his harness to accept his treat. In contrast, Aegis daintily took the fish from Lainey's hand.

"Now we give them a going over to make sure there aren't any strains or injuries," Scotch said. "Nothing too extensive—that's only for when you stop for a few hours rest. But if you're snacking the dogs to take a quick break, you still want to make a cursory examination."

Lainey nodded and went back to her team. Again she started with her leaders. She checked the leads from their collars, examined the area where their harnesses created pressure across their chests and gave each animal's shoulders a swift massage. When she was done, she stood. "They all look good."

Scotch grinned. "Yeah, they do." She shrugged her pack over her shoulders. "Ready for the return trip?"

"I guess so." Lainey packed up her things.

"Lead the way," Scotch said. "Just remember to turn left at the trailhead."

Lainey blinked. "Me?"

"You're going to have to learn all these trails before winter hits. Best start now." Scotch boarded her ATV and looked back over her shoulder. "By snowfall, you should know enough about your team to gauge how far to travel in your training. You don't want to overextend your team by going too far too early—it'll cause injuries."

Lainey turned to stare at her dogs. Bonaparte was the only one watching her. Kaara watched him, Jonah rolled on the grass, and Aegis delicately finished her snack. Trace and Sholo seemed more interested in Scotch's doings, probably wondering why they weren't on her string. They had no idea Lainey was a novice. What would happen if they ever figured it out? A "riot" as Scotch called it?

Bonaparte sniffed and looked away.

Irritated with his canine challenge, Lainey smiled in feral anticipation. No way was she going to let some snotty mutt run the show. With a renewed sense of purpose, she marched up to Sholo and Trace, taking the mainline and bringing the dogs around until they faced back the way they had come. She climbed aboard the ATV, cranking the handlebars to the left as far as they would go. Her team, used to such activity, seemed ready to move out. Lainey made certain the ATV brake was set and then started the vehicle.

"Ready!"

Trace and Sholo pulled forward, forcing the other dogs to straighten their line. Jonah's hindquarters flexed as he tried to get the ATV moving by sheer will alone. Kaara gave Bonaparte a quick nuzzle before settling down to business.

Lainey glanced at Scotch, grinning when the woman tipped her baseball cap at her.

"Let's go!"

CHAPTER FIFTEEN

"What're you reading?" Scotch asked.

Lainey sat up from her sprawl across the couch, making room. "*The Call of the Wild.*" She waggled the book at Scotch, taking care to keep her place with one finger.

Scotch chuckled and dropped into the vacated space. "Trying to get a dog's eye view of an Alaskan winter?"

"Something like that." She marked her page with a scrap of paper and set the book down on the rough-hewn coffee table.

"While the story is historically accurate, don't go basing the Iditarod on it. Modern dogs are way different."

"Okay." Sitting back, Lainey propped her feet on the edge of the table and regarded her roommate. "How'd it go on the day trip? Get any sponsors?"

"Investors only, this time." Scotch turned on the couch until she faced Lainey, her legs stretched out along the floor beneath the woman's feet. Frowning, she stared at the ceiling in calculation, silently counting on the fingers of one hand. "I got enough bootie money for all the dogs two times over."

Lainey did the math. A buck per bootie, four booties per dog, times sixteen dogs and doubled. "That's not bad. Only about a thousand more to go."

"Not bad at all considering it was all from the kids. They saw our website and started saving their allowances last year when their family planned a vacation up here."

"Wow. That is impressive."

Scotch stretched and yawned. "Yeah. They studied the Iditarod in school last year. I promised to list them as supporters on the website next time we update."

A slight smile on her face, Lainey watched her. It would be nice to cuddle with her. Maybe she would take a series of candid photos of Scotch, something she could take with her when this assignment was over. Her throat thickened in sudden remorse at the thought. *What the fuck; it's just a gig. She's just a subject, maybe even a friend. Nothing more.*

"What?"

She forced a wide grin at the suspicious look Scotch was giving her. She was perpetually getting busted daydreaming around the woman. "How much more in donations do you think you'll need to cover the costs of running the Iditarod this year?"

Scotch eyed her with a mixture of amusement and exasperation. "Is this an interview question?"

"It could be."

"I thought Don was the one doing the articles on me. You're supposed to be reporting about your training."

Lainey lifted her chin in defiance. "It's still my gig. He wouldn't be here if I hadn't agreed to the initial pitch." Her lips curved as she saw mischief reflected in Scotch's demeanor. Scotch's confidence always ran hot or cold, either emanating from the depths of her soul or completely absent, depending on the situation. At the moment, it radiated from her lanky form in waves. Lainey found it quite a turn-on.

"I'll answer you if you answer a question for me."

The glint in Scotch's eye gave Lainey pause. She hid her wariness behind humor. "What's this—an Alaskan version of Truth or Dare?"

Scotch grinned. "Well, we could do that too."

Lainey felt a moment of dizziness at the thought of playing Truth or Dare with the woman who starred in her wet dreams. *What a game that would be! Yowza!* She forced her overactive imagination away. "All right. A question for a question. I asked mine first."

With a satisfied air, Scotch relaxed further onto the couch. She draped one long arm across the back of it, not quite able to reach

Lainey's head. "Technically, I'm all set for the race. Figure it runs about ten grand after entry fees, gear replacement, food and freight. When you made the deal to train for the race, the money you brought covered both of us."

"Yeah?" Lainey felt a sense of pleasure.

"Yeah. This is a year of plenty. The formula for running a kennel is a buck-fifty per dog per day. And we have almost a hundred dogs."

"Have you ever done this before? Taken on a rookie to train?"

Scotch grinned. "That's two questions, and it's my turn."

Lainey held up her hands in surrender. "Fire away."

"What's it like to report from a war zone?"

"Oooh." She winced, not having expected that particular query. She had made a lifestyle of avoiding that time in her life. "Man, you shoot from the hip, don't you?"

A contrite look crossed Scotch's face. "Sorry. You don't have to answer. It's none of my business."

Lainey reached out and patted Scotch's thigh. It took effort to withdraw it. "No, that's okay. It just surprised me." She drew one foot up to the edge of the couch, wrapping her arms around her shin in thought. "It's one part challenge, one part terror, and three parts excitement—shaken, not stirred."

"On the rocks?"

She laughed, breathless from the dread coursing through her system. "Yup. You got it." Sobering, Lainey forced herself to remember. "You hear an explosion or gunfire in the distance, you grab whatever transportation you can find to get to the scene. Your heart is pumping, your nerves jittery. Your destination smells of dust, faint gunpowder and blood. If you're lucky, the perpetrators are long gone. And if you're luckier, they're still there, shooting it out with whoever claims that area.

"Nothing is truly real. You see it all through the viewfinder. It's a photo op—the destruction, the death. There's no time to feel. You record the event as it unfolds and hope to God you'll be in one piece afterwards."

"Did you enjoy it?"

Lainey's mind's eye returned to the cabin. She waggled a slightly shaking finger. "Ah, ah, ah. My turn."

Scotch grinned and shook her head. "You want me to answer your last one?"

"Nope. I retract it. Why do you run the Iditarod? What's the draw?"

Scotch pressed back against the arm of the couch, crossing her arms over her chest. "I think you've already said it: one part challenge, one part terror, and three parts excitement, though it's stirred in this case."

"On the rocks?"

"Only in warmer years with little snowfall."

Lainey snorted when Scotch didn't continue. "Oh no. Now's not the time to become terse. Give me something to go on here."

Scotch chuckled. "Okay, give me a minute."

As she became lost in contemplation, Lainey's fascination grew. The aura of strength solidified and grew around Scotch. The race or the dog sledding was the root of her confidence. Lainey's heart thumped with the realization. Why? How? Not everyone carried themselves this way after merely finishing. She had met many mushers last year, including women, and hadn't seen this with any of them.

"You're alone with sixteen dogs, crossing the tundra or weaving through trees and brush. It's so cold and the air so crisp you can actually see better than at any other time, crystal clear. There's nothing but the dogs panting, their feet crunching in the snow and the next turn of the trail. You feel so small and so insignificant, but the dogs rely on you as you rely on them. I can't really explain it. It's the ultimate high."

They sat in silence for a moment, Scotch mulling over her memories and Lainey soaking in the feelings those recollections evoked.

"My turn."

Lainey ducked her head in a nod. She watched Scotch shift her gaze away and chew the inside of her cheek. A frown rippled across her fair features. Lainey braced herself for the next question, sensing it wouldn't be easy.

"It's been bugging me since you got here. I know it's none of my business, but I can't seem to shake it." Scotch looked back at her. "Where did you get shot?"

She stared blankly at her roommate. Here she thought she'd have to answer something really tough like, "Are you really drooling every time I walk by or do you just have an advanced case of rabies?" When Lainey didn't give a prompt answer, Scotch seemed to withdraw from the conversation. She hastened to reassure her. "It's all right. Really."

Sitting up, Lainey dropped her feet to the floor, upsetting Scotch's legs beneath her. They laughed uneasily as they readjusted their positions. Lainey stood, and turned so her right side faced Scotch. "I was out with a US military patrol in Kosovo. They were ordered to do a standard sweep through a village for insurgents. Luck was with me then." She lifted her shirt to reveal the six-inch-long keloid marring her torso. It started beneath the lowest rib, coming up at an angle toward her breast, ending just below. "There was an ambush. I got a lot of really good photos of the action."

Scotch grimaced at the jagged scar. "Damn, that must have hurt."

Unaccountably nervous, Lainey laughed. "Not at the time." She peered past her shirt at the cause of her sudden career change. "I was prone on the ground behind cover. Nobody realized there was a flanking fire team until we started getting shot at from behind. The bullet came in at a very low angle." She touched the bottom of the scar and traced upward. "He was aiming for my heart. Instead it hit and shattered my ribs, poking holes in my lung, and then what was left of the bullet lodged along the bone."

"Ow," Scotch said in soft sympathy, engrossed in the damage. She reached out and traced the raised tissue with gentle fingers.

Lainey hadn't expected her to take the liberty. She swallowed against a sudden urge to cry. *What the hell?* Shaking her head, she forced a chuckle. "Anyway, I hardly felt it, just a sharp sting in my side. When I tried to get up to follow the rest of the fire team to safety, I couldn't. That's when I passed out. One of them realized I was wounded and carried me out." She eased out of reach and pulled her shirt down. "I don't remember much else until I woke up in the hospital."

"You were out for a year. Was most of it spent in the hospital?"

Despite the fact it was Lainey's turn, she answered. "I was in Kosovo for about two weeks before shipping back to the States. Spent another month in a hospital in Washington before being released as an outpatient." She sat down, resting her elbows on her knees rather than resuming her previous position. "Had some counseling and some physical therapy, got a clean bill of health after a couple of months. I guess I just needed some time to think about what had happened." She didn't volunteer that she had spent a good portion of the rest of the year attempting to pickle what few inner organs hadn't been damaged. *What I wouldn't give for a drink right now.*

Seemingly at a loss for words, Scotch remained silent. Lainey pushed away the sudden vulnerability that had reared up at Scotch's touch. She didn't know what that was and had no time to investigate it. After a deep breath, she propped her feet on the coffee table. "My turn."

Smiling, Scotch went with the change of subject, visibly relaxing.

"Have you ever been hurt on a race?"

"Oh yeah," Scotch confirmed. "Though nowhere nearly as bad as you. When I was seventeen, I was finally eligible for my first adult race. Ran the Yukon Quest 250 that year. It was my first overnighter on unfamiliar territory."

"What happened?"

"Frostbite. I set my gloves down while feeding the dogs during a break. I haven't a clue where they went. It was warm out when I left the checkpoint, so I didn't even notice they weren't with me until it started to cool off."

"Ew." Lainey wrinkled her nose.

Scotch grinned, holding out her hands to study them. "Yeah. The 250 takes about two and a half days to run. I lost the gloves on the second day, had to go through the night and into the next morning to get to the finish line."

"Looks like your hands survived."

"They did. I was lucky it was such a warm year. I had some leather work gloves with me. My sled wasn't in the best shape, so I was prepared to make repairs on it. Those and a couple of pairs of socks for mittens prevented the frostbite from being even worse." Scotch leaned closer, showing the side of one hand. "You can see where I lost a bit of skin there. The seam on the gloves was worn, and the damage too great to recover from."

Lainey shivered and shook her hands in empathy. "Yuck! That gives me the willies."

"It's just a bit of skin! One of the race vets did the job." Scotch leaned back and laughed. "It's not as bad as what you went through."

"Yuck," Lainey repeated.

"My turn."

"Anything you ask now will seem anticlimactic."

"Probably."

Lainey smiled. "How about we head over to the main cabin for dinner instead? I believe I have a date to beat you at Monopoly."

Scoffing, Scotch stood and offered her hand. "You wish. I am the Monopoly kingpin in this family."

Lainey accepted the assistance, enjoying the touch too much as she rose. "Time for me to topple your funny money empire, sister."

They shared an amused look before bursting into laughter.

CHAPTER SIXTEEN

August

Lainey sat at the dining table in Scotch's cabin, staring at the blank legal pad before her, a pen rapidly waggling back and forth between her index and middle fingers. Normally she would have typed her work into her laptop, but she wanted to conserve the battery. Her computer stayed at the main cabin for the most part, keeping itself juiced up and available for final copies and email correspondence.

Daylight poured in from the high windows above as it did almost twenty hours a day. Getting used to the constant sun had been difficult. Lainey had been told that she might see darkness go beyond twilight before she fell asleep. The idea that January would find her sitting here with a lantern at three in the afternoon to ward off the constant night seemed a fantasy.

She had eighteen dogs assigned to her now. With help from Scotch and Rye, Lainey had created an elaborate training schedule to keep all the animals working together. She'd graduated to driving eight dogs at a time and rotated among her canine companions to ensure each received the proper workout. Lainey was the only one allowed to feed her dogs, the only one to spend any significant amount of time with them. Miguel Sanchez, the kennel's handler, helped with all the animals, but those on Lainey's team looked to her as their pack leader.

Lainey tossed down her pen with a grunt and leaned back in the chair. A torn piece of vinyl poked her in the back, and she adjusted herself, flattening the flap with her shoulder. She had to have something to give her editor by the end of the week. There would be hell to pay if she missed her deadline, but she couldn't seem to focus. Instead of thinking about the writing, her mind drifted to her favorite subject.

Scotch was a wonderful instructor. Lainey had learned so much from her, not just about discipline but about how to get the dogs to want the same things she did. They spent most of each morning together doing chores. Scotch had coerced Lainey into a physical fitness regime consisting of long runs and light weight training. Afternoons were for training dogs or entertaining tourists, usually separating the pair. Lainey still didn't know all the trails well enough to go out alone and wasn't allowed to take guests out on cart rides. On those days, she took members of her team out with Rye or Irish. Evenings consisted of another round of feeding and poop scooping, followed by dinner and time with the Fullers and Howry. At bedtime, Lainey and Scotch made the trek to their cabin, swapping stories about their day.

There had been many times Lainey had wanted to take Scotch's hand along the trail or give her a hug or a kiss when lounging in the cabin. She really liked Scotch. Much to her chagrin, their friendship didn't dampen her desire one bit. If anything, she wanted Scotch more now than when she had started the assignment. She laughed at the thought. *I'll take any Scotch I can get at this point.*

She forced her attention back to the notebook. She had never missed a deadline and didn't plan on starting now. *Maybe if I start with a description of one of my runs...* Retrieving her pen from the middle of the table, she began to write.

The wind rushes past me at a whopping eleven miles per hour. I hear nothing but the sound of panting dogs and rubber tires crunching across the previous season's detritus. The smell of pine and loam fills my nostrils, competing with the ever-present odor of dog fur that has become the center of my world for the last forty-five days.

This is one of my first lessons as a musher. I have no license here, no insurance. My only company is a team of eight canine athletes who have decided to give me a shot at leading them. Up ahead is another all-terrain vehicle disappearing around a bend. My partner in crime—my mentor, Scotch Fuller, three-time Iditarod finisher—is leading the way. I have no idea where I'm going, just that I'm to follow her lead. Oh, and to make sure my team thinks I'm in charge.

So begins my training for the Iditarod sled dog race, which takes place every March in Anchorage, Alaska. I am one of thirty-eight rookies signed up for the next one, thirty-eight novices taking on the challenge of what is billed as the Last Great Race in the World.

The days all run together here. The constant sunlight doesn't help my sense of time; I've yet to see full dark since my arrival at the end of June. I hear it might make an appearance by the end of August, at least for a little while. Until then, I go to sleep in daylight and wake to daylight, even at 10 p.m. and 5 a.m.

In the morning, the dogs are seen to first. There are almost a hundred of them at Fuller Kennels. You'd think with that number they would all sort of run together in the mind, a mass of wet fur and wagging tails with little in the way of distinction other than the markings on their coats. That's not the case, however. As I've discovered in the last month and a half, each animal is different from the other, with his or her unique foibles and strengths. The ones I know the best are my team.

Trace is all white, with bright blue eyes flickering with intelligence. He's finished the Iditarod twice before, leading the team for a part of the way. His experience will be a tremendous asset to us when we get to Anchorage.

Sholo is Trace's diametric opposite in appearance. His black coat and eyes will make him difficult to see in the dark (providing I ever see him at night; some days I have my doubts). He's a hard worker who has little patience for incompetence, though he's at least polite when I exhibit mine. His ability to stick to a trail is astounding. I've found he'll refuse orders from me and, when I try to call him on it, I discover I was the one in the wrong—the trail didn't go the direction I wanted or an obvious obstacle that I couldn't see blocked our way. I swear this dog is a barking, shedding, dowsing rod.

Behind the lead dogs are another couple of characters. Meshindi is a rookie at age two. His only experience has been in sprints last year. His brown eyes are almond-shaped, making him seem more Asian than canine. He's not "inscrutable," by any means. I have no doubts about his opinion on anything as he grins or grumbles at me. Most of his grumbling has to do with me interrupting his naps during our training breaks. His grins are for frozen moose liver treats, his favorite.

A leader in training, Montana has had experience in several mid-distance races. This will be the first Iditarod for him too, but I'm hoping Trace will take him under his...paw and show the new guy the ropes. He has a tendency to swagger as he runs, as a young male is prone to do, and is more than willing to wrestle with anyone willing to play.

Behind them is Bonaparte. Almost no one else is allowed in his section of the mainline; he'll balk if he's not treated with proper deference. He's a small dog with a big attitude, and God help the handler who doesn't give His Majesty his due. Despite the regal behavior, he doesn't want to lead—such is the job of mere mortals. Instead, he follows just behind the leaders, keeping the rest of the team in line.

His consort is Kaara. Her name means "shining light of the morning" and it's so apt. Off-white with mottled browns and grays, she gives off a calm and cheerful aura. She's the only dog in the kennel that doesn't call Bonaparte on his snotty attitudes. In fact, she adores him, playing Josephine to his highfalutin ways. It's rumored that she's in love with him. If ever there was a living example of puppy love, Kaara carries it with pride.

Just in front of my ATV are Jonah and Aegis. Male and female, they're the largest dogs on my team, weighing in at a total of one hundred fifty-seven pounds. They're that big because they're the wheel dogs—the animals right in front of the sled. They need the extra power to keep control of a six-hundred-pound sled during turns. Yet they also must be fast enough to avoid getting run over.

Jonah is a wild and wooly fellow, the mountain man of the team, with shaggy hair and an obsession with pulling. Given the chance, he'd be happy to do all the work and leave his mates back at home. When the rest of the team hears the command, "Ready," he's the one who leaps forward with the most eagerness to get going.

Aegis is my sweetheart. Her size makes her appear somewhat threatening, though all the dogs are thoroughly adapted to humans from the time they're born. In reality, she's nothing more than a big mushball who enjoys tummy rubs and daintily nibbles on her treats while the others wolf theirs down.

The cabin door opened, interrupting Lainey's thoughts. She looked up at Scotch clattering down the steps.

"Want to go swimming?" Scotch's eyes sparkled.

She was without a cap, her tawny blonde curls unconfined. Her skin had taken on a light gold color from her constant exposure to the outdoors. From the looks of her peeling nose, perhaps she'd had too much time in the sun. Lainey smiled in return, wondering how much longer she could take this unrequited yearning. The desire for a drink paled in comparison. "I don't have a swimsuit."

Scotch sat down across from her. "Doesn't matter. You can use your sleep clothes. All you need are shorts and a T-shirt. That's what I wear."

"Who's going?" Lainey asked, more to keep Scotch talking than to get an answer. She enjoyed hearing the woman's voice, savored the undertone of happiness in it.

"Pretty much everybody. You know the trail near the river?" At Lainey's nod, she continued. "About a hundred feet around the bend there's a cove. We swim there every summer."

Lainey looked at her article, chewing her lip. "I don't know. I've really got to get this done."

Scotch leaned forward, elbows on the table that wobbled under her weight. "There's a rope swing." Her voice held a slight wheedling tone.

Lainey saw flecks of dark mixed with the light blue of Scotch's irises. At this range, the freckles dusting Scotch's slightly crooked and peeling nose were adorable. She felt her resolve waver, the call of playing with this woman far louder than the professional demand to get her job done and in on time. "You're evil."

Realizing she had won, Scotch jumped up with a whoop. "All right!" She headed toward the stairs. "You can change here or at the river."

Lainey stood, refusing to look at the article lest it cause her to change her mind. "Where do you change?"

Past the door and almost to the loft, Scotch grinned down at her. "At the river. Nothing like getting nekkid in the great outdoors." She disappeared into her half of the sleeping loft.

Staring after her, Lainey alternately felt hot and cold. Surely Scotch was joking, not flirting. Wasn't she? She carefully put the vivid image of a naked Scotch out of her mind. Her skin flushed and she muttered under her breath, "God help me. Seven more months of this."

CHAPTER SEVENTEEN

The dogs weren't pleased to be left behind. As the ATV roared away without them, they set up a clamor loud enough to be heard above the engine. Scotch played daredevil, accelerating along the familiar trails at speeds Lainey hadn't attained before. She clutched at Scotch to keep from tumbling off. Not that holding her was such a hardship. Had she known she would be allowed to cuddle against Scotch's back, arms about her slim waist, she would have leapt at the chance to go to swimming.

As they traveled, Lainey tried to keep her lascivious thoughts in line. Her lack of success left much to be desired. She mentally tried to follow the trail, noting familiar landmarks, known distances and turnoffs to other paths. Scotch's belly had just the right amount of give to it, indicating a muscled figure with enough curvature to be interesting. Even with the wind whipping by, the smell of Scotch's hair was strong enough to induce hyperventilation in Lainey as she inhaled deeply again and again. The vibration through the seat didn't help either. Feeling deliciously illicit, she leaned her cheek against Scotch's back, soaking in her proximity. Without thought, she gave Scotch a gentle hug, only realizing what she'd done when Scotch responded with a squeeze of her arm on Lainey's. Horrified at her faux pas, Lainey attempted to release her but was held firmly in place.

"Hang on!" Scotch called back.

Lainey, her insides as jittery as her emotions, signaled her understanding with another hug. Scotch patted her arm and returned her attention to the trail.

She closed her eyes, adding this latest interaction to the host of others she'd stored over the last month and a half. Sometimes it seemed Scotch was definitely gay. She often made comments that could be construed in such a way if Lainey were inclined. If she were straight, her remarks would also seem appropriate in everyday conversation. Howry had noticed, as well, and the two of them had spent quite a bit of time comparing notes. It was enough to make Lainey cry.

"Almost there."

In an effort to distract herself, Lainey returned her attention to her surroundings. She recognized the trail, though she hadn't taken the turn that Scotch was driving toward. They dropped fairly quickly down an incline and she clutched at Scotch, feeling a rumble of laughter through her arms. The air immediately cooled as they leveled off onto a trail that paralleled a river.

"When the river's frozen, we take the dogs through here," Scotch yelled. "There are more trails on the other side."

The trees drew back as they pulled into a clearing already occupied by most of the Fuller clan. One of the trucks, sans dog trailer, sat off a dirt road with its tailgate down, its bed filled with a couple of coolers, an assortment of towels, and Bon playing with an inflatable ball. Helen was rummaging through one of the coolers for drinks. The clean smell of fresh water held an underlying scent of mesquite charcoal smoke. A barbecue squatted nearby, manned by Miguel. Two folding tables and a number of deck chairs clustered together, a variety of picnic items resting on their surfaces. Scotch parked beside the truck and turned off the engine.

A whoop of sheer joy exploded into the sudden quiet. Lainey turned and saw Howry, wearing a pair of shorts and ratty tennis shoes. He swung on a rope attached to a tree looming over the water. At the apex of his swing, he released his hold to fly a short ways, hitting the water like a cannonball. Swimming nearby, Irish and another girl her age yelped at his boisterous arrival.

Lainey's brow furrowed at seeing the stranger. She reluctantly released Scotch and dismounted the ATV, taking a closer look at the clearing. Of its own accord, the rope was moving back to the top of the embankment. Lainey followed the action with confusion until she realized there was a thinner rope attached to it, allowing someone to hoist it back up. A young man stood there, long brown hair tied back in a tail, a light beard sprouting on his jaw. He wore less than Howry, who had surfaced with another shout.

"Who's that?" She nodded toward the man, not too pleased with his physique. Obviously he worked out with regularity, and his tight swim trunks left little to the imagination.

Scotch looked up from rummaging in a carry sack she had cradled between her legs for the trip. "That's Martin Schram. His family lives right over that ridge." She waved. "Hey, Martin!"

The man turned toward them, smiling when he saw Scotch. He waved back. "Get up here, Scotch! Let's show these *chechakos* how to swim in Alaskan waters!"

Laughing, Scotch nodded and returned to her bag, pulling out her swimming gear.

Disgruntled, Lainey tried not to show it. "*Chechakos?*"

Scotch chuckled. "Newcomers, greenhorns, people who haven't lived in Alaska before."

"Oh."

"Where's Dad and Rye?"

Helen played catch with her youngest son in the bed of the truck. "Soaking around the bend. Phyllis is with them."

Scotch saw the question before Lainey could utter it. "Martin's mom. And the girl with Irish is his sister, Teresa." She scanned the vegetation a safe distance from the river. "We can change over there. If the others are soaking, they'll be on the other side of those boulders."

Lainey ignored the stab of jealousy as she watched Martin sail gracefully through the air to splash into the natural pool. *It's not like I have any claim on Scotch's attention. Hell, I still have no idea if she's straight or not.*

"Lainey?"

She spun around. "Um, yeah, over there is fine." She didn't know whether or not her sudden forced cheerfulness registered with Helen, but the smile Scotch gave her triggered Lainey's apprehension. She promptly busied herself with her daypack, extracting her shorts and T-shirt. "Shall we?" She did her damnedest to look innocent.

Scotch led the way. Behind them, the girls squealed at some game they were playing. Lainey's last sight was of Martin picking his way over the stones at the riverbank, rubbing his muscular upper arms.

He looked cold, and Lainey suddenly wondered about the wisdom of swimming in an Alaskan river, even in August.

"You can change here." Scotch gestured to a sheltered area behind some huckleberry bushes. "Keep your eyes open. The hot springs are right through there. Sometimes people cut through here to get to the swing."

Lainey blinked. "Hot springs? Now that sounds like fun."

"It is." Scotch grinned. "And when you get too hot, you can take a dip in the river. It's a hell of a wake-up, let me tell you."

She laughed. "Where are you going to change?"

Scotch pointed to another cluster of berry bushes. "Right over there. See you in a couple of minutes."

"Okay."

Lainey waited until she saw Scotch disappear into her impromptu changing room before beginning to undress. She shucked out of her clothes, keeping a wary eye on her surroundings as she donned her sleep shorts and a black T-shirt. Folding her clothing, she set her boots on top of the pile. On her feet were the tennis shoes she had purchased at the general store in the village for working in the dog yard. Her attention drifted toward the cluster of bushes where Scotch had disappeared. She saw movement, caught a tantalizing flash of pale skin, but nothing more. Unable to help herself, she took a step closer, standing on her toes to catch sight of her libido's desire.

"See anything interesting?"

Startled, Lainey jumped and spun around at the loud voice. Howry stood on a passing trail, water still dripping from his body. Shivering, he clutched a towel tight across his shoulders. His obvious discomfort didn't lessen his joy at busting her in a little Peeping Tom action. His grin insolent, he wiggled his eyebrows at her.

Lainey scowled at him. She couldn't respond the way she wanted, being so close to Scotch's hiding place, and he knew it. "Nope, just waiting for Scotch to finish." She waved at him, urging him to move along.

Howry's smile widened. "Hey, Scotch. Need any help in there? Lainey's offering."

Her mouth dropped open and she glared daggers at him, taking a step forward, intent on strangling him with his towel.

"Naw, I'm done."

Lainey plastered a pleasant expression onto her face as she turned to see Scotch emerging from her hiding place.

"What do you say we drop these at the truck and then go to the springs?" She indicated the clothing in her arms.

"I'll see you there." Howry winked at Lainey before continuing down the path.

"Sounds like a plan." Lainey felt relief as he left but dreaded that he'd lay in wait for her later.

At the truck, Lainey was formally introduced to Teresa. The two girls were eating hot dogs, ignoring Bon making a mess of his ketchup and mustard just out of reach. The handsome Martin was nowhere to be seen. Lainey figured he was with the others at the hot springs.

There's still time to back out. Scotch won't mind if I take the ATV back, will she? Howry would be a pest, Lainey knew, but his teasing was a known entity. What if this Martin fellow had designs on Scotch? She was a beautiful—and single—young woman. He'd be a fool not to notice her. What if Scotch felt the same way toward him?

Lainey's heart sunk as Scotch showed her the way to the springs. *Well, you wanted to know where you stand*, she thought, castigating herself.

The air became more humid as they neared the springs just past the boulders, an area having both natural and manmade features. Sturdy wooden steps led down to the water, ending at a long deck flanking the two edges. Large flat stones circled the remainder. Lainey saw Thom, Rye and a woman who had to be Phyllis Schram. Martin and Howry sat shoulder-deep in the water, warming up after their dip in the river.

Scotch called a greeting as she went down the steps toward the deck. Lainey followed, displeased at the overt interest she sensed in Martin, who swam closer.

"Lainey Hughes, Martin Schram. Martin, Lainey." Scotch slipped into the water with an audible sigh, not waiting to see whether Lainey joined them.

"Pleasure to meet you."

Up close, Lainey was heartened to see that at least the man had bad teeth. Unfortunately, that was the only negative thing she noted about his appearance. "Nice to meet you, too," she lied.

It was deep enough that Scotch treaded water as she moved away from the deck. "You coming in? It's cooler over here. Warms up as you make your way to the rocks."

"Sure." Lainey sat on the deck and put a tentative foot in the water. Her tennis shoe immediately became sodden. Warm water washed over her ankle. "Oh, it's nice." She smiled, forgetting Martin's presence. She eased over the side, holding the deck to keep afloat.

"It's really good in winter," Martin said.

Scotch agreed, and they shared a smile. Lainey's lip curled. When the woman looked back at her, she ducked under the water to hide her expression, surfacing with a grin. "I'll bet it is."

"Come on." Scotch began swimming toward the others.

Lainey had little choice but to follow.

* * *

Scotch lounged in the back of the truck, her youngest brother napping beside her. Irish and Teresa had left with Phyllis to stay the night at the Schram cabin. Helen had taken the ATV home to check on one of her canine patients at the clinic. The coals in the barbecue had long since burned out, and the men idled around the clearing in patio chairs, digesting a heavy lunch of potato salad and hamburgers as they discussed life, evolution and politics.

As Scotch had expected, Martin had put the moves on Lainey. Scotch felt a combination of relief and displeasure at his antics. He'd always been a player, even when they were children. She had fended off hundreds of advances from him over the years, so his distraction today had been a joy. Still, she didn't care for it when he had begun flirting with Lainey.

She watched him walk with Lainey along the river. Scotch didn't know whether Lainey's suggestion of a stroll had been to spend more time with the outgoing young man or to be rid of him. Lainey was a healthy woman. Surely she would want to sow some oats here and there. It wasn't as if she had a steady boyfriend. Traveling the world as she did, she probably had a man in every port and no strings attached.

Did this particular port have to hold Martin though?

What if Lainey had meant to take a walk with Scotch instead? There was a moment there when Scotch couldn't tell. She'd had difficulty reading Lainey's signals all day. After a month and a half of close quarters, she thought she knew Lainey pretty well. Today every look or word made her question that supposition. It was like Lainey was hiding something from her. Did she think Scotch and Martin had a thing for each other and didn't want to cause a scene between them? What else could explain this sense of duplicity?

Scotch saw them returning. She eased out of the truck bed, careful to not wake Bon. Strolling over to one of the tables, she stood and nibbled at potato chips until Lainey and Martin were near enough for her to talk to them without yelling. "Welcome back. I'm going to head home and catch a nap before feeding the dogs. Want to come?"

"That sounds like a great idea!"

Lainey's instant agreement buoyed Scotch's spirits. "Mom took the ATV, but we can walk."

"I'm in." Lainey turned to Martin. "It was really nice meeting you." She offered her hand and gave him a handshake.

Scotch grinned at the reappearance of her friend's ultra professionalism. Apparently Martin hadn't swayed Lainey with his attentions after all.

Under the watching eyes of the others, he could do nothing but respond in kind. "Sure. Let me know if you want to go fishing. I know the perfect spots."

"I'm sure you do. We'll see how it goes."

Howry snorted in amusement and Scotch glanced at him. She wondered what was funny, but let it go as Lainey returned to the truck to gather her clothes and change back into her boots.

"Ready?"

Scotch hastily grabbed her belongings. "Yeah. Let's go." Feeling light of heart and not knowing why, Scotch joined Lainey at the trailhead.

CHAPTER EIGHTEEN

September

Scotch burst through the tree line and into the dog yard. Hands on her knees, she panted heavily. Most of the dogs not on a tour with Miguel and Rye lounged about their shelters, tongues lolling in the unseasonable warmth. Scotch's dog team paid close attention to her arrival, Sukita and Trace standing to yip at her. Still breathless from her run, she chuckled as she approached to give Sukita some attention. Nearby, Trace whined, tail wagging.

"Sorry, son. You're on Lainey's team this year. You know it's hands off until the race." Trace whined again, blue eyes begging. Scotch glanced around, ascertaining there were no witnesses in the area. She furtively gave the dog a deep scratching. "Now don't tell anybody, okay?" She laughed, pulling her face away from the questing tongue. "I know! I miss you too, buddy."

Not wanting to be busted fraternizing with Lainey's lead dog, Scotch stepped away, her legs reminding her she had just finished five miles. She walked a bit around the back porch of the main cabin, cooling down.

Lainey had run with her for part of the way. She didn't yet have the endurance to keep up. Lainey freely admitted that most of her adult life had been spent in pursuits other than physical exercise. She would have a lot of training to do if she ever planned on achieving the same level of fitness as Scotch. Lainey had turned back at the one-and-a-half-mile mark, leaving Scotch to continue alone. Scotch smiled. Lainey's expression upon learning the dogs weren't the only ones physically training for the race had been entertaining. As with most things, Lainey initially balked before throwing herself headlong into the activity.

Scotch figured that some folks were natural "yes" people, and others gravitated toward "no." Whether or not a "no" person could go against his or her negative instincts was the question. Many simply couldn't break out of their restrictive boxes. Lainey was a "no," but she never held back from a challenge. Scotch respected that. She had known others who couldn't get past their initial inclinations, sometimes with disastrous results. Her mind flashing back to a couple of years earlier, bile rose in her throat and a chill ran down her spine. *Like Rye said, Lainey's not Tanya.* With a shaky sigh, she pushed the image and emotions away.

Using the deck steps, she stretched her legs for several minutes, then headed up into the cabin. The house rang with the silence of emptiness. Her mother was working at the clinic next door, probably with Bon playing under an exam table, but Scotch thought she would at least run into Irish. The girl was too young to run dog tours, spending the majority of her non-kennel time doing schoolwork or chores around the house.

Scotch went through the kitchen, stealing a snickerdoodle from the cookie jar as she passed. She debated putting away the dishes drying in the rack but instead rummaged in the refrigerator for the milk jug. Movement from the dining room window drew her attention as she retrieved a glass from the cupboard. Leaving the milk and glass on the counter, she went over to see what was in the front yard.

The drive-around circled an island of grass. Irish and Lainey romped there with the youngest pups. Now weaned from their mother—Miguel's swing dog, Sazu—they each wore a small halter attached to a chunk of wood. The four puppies rollicked around the central clearing, happily towing the "light weights" as Irish and Lainey called them back and forth. Scotch grinned, focusing on her roommate.

Lainey still wore her workout clothes—running shorts and a tight tank top. As Scotch had expected, Lainey's dark complexion had deepened to nut brown from constant exposure to the sun. From this distance, Scotch couldn't see the traces of silver shooting through her dark curly hair. It had grown long. Lainey would be able to put it into a ponytail by the time the Iditarod rolled around.

One of the pups made a break for freedom. Lainey, seated on the ground, lunged for the dog as it passed. She barely snagged the small log as it went by. Sprawled across the grass, tank top riding up to bare her midriff, she reeled the pup in by its lead. She laughed and squirmed as she received a thorough face bath from the exuberant animal.

Scotch licked her lips. Unobserved, she allowed herself the liberty of fully enjoying the lithesome body rolling in the grass. Lainey was small-boned, barely topping five foot three, but even in uncertain circumstances she radiated self-assurance that belied her short stature. Her sense of humor had sent Scotch into stitches on many evenings as she regaled the Fullers with tales of her travels. Scotch liked the sound of her voice and laugh—low, a little on the husky side. She liked it even better when they spoke alone on the trail or in the cabin. At those times Scotch liked to think it held a level of intimacy, just for her.

She knew that was ridiculous. At no time had Lainey ever extended more than friendship to her. That didn't keep Scotch from developing a crush. She had initially taken to doing whatever possible to exhaust herself before bedtime rather than suffer insomnia with the object of her lust sleeping on the other side of a thin curtain. That tactic hadn't lasted long. It kept her from spending time with Lainey, so she had stopped. When she did get to sleep at night, her dreams centered on Lainey, each more erotic than the last.

Outside, Lainey sat up, arms full of excited puppy. The energetic bundle jumped up in her lap, its tongue a whirlwind as it continued to wash her face. *Wish I were that dog.*

"Is this yours?"

Flushing, Scotch spun around. Her mother stood in the kitchen by the abandoned glass and milk jug. When had she come in? Scotch struggled with her voice, clearing her throat. "Uh. Yeah. I just got back from my run." She hastened forward, feeling the burn along her cheeks as she shakily poured a glass.

"Me too! Me too!" Bon hugged her leg.

Thankful for the distraction, Scotch plucked a plastic cup from the dish drainer. "What do you say, Bon?" She fought nervousness as her mother took up her former position at the dining room window.

Bon studied Scotch a moment. A grin spread across his face as he held out his arms as wide as they would go. "P'ease!"

Smiling, Scotch poured her little brother's milk. "Go get in your chair."

He ran to the high chair. With expert hands, he pulled the tray off, carefully set it on the floor, and clambered into his seat. Clapping his hands, he sang some song he had picked up from a children's television show.

Scotch put the glasses down on the dining room table. After an anxious glance at her mother's back, she put the high chair tray in place. She handed Bon his cup. "And now?"

"T'ank you!" he yelled.

She ruffled his hair. "You're welcome."

Helen turned around, her intense gaze falling on her daughter. Scotch did her best not to fidget. "Can he have a c-o-o-k-i-e?" she asked, spelling it out to avoid a tantrum if the answer was no.

"Yes. He's been a good boy today. Let's all sit down for a treat." Helen went into the living room and opened the door to call Lainey and Irish inside.

Relieved that her mother hadn't made the connection between the view outside and her discomfort, Scotch returned to the cookie jar.

* * *

The breeze felt good as it ruffled through Scotch's hair. She slouched in the passenger seat of the truck, one foot up on the dashboard. Beside her, her father navigated toward Anchorage and the feed and seed store to load up on dog chow. Usually Rye went along on these excursions, but he had begged off to attend a junior sled dog racing meeting.

Scotch expected the weather to begin cooling in a couple of weeks. Soon they'd be able to take the dogs out on longer runs. She looked forward to showing Lainey some trails she hadn't encountered before, with the eventual addition of overnight expeditions. Scotch enjoyed her solitude but liked the idea of having Lainey's company on the trail this winter.

"So, how's training going?"

She grinned at her father. "Pretty good. I think Tori and Senshi are finally beginning to get their act together."

He nodded as he stared out the windshield. "Good. You sure you don't want Lainey running the first years instead?"

Scotch laughed. "She's got enough on her plate learning to race dogs. Besides, she has Chibee. He's more than enough of a handful."

"Good point." They rode in silence for several minutes, then he added, "How are you two getting along?"

Something in the tone of his voice drew Scotch's attention. She glanced at him, unnerved to see a set to his jaw that indicated his question wasn't casual. "She's a nice lady," she finally allowed. "It's working out better than I thought it would."

"Yeah?"

Scotch sat up, dropping her foot to the floorboard. "Yeah."

"Your mother says the two of you are getting close."

Face scorching, she quickly looked out the passenger window, the cool wind doing nothing to battle the flush. *Damn it. Mom did notice something.* "She's a good friend."

"What?"

Scotch huffed a breath and spoke louder, turning her head back toward him. "I said she's a good friend." After a pause, she added, "Nothing more."

Again he gave a thoughtful nod. "You know, there's nothing wrong with there being…more."

Groaning aloud, Scotch closed her eyes, her head dropping back on the seat. "Dad." Her stomach churned with acid, the big breakfast she had enjoyed now turning into a weighty lump.

He cut her off. "I'm just saying that your mother and I…well, we worry about you, out there in that cabin all alone."

"I like living alone." She opened her eyes to see him wave his hand dismissively in her direction.

"I know, I know." He risked a quick glance at her, a slight flush in his cheeks. "And it's none of our business. We get that."

Lips set in a frown, Scotch knew better than to think that was the end of the discussion. She didn't know whether to feel pleasure or annoyance as her father continued speaking.

"You probably don't know it, but she watches you when she thinks no one is looking."

Blinking, she sat up a little straighter. "Watches me? What do you mean?"

"I think she likes you, honey. And I know you like her." He chuckled as flame seared across her face. "All right, I'll drop it. We just wanted you to know that it's okay. We love you, and we are proud of you."

"I know, Daddy." Scotch swallowed against a lump in her throat, her eyes stinging.

"Don't let what happened in the past color what's going on now, okay? I know it's hard, but give yourself a chance to live again." He reached over and patted her knee. "You deserve all the good things life has to offer."

As his hand returned to the wheel, Scotch fought the urge to cry. The burden she had lived with for two years seemed to lighten, despite the fact that nothing had really changed. She stared out the passenger window, wondering why that was.

Lainey watches me?

CHAPTER NINETEEN

October

Lainey woke before Scotch's alarm went off, the elusive taste of whiskey on her tongue. She grunted at the fading dream of her favorite Jersey pub, once again wondering whether Strauss was right. It seemed she couldn't go a single hour, day or night, without desiring a drink. Sometimes the yearning caused her to sweat and shake for the want of it. Pushing aside the familiar, smothering ache, she opened her eyes.

The room was gray, a product of the inevitable return of winter. If she stayed up late enough at night, she would be treated to full dark instead of the impending nightfall that had been all she had experienced since her arrival. Stretching in the warmth of her bed, she noted the chill on her face. Was it colder than usual? Knowing from experience not to delay the torture, she sat up and tossed off her blankets. It was colder. She cursed under her breath as her bare feet came in contact with chill boot leather. Time to sleep with a change of clothes underneath the blankets. *I'd kill for warm socks right now.*

She shivered, feeling the ache beginning in her ribs. Her breath fogged the air as she stood and tiptoed toward the stairs, quietly easing past the curtain dividing her half of the loft from Scotch's. She smiled as she passed through the room, unable to keep from studying her sleeping roommate. This was one of the reasons Lainey enjoyed waking so early—it afforded her an opportunity to examine her favorite subject unawares.

Despite the appearance of not noticing the cold, Scotch had graduated to a long sleeved T-shirt instead of the sleeveless ones she had worn through summer. She lay sprawled across her bed, blankets gathered at her waist. Lainey saw an appetizing flash of skin where the T-shirt had hiked up from the waistband of her sleep shorts. Glimpses like this fueled Lainey's desire. If Scotch had flaunted nudity, Lainey supposed that she would have become inured to its effect. Instead, seeing bits and pieces teased her almost to desperation.

She resisted the urge to cover Scotch with her blankets. She had no illusions about her desire. What she wanted was to touch and explore the available skin, to finally taste it and to see what remained hidden beneath the layers of cloth and personality. She swallowed, her mouth suddenly dry. Scotch seemed to respond to Lainey's surge of desire. Sighing, she rolled over onto her side, facing her voyeur, the blankets falling farther to reveal the incredible curve of waist, swell of hip and the barest hint of a pale thigh.

Lainey fled. Considering the strength of her yearning, it was safer to stay far, far away. She wasn't sure she could fight the impulse in any other manner. It helped that Scotch hadn't returned her interest.

At the door, Lainey grabbed a jacket and stepped outside, closing the door softly behind her. *Christ! This is the worst case of infatuation.* She leaned back against the door, its solidness a balm to her unsteady emotions. She tried to recollect the number of times she had felt this way about anyone and wasn't pleased to realize the answer. *Never.* Part of her uneasiness stemmed from the fact that she was floundering in completely new territory. Even her best friend and fuck buddy, Carol, didn't cause this sort of confusion and desire.

There was nowhere to go, nothing to be done about it now. The Fullers had entered into a contractual agreement with Lainey to train her for the Iditarod. She had authorized the transfer of money from her magazine, *Cognizance*, months ago. Everything was signed, sealed and—while not necessarily delivered—she expected to run the race of her life in March. If Lainey folded now, she would owe her editor a lot of money. Running wasn't an option. *Besides, I'll be damned if I prove Ben right.*

The realities of her situation firmly in mind, Lainey took a deep, bracing breath. As soon as the snow hit, things would be different. Training would fill most of her days and nights. Rye had said that winter was a very busy season for the kennel in terms of weekend tourist outings, preparing for the larger races and attending small sprints and the like. Lainey would just have to make an extra effort to exhaust herself over the coming months. Once the Iditarod was over, she and Howry would take their leave and she could lose herself in Carol's arms. *For about a month.* All those unspent hormones of hers had to go somewhere. Certainly that had everything to do with her volatile emotions and cravings now.

Heartened by the plausible explanation, Lainey stepped off the porch. The ground squeaked beneath her boot and she focused on the clearing around her. A thick layer of snow covered the ground, seeming to glow in the growing daylight. A stream of smoke through the crisp air was rising from the other side of the hill where the main cabin lay. Huddled within her jacket, she trudged toward the outhouse. *Oh, yes, it is definitely colder today.*

* * *

A light sprinkle of snow continued to dust the kennel as Scotch and the rest of the crew started their morning chores. She tried to assess how much snow had fallen during the night, whether the trails were thick enough to warrant a shakedown run with the sleds and which dogs to take on the first official run of the season. Irish and Rye no doubt were thinking along the same lines as they went about their jobs on autopilot. Scotch shared glances of anticipation with her siblings, knowing nothing would keep them off the trails today. They had no tour reservations this morning, and any sightseer in the area might be too caught up in the beauty of an Alaskan snowfall to consider dropping by the kennel.

Howry was equally distracted. He had brought his camera with him this morning, pausing in his chores to grab several shots of Scotch and her dogs excitedly playing in the powder. The animals knew what the change of weather meant and showed it with an extra level of exuberance. Having become accustomed to the endless attention, Scotch ignored Howry's activities. His constant presence was the price she paid for agreeing to the magazine articles. She had to admit that some days were very trying. Having a bad day sooner or later was inevitable; having one with an observer photographing her every mistake or temper tantrum didn't improve matters.

She glanced at Lainey. The shorter woman stood on the step stool, shovel in hand as she used the edge of the tool to break up the fish. It was a far cry from her first day, cringing away from the idea of feeding fish, heads and all, to the dogs. Scotch grinned at the recollection. She remembered Cliff, the bush pilot, and his remark that Lainey appeared high maintenance. Scotch was relieved that this hadn't turned out to be the case. If anything, Lainey was more than capable of rolling up her sleeves and digging into whatever was required to complete a task, regardless of the level of filth involved.

She watched as Lainey finished the chopping and Rye put the lid back on the kettle. As soon as Lainey was clear of the stool, she retrieved her camera from a hook. Lainey's hazel eyes met hers, a puzzled cast to the brow. Scotch blushed, grinning foolishly at being caught staring. Lainey promptly took a picture. Laughing, Scotch waved her away, stepping into the dog barn to consult the daily lists.

Since her conversation with her dad, her parents hadn't said a word about their suspicions or hopes. After a few days walking on eggshells, Scotch relaxed back into the normal flow of kennel life. Aware of her father's observations, Scotch had discovered that he had some basis for them. Since then, she had busted Lainey watching her multiple times. After several weeks of this, it had become an unspoken game between them, one that Scotch enjoyed. Her mind drifted off to a series of mental images of Lainey, some remembered and some fantasy.

"Hey there. Anything new?"

Startled, Scotch glanced up to see her lust object had entered the barn. "Nope. Same old, same old. We can start gathering the additives." She shared a grin with her friend as they opened a cabinet to pull out large measuring bowls. They worked in silent tandem, almost as an extension of one another as they retrieved vitamin supplements, rice and bone meal to add to the morning stew. The ease and familiarity with which they moved soothed Scotch.

"We'll have to alter the dogs' diets for the weather, won't we?"

Scotch nodded. "Eventually. More fats and proteins, less filler. That'll take place once we get them past seven miles a day."

"And when will that be?"

"Soon." Scotch finished measuring out bone meal. She turned toward Lainey, resting a hip on the edge of the counter. "I think we'll skip the run today. Let's take the snow machines out of storage and out on the trails to pack the snow down a bit. It'll give us an idea of how they're faring and how deep the snow truly is. If we're lucky, it will keep snowing for a few more days. That would give us a healthy base to run on."

"Sounds like a plan. I take it there are no tours today?"

"Nope. And even if there are visitors today, Miguel can do the deed. Once the snow flies, training begins. He and Dad are going to take up a lot of the slack as our winter tourists come through."

Lainey frowned. "But your dad works."

"Construction," Scotch reminded her. "Business slows down enough that he can leave a lot of the work to his foreman. There's some interior work to be had, but he'll have fewer jobs until spring. If the snow holds, work will taper off enough that he'll be home a lot more."

When Lainey smacked her forehead lightly at her momentary lapse of insight, Scotch smiled. Despite the heavy coveralls layered in dog hair and mud, Lainey looked adorable. Her expressive features and dark eyes always reflected cheer. *Do they reflect something else as well?*

"What?"

Scotch pushed away the sudden desire. "Sorry. Just thinking that I'm glad you're here."

Lainey's grin softened. "Thanks. I'm glad I'm here too."

Heart thumping, Scotch took a step closer. "That's good to know," she said, her voice husky. She focused on Lainey's face. Fascinated, she watched as her friend's lips parted ever so slightly.

Irish came into the dog barn. "Are you guys ready yet?"

Bewildered, Scotch turned, barely noting Lainey taking a smooth step away from her. "Just about."

Irish stopped and stared at them. "What's going on?"

Lainey smiled at her. "We were just talking about what to do today."

"Check the trails, of course." The girl acted as if it were a foregone conclusion. She continued forward and took the tin of rice. "Rye says it's time."

"Then let's go. We have a lot of dogs to feed." Lainey scooped up the bone meal and followed Irish. At the door, she paused. "Are you coming?"

Scotch took a deep breath, regaining her equilibrium. "Yeah." She turned to study Lainey, seeing a flush cross the woman's tanned skin and knowing a similar blush tinted her own. "I'll be there in a minute."

On the verge of saying something, Lainey loitered a moment.

"Hey, where's the rest?" Howry called from outside.

The moment passed. "On my way!" Lainey's expression flickered with regret, and she gave a little half shrug before disappearing outside.

Scotch turned back to the counter, placing her hands on the edge. *Was I going to kiss Lainey just now?* In answer, her mind delivered up an erotic vision of just such an action. Her body responded with a rush of sensation that swept from her heart to her groin, and she swallowed hard. *Good God, yes!*

Irish marched up to the counter. "What's taking so long?"

"Nothing. I…" Scotch picked up the nearest clipboard. "I was wondering whether or not to start the dogs on the extra protein now."

Irish quirked an eyebrow in question. "Don't we want to wait until they've been training first?"

Scotch nodded. "Yeah, you're right." She slid the measured additives toward her little sister. "Here. I'll get started on breaking out the snow machines until the stew's ready for the dogs."

"Okay." Irish took the tin and left, unaware of Scotch's confusion.

Using the opposite door, Scotch walked to the storage barn, avoiding the dog kitchen completely. Entering, she switched on the overhead lights and located the vehicles, automatically reviewing the process of preparing them for use. It had been a long time since she had experienced such a strong attraction to anyone. The last time had ended with disastrous results that still gave her nightmares. A chill crept down her spine and she shivered. This was more than simple infatuation. *When the hell did that happen?*

Scotch pulled the tarps off the vehicles, her nose itching at the dust that flew. A healthy round of sneezing later, she had the coverings folded up and set aside, and she began preparing the snow machines for use. She grumbled under her breath as she forced open a sticking gas cap. Even if she had made the attempt to kiss her roommate, that didn't necessarily mean Lainey felt the same way, regardless of what her parents thought. What were the odds? *But she didn't look like she didn't want it.* Closing her eyes a moment, Scotch recalled what she had assumed was arousal in Lainey's eyes.

With a groan, she forced the image away. "What difference does it make?" Once the Iditarod was over, Lainey would move on to other gigs. Scotch would return to living alone. Maybe Lainey could have a woman in every port—providing she was into women—but Scotch wasn't built that way. She gave too much of her heart. Casual liaisons were impossible for her. Besides, the Iditarod was far too important to screw up for a roll in the hay, no matter how appealing that roll might seem.

"Hey, Scotch."

"What!" She glared at the interruption.

Howry raised his hands defensively and took a step backward. "We're getting ready to feed the dogs."

She slumped and gave the reporter a contrite look. "Sorry. Guess I got up on the wrong side of the bed. Didn't mean to snap."

He shrugged. "Don't worry about it. It's an exciting day for you, I'm sure."

Chuckling at the unintended irony, she said, "You don't know the half of it."

CHAPTER TWENTY

Lainey kept the pleasant expression plastered on her face as she left Scotch in the dog barn. She poured the bone meal into the kettle, her motions on automatic as the sight of Scotch leaning closer filled her mind. Damn, that had been close! She had almost thrown herself at Scotch. *Or did Scotch make the first move? Is that wishful thinking on my part?* Had Scotch initiated the seduction?

"Where's the rest?" Rye asked, stirring the mixture.

"Scotch has it." Lainey made no move to return to the barn, not wanting to face her friend just yet. Her first priorities were to slow her thundering heart and quell the rich wave of yearning rolling through her.

Irish pursed her lips in preadolescent aggravation. "I'll go get it." She took the measuring bowl from Lainey and stomped toward the door.

Rye rolled his eyes at his sister as he continued to mix the stew, saying nothing.

At loose ends, Lainey took the opportunity to flee, picking up her camera and heading into the dog yard. Standing behind the lens calmed her erratic nerves, allowing her to detach from her immediate surroundings. After she had been shot, the psychiatrist had said the camera was a crutch, protecting her from reality. *No argument there.* At least this way she was able to chill out enough to contemplate what happened.

What had happened?

First, they were talking, working side by side as they had for months, comfortable in their proximity. Then…Scotch had put the move on her.

"No. That can't be right." Lainey shook her head and returned to finding the right shot through the viewfinder. Bonaparte demanded a state portrait with his elegant profile, and she snapped the picture.

As far as she had been able to ascertain, Scotch was straight. Certainly there had been times she wondered if perhaps she was wrong. She had chalked it up to wishful thinking on her part. Every instance of ambiguity could be chalked up as a simple misunderstanding. Living with a person for three and a half months had to count for something. She would know if Scotch shared her attraction to women, right? Even Howry had done his fair share of talking with Scotch, attempting to discover the nature of her sexuality. He had shared his conclusion with Lainey that Scotch was a very sheltered, innocent, straight woman.

So, what had just happened in the dog barn?

Lainey growled under her breath. Nothing but the obvious could explain it. She'd had too much experience in the art of seduction not to recognize an attempted kiss. Scotch had made the first move. But why? *And, more importantly, why now?*

The steam from her sharp exhalation clouded the vision through her lens for a moment. It was no wonder she was constantly confused about Scotch's intentions. That could only mean that Scotch was probably just as confounded. Which indicated, at the very least, that she was only now discovering who she was. Great. Not only did Scotch not have the common decency to know her own sexual orientation at the age of twenty-four, she had to complicate Lainey's attraction by figuring it out now. *The last thing I need is a virgin.* Despite that sardonic thought, she felt a tremor of excitement at the possibility.

"Stop it!" She forced away ribald visions of what "lessons" she could teach Scotch. "Dirty old woman." Kaara cocked an ear at her. "Not you, girl." Lainey rubbed the dog's head.

What to do? It was one thing to have a crush on a straight roommate. Lainey had experienced such unrequited fiascos in her youth. This one might be stronger than anything she had felt in the past, but all she needed to do in such a case was keep a tight rein on her desires and suffer in silence.

If Lainey's suspicions were correct, however, Scotch was waking up to something fundamental about herself. Such a realization was difficult enough in the best of times; here in the backwoods of Alaska, it could cause major trauma. Lainey really liked Scotch. She didn't want to lose their friendship because of a mistake. Scotch might make a pass at her in experimentation, and Lainey wasn't sure she could resist.

She snorted to herself, grinning when Jonah did the same as he nosed his empty bowl. "You'll be fed soon." She scratched his back.

Irish's timely interruption was the only thing that had saved the morning. Now aware of Scotch's attraction, Lainey knew it would be three times harder to deny her own. Perhaps she should move into the main cabin. She could cite the cold as a reason. Scotch knew about her ribs; it would be nothing to expand a bit on that to feign a need for a steady form of heating through the winter. *Unless Scotch offers a more entertaining manner of keeping warm in the evenings.*

"Ugh!" Lainey wished there was something to pound her head against. *I need a fucking drink!*

"Lainey! Breakfast time!"

She sighed and turned toward the dog kitchen. Waving to Rye, she returned to the dog kitchen.

* * *

Lainey refused to believe that Howry's insistence on riding with her was just to get better shots of Scotch on her snow machine. She had seen him watching her at breakfast. He knew something was up and, like any good journalist, wouldn't let it go until he got the scoop. She forced a smile and agreed to take him as a passenger, unable to come up with a valid reason to deny him.

After a quick lesson on the operation, she saddled up on the snow machine with Howry behind her. The controls weren't much different than the ATVs she had used all summer. *Too bad*, she thought. *If I couldn't drive one, maybe I'd have ridden with someone else.*

Rye, Irish and Scotch each rode a machine, and the yard was filled with the whine of engines and the barking of the dogs. Scotch looked back and gestured for Lainey to follow her. Her brother and sister each went in different directions, off to check the snow levels of their favorite stretches of trail.

Lainey surged forward with a jerk, causing Howry to clutch at her and curse. She grinned despite her trepidation at his upcoming questions. As she became used to the vehicle controls, he relaxed his grip and she heaved a sigh of relief. Her ribs were definitely giving her trouble today, and her passenger's death grip didn't help. She could tell she would spend a lot of her free time at the hot springs in the coming months.

Though she had just been on them the day before, the trails were almost alien. White powder covered the familiar landscape, transforming it into a different realm. Branches which had previously been above her head now drooped under the weight of snow. In some places, only brightly fluttering plastic markers jogged her memory and indicated where she should go. Scotch rode ahead of her, breaking the trail, and Lainey gave her plenty of lead space to keep from running into her when she occasionally bogged down in snowdrifts.

"So, what happened this morning?"

Lainey pursed her lips. "What do you mean?"

"Don't be coy, Lainey. You don't wear it well." Howry raised his voice to be heard over the engine. "We both know what I'm talking about."

"What if I don't want to talk about it?"

He remained silent behind her for a full minute. "Think I should talk to Scotch instead?"

"Bastard," she said under her breath.

Howry hugged her closer. "What was that?"

Lainey looked over her shoulder. "I said you're a bastard."

"Good to know I haven't lost my touch."

His laugh triggered her sense of the absurd, and she laughed along with him. It was far better than crying.

"Seriously, Lainey, what's going on? You two have a fight or something?"

She sobered. Before her, Scotch took the left branch of a trail, standing on the machine as she disappeared down an embankment. Lainey braced herself and followed. Once they were back on level ground, she slowed to give Scotch more room. "I don't think Scotch is straight."

"What? I don't think I heard you right. Scotch isn't—"

"Straight!" Up ahead, the subject of their conversation must have heard something because she glanced backwards. *No!* Surely she hadn't shouted loud enough for that. Scotch was only checking the distance between them.

"Really?" Howry drawled. "How do you figure?"

"Oh, I don't know, Don. I guess when she tried to kiss me, I kind of figured things were off."

He loosened his grip slightly, pulling away. "You're joking."

Lainey grumbled to herself. "I wish."

He didn't need to hear her to understand what she said. As he digested this new information, she concentrated on driving. Scotch pulled onto another trail, waving Lainey toward one that paralleled her course. She gave the snow machine more gas and caught up to her. Breaking her own trail made the journey a bit rougher, but no less enjoyable. A thin line of deciduous trees flickered between them, giving Lainey the weird sensation of watching a reel of film at slow speed. Her heart warmed as she saw Scotch smile at her. At least the morning's oddness apparently hadn't affected their friendship.

Howry took advantage of their proximity to take a rapid series of photos.

"How're you doing?" Scotch yelled.

"Great! Where to next?"

"Let's head to the river, see how it's doing there. We'll need to slow down some."

"Okay. Lead on!"

Scotch nodded agreement and pulled ahead. At a break in the tree line, Lainey crossed over to the other trail, feeling the fine mist of granulated snow as Scotch picked up speed and rooster tailed. Howry laughed and she did too.

"So, she put the moves on you, huh?"

Lainey rolled her eyes. She had hoped he would drop the subject, but she supposed she hadn't made allowances for the fact that he was a newsman, through and through. "Yeah. She said she was happy I was here, and the next thing I knew, we were closing in for the clincher."

"Did she come to her senses and realize I'm a far better catch than an old, broken-down warhorse like you?"

Despite the churning of emotions, Lainey smiled. "Actually, we were saved by the sister. Irish interrupted before anything could happen."

"Hmmm, my sympathies to you then."

"Don—"

"I know! I know! Even though you've moped around for months mooning over her, you can't conceive of slaking your passions in her bed. I understand."

She wondered whether she could find a ditch to jump and dislodge him from behind her.

"No. Scratch that. I don't understand," he continued. "What's the problem? I'd think you'd be shedding your parka and skipping into her arms by now."

"God, you're an idiot."

"That's not news."

She chuckled. "You don't get it. Scotch has just figured out she's either gay or bi. This is all new ground for her."

Howry whistled. "Lucky for her you're here to show her the ropes, huh?"

"Don!"

"What?" he asked in the same sharp tone. "I'm just a straight man; I'm not getting it here. Enlighten me."

Lainey refused to speak. Howry wasn't dense. If he couldn't figure it out, she certainly wasn't going to explain it to him. Scotch took the trail to the right and Lainey pushed the snow machine to its limit as she turned and followed, causing Howry to clutch at her in abrupt fear of being thrown.

"Holy shit."

At first, she thought he was swearing because of her attempt to dump him in a snowdrift.

"You *love* her."

Lainey swallowed, her lungs suddenly not big enough to pump sufficient oxygen. She wheezed a couple of times, her heart thumping so hard that she was certain he could feel it through his thick gloves and her parka.

Love.

As she regained control of her respiration, a sardonic grunt left her throat. Of course. Infatuation was the wrong word entirely. Being a journalist, she needed a good command of the language. Funny how her mind had danced around the term, never allowing her to focus on it.

Her mother had always said, "If you can name your demons, you can control them." Lainey wondered how she could control this.

CHAPTER TWENTY-ONE

Irrespective of her sudden emotional revelation, Lainey spent the rest of the expedition doing her damnedest to banish her demon. She doubted she was a hundred percent successful when every time she got a good look at Scotch racing ahead of her, her heart thumped in muted joy. As they neared the kennel, she felt she might have gotten a handle on her ardor. It helped that Howry had let her stew in silence after his observation. Not having to defend herself to him gave her plenty of time to work through her available options and come up with a plan. Not that it was a good plan, but at least she had something.

The last thing Scotch needed was a distraction. She was aiming to finish in the top ten or better in the Iditarod this year and needed to stay focused on her dogs and their training. It was never easy for someone to question her sexuality. Coming out to oneself was worse than coming out to family or friends. Lives had a tendency to fall apart as the soul searching took over, and Scotch could ill afford the time or heartache. Moving out of the cabin, while the easiest way to achieve space between them, would make Scotch question Lainey's reasons. Even the excuse of requiring warmth for her "football injury" would fall flat. They would both know the reality of the situation. It would only serve to highlight the attempted kiss in the dog barn. Lainey had to draw the focus away from that.

No, she had to be the adult here, the experienced one. She had to stay put to allay Scotch's fears, yet not get intimately involved with her. It would be hell, but Lainey would just have to hang on to this demon for all it was worth. When the race was over, then and only then could she consider sitting Scotch down for a real heart-to-heart discussion about what was going on with her.

Lainey felt vaguely pleased with her decision, though a bit perplexed at the self-imposed distance she would have to place between them. She would much rather do exactly what Howry had suggested—teach Scotch all the joys of loving a woman. She consoled herself with the knowledge that after the race, things would be different. If Scotch truly felt desire for her, Lainey would be more than happy to reciprocate.

She pushed away the rush of arousal that followed that particular notion. Hot on the heels of that came a strong yearning for another kind of scotch, one that didn't cause so many problems.

Or does it?

By the time they returned to the kennel, Lainey had set aside her internal debate. Her nerves still fluttered, but she was resolute. She drove the snow machine into the yard, to the welcome clamor from the dogs. Pulling up next to Scotch, she saw that Irish and Rye had already returned, their vehicles covered with a light dusting of still-falling snow. She turned off the engine and glanced at the woman beside her.

Scotch's cheeks and nose were red from cold, her eyes sparkling as she grinned. She had yanked back her hood and tawny curls stuck out about her face, flakes of snow starting to settle there. Lainey's heart ached as she returned the smile. *Stay away from this? God is a cruel, cruel being.*

"It's looking really good." Scotch climbed off the snow machine. She pulled off her thick gloves and opened the neck of her parka. "We can only hope the snow stays like this for the entire season!"

The vehicle shifted as Howry got off. "I think it's time to switch to manual cameras." He pulled a plastic bag from his pocket, stuffed his camera inside and zipped it closed. "I ran out of film on the run. If I wind it now, it'll shatter."

"You can always switch to digital," Lainey said sweetly, revisiting an old argument between them.

"Blasphemy! A camera without real film is an abomination in the sight of the gods."

Lainey smiled and swung her leg over the snow machine, remaining seated. She too removed her gloves. "Are we taking the dogs out today?"

"No. Let's give the trails another run after lunch. Pack 'em down some more. If it keeps coming down, we'll do more tomorrow. The tighter we pack the trails now, the longer they'll last if the temperature rises. It's still early in the season. Who knows what the weather will do."

Standing, Lainey stretched with slight misgiving as her ribs gave her a sharp jab. The pain was far less than it should have been after the extensive ride. They had spent a good three hours roaming the trails. By all rights, she should be emulating a rheumatic old woman.

"You okay?"

Lainey nodded at Howry. "Surprisingly. I'm glad I heeded Thom's advice. That jacket I had last March was crap."

Without warning, Scotch reached out and grabbed her right hand, forcing it up above Lainey's head. The ache was bearable and completely overshadowed by the feel of Scotch's skin against hers.

"You know that liniment we use for wrist injuries?" Scotch concentrated on Lainey's ribs.

Lainey blushed at Howry's smirk. "Um, the one for strains and sprains?"

"Yeah." Scotch released her. "I bet it'd work on your ribs."

Howry snorted, no doubt entertained by the notion of Scotch offering to apply the balm to the injury. Lainey so wanted to kick him in the shin but knew she'd have to explain herself to their witness afterward. Instead, she rolled her eyes. "It's for dogs," she reminded Scotch.

"It's been used on people upon occasion." She chuckled. "It might do the trick. You should give it a try."

Scotch's matter-of-fact tone made Lainey view the salve in another light. Its primary purpose was to ease joint aches in the wrists and shoulders of overworked dogs. It was a homespun remedy created by God-only-knew-who, but it seemed every musher worth his or her salt had a variation of the recipe. An herbal mixture, it was blended with petroleum jelly to give it substance and make it easy to apply. Scotch and her brother both swore by the stuff.

"All right. I'll think about it." Scotch opened her mouth to say something, and Lainey interrupted her. "I'll think about it! Right now, though, I'm starved. Let's get some lunch!"

"That sounds like a great idea." Howry moved toward the back deck.

Scotch grinned and nodded, dropping whatever she had planned to say.

Lainey followed them, relief coursing through her. She had known exactly what Scotch was going to say. Despite Lainey's recent pledge to avoid awkward situations with Scotch, there was no way she could deny her if she offered to apply ointment. And that would be a bad, bad idea.

* * *

Scotch idled in front of the fire, her feet propped up on an old footstool she had rescued from a thrift store years ago. She wiggled her sock-covered toes and sipped from a cup of hot chocolate.

The first snowfall of the season had been a good one. If conditions held up like this, training would be a breeze. She recalled the winter before last, unseasonably warm and no major snowstorms to speak of. The first third of the journey had been treacherous, with bare ground and freely flowing water. A lot of mushers had been forced to scratch from the race because of broken equipment or injuries to themselves or their animals. Not this year.

Scotch relished her contentment. Even if it warmed up a bit, chances were it wouldn't interfere with the hardening trails. After lunch, they had gone another round, packing the trails down for future runs. Tomorrow the sleds would come out and the training would begin in earnest.

The cabin door opened and Lainey stomped inside. A draft followed her, but Scotch was warm enough that the cool air felt nice. "Still snowing?"

Lainey glanced over her shoulder as she hung her jacket on a peg. "No. It finally stopped." She laughed at Scotch's expression as she moved down the stairs to return to the couch. "Give it a rest, Fuller! We got two feet today, maybe more."

Scotch's petulant frown eased into a smile. "Yeah, I guess."

Snorting, Lainey kicked off her boots. Tucking her feet underneath a quilt, she leaned forward to pick up her mug of tea and then sank back with a sigh. "You know, there's something I've been meaning to ask you." She stared into her cup.

Sudden wariness disrupted Scotch's composure. She had been expecting this all day. Initially she held hopes that Lainey hadn't realized how close Scotch had come to kissing her. As the day progressed, however, there had been several moments where it seemed as if she wanted to discuss something. What was she going to say when Lainey asked what had happened? *"Sorry about the pass, but I've got a crush on you that just won't quit."*

Her silence was noticed, and she looked up to see Lainey watching her. "Uh, yeah?"

"Have you ever considered the benefits of a chamber pot as opposed to an outhouse?"

Scotch stared at Lainey, her mind stuttering to a halt. She blinked and shook her head. "What?"

Lainey grinned and sat up. "Chamber pots. You know—porcelain pots that you squat over rather than shuffling around in the dark and cold, baring your ass to freezing temperatures." She shrugged, waving one hand in the air. "I, of all people, understand the rustic life here. I've lived and worked in Third World countries. But even in Africa they have a version of the chamber pot. Why don't you?"

Her trepidation was replaced with a healthy dose of relief and amusement as she registered what Lainey was saying. Scotch ruefully ran her hand through her hair. "They're called honey pots around here, and I don't know why I haven't got one. Can't say it's ever come up in conversation."

"Well, it has now," Lainey replied in crisp tones.

Warming to the conversation, Scotch shifted in her chair. "What do you suggest, O Worldly One?" Scotch laughed when Lainey stuck out her tongue.

"Funny you should ask. I couldn't help but notice that there are a lot of five gallon buckets over by the dog barn. I think one of those would make a wonderful indoor privy for those of us without ice in our veins."

"It's you who's cold-blooded."

Lainey's brow furrowed. "How do you figure?"

"It's a scientific fact that cold-blooded animals get sluggish in lower temperatures. If that doesn't describe you in the morning, I don't know what does."

Lainey stuck out her tongue again and Scotch barely refrained from asking her if she was offering her services. She blushed and shied away from where that would lead the conversation. "So, what are you wanting—my permission to set up a honey pot in the cabin?"

"You live here too." Lainey shrugged. "I realize that no matter how often it's emptied or how clean I keep it, there'll be some odor involved."

"It really wouldn't be that bad." She gave Lainey an inquiring look, receiving a nod in return. "We could go into town tomorrow after lunch and pick up plastic bags and some lye or something to help control the smell."

Lainey's smile was beautiful. "That'd be great!"

Scotch returned her grin, an ache in her heart. She would love to snuggle under that quilt and kiss Lainey senseless. She ducked her head, unable to shake her desire, and brought her cup to her lips instead. Of all the people to fall for, it had to be an international photojournalist who would soon be off on another adventure.

"What are you thinking?"

Startled from her thoughts, Scotch groped for something to say. "Just thinking about Don." Lainey cocked her head in silent question. "He's going to have a tough time keeping up with me now that the snow has fallen."

"Yeah." Lainey chuckled. "Yeah, he will. But don't underestimate him. He'll probably follow you around on a snowmobile every day if you let him."

Scotch held her cup in her lap, a stern expression on her face. "Snowmobile? What the hell, Miss Hughes!"

"Snow machine! Snow *machine*!" Lainey raised both hands in surrender, almost upsetting her tea. "I'm sorry, master! I had a momentary lapse!"

"Damned right you did," Scotch groused. "By the time you leave this great state of Alaska, you'll be able to pass for a native." She enjoyed their shared laughter. It was less than what she truly wanted, but good friendships were hard to find. She didn't want to screw this one up.

CHAPTER TWENTY-TWO

November

Lainey went over her sled with care, checking the plastic runners for damage and tugging this way and that to test the rigging. As soon as everything had passed inspection, she pulled the tow lines from the sled bag and laid them out on the icy ground. A few feet away, Scotch mirrored her activities.

Rye and Irish were already gone. Having left immediately after breakfast, they were driving a truck full to the brim with excited mutts and three racing sleds. There was a junior event in nearby Wasilla, and they had each entered a handful of sprints. It was now after lunch. Chances were good that one if not both of them had placed well and were finishing their last race before returning home.

Once Lainey had the line in place and tested for wear and tear, she set her snow hook and stomped it deep into the snow. For the most part, the large curved metal hook served as an anchor to keep the sled immobile. Mindful of the fact that she was running Jonah today, she also tied her snub line to a post. She had learned the hard way that her muscle man wheel dog had a tendency to pop the hook. It took a single morning of chasing her team down on foot to ingrain that particular lesson.

It was a weekend so there were no tourists scheduled. The handler, Miguel, had a group of amateur mushers on a weekend excursion. By now six eager teachers from Minnesota had left a filling and educational lunch at Lafferty's fish camp and were on their way to the other side of the river for an overnight stop at the hot springs.

Lainey had been surprised to discover that after the snow fell, visitors became more plentiful, not less. Not only were nearby schools bussing their students to outlying kennels for field trips, but Helen received a fair share of veterinary classes from Anchorage. Apparently hers was the only local animal hospital attached to a racing kennel, and the graduate students came from miles around to see the complete operation.

Then there were the neighbors. Everyone in and around the nearby village had stopped by at least once since the snow began, many of them on dog sleds. Of those, most used their dogs as winter transportation, a string of three or four animals hauling them around the area. One man lived in the bush, trapping and fishing for a living, and he followed his trap line like clockwork. Three others were in training for various races, including the Iditarod. While they idled over the requisite cup of coffee, Lainey listened raptly to their tales of races won and lost, gleaning as much as possible from their experiences.

Lainey pulled a small notebook from her pocket and flipped it open. She now had twenty dogs to train and had worked up a running schedule with Scotch's help. When it came down to the race, she would only be allowed sixteen dogs, but Scotch had made certain she had a decent pool from which to draw her selections. This early in the training season, they were each running a ten-dog team, mixing and matching the animals to get them comfortable working together. She checked her list for Saturday afternoons and went to round up her team.

Soon a mass of furry, barking animals tugged on the sled, their vocalizations echoed by Scotch's team and the anguished demands of those being left behind. Though Lainey had been driving dogs for a month, the excitement of the dogs remained contagious. She wanted to hurry through the final checks. Instead, she quieted her exhilaration and went down the line, rechecking tug lines, neck line and the heavy rubber shock cord.

At her sled, she did a quick inventory of the mandatory items required for the Iditarod. She had eighty dog booties, a cooker with three bottles of fuel, a three gallon pot and a cooler for cooking and soaking dog chow, another pan for people food, ten plastic bucket lids for dog bowls, an arctic weather sleeping bag, an axe, eight pounds of emergency dog food, a pair of snowshoes and a plastic bag of frozen whitefish to snack the dogs. It seemed like a lot to haul in light of the fact she was only going to be gone for three or four hours today, but Scotch had insisted on these items as well as some odds and ends of survival gear, explaining that a sudden blizzard would kill her just as quickly whether she was two miles away from home or two hundred. The one thing Lainey hated to carry was the holstered .44 automatic. She'd had enough nightmares about guns after her injury; she saw no reason to drag the weapon along, regardless of the danger of wolves or moose on the trail. Though the gun was not mandatory for the Iditarod, Scotch had put her foot down, threatening to renege on their contract if Lainey refused to carry it. Given no other option, Lainey kept the loathsome thing buried at the bottom of the bag.

She zipped up the sled bag and checked the munchie bag hanging between the handles. There was a thermos of warm Gatorade, a couple of bags of hard candy and some trail mix. Another lesson learned— the dogs weren't the only ones working on a run. Tangles with brush, barking dogs and running behind the sled to lighten the load would give her lots of exercise. The mushers at the finish line the previous March had made the entire process seem easy. Lainey had discovered how much work was truly involved for the human element of the team. She was glad she had let Scotch bully her into running every day through summer and fall.

Lainey looked over at Scotch, who had finished her last-minute checks. They had agreed to head out together and then split up about three miles out. Scotch wanted to take her dogs through the ravine, driving them along a narrow creek bed and up onto the road near the kennel. Lainey hated that run. More than anything else, it reminded her of an Olympic toboggan chute. If something happened, she would never be able to muscle her dogs and sled out of it; she'd probably be dragged behind them. She had already had a couple of experiences of eating snow and she didn't wish to repeat them.

She planned on hitting a milder trail near a snow-covered meadow. There was a loop there with several trails sprouting from its central path that the Fullers had dubbed Dupont Circle, after the notorious traffic circle in Washington, DC. Lainey's leaders had to pay attention to her spoken commands or likely go off on the wrong trail. The run was not as hazardous as Scotch's route, but there were some wonderful switchbacks along the route Lainey had chosen. The Iditarod was over a thousand miles long, and she needed to prepare her dogs for any eventuality.

After the run, she and Scotch planned to meet up at the hot springs to greet Miguel's overnighters and snack the dogs. They would have a rest break there and then take their teams home in time for dinner.

Everything ready, Lainey glanced over at Scotch, who stood on the runners of her sled, grinning expectantly. She smiled and waved back, copying the woman's stance. With one hand on the handlebar, Lainey crouched down to pull the snow hook, placing it in the specially made pouch at the back of the sled bag. She heard Scotch call out commands and watched as her team pulled out of the yard.

Not wanting to be left behind, Lainey's team lunged forward, barking for all they were worth. Still attached to the pole by the snub line, the sled skimmed sideways and she clutched the handle tightly. "Ready!" she called. Cochise and Sholo, her leads, pulled forward, straightening the line of dogs. Lainey released the last mooring and yelled, "Let's go!"

Free to run, the team shot forward, tails wagging and tongues lolling. Within minutes they were out of the yard, the clamor of those left behind fading in the distance. The dogs always went quiet when they began running, and Lainey sighed at the silence broken only by panting dogs and the swish of a sled tracking over snow. This was so much better than with an ATV—no running motors, just her and the dogs and the wilderness. Lainey had worked in the bush in many different countries, always enjoying the chance to be alone with nature. It was with some delight that she realized she would be afforded an even deeper sense of solitude during the race.

She barely caught sight of Scotch as she rounded a bend up ahead. *Small wonder, considering the distance.* Cochise and Sholo were about twenty feet in front of Lainey, and there was a thirty-foot gap between them and Scotch. That was another thing about sledding—she could be driving dogs with all three Fullers and rarely catch a glimpse of any of them unless they passed one another on parallel trails.

The dogs were going at a good clip. Lainey figured they were running at about ten miles per hour. That was expected, since they were all well rested and eager. They would pass a couple of more trails, and then she would cut off this one and onto another, leaving Scotch to her breakneck roller coaster ride.

The trailhead came up, its entrance marked by a fluttering strip of red cloth. As Cochise came abreast of it, Lainey called, "Haw!" The husky and his all-black partner automatically turned left, onto the path. Behind them, the swing dogs—Montana and Meshindi—followed the smooth arc, leading the rest of the team forward and into the turn. Dablo, Bast, Tecumseh and Heldig trotted along dutifully. When the sled arrived at the turn, Jonah and Aziz, the burly wheel dogs, put their formidable strength into it, yanking the sled onto the new trail with relative ease.

"Good dogs!" Lainey watched ears prick back to hear her praise. She grinned against the chill wind along her cheeks. Had anyone told her she would one day relish being in below-freezing temperatures on the back of a dog sled, she'd have laughed in their face.

All in all, it had been a good idea to arrive at the end of June. It had given her an opportunity to become acclimated to the gradual change of seasons and cooler temperatures. The weather didn't affect her nearly as badly as it had during her previous visit, when she had come from sweltering sun to the icy expanses. With Thom Fuller's help, she had purchased the proper arctic gear, and now she rode her sled with little discomfort. Native mukluks encased her feet, and she wore bibbed snow pants recommended for mountaineering. Her parka was a pullover, like Scotch's, the lack of zippers and snaps giving added protection as wind and snow had no points of entry. Helen had sewn an extra pocket high up on the right side, its size perfect to accommodate a hand warmer nestled against Lainey's ribs.

Toasty and warm, she watched the world open up as the team pulled into Dupont Circle, each of its half dozen trails marked with a different colored flag. The one she wanted flickered green, but Lainey allowed her team to pass it without command. There had been another spate of snow the night before, and the dogs took the opportunity to bite at snowdrifts as they passed, quenching their thirst and cooling off. She looked over the lot of them, careful to note their body language, searching for anything out of the ordinary that indicated discomfort or injury.

The dogs ran well, loping back around the circle. Sholo glanced over his shoulder as they passed their point of entry. Lainey could imagine what he was thinking—*You brought us here. Where the hell are we going?* She laughed aloud and called the command when they got to the proper trailhead. "Gee!"

Like a well-oiled machine, the team turned right, leaving the meadow for a run through dense brush. Lainey paid more attention to her surroundings as trees crowded closer. There was a real danger here of sweepers—limbs hanging low enough to knock the musher from the sled. The close confines caused the dogs to slow a bit and Lainey hopped off the runners, trotting behind the sled to lighten the load. Up ahead she saw orange paint on a tree trunk, indicating the first switchback.

Sholo and Cochise easily navigated the trail as it doubled back on itself. Of course, they had the benefit of years of experience on the paths around the kennel. They ran beyond her line of sight, and Lainey watched the rest of her team disappear around the bend. When the swing dogs were the last, she jumped back on the runners, leaning hard to the left. The sled jerked left, the momentum forcing her to the right like the end of a whip, but her preparation kept her upright and on course. Exhilarated, she stepped off the sled and ran again, her breath steaming in front of her. The dogs, tails wagging, continued to the next hairpin turn.

After the third turn, Lainey noticed the team's attention had diverted from the trail. Their ears pricked toward the right and she peered in that direction, unable to see anything through the undergrowth. Maybe they smelled a rabbit or another dog team in the area. In any case, their divided attention became a concern. She kept a close eye on the dogs. One or two of them were young and untrained enough that a romp through the woods in search of an elusive rabbit would be quite entertaining. Something like that had the potential to cause a mutiny in the ranks or major damage to the sled and gear should they make a run for it. Lainey reached into the sled for the snow hook, hanging it over the back of the sled bag for easy accessibility.

Pulling through the next turn, Lainey heard Sholo and Cochise barking before she rounded the bend. The sled jerked forward as the dogs pulled with more enthusiasm, more of her team taking up the baying. The dogs had never acted this way before. What could have them in such a tumult? Lainey felt the cold tickle of apprehension as adrenaline pumped through her veins. She leaned into the turn, and the thing setting off the dogs came into view.

A bull moose stood near the next switchback, right in the center of the trail. He looked huge, the velvet covering of his antlers long since rubbed off, revealing heavy bone. Lainey knew from lessons with Scotch that rutting season was over. The bulls had finished their annual mating confrontations and were now back to regaining the weight they had lost. The dogs had caught this one stripping bark off a tree that quivered nearby. He turned from his task to glare at them, but he didn't seem daunted by being outnumbered.

Lainey noted all the details in split seconds, the hormones flushing her system giving her a crisp, clear image. She saw a snort of steam rise from the moose's flared nostrils, saw his shoulders give a shake, the coarse hair bristling, and the slight change of stance as he moved the weight off one of his front legs. A distant part of her mind regretted there was no time to get a decent photograph; she had left her camera in the cabin.

Sholo and Cochise were almost upon the interloper. "Whoa!" she bellowed. Time slowed further as her feet left the runners to stand on the brake and drag between them. The first was a metal bar with two hooks that dug into the snow, the second, a rubber mat with bolts on the underside. She held on to the handlebars with one hand, simultaneously pulling the snow hook from its temporary placement. Squatting, she forced the tines into the trail beside her, then stood to stomp it down.

The dogs pulled up short, their clamor interrupted by a collective grunt as their chest harnesses held them back. The shock cord did its job, and none of the animals appeared injured by the abrupt stop. They barked joyously at the interesting obstacle in their path, tails wagging in furious anticipation of more fun.

Her leaders stood less than thirty feet from the moose, riding high on the exhilaration of their comrades, telling the bull off for blocking their trail. Knowing the danger, Lainey wildly looked about her for something sturdy enough to tie her snub line to. Her heart sank when she realized she would have to get off the brake to reach the nearest tree. The sled jolted as the dogs tried to surge forward, and she stamped harder on the brake and drag. Tears of frustration and stress stung Lainey's eyes as she returned her attention to the moose, praying he would decide to leave the trail.

The bull eyed the noisy gathering, snorting again as he considered his options. Lainey could almost see the thoughts on his big ugly face. His tormenters didn't close in, and he was in a foul mood from a combination of their noise and his hunger. Obviously he had the upper hoof, so to speak. Horrified, Lainey watched the bull step forward, her dogs barking louder in response. His next step was quicker and he dropped his head, preparing to charge, his formidable antlers lunging toward them.

"Hard gee!" she screamed. "Sholo! Hard gee!"

Her voice, high and panicked, pierced the ruckus. Amazingly, Sholo tugged to the right, yanking Cochise with him. As the moose rushed the team, the leaders began to double back toward the sled.

No longer needing to stay on the brake, Lainey scooped up the snow hook, yelling at the dogs, "Hurry, hurry!" The bull had a head start, however, and Cochise yelped as the deadly antlers tossed him into the air.

The carefully regimented line of dogs fell apart. Sholo continued to pull, Montana and Meshindi doing what they were trained to do. Unfortunately, that meant all of Lainey's dogs were moving forward, into the turn, and closing with an angry moose. The team slowed, Sholo dragging Cochise's limp body along as the wild animal made another lunge, tangling his antlers in tug lines.

The pistol!

Lainey dove over the handlebars, unzipping the sled bag with clumsy hands. It took forever before she rooted it out. She knelt in the sled, the cold heavy steel of the .44 in her hand. There came a moment of terror when she couldn't reach the trigger. She swore, ripping her mitten off with her teeth.

Her first attempt did nothing and she stared blankly at the weapon. *The safety! The safety's on!* With a quick flick of her finger, she released the safety catch and fired.

CHAPTER TWENTY-THREE

The sound of a gunshot echoed across the wilderness. Scotch cocked her head. Hunting season was over for most game. Besides, had there been hunters in the area, someone surely would have mentioned seeing them during the many evening visitations winter always seemed to draw. The only people with guns in the immediate area were her, Miguel and Lainey.

Another shot rang out and Scotch felt her heart jump in her chest. With hunters ruled out, the only reason someone would shoot a firearm would be to defend themselves. Providing Miguel's tour was following his usual route, they were much too far away for the shots to be from that group. Those shots had to have been fired by Lainey. It had been like pulling teeth to get her to carry a pistol in the first place. Something dire must have happened for her to actually shoot it.

Scotch scanned the trail ahead of her, visualizing the paths that branched away. Her team had yet to reach their destination; the creek bed was several miles from the kennel. She knew where Lainey had been heading, now she had to find a way to get there. Shaking her head with a grimace, she realized her only route would be too roundabout, delaying her arrival at the switchbacks. All the nearest side trails led away from Lainey's position.

"Whoa!" She put on the brakes. As soon as her team halted, she jumped from her sled and ran to the head of the line. She grabbed the collars of her lead dogs, Cleatis and Sukita, and brought them around. The rest of the team followed until they faced back the way they had come. Muscling the sled about, when everything was ready Scotch popped the snow hook and yelled, "Let's go! Get up!"

The dogs happily sped along at a brisk pace, per Scotch's command. She heard no more gunshots, but that did little to ease her mind. What could have forced Lainey to use the pistol? Scotch wasn't even sure Lainey knew how to use the thing. She had flat out refused to do more than listen to a general run-through about the weapon before putting it in her sled bag with a distasteful expression. Only Scotch's threat to terminate their contract made Lainey accept the gun as part of her racing gear.

The team wasn't moving fast enough. "Get up!" she called again. "Let's go!" Her team put forth a little more effort, but she knew it wouldn't last for long. This speed was primarily for sprints, not extended runs. She fought the urge to jump off and run with them, knowing they were gliding along faster than her feet could carry her but feeling an overwhelming need to do something to get to Lainey faster.

Anxiety raced through her as she conjured up all manner of scenarios, none of them pretty. As the possibilities ran through her mind, she automatically gave the commands to get them to Dupont Circle. Several minutes passed before they pulled into the meadow, and she wasted no time getting the dogs onto the proper trail. She heard a snow machine approaching from a distance and a profound sense of relief washed through her at the added assistance on the way.

The switchbacks were fairly hazardous on the best of days. Going at breakneck speed increased the danger of tangles and falls. Scotch and her team had extensive experience with the even more perilous trails of the Iditarod course and the Yukon Quest. Still, she barely managed to remain upright as the dogs took the fourth turn. Jubilant barking met her ears, and she barely registered Lainey's team before she stood on the brakes and halted her dogs beside Lainey's sled.

Setting the snow hook was an automatic procedure as Scotch flung herself from the sled. Lainey sat in the snow amid a tangle of tug lines and dogs. She seemed okay enough and Scotch looked over the mess, glad to see that none of the animals were so snarled that their lines were choking them. A few feet away, blood stained the snow where a moose had collapsed. She carefully noted it was dead and dismissed it as a non-threat. She almost swooned as the weight of fear lifted. Lainey was safe. Scotch's knees became rubbery with relief, and she stumbled as she rushed forward. Lainey held a bleeding dog in her lap, and Scotch's initial relief morphed into dread. The pistol lay nearby, its black metal sunk into the snow.

"Are you all right?" She knelt in the snow beside Lainey, grimacing as she saw the wounded dog was Cochise. He panted and whimpered, but held still in Lainey's arms. His snout was bloody and one eye had swollen shut. Scotch couldn't tell if he had a simple head injury, or if the blood around his mouth was from internal bleeding.

Lainey barely nodded in response to her question. "There wasn't any time. The moose was only a few feet away when I came around the bend."

Scotch hugged the distraught woman, resting her cheek on the dark head. "It's okay. It's all right. It's over."

Lainey sobbed and burrowed closer, her hands never leaving Cochise, gently stroking his fur.

The snow machine drew closer and stopped. Scotch heard the motor drop into an idle and a voice call out in question. "Hang on, help is here." Though reluctant to release Lainey, Scotch stood to yell back, "Over here! In the switchback!"

She received an answering shout as she heard the motor rev. As much as she wanted to return to Lainey, this disaster had to be cleaned up. The smell of blood would draw any predators or scavengers in the area, and the dogs needed to be straightened out and returned to the kennel. Scotch bent and unhooked Cochise from his neck line as the snow machine came into view from the other side of the switchback.

"What the hell!" Ray Lafferty exclaimed, swerving at the last minute to avoid the bull in his path. He turned off the engine and clambered from the snow machine. "I heard the shots. Everybody okay?"

"For the most part." Scotch stepped forward to shake his hand. "I'm glad you're here. Cochise has been injured and I don't know how bad."

"I'll take him to your mom." He looked over her shoulder at Lainey. "Should I take her too?"

Scotch turned to regard the woman who quietly wept. "Yeah. Maybe you should. I can rig the dogs together and pull her sled in."

Lafferty nodded his grizzled head. "Let's get going then. Time's a wasting." He went back to his snow machine.

"Lainey?" Scotch returned to her friend. "Ray's going to take you and Cochise to Mom's hospital."

"What?" Lainey asked, confused.

"Ray's here." Scotch gestured to the old timer who was bringing up his vehicle. "Cochise needs to get to a vet. Ray will take both of you to Mom."

Lainey studied Ray as he dismounted and neared, then the dog in her lap. She scanned the tiny clearing. "What about my team?"

"I'll get them in. Don't worry about that." Scotch's voice was calm, soothing. Lainey was obviously in shock. With the right tone, she would be compliant and follow orders. Killing wasn't an easy thing to do, regardless of the situation. The photojournalist had seen a lot of death during her career but had never been its perpetrator. It had to be messing with her head.

"No."

"Excuse me, miss?" Lafferty asked. "The sooner we get in, the better chance that dog has to survive."

Lainey wiped her face, lifting her chin. "I'm not going with you. It's my team and my mess. I'll help clean it up."

Lafferty blinked at her, taken aback by her suddenly defiant attitude. He shook himself and gave Scotch a rueful grin. "Whatever you say, ma'am."

She glared up at them. "That's what I say."

Scotch regarded her for a long moment, seeing Lainey's stubborn need to follow through, no matter how difficult the task. Women of a less hardy nature would take the offer for what it was—an escape from the emotional upheaval of dealing with the issue. Lainey had not only overcome her fear of guns but had successfully defended herself with one. She kept her head when others would have crawled under a rock, defeated. Her opinion of Lainey Hughes, already high by most standards, went up a notch. This was one tough lady. If any Outsider rookie had a shot at completing the Iditarod, this one did. "All right. Let's get a move on."

Her words were a catalyst, and Lainey squared her shoulders. With Lafferty's help, Lainey wrapped Cochise in her sleeping bag and helped him cradle the dog between his legs on the snow machine. When they were ready, he promised her that he would take care of her lead dog and slowly drove the vehicle toward Fuller Kennels.

Scotch used the time to untangle the dogs and get both teams facing toward home. She tied off the snub lines on both sleds. Lainey snacked her dogs on frozen whitefish, heaping praise on them for their level heads. Scotch did the same. Once the muddle was cleared up, Scotch approached the moose. Close inspection showed two bullet wounds, one on the forehead and one in the neck. From the amount of blood, it looked as if Lainey had hit an artery. She heard the crunch of snow from behind her as Lainey approached.

"Damned good shot for not knowing what to do." Scotch poked at the head wound, noting a streak of damage that went up past its ear. "Looks like your first shot hit him at just the right angle to deflect the bullet. It was your second shot that did him in."

"He reared up. He didn't look like he was leaving and I didn't want him trampling the team, so I fired again."

"You did what you had to do. Now you're going to learn what to do if this happens again. If you kill a game animal on the race trail, you're required to gut it and then report it at the next checkpoint. Here at home you have to report it to the Fish and Game Department."

Lainey swallowed, her complexion growing pale. "How often does this happen on the trail?"

Scotch heard the tremor in her voice. "On the Iditarod itself? Not often. Maybe once every couple of years. For the most part, a moose will leave the trail rather than fight it out. If you were as close as you say you were, he probably didn't think he had any other alternative." Unable to stop herself, she reached out and cupped Lainey's cheek. "I don't think this will happen to you again."

Lainey closed her eyes and nodded, leaning into the touch. Scotch was familiar with the forceful steel of Lainey's personality. This hint of vulnerability had slipped free of that, and the rare moment called to her. Ever since her aborted attempt to kiss Lainey, she had forced herself to stay aloof. They had never discussed what had happened in the dog barn, and for a time Scotch wasn't even sure Lainey had realized what had almost occurred. This moment felt too right to pass up. Scotch leaned forward and brushed her lips against Lainey's, her desire overwhelming her vow of abstinence and fear of driving the woman away.

Far from being appalled at the forward behavior, Lainey returned the kiss, her hand drifting up to touch Scotch's. It was sweet and gentle, and Scotch fought the urge to demand more. Now wasn't the time. She only wanted Lainey to know she was there for her, a friend to support her rather than a sex-crazed roommate. She ended the kiss and leaned her forehead against Lainey's a moment, regaining her equilibrium. "Are you okay?" Scotch opened her eyes to see Lainey peering at her.

"Yeah. I'm good."

Nodding, Scotch released her and sat back. "As I said, you have to learn to gut the carcass. Watch closely." With businesslike movements she began the process, deliberately not speculating on Lainey's lack of protestation at the liberty she had taken.

CHAPTER TWENTY-FOUR

When they arrived at the kennel, they were met by friends, family and neighbors alike. Howry, Thom and Lafferty, alerted by the dogs in the yard, stood out on the back deck. Rye and Irish were back from their races and promptly set to work taking over Lainey's team, despite her insistence that she was supposed to care for them.

"You've done more than enough today," Irish said in a voice that brooked no refusal. Her manner was brisk and business-like as she turned Lainey away. "Get over to the clinic and check on Cochise."

Still numb from the ordeal, Lainey nevertheless recognized Helen's mannerisms in the nine-year-old.

"Don't argue with a Fuller woman." Thom draped an arm around Lainey's shoulder. He and the other men had gathered at her sled to look over the moose carcass. "It's a hopeless cause."

She glanced at Scotch, who was snacking her dogs again before kenneling them. Her lips tingled at the remembered kiss, knowing that her resolve to not come on to the woman hadn't been as strong as she had thought. It had shattered in that instant, like the thin, beautiful icicle it was. There was no going back. Scotch glanced up from checking one of her dogs and smiled at her. A shiver of dread swirled through Lainey. "I think you're right."

Thom chuckled. "I'm right. I've just had plenty of years to get used to the idea." He gave her shoulder a squeeze and then turned to Lafferty. "Let's get this carcass off the sled and call the Fish and Game people. Since you were kind enough to help out, what do you say to staying for dinner tonight?"

"That sounds like a fine idea." Lafferty licked his lips. "A man can get mighty tired of his own cooking."

As she stared down at the moose, Lainey once again experienced the terror that had flooded her system. The bitter taste of burnt metal lingered on her tongue, making her want to spit. She felt again the ice cold metal of the pistol against her shaking fingers. A surge of revulsion rolled through her, followed by such a strong physical desire for a drink that she grew lightheaded. She shuddered and took an unsteady step away from her sled.

Howry, unencumbered by chores, took up pace with her. "How are you?"

She gave him a wan smile, swallowed against the bile. "I've been better."

He kept his hands in his pockets. "I heard Lafferty say you got a hell of trophy there. He thinks that moose is close to a thousand pounds."

"It sure felt that way." She shook her head. "I'm going to be so sore tomorrow. I'm surprised Scotch and I were able to get it onto the sled at all."

He was silent a moment. "How did you get it loaded anyway?"

"After trying a lot of other methods, we harnessed our wheel dogs together, wrapped rope around the carcass, and used the dogs to roll it into the sled."

"Should prove to be an interesting article, huh?" he said. "Intrepid Reporter Takes Down Bull Moose in the Wilds of Alaska."

Lainey trembled. "It might sell copy, but it's not something I ever want to repeat."

"Were you scared?"

"Terrified."

"I would have been too."

She debated whether or not to admit that Scotch had kissed her. A featherlight touch of panic wove through her already unstable heart, and she chose to remain silent. He would figure it out sooner or later; he was an astute man. Until then, it would be her secret, hers and Scotch's.

They took the steps up to the cabin that housed the veterinary hospital two at a time. Though the waiting room was empty, the lights blazed against the early Alaskan sunset. Lainey stomped snow from her mukluks and shed her bloodstained parka.

"Helen?"

"In here," came the answer. "Second door on the left."

Howry on her heels, Lainey hastened down the hall. Cochise lay on the table, his breathing easy. Stark white bandages covered his eye, a hint of pink blushing in the center. His chest was tightly wrapped, and he was unconscious. Tears stung Lainey's eyes as she ran her hands over his fur. "How is he?"

Helen, wearing a white smock over a heavy ribbed sweater, smiled. "Actually, quite good. He's got a couple of cracked ribs, but I think they're nothing more than hairline fractures. No internal bleeding. There's damage to the eye. It will be a couple of weeks before we know whether he's lost his sight. He'll have a grand headache when the drugs wear off."

Lainey's shoulders slumped in relief and tears spilled down her cheeks. "Thank God." Cochise would live through his injuries, maybe even heal well enough to pull a sled again. She had been so worried that the moose had done him mortal damage.

"What happened?" Helen asked. "I know there was a moose in the trail, but how did Cochise get hurt?"

Lainey explained the incident to her and Howry—seeing the moose too late, trying to get the dogs out of danger, and the ultimate act of killing the animal as it began a rampage through her team. By the time she finished, she found herself sitting on a stool, shaking and weeping, feeling like a complete idiot. Howry handed her a handkerchief and she blew her nose while he rubbed her shoulders. She heard footsteps and looked up to see Helen returning from somewhere with a glass of clear liquid in her hand.

"Here. Drink this down. Doctor's orders."

Lainey caught a pungent whiff of alcohol. Her entire being sang with the need to bring it to her lips, the yearning overpowering in its strength. A tiny voice told her to turn it down, hand the glass to Howry beside her, "cowgirl up" and avoid proving Strauss right. Unable to help herself, she took the drink, draining it in one swallow. *Fuck Ben Strauss!* Wheezing, she held the glass out. "More." Helen gave her an odd look, but went to get a refill.

"Lainey—"

"Butt out, Don."

* * *

Scotch sat on her front porch, steaming cup of coffee in hand and trusty thermos on the floorboards at her side. It was long past dark. *Hell, it's long past bedtime.* The cabin was disturbing in its emptiness. She couldn't stay inside. She had returned after dinner with every intention of getting some sleep. Instead, unexpected loneliness seeped into her soul, making rest impossible. She'd brewed some coffee, donned her cold weather gear and settled out here to look at the stars, waiting for her roommate to come home.

It had been a week since the moose attack on Lainey's team. Cochise was doing well, though it was doubtful he would regain full sight in his injured eye. Once he finished healing and they knew for sure, he would be retired from the racing string. He was a good dog; he wouldn't be put down when he could breed other race dogs. He would spend the rest of his life running tour sleds. It would be a good life for him. Lainey was the concern.

The night of the attack, she had gotten plastered on white lightning. Scotch had been somewhat surprised, since Lainey hadn't touched a drop of alcohol her entire stay. She knew Lainey needed something to blow off the stress and fear of the encounter. When the following morning found Lainey too hung over to get out of bed, Scotch had cut her some slack and let her take the day off.

After a decent morning run with her team, she had returned to hear that Lainey had borrowed the dog truck and gone into town. Worried for her friend, Scotch decided not to go on an afternoon run. She remained at the cabin, shoveling snow from the back deck and pathways and doing other tasks around the kennel. Lainey had showed up just after dinner, already drunk, a brown paper bag under her arm. Rather than spend time with the Fullers at the main cabin, she pleaded exhaustion and went home. Scotch arrived an hour later. Lainey was passed out on the couch, a half-empty bottle of whiskey on the floor beside her.

Such had been the week. Lainey rarely ate anything, was too hung over to get up in the morning for chores, claimed illness rather than train her team and drank herself into oblivion every evening. Tonight she had borrowed one of the dog trucks and hadn't yet come back. Thom Fuller's glances were becoming less sympathetic and more disapproving as the days passed. Helen had taken Scotch aside tonight to apologize...*apologize!* for handing that first glass of alcohol to Lainey the night of the attack.

Scotch sipped her coffee, fighting a sense of foreboding. She knew having to use the pistol to kill the moose had everything to do with Lainey's breakdown. She couldn't help wondering whether the kiss she'd given Lainey out on the trail had helped push her over the edge. *I should have vetoed the contract when it was first proposed. Let her find some other kennel to train her for the race.* Second-guessing and regretting past choices were still new strategies for Scotch, having only been experiencing them for a couple of years. The lack of experience didn't diminish the oppressive weight of depression sinking into her bones.

A flashlight beam caught her eye. Relief rippled through her, her heart pounding with sudden adrenaline as someone came up the path toward the cabin. The moon was full enough to illuminate the clearing. When the person came out from under the tree-lined path, she felt her stomach drop. It wasn't Lainey returning home but Don Howry trudging up the path. She must have made some sort of noise because the light swept up and pinned her. The beam immediately dropped.

"Hey. Mind some company?"

To be honest, she did mind. She wanted to be alone with her regrets, her dread and the haunting sound of a creaking rope. Her parents had raised her properly, however. "Sure. Want some coffee?" She held up the thermos.

"No thanks. I had too much at the main cabin tonight. I'm sloshing." He crossed the clearing and stepped onto the porch, dusting snow off the other side of the bench swing before sitting. His flashlight clicked off.

Scotch gave him a vague welcome, taking another drink of coffee as her eyes readjusted to the moonlight. She didn't know why he had come, and she didn't care. Nothing really mattered until Lainey got back safe and sound. *And what about tomorrow night? Or the night after that? How long can this go on?* They sat in silence for such a long while that Scotch had forgotten his presence in the shadows beside her. When he spoke, she gasped in surprise.

"I've known her since she was a snot-nosed war correspondent. The kid had a knack, you know? Always seemed to be in the right place at the right time, picking up the award-winning shots that everyone lusted after." He paused, brushing at his jeans. "I was on the fringes of that crowd, not much into reporting on the violence. I preferred the human interest stories in the background. But when the money was good, it was very, very good. Anyway, she was a hard partier even then."

Scotch swallowed, intrigued despite herself. She had wondered what Lainey had been like before the firefight that had wounded her. It hadn't occurred to her that Howry had known her then. She looked over, catching a faint smile on his face.

"Don't get me wrong, she was a responsible drinker back then. Didn't get totally trashed or anything. It's not something that's done on the battlefield. Get too blotto and you might miss that perfect shot." He blew out a breath. A fog of heated air emitted from his mouth and expanded outward, dissipating into the night. "She saw too much. We all did. It's part of the job. But that whole Rwanda thing was...it was just brutal. Not long after that, she picked up a gig in Bosnia. That's when she was wounded in action." Howry looked over at her, gesturing to his side. "You know, the rib thing?"

She cleared her throat. "Yeah. I've seen it."

Assured she was paying attention, he looked back out into the clearing. "The fire team she was with got her out of the kill zone, but another reporter had to do some fast talking at the border to get her out of that part of the country. He's the guy who hired us for this gig— Ben Strauss from *Cognizance*. Lainey wouldn't be alive now if it wasn't for Ben." He seemed to have run out of words.

Scotch considered a long moment before speaking. "She didn't work for a year after that. She told me her wound took a few months of healing."

"That's one reason." He scrubbed his face with a gloved hand. "She's gonna kill me," he muttered.

"Why? What happened?"

He ignored the question. "Military personnel who see action, police officers, war correspondents...we have a high rate of depression and suicide. We see too much of the violence, the bad shit no one else sees, and it changes us. A picture may speak a thousand words, but the reality is...well, it's Technicolor, surround sound and inescapable." His hand dropped to his lap. "She changed. The warfare she witnessed, the violence of being injured in action—it changed her, warped her. It changes all of us."

The mention of suicide brought Scotch's pounding heart into her throat. *No. Not Lainey.* "What happened?" she demanded, voice harsh. "What happened that year she wasn't working?"

Howry returned his attention to Scotch. He shrugged, hands gesturing his helplessness. "She drank. Constantly. Once the docs gave her the green light, she didn't come up for air for months."

Alcoholic. She's an active alcoholic. Scotch slumped in her chair, staring into the darkness surrounding her cabin. She understood why her mother had apologized for offering Lainey that first shot of liquor. *What the hell am I going to do now?*

"I don't know."

She looked sharply at her companion, surprised that she had spoken the thought aloud.

He continued without noticing. "She normally doesn't drink on gigs, but this one is lasting three times as long as any normal contract. With the stress of the...of what happened, I doubt she could have helped herself." He gave Scotch a worried look. "Our editor, Ben, has joined AA. He's been trying to get Lainey to go too. I don't think she's ready to admit she has a problem."

"You think she does?"

"Don't you?"

Scotch only had the last week of experience to go on. Alcoholism was rampant among the people of Alaska, either due to genetic predisposition or the depression triggered by the constant lack of sunlight. While no one in her family suffered, Miguel was a member of Alcoholics Anonymous, attending meetings twice a month in Anchorage. She herself had gone on a three-day drinking binge once, but even the crushing grief she had experienced hadn't kept her drunk for long.

Reluctant to speak the words, she leaned forward, elbows on her knees, the swing swaying crookedly at her movement. She looked away to hide her expression from Howry. "I think you're right."

Silence reigned for several more moments as Scotch fought against an urge to cry. The woman she thought she knew didn't exist. The Lainey she was attracted to was a fake, a mask to be worn until she was off the job and back in the bottle. That inadvertent kiss had nothing to do with the events at hand. It didn't matter whether it had meant anything to Lainey, because alcohol held control over her. *I can't live this way.* "Why did you tell me this?" She sniffled, annoyed at the cracking in her voice.

Howry sighed. "Because she cares about you."

"What?" Scotch's head swiveled around, a tear spilling over to freeze against her cheek.

"I've never seen her like this with anyone else. I think she loves you."

She glared at him for long minutes. "Whatever gave you that idea?"

Howry grimaced. He looked away. "Scotch, we're only here because of you. She's the one who suggested you to Ben when he pitched the deal. I think if you had turned down her request to train her for the Iditarod, she'd have canceled her end of the contract and gone home."

The tangle of emotions in the pit of Scotch's stomach defied identification. The old accusations and guilt were the strongest, nearly overwhelming her in their comfortable familiarity. Depression, castigation and self-reproach—she had lived shoulder to shoulder with them long enough that turning them over in her mind was a familiar pastime. She had been the cause of the situation that created the feelings, so it was only right she "suffer the slings and arrows" that resulted.

Lainey's predicament was of her own choosing, not Scotch's. Though Scotch felt her heart reaching out to take responsibility for Lainey's current drinking binge, a part of her rebelled. For the first time in years, anger sparked, flared and caught hold in the kindling of past remorse. This was not her fault. Lainey possibly loving her didn't make Scotch accountable for her drinking problem. Scotch's feelings for Lainey didn't automatically obligate her to accept the blame.

The fury burned clean. For the first time in forever, Scotch didn't fall back on uncertainties, didn't deny her senses. She flat out refused to take on any more of a burden than she already carried. That now-stale burden wasn't even hers, she realized. The epiphany of the simple thought nearly blinded her with its truth.

In the distance, she heard the dogs barking like mad. They only did that when one of the dog trucks came or left the property. "She's back." She stood.

Howry rose. "I should go, make sure she gets back here." He took a step off the porch, stopping when Scotch grabbed the sleeve of his parka.

"No. Let her get here on her own. I'll stay out here. If she's not back in half an hour, I'll go find her." At his puzzled frown, she shrugged. "If she's a drunk, she needs to learn to take responsibility for her actions. She gets bruised up out there, it's her problem, but I'll make sure she doesn't pass out and freeze to death."

"That sounds pretty harsh."

Scotch pursed her lips. "Harsh is what she needs. I've coddled her long enough. She has a race to run, just like I do. Either she sobers up and gets back to it, or she's out."

He looked at her, eyes wide, seeing something he hadn't seen before. With a slow nod, he turned on his flashlight. "All right."

She swallowed, her throat tight as the anger faded enough to let her heart shine through. "She's my friend too, Don. Maybe more. Talk to Miguel. He'll understand."

Howry sighed, shoulders slumping. "I'll see you tomorrow morning."

"We'll be there." She watched him leave, following the circle of light on the path when she could no longer see him in the darkness of the trees. Sitting down, she poured another cup of coffee...and waited.

CHAPTER TWENTY-FIVE

"Get up."

Lainey growled, rolling herself tighter in her warm blankets. The usually pleasant tones of her roommate boomed against tender ears, setting her head to pounding. She mumbled in response, though even she didn't understand a word she said.

"I said, get up. We have to get to the dog barn."

Lainey groaned, pulling the covers down enough to peer over the top of them. A fully dressed Scotch stood beside her bed, a bright lantern in her hand. Shards of light pierced Lainey's eyes, and she squinted them shut before they bled. "I don't feel well. Go without me." The light across her eyelids faded. As she relaxed back into her cocoon, already beginning to drift off into a hazy sleep, she felt swift, swooping motion beneath her.

Landing on the cold floor, Lainey struggled with her blankets as the weight of the mattress pressed down upon her. She squawked as the morning's chill woke her far more cruelly than Scotch had a few seconds earlier. Crawling out from under the bedding, she scowled at Scotch, who picked up the lantern from where she had set it on the floor. "What the fuck, Fuller?"

"Get dressed. Downstairs in five minutes or I will throw you in a snow bank." She turned and strode out of the room.

Lainey gaped after her, doubt warring with conviction. *She wouldn't do that. Would she?* The uncertainty was enough to get her moving. Her raging headache roared when she bent to get socks from her drawer. Standing stock still, she massaged her temple.

"Four minutes."

Narrowing her eyes, Lainey growled at her friend's callous call from below. "Stuff it." *I need a drink before I can deal with her temper tantrum.* Opening her top drawer, she found...nothing but clothing.

Panic washed through her, the hangover fading. *Where the hell is it? I left it here. I know I did!* She scrabbled inside the drawer, then the next and the next, not finding the fifth of scotch she had stashed there for her morning fortitude. When her search proved fruitless, she looked under the partially dismantled bed and began rooting through the blankets. "Where the hell is it?"

"Looking for this?"

Lainey whirled around. Scotch stood at the curtain separating their rooms. She held an empty bottle. "What did you do? You went through my stuff?" Fury bloomed in her chest. "Who gave you the right to go through my things? I bought that with my own goddamned money!" She swiped at the bottle, becoming angrier when Scotch easily kept it from her reach.

"You have three minutes to get dressed. If you're not with me when I leave for the dog barn, pack your things. I'll take you to the Anchorage airport as soon as breakfast is finished."

Her wrath dissipated with such speed that Lainey stumbled. She barely made her voice work. "What?" The blue eyes before her showed confidence and conviction, as well as something else.

Scotch handed the empty bottle to her. "You heard me. I have a race to run in March, and so do you. Either you get back into training, or you're out. I don't have time for this bullshit, and you don't either." She turned her back and stomped away.

Lainey looked at the bottle in her hand, trying to wrap her mind around the stranger who had just left the room.

"Two minutes."

She had never dressed so quickly in her life.

* * *

The aura of fearlessness that had originally drawn Lainey to Scotch had become magnified since last she'd noticed. While Scotch would occasionally evince uncertainty in the safety of her family and home, such doubt was completely absent now. Lainey attempted to dredge up her former anger at the invasion of her privacy, needing to start a fight, if only to share her misery. Scotch refused to take the bait, insisting they would talk later or not at all. She left Lainey standing on the porch, picking her jaw up off the ground. Of half a mind to go back to bed, she mulled over Scotch's threat to send her away. Not wanting to test her roommate's resolve, at least not yet, Lainey hastened to catch up.

Irish and Rye were the only ones to show their surprise at Lainey's arrival, the girl's expression more disapproving than her brother's. Howry gave Scotch a grudging, respectful nod and proceeded to dump frozen salmon into the dog stew. Lainey wasn't sure what was worse— the raging headache exacerbated by exposure to the halogen lamps set up in the dog yard, the overpowering demand of her body for another drink or the growing apprehension she felt when looking at Scotch.

Still shaky, Lainey made a half-hearted attempt at taking over the job of stirring the stew pot. Howry took the shovel "spoon" out of her hands without a word. As he climbed the step stool, Lainey swallowed against a lump in her throat. She wasn't needed; they had all gone on without her. Scotch came out of the dog barn, her blue eyes mistrustful as they landed on Lainey. Oppressive weight bowed Lainey's shoulders.

She recalled their kiss on the trail, the expression of tender compassion on Scotch's face. It had finally happened and, rather than dealing with the poor woman's sexual confusion, helping her understand what was happening with her, Lainey had gotten smashed. *I threw our friendship away, hurt her when she was most vulnerable. Any chance I had with her is gone now. All because I had to have a damned drink!* Self-pity welled up inside, swamping her anger and spilling over as tears. She spun around, intent on running, though she didn't know where she would go. After she had taken no more than a handful of steps, a hand grabbed her arm.

"Lainey."

Pulling away seemed impossible. Her traitorous body wouldn't move at her command. Scotch turned her around and wrapped Lainey in her arms. The tears of regret and fear broke through Lainey's emotional dams. Despite the turmoil, a distant part of her relaxed into the embrace.

Some time later Lainey's thoughts returned to her surroundings, snot and tears cooling unpleasantly on her face, familiar shame supplanting the sense of worthlessness. Though she wanted to remain in Scotch's strong arms forever, she remembered the disgusted expression that morning. Lainey weakly pushed away, using one hand to wipe at her face. A handkerchief appeared, and she mumbled thanks as she used it to clean herself up.

"You're welcome."

Bracing for the expected expression of contempt, Lainey looked up at Scotch. Though the wariness remained, there was no censure in the return gaze. She fought against a fresh desire to weep, this time in relief. "About this morning— "

Scotch held up a hand, stepping back. "I said we'd talk after breakfast. Right now, you need to get out to your dogs and remind them you're still part of the pack."

Lainey looked over her shoulder at her string of dogs, Cochise conspicuous by his absence. Napoleon ignored her as he stood atop his doghouse to watch the dog barn. She felt a stab of self-hatred; she hadn't even checked on her injured lead dog since the night of the accident. "Cochise?"

"He's fine." Scotch glanced back at the dog barn. "He's inside, where it's nice and warm." She waved at the dog yard. "They haven't been out since...since the attack. We're taking them on a run either late this morning or after lunch." Her tone brooked no argument.

Late this morning. After our talk then. "Okay. I understand." Lainey nodded, a tenuous tendril of hope wrapping around her heart. She straightened, squaring her shoulders. "Call me when the food is ready."

"Will do."

Lainey marched toward her dogs.

* * *

With the dogs fed, Lainey assisted with the scooping. She made no complaint, knowing she had forced everyone to take up the slack caused by her lack of assistance for too long. When it came time to go into the main cabin for breakfast, her stomach tied itself up in knots. Irish's obvious condemnation had to have come from somewhere. Lainey wasn't keen on facing the Fullers to discover its origin, but Scotch stood at the back door, waving Lainey in ahead of her, not giving her a chance to escape.

The vestibule was crowded with people, shoes and clothing as everyone divested themselves of their excess coverings. They spilled into the kitchen from the mudroom. The smell of biscuits and gravy nauseated Lainey. Her being there was a waste of time. She turned to tell Scotch exactly that. Arms crossed, Scotch was guarding the back door, lifting an eyebrow at her. She raised a single arm, gesturing toward the door to the kitchen. Shoulders slumping, Lainey moved into the house.

Lainey washed up at the kitchen sink with the others and sat at her place at the table. She wondered whether or not it had been set every day. Guilt coursed through her. She stared at her plate, trying not to wince as Bon's shrill voice cut through her headache. Around her, the rest of the household chattered and settled around the table to enjoy breakfast like any other day. Someone placed a cup of coffee before her, rubbing a hand on her upper back. Lainey peeked up at the offering, blinking at Helen's kind face.

"Welcome back, dear."

Lainey ducked her head, blushing. "Thanks." Helen patted her shoulder and moved on.

As food was passed around the table, Lainey avoided taking any as a queasiness took over. Scotch circumvented that tactic, placing a single biscuit on Lainey's otherwise empty plate. She scooted closer, leg touching Lainey's beneath the table.

"You need to try to eat something. I won't push it if you can't."

A glance at Thom showed where Irish's unfavorable judgment was coming from. Rather than fight the inevitable, Lainey nodded and picked at the fresh bread. The biscuit helped settle her stomach.

At Scotch's request, Helen unearthed a bottle of ibuprofen. Lainey washed down three pills with her cooling coffee, hoping that would be enough to eradicate the headache. As everyone finished, Howry asked Miguel if he needed help with a day tour scheduled that morning. Helen and Thom collected their two youngest children for a shopping trip to Anchorage, and Scotch swapped her dishwashing duties with Rye for the morning.

"Come on."

The earlier dread surged again as Lainey rose to follow Scotch. They dressed in thick silence and stepped outside into a light snowfall. Miguel and Howry were already in the yard, preparing the non-racing string for an outing. Several dogs barked in excitement at the sound of Helen's four-wheel-drive truck starting up, causing Lainey to cringe from the remnants of her headache. "Where are we going?"

"To the cabin."

Struggling to keep her emotions in check, Lainey trailed after Scotch. Neither spoke as they walked, giving Lainey plenty of time to imagine the coming conversation. It started with something along the lines of *"You're not needed here"* and ended with *"Get the hell off our property."* Too soon, they arrived at the squat cabin. Lainey's already racing heart jumped into her throat as they stepped inside.

The living area was still warm from the morning fire. Scotch removed her dog yard boots, hung her jacket on the hook by the door and headed downstairs to stoke the fire. Hesitant, Lainey discarded her outdoor clothing and followed Scotch. Once on the ground floor, she hovered, not certain if she was still welcome.

Scotch added wood to the fire. When it was burning to her satisfaction, she stood and turned, puzzlement etched in her face. "Sit down." Lainey chose the overstuffed armchair. "You want more coffee?" Scotch headed to the kitchen.

How about something a lot stronger? Lainey clamped down the thought. "Sure." She fidgeted, eyes roaming the living area as if she'd never seen it before. Her gaze landed on one of her early photos, framed and sitting on the mantel. It had been there when she had arrived in June. At the time Scotch, sweet in her embarrassment, had claimed it was her favorite. Lainey looked up at Scotch's return, not seeing the shy young woman she had thought resided in that lanky form.

Scotch handed Lainey a steaming mug, holding her own in her other hand. Rather than sit alone on the couch, she settled on the sturdy coffee table across from Lainey. "How are you feeling?"

Lainey snorted. "Like an idiot." She noticed Scotch didn't argue the point as she sipped at her coffee.

"Are you in, or are you out?"

The uncharacteristically bald question startled her. A vestige of her competitive nature struggled through the morass of self-pity. "I'm in."

"Good." Scotch studied her. "Here are the conditions: no more drinking; no alcohol anywhere on the property. You're not allowed to borrow any vehicle for any reason. If you touch a single drop of booze between now and the end of the Iditarod, you're leaving on the next plane out of Anchorage."

Lainey stared at Scotch. "Wh...*What* did you say?"

"You heard me."

She sputtered, indignant at the threat. She stood, coffee splattering out of the mug at her sudden movement. "Who the hell are you to order me out if I want a beer?"

Scotch stood with her. "I'm your trainer," she growled. "And you're training for a race that could kill you if you're drunk on the trail. I won't be party to your suicide attempt. You want to kill yourself slowly with booze, go ahead. Leave me out of it."

Lainey blinked in surprise, belated in her realization of the depth of wrath in Scotch's voice.

Unaware her protegé had stopped arguing, Scotch continued. "You're going to get your shit together, and we're going out on the switchback trails today. I know the ordeal with the moose traumatized you, but that's no reason to let it rule over you forever. Get on with your life!"

Lainey's brow furrowed. *Is she talking to me, or someone else?* "Scotch?"

Scotch sniffled and turned away. She took a step toward the fireplace, leaning against the mantel to stare into the flames.

Lainey moved up behind her. Hesitant, she touched the tense shoulder. "Are you okay?"

The shoulder twitched, as if Scotch wanted to shrug her off but was holding back. "I'm fine." She sniffed and straightened. "I'm sorry. I shouldn't have unloaded on you."

"No, it's okay. I'm sure I deserve worse." Lainey moved around to see Scotch's profile. Unshed tears glistened in the firelight. Despite the evidence of sorrow and anger, the self-assurance hadn't faded. *What changed? Was it me? Did I cause this?* More importantly, was this fundamental change within her friend a good thing?

Scotch turned her head to look at Lainey. The anger had dissipated, though it still lay beneath the still surface. "You know I care a lot for you."

Lainey frowned. This had been what she'd been trying to avoid, perhaps even more so than the terror of holding an instrument of death, of using it to kill for the first time, self-defense or not. She dropped her hand and stepped back toward her chair. "I know."

"Do you?" came the whispered response.

"I remember the kiss." Lainey stopped at the armchair, arms crossed over her chest, back to the fire. The long silence was broken only by the crackle of the fire and the sounds of their breathing. A light shuffle warned Lainey of Scotch's approach, then she was spun around.

"Remember this one too."

At first, the kiss was as gentle as it had been on the trail. Unable to resist, Lainey relaxed into the strong arms encircling her waist and shoulder. Scotch's tongue brushed her lower lip in request. Her mouth opened and Scotch slipped inside to explore with lazy insistence. Lainey moaned at the welcome invasion, vaguely amazed at Scotch's apparent experience. The thought swept away as her fingers finally enjoyed the softness of the tawny curls that had so interested her from the beginning. They stepped into each other and Scotch tasted her, warm hands roaming her back and sides.

It seemed to go on forever, yet hardly lasted the blink of an eye before Scotch drew back, resting her forehead against Lainey's. "I've been wanting to do that for a long time."

Lainey's fingers stroked the back of Scotch's neck, not sure whether she should laugh or cry. "I've been wanting to do it longer."

Scotch pulled back enough to look at her. "Yeah?"

"Yeah. Ever since the first moment I saw you."

She tilted her head. "At the banquet in Nome?"

Lainey chuckled, realizing it was time to confess. "No. Before the banquet. You helped a klutz of a woman to her feet that afternoon and received nothing but an attitude as thanks."

Scotch looked blank for a moment. When she recalled the incident, she jerked back further. "That was you?" A mixture of amusement and annoyance replaced the somberness on her face.

"Guilty." She watched a myriad of emotions flit across Scotch's face and winced a little. "I made that bad of an impression?"

Scotch hugged her. "At the time, yes. I think I can forgive you now, though. You were in pain from your ribs, weren't you?"

"Yeah, but that's not an excuse for rude behavior."

"Not in this family," Scotch agreed. "But you were an unsophisticated rube from Outside at the time. I can cut you some slack."

Lainey dropped her head against Scotch's chest. "Gee, thanks." She received a hug in response. "About last week—"

"It's done, Lainey. Over. There's nothing more to talk about." Scotch sighed, hugging her friend close. "This doesn't change my conditions. I'll go into debt paying the money back to the magazine if I have to, but I won't allow you to compromise the race."

Troubled, Lainey considered her options with a clear mind. She forced herself to recognize she wasn't the victim here. She had taken that drink from Helen on her own and had let it rule her. Again. She inhaled deeply, fixing Scotch's scent in her memory. *Ben's right. I...have a problem.* Swallowing against the lump in her throat, she fought the urge to cry. She had done too much of that already. "I'll abide by your conditions."

Scotch nodded, caressing Lainey's hair and cheek. "Then we need to get dressed for the trail." She kissed Lainey's forehead and released her. "Your dogs haven't been on a run in a week. It shouldn't make that much of a difference in the long run, but we'll be running them morning and night for a few days."

"Yes, ma'am."

CHAPTER TWENTY-SIX

December

"Are you ready?"

They were in the parking lot of an Anchorage hotel. Lainey smiled at Scotch. "You bet."

"Let's go then." She gave Lainey's hand a quick squeeze and climbed out of the truck.

Following suit, Lainey grabbed her notebook, camera and paperwork before stepping onto the lot. Howry, Rye and Helen waited at the lobby doors. Lainey splashed her way through the slush and snow toward them, Scotch behind her.

The past couple of weeks had been another learning experience altogether. Emotional consequences aside, Lainey was amazed how a single week of a drunken binge had affected her physical stamina. She staggered out of bed every morning, sore and exhausted, went through the day doing chores and sled runs and fell back into the sack at the first opportunity. The dogs were racking up forty miles a day, six days a week, with training sessions lasting through lunch and into the afternoon. Soon they would graduate to overnight sessions. Lainey's muscles constantly ached or burned, and the headache between her eyes and at the back of her head never seemed to quit.

Scotch had been a saint. She hadn't complained about the slowing down, but she also didn't allow Lainey to shirk her training and chores. Once she had realized how much pain Lainey was in, she'd insisted on nightly trips to the hot springs. There they would soak in the heated waters, allowing Lainey's muscles to unwind, talking and looking up at the stars. There had been nothing as intimate as the kiss in the cabin, though Scotch didn't have a problem with public displays of affection. They held hands—even in the presence of Scotch's parents—and walked arm in arm everywhere these days. Thom's disapproval became less apparent, though he still cast worried looks at his daughter when he didn't think Lainey would notice. She didn't blame him.

Howry held the door open. "Got your paperwork?"

"And a whole lot of paper for notes." Lainey held up her notebook.

"Some techno geek you are," he snorted. "I thought for sure you'd make a digital recording of the entire meeting."

She grinned, fishing an iPod and companion microphone from her pocket. "Might not get it all, but I should be able to get half of it before the batteries go."

Howry shook his head as the others laughed.

Lainey wondered whether everyone lounging in the lobby was attending the mandatory rookie meeting. Thirty-eight rookies had registered, but far more than that number milled around the foyer. Since December in Anchorage was not the ideal vacation destination, they had to be present for a reason.

Rye returned from the front desk. "Meeting's in the Redington Ballroom."

Scotch led the way to the meeting room, stopping at a registration table outside. The Inuit woman seated there stood, a smile on her broad face. She bustled around, arms wide. "Helen! I heard you were speaking today! It's so good to see you!"

"And you." Helen returned the hug. "Doris, you remember Scotch and Rye, my children?"

Doris beamed at the siblings. "I most certainly do. Scotch, you did a wonderful job last year. I bet Rye will give you a run for your money when he's old enough to enter."

"I doubt that." Scotch laughed.

Rye grinned, though his face reddened. "Bet on it, Sis."

"This is Don Howry. He's doing a series of articles on Scotch for *Cognizance* magazine." Howry shook Doris' hand. "And this is Lainey Hughes. She's also a photojournalist for *Cognizance* and is our resident rookie this year." Helen turned to the reporters. "Doris is one of our most enthusiastic volunteers. She has assisted the vets at the checkpoints for…how many years?"

Doris waved away Helen's praise. "Fourteen, but who's counting?" She bobbed behind her table, suddenly all business. "Lainey Hughes?" Peering closely at her paperwork, she located the name on her list. "Ah, here it is. I'll need you to sign in, dear."

Lainey signed the sheet of paper, handed over her required paperwork and received more in return.

The transaction completed, Doris shook her hand. "Welcome to the Iditarod, Miss Hughes. I hope you have a wonderful race. There's a coffee station right there, and then you go on in and have a seat."

"Thank you. It was nice to meet you."

The room was spacious, with a stage and podium at the front. Several narrow tables sat in regimented rows, giving the place the appearance of a schoolroom. Additional chairs lined the back wall; Rye and Howry found seating there. Scotch directed Lainey forward.

"Mom and I are speaking, so we're in the front row. You want to sit behind us?"

"Sure." They found places and dropped their heavy coats.

"Scotch Fuller!"

They both turned to see a man waving at them from across the room. Grinning, Scotch squeezed Lainey's shoulder. "I'll be back."

Lainey nodded and sat, watching Scotch greet the man with a hug. It was fun watching Scotch as she worked the room. She encountered friends and acquaintances and met newcomers, greeting each as long-lost comrades. Sighing, Lainey enjoyed the show. Every once in a while, Scotch looked back her way and they shared a smile that warmed Lainey's heart. With Scotch busy, Lainey allowed thoughts of training to take over.

Cochise had been benched for the season, leaving her with only two fully trained lead dogs. He still resided in the heated dog barn rather than out in the kennel. Fortunately he wasn't alone, as there had been a late batch of puppies born. They and their mother were in one of the neighboring stalls. As things now stood, her leaders—Trace and Sholo—would make the final cut, barring accidents. One of her swing dogs, Montana, was also developing into something of a leader. She had started putting him in the harness with one of the others to give him experience at the front of the pack. It was a balancing act to keep his spirits up without undermining his confidence when he made mistakes.

If she took Bonaparte, she'd have to take Kaara; they were a package deal. Meshindi worked well with everybody, but Bonaparte was a snob. Lainey wasn't sure his skill as a swing dog outweighed the hassle he could create when his back was up. She had learned that the hard way a couple of days after she'd returned to training. In her fuzzy-mindedness, she had forgotten his favorite snack and had been stuck out on the trail one stormy afternoon when the stubborn mutt staged a mutiny. In retaliation, she refused to run him for three days. It seemed to have done the trick. Bonaparte had the brains to make the connection between his behavior and the punishment. If he pulled a stunt like that during the Iditarod, Lainey could be stuck for hours in the middle of nowhere. Granted, her chances of winning a thousand mile race were minuscule, but those hours could make the difference in keeping her from being the last musher into Nome.

More people filtered into the room. She watched them idly, her mind still on her team.

Everyone else worked up fine. She had six wheel dogs to choose from. Rye had suggested she keep four of them. Some parts of the trail held steep inclines, and the Farewell Burn was notorious for abrupt changes. She would need the extra muscle. Jonah and Aegis were definitely going. Both had finished the Iditarod with Scotch, Jonah for three years running. His experience on the trail would be most welcome.

Of her seven team dogs—those animals who had not shown aptitude for leadership or did not have the extra strength needed for a wheel dog—she had serious misgivings about Dablo. He was Trace's brother, twin to him right down to the bright blue eyes. That was where the resemblance ended. Trace seemed to be the go-getter in his family line. More times than Lainey could count, she caught Dablo's tug line slackening. He ran with the team, letting the others do the work, not pulling his weight. Occasionally she could urge him into taking the load, but only when he knew they were heading back to the kennel for dinner.

"Anybody sitting here?"

Lainey looked up at a young man standing by the chair next to her. "No. Go ahead."

He grinned his thanks and draped his jacket over the chair back before sitting down. Turning toward her, he offered his hand. "Roman Spencer, Iditarod rookie."

She smiled. "Lainey Hughes, the same."

Spencer cocked his head. "Lainey Hughes? The reporter for that magazine?"

"Yeah. That would be me. My checkered reputation precedes me." She shrugged ruefully. "And you? Spencer sounds familiar."

He blushed. "My dad and older brother are Iditarod veterans."

"Ah. Looks like I've got some well-trained competition then."

His skin darkened, but he was saved from responding by Scotch's return.

"Hey, Roman! Good to see you. How's your dad?"

Their conversation fell into the typical topics for mushers—ones that Lainey was quite familiar with after six months' experience— namely dogs, trails and races. Scotch sat in her first-row chair, straddling it to face them. She had worn jeans and a powder blue cable-knit sweater, her ubiquitous baseball cap on the table behind her. Their conversation drew a couple of other rookies closer, and they threw in their questions and comments.

Lainey contentedly watched Scotch hold court. Thoughts of dog teams and races faded away as she basked in the fervor her friend felt for her subject. Scotch's eyes sparkled with delight at someone's comment. When she looked at Lainey, she winked, her gaze reflecting something else entirely. Lainey tried not to sigh like a schoolgirl, thankful that no one seemed to have taken note of the interaction.

The discussion was interrupted by Helen Fuller's arrival. Lainey saw the room was packed, all the tables full and most of the chairs in the back occupied. These were definitely not all rookies. She recognized some of the faces from the race sign-up in June as well as from the awards banquet last March.

The president of the Iditarod Trail Committee took the stage. Clearing his throat at the podium, he began. "Well, everybody, welcome to the mandatory rookies meeting." There was a smattering of applause, and his thick white mustache twitched in embarrassment and pleasure. "We've got a lot of ground to cover, so let's get started."

Lainey put aside her gentle desire for Scotch and activated her iPod as last year's winner took over the podium. She caught Roman's envious glance at the recording instrument and gave him a crooked grin. Then she focused on the rawboned man on the stage as he explained the realities of running the Iditarod trail.

* * *

"Well, what'd you think?" Howry asked as they stepped outside.

Lainey juggled her notes and iPod and whistled. "I learned a lot." Scotch came up behind her, and she looked over her shoulder at the woman. "I mean, you've taught me a lot about how to care for the dogs and get them to want the same things I do, but not much about the trail itself. Or running long distances. Or the true importance of pacing. Or much about a lot of other things."

"You have to learn to walk before you can run." Scotch reached for Lainey's paperwork with a smile. "Now that you've gotten the basics down, we can start branching out into other areas. In fact, I've made arrangements next week for a road trip with the dogs. It'll be good to get them in an area they don't see often—different trails, different smells. Once we increase their mileage, you'll learn more about long distance running and pacing."

"You're doing about forty miles a day now," Howry said. "When do you increase the mileage?"

"This month." Rye joined the conversation. "Lainey's got qualifying races in January and February, and she needs to be ready for them."

"By Christmas we'll be pushing for seventy miles a day and running larger teams. It's going to be hectic. Rye and Irish are prepping for the Two Rivers Solstice junior races too." Scotch grinned at Howry. "This is the month from hell. The pressure's starting to heat up, and tempers are going to be short."

"Well, before you become a prima donna and start throwing tantrums, how about I buy dinner?" Howry offered.

"You're on."

CHAPTER TWENTY-SEVEN

January

"On by!"

Another team overtook Lainey on the trail, the third in as many hours on this stretch of the Kuskokwim 300. Montana, Chibee and Himitsu bitched at the passing dogs while she gave the musher a friendly wave. Gritting her teeth into a semblance of a pleasant smile, she eyed Georgio Spencer's team as they drew ahead. They looked healthy and eager, much like hers. As soon as the sled was safely past, she let up on the drag, allowing her team to increase speed. She struggled with her competitive nature, wanting to urge her dogs forward and retake their position. Instead she called out praise to her team, quieting her three trash talkers as their ears flipped back to listen to her voice. Spencer was a two-time Iditarod champion; she would never be in his league.

From what she gathered, she was close to the halfway mark, between Tuluksak and Kalskag, with about seventy-five miles behind her and roughly twenty-five to go. She had taken a four-hour break in Tuluksak, more interested in keeping her relatively green team rested than being the first across the finish line. Fourteen of her twenty Iditarod trainees were with her on this run, four of the dogs with no more experience than what she had put them through around the

Fuller Kennels this season. She wasn't much more seasoned than they, having only three weeks of overnight sledding runs under her belt.

Checking her watch, she saw it was nearing seven in the morning. The sky hadn't lightened much, dawn just a dream until later in the day. The three hundred mile Alaskan race from Bethel to Napalmute and back had started the previous evening. She'd had a short nap while in Tuluksak. When she reached Kalskag, she planned to take a six-hour layover. That would net her another four hours of sleep if her luck held.

Scotch was somewhere ahead, probably already out of Kalskag. She'd drawn a higher starting number than Lainey and hadn't looked back. Georgio Spencer's sled pulled out of sight, the flash of his headlamp no longer visible in the dark. *Hope she kicks his ass.*

Lainey ran a practiced eye over her team, alert for evidence of injury or exhaustion. They trotted along, panting, tails wagging in the chill, setting a brisk pace. The test would come after her upcoming six-hour break. How many mushers would wake up from a short nap and be ready to run another few hours? *And will I be awake enough to do all the necessary chores?*

Her eyelids heavy, she yawned as she rolled her shoulders. Despite a full night's sleep at a volunteer's house the evening before the race, spending the night on the trail had drained her. She understood why the Iditarod Trail Committee insisted on mushers completing mid-range qualifying races. Experiencing some of the realities of the situation could cause many rookies to drop out before the Iditarod started. This was just a taste of the sleep deprivation she had to look forward to in March. If two or three nights out during a race were this bad, how could she survive up to two weeks of the same?

She shivered. "I'll be a freaking zombie." Furry ears flicked back at her voice and she grinned. "At least I'm not alone, huh? You guys are the best team on the trail. It's an honor to mush with you."

Light from her headlamp reflected off water across the trail, drawing her attention. *Water on the trail?* She stood on the drag and brake, stopping her team to get a better look. Setting her snow hook, she pulled a bag of frozen treats from her sled bag. "Might as well give you guys a snack while we're here, right?"

Tails wagged as she made her way up the line, snacking and checking all the dogs. Passing Trace and Montana, she continued forward to study the trail. It went right through the pool of water and up a slight incline on the other side. There had been a light powdering of snow here since the start of the race, and she saw Spencer's tracks going right into the pool.

Closer inspection revealed a frozen creek. Lainey dug into a parka pocket, pulling out her race notebook. Scanning her scribbles and a small map, she realized this was probably Bogus Creek. She frowned as she looked at the trail again. It appeared the ice was thick enough to take the weight of a laden sled, but somehow water had seeped up to cover the surface. *Well, it's not that big a deal. If it can hold Spencer and the three million other people ahead of me, it'll hold me, too.*

Lainey trudged back to her team. Checking the small thermometer dangling from her goodie bag, she noted the temperature was right at freezing. She packed away the snack bag and popped the snow hook.

The dogs had enough traction on the snow to get the sled up to speed before hitting the water. She watched her leaders slip and slide across the pool until they reached the opposite bank. Everyone followed in line until her youngster, Chibee, reached the midway point. He slipped, straddled and sprawled. His yelp was part excitement, but also maybe pain. Lainey couldn't tell. He dragged a couple of yards before regaining his feet, and then the sled reached the edge of the creek.

She held her breath as water sprayed up from her sled runners, tense as she waited for an ominous cracking of ice or the sensation of slipping. Ahead, Chibee looked fine as he helped pull her across and up the slight embankment. In a heartbeat she was on the other side. Her glance back at the rippling water was her undoing. The sled jerked as it hit an abutment next to the trail. Unprepared, Lainey spun her head around, mouth open to call a command. Before she could speak, the entire sled tipped to the right, crashing on its side without stopping.

Clinging to the handlebar, dragged behind the hardworking team, she started to call another halt. Instead she ducked her head away from a looming snowbank, cursing as snow rushed over her head and down the collar of her parka. "WHOA!"

The sled dragged to a halt. Shaking, Lainey picked herself up, her first action the setting of the snow hook in the ground below. She swore under her breath, digging snow out from the neck of her parka. The team sat along the line, grinning at her as she completely removed her outer garments to clear away the snow and check for damage. Even Napoleon seemed to find her tumble humorous. "Yeah, just wait, mutt. You'll get yours."

Freed of winter's bounty, Lainey walked down the line, checking dogs, especially Chibee. He showed no injury from his waterlogged fall, licking her face with wild abandon as she explored his muscles and bones. She couldn't help smiling at his excitement, her annoyance melting away. "All right. Let me get the sled back up and we'll go."

It was a bit of a struggle to hoist the six-hundred-pound sled back onto its runners. She had to unpack part of it to lighten the load. When everything was back in place, she picked up the snow hook. "Ready? Let's go." The team started off, and she rolled a stiffening shoulder. *If this is the worst I have to deal with on this trail, I'll be lucky.*

* * *

Lainey climbed out of the vehicle, exhausted and exuberant. The dogs in the yard greeted her, and her team responded with fervor from inside the dog truck. On the deck, Thom held Bon in his arms, Miguel standing beside him. The second dog truck pulled up beside her and emptied out its tired occupants.

Thom called, "Well, rookie, how'd you do?"

For a moment, Lainey didn't know how to respond. Since her drinking binge, things had been strained between herself and the patriarch of the Fuller clan. His disfavor had diminished with time, but it hadn't completely vanished.

Howry saved her from having to answer as he yelled from the other truck, "Twelfth place!"

"And she's officially finished one qualifying race for the Iditarod." Helen went up the steps, silencing Bon's cries of "Mama!" by taking him from his father.

"One down, one to go." Scotch threw her arm around Lainey's shoulders.

Lainey blushed at the public familiarity but didn't move away, despite the gentle ache in one shoulder and her ribs. They had spent the last week either sleeping in the living room of a family friend or out on the race trail. Quiet moments alone had been hard to come by, and she craved the contact. "Scotch placed third."

Thom trotted down from the deck, Miguel on his heels, and gave them each a hug. "Third place? Fantastic! What was the purse?"

"Ten grand." Scotch proudly pulled a check from the pocket of her parka and handed it to her father. Miguel whooped in congratulations and Scotch turned bright red. A smile split her face as he clapped her on the back.

Thom gave both women another rough hug. "You two must be exhausted. Get on over to your cabin and catch some sleep. We'll take care of the dogs."

"Thanks, Dad." Scotch released him and returned to her truck for her gear.

Lainey drew her winning check from her pocket. It was decidedly less than ten thousand dollars, but still a tidy sum. She handed it to Thom. "Here. I want you to have this too."

He didn't take the check. "I can't do that, Lainey. You paid your own entry fee. You won that money fair and square."

"That's right, I did. So I get a say on where it goes." She raised an eyebrow. "Consider it a donation to the kennel. You've all worked so hard to make me feel welcome and to train me for this." *And put up with my shit.* She didn't mention the weeklong drunk, knowing it crossed his mind with regularity without any reminder. "I'd never have been able to do it without your support and encouragement."

Thom looked tempted but still made no move to accept the money. "You contracted for the training and team; you're only getting what the magazine paid for to begin with."

Lainey thrust it closer to him. "Fine. I'm sponsoring Rye for the Yukon 300. How's that?"

He blinked, a grin crossing his face. "I'll let him know who to acknowledge," he said as he took the check.

"Thanks." Unable to help herself, she stood on tiptoe and kissed his bearded cheek. "For everything."

He turned as beet red as his daughter had only moments earlier. "No. Thank you, Lainey Hughes."

"You coming or what?" Scotch called.

"Yeah." Lainey winked at Thom before getting her bag from the truck, and then together she and Scotch walked toward the trail leading home.

It was cold inside the cabin, so they kept their parkas on as they set about lighting fires and lanterns. While Scotch worked at the hearth, Lainey built a fire in the wood stove to start a pot of water on the boil. Soon the interior warmed up enough that they shed their outer layers. Not long afterward they sat together on the couch, sock-covered feet propped on the coffee table and mugs of hot chocolate in hand.

"That was fun."

"Yeah, you did pretty good for being from Outside."

Lainey grinned. "I had an excellent teacher."

"I totally agree."

She laughed and kissed Scotch, losing herself in the gentle caress. Long moments passed as they reacquainted themselves with one another, drinks forgotten as they relaxed together. Eventually the kiss ended, and Lainey snuggled against Scotch, a smile on her face. They lounged on the couch, the heat from the fire easing the last of the tension from Lainey's sore muscles.

"I heard you tell Rye you fell near Bogus Creek."

Lainey, whose eyelids had drooped closed, grunted lethargically. "Yeah. You saw the overflow?"

"Yup."

"Coming up out of that I missed the trail by a couple of feet. The sled went on its side."

"Ate some snow?"

Her expression sour, she nodded. "About ten feet of it before the dogs stopped."

"Well, you are a rookie." Scotch's voice held a note of superiority.

Lainey's weariness rushed away at the insult. "A rookie, huh?" She sat up. Before Scotch could respond, Lainey had taken their cups and set both on the table. Her fingers unerringly found the woman's ribs, tickling her. "I seem to remember you eating snow a couple of weeks ago in that sprint in Wasilla."

Scotch recoiled from Lainey, curling her long limbs to avoid the attack, laughing. "No! That wasn't me, that was someone else. Stop!"

"Hah! Don got photos. Admit it or I'll make sure the next article *Cognizance* runs will have your snow-covered butt plastered all over it."

"All right! All right! I admit it!" Lainey stopped tickling and Scotch slumped in relief. She sprawled across the couch with Lainey on top of her. As she caught her breath, they adjusted themselves into a more comfortable position.

"That was mean."

Lainey grinned, eyes closed. "Journalism is a brutal world, my dear. You've got to learn to swim with the sharks."

Beneath her, Scotch chuckled and yawned. "I think I'm going to fall asleep right here."

"Nothing wrong with that." Lainey sighed with pleasure as Scotch wrapped her arms around her, turning until they lay on their sides.

"That's good, because I don't think I can move another step."

"Shhh, go to sleep."

CHAPTER TWENTY-EIGHT

The following afternoon Scotch and Lainey wandered down the path, hand in hand. "I don't know how you didn't get a crick in your neck, sleeping on the couch like that."

Scotch laughed and squeezed her hand. "I could say the same about you."

"I had a nice soft pillow." Lainey smiled. "I can't believe we slept so late. Everybody's going to be ticked off that we didn't feed the dogs this morning."

"Naw. You always get a day off after a big race. Next month it'll be you and Rye lounging about while the rest of us slave away."

Rounding a bend in the path, they came into sight of the yard. Lainey tried to release Scotch's hand, offering discretion in dealing with her family, but Scotch held tight and winked at her.

They hadn't discussed their relationship beyond the need to concentrate on the Iditarod but hadn't refrained from expressing their feelings with one another either. Early on, Lainey had realized that Scotch wasn't ignorant of her sexual orientation. Nothing she said or did startled Scotch. No reference to gay topics befuddled her, no flirtatious remark or action caused more than the expected blush. Besides, no one could kiss like that without at least some experience.

With her concerns in that area dispelled, Lainey allowed herself to relax into their burgeoning romance as other demons rose to haunt her.

Training the dogs was a full-time endeavor, and Lainey had found little opportunity to open a conversation with Scotch about what was growing between them. In her darkest moments, with the craving for a drink at its strongest, she castigated herself for even thinking they could ever have a relationship. How she felt about Scotch, or vice versa, meant nothing. After the race in March, she would move on, return to her tiny Jersey flat and drink herself into oblivion for the next year. A small voice spoke deep inside. Silenced for years by the shame and anger that was her soul, it had grown stronger as the daylight grew weaker. *It doesn't have to be that way.*

When the time for talk did present itself, the two of them would have to sit down and discuss things in detail. If they were to have more than just a fling, there were things that had to be figured out.

Howry came into view, pulling a plastic children's sled piled with packages. It apparently weighed a lot, for he had removed his parka and was bent over in exertion. He stopped when he spotted them. "About time you two got up. We've got a meat delivery out front. All hands on deck."

Scotch came to rigid attention and saluted. "Yes, sir!"

He wiped sweat from his forehead, snorting at her. "Get going, you two. You've slacked off enough today."

"But we haven't even had breakfast." Lainey's words were cut short as Scotch yanked her along.

"It's almost lunch time." Scotch walked past the back deck and around the side of the main cabin. "And I seem to recall you having a toasted cheese sandwich an hour ago."

Lainey grinned, lowering her voice. "He didn't know that." She laughed with Scotch, who raised their linked hands and kissed them.

Irish hustled past with another sled, dragging it behind her with both hands. Her load was smaller, but she put as much effort into it as Howry had. "About time," she grumbled without stopping.

They came around the cabin. "Oh. My. God." Lainey stared at a large semi in the parking area of the circular drive. Three men—the driver and two helpers—had half the contents emptied onto the snowy ground. Thom stood by with a clipboard, making check marks on it as items came off the truck. Rye and Miguel each took a sack of meat and carted it off toward the kennel. "Are we getting all of that?"

"Yup, and then some. This is just the first delivery. We'll each be using about nine hundred pounds apiece through the racing season. Of course that doesn't count dry or canned food or rice. Come on. We've got to get everything stored against scavengers before it gets dark." She released Lainey's hand and strode forward, calling and waving to the deliverymen.

* * *

Three days later, Lainey huddled over two cookers. One held boiling water in which a plastic bag of beef stroganoff was being heated for lunch. The other carried a quart of water, a pound of lamb and a half pound of fat. Nearby, a ration of dry dog chow sat in readiness. The dogs had already eaten. They lay on the line, curled up to sleep while they could. She had already examined each for signs of stress and strain, fed them and released their neck lines to improve their comfort. The batch of food she made now would go into the cooler she carried for their next stop.

She had to be forty or so miles from the kennel. Somewhere out here, Scotch was performing similar tasks. Her team was faster and more experienced. Chances were good that she was at least another five or ten miles closer to home.

Despite being alone in the wilderness, miles from civilization, Lainey smiled. She could see the draw of long-distance racing. Only the hardiest of souls, those not afraid to be by themselves for extended periods of time, could attempt the solitude. Lainey had heard many stories about newcomers who arrived in Alaska determined to live a rustic life, to build a cabin in the wilds and live off the land. The majority never succeeded, the constant silence and darkness of winter too hard to bear. Not everyone could live in their heads without going crazy—it forced a person to take a serious look at herself—and many soon fled for civilization.

After a month of this, Lainey had come to some rather severe conclusions about herself. The smile faded, turning to a frown. She had turned to the bottle to drown the grisly memories of her career, to silence the questions of right and wrong that inevitably came up as she photographed the latest atrocity committed by some dictator or general. The drinking released her from responsibility, enabling her to witness the shit man heaped upon man and ignore her natural human desire to change things for the better. *Ben's right. I have a problem.* That thought was becoming a litany. She had yet to voice it aloud and wasn't sure what the next step should be.

Setting aside the worry, she turned off the cooker and added the measure of dry chow to the hot mixture. With mittened hands, she took the pot to the sled, pouring its contents into the cooler there. Once the lid was secure and the empty pot was cooling in the snow, she made another trip up the line with the hot water from her lunch, giving her team a warm drink. When she returned, she opened the bag with a pocketknife and ate hungrily. She used no utensils, squeezing the food up to the opening. She deposited the empty container in a trash bag inside her sled. Making another trip along her team, she collected their plates.

Only after all chores were completed did she curl up in her sleeping bag, seating herself on the cooler and leaning backward to drowse. She had about three hours before her wristwatch alarm would go off. Then it was back on the trail. As she drifted to sleep, she saw Scotch smiling at her, a promise in her blue eyes and laughter on her lips. In her hands was an unopened bottle of Glenlivet.

CHAPTER TWENTY-NINE

February

The yard resembled a disaster area. Earlier in the week Rye had stapled paper plates to wooden stakes, each one labeled with the name of an Iditarod drop site. At each marker sat two piles of goods for each of the mushers entered in the race. Eventually these heaps would be consolidated into two or three large bags apiece to be shipped to the various checkpoints along the Iditarod trail, a delivery of doggie groceries made available as Lainey and Scotch took the arduous trek to Nome. Until that time, however, they were semi-contained mounds of sealed plastic bags.

Lainey took her turn at the meat saw in the dog kitchen. She wore heavy work gloves and goggles, the sound of the table saw buzzing loud across the kennel. In her hands was a haunch of frozen horsemeat which she diligently sliced down to manageable chunks. The goal was to keep the meat frozen, but in small enough pieces to easily boil up for dog stew. Her arms trembled unpleasantly with the vibrations, but she kept working. She tossed the meat into a nearby bucket that Howry occasionally swapped out with an empty one. He weighed the meat on a scale, handing it off to Miguel when it reached the one-pound mark. From there, the dog handler transferred it into heavy-grade plastic bags. He used a vacuum sealer to remove the air and then heat seal the bag, passing the finished product to Scotch.

Working from a clipboard of notes, Scotch deposited the package at one of the thirty-six growing piles. She prowled the yard constantly, checking and rechecking the eighteen drop points, muttering under her breath and adding notes to the margins of her checklist.

Lainey finished dissecting that haunch of meat and stepped back, rolling her shoulders and shaking out her arms. She was glad she'd had the summer to get into shape; she could well imagine the pain she would be in had she just arrived to enter the race.

"Want me to take a turn?"

She considered the extent of her soreness before answering Howry. "No thanks. I'm still good. Besides, it's Scotch's turn next." With a resigned exhalation, Lainey reached for another chunk of meat, not letting her mind settle on the animal from which it had come. When she'd seen the donation request form in June, she had almost thought it a joke. Horsemeat? Really? Now she slogged through four hundred pounds of the stuff.

Time passed as she fell into the routine: running meat through the saw, brushing away meat dust to keep it from clogging the machine, dropping chunks into a bucket, turning away for more and starting again. She saw movement from the corner of her eyes— Howry replacing her bucket with an empty one, Miguel sealing bags and Scotch taking the bags into the yard. Her world was motion and sound, the buzz of the saw blocking out all other conversations. A pat on her back broke her reverie. Looking up in surprise, she saw Miguel and Howry halfway across the yard. Lainey turned off the saw and looked up at Scotch.

"Come on, it's lunch time." She squeezed Lainey's shoulder.

Lainey groaned as the touch massaged tender muscles. Scotch stepped behind her and kneaded Lainey's tense shoulders. She sighed in pleasure. "That feels wonderful."

"I believe it." Scotch chuckled. "When we get back out here, we'll rotate. I need to change the blade anyway."

"Okay." Scotch moved away and Lainey stretched. She removed the safety goggles and glanced at the horsemeat, amazed at how much she had gotten processed. "Wow. Time flies when you're having fun."

"You're a cheap date." Scotch ducked the swat Lainey aimed at her. "Let's go. I'm starved."

"You are so going to pay for that remark," Lainey promised as they walked to the main cabin.

Scotch gave her a sultry smile. "Good."

Lainey felt a surge of arousal. She would have given anything to be able to drag the woman back to their cabin and quench her lustful thirst. But they had a training run scheduled at midnight, and she knew she would never make it through the night without a decent nap. There was still too much to do, so much riding on the dogs and training and preparation. "You'll pay for that too."

Scotch grinned as she climbed the steps to the deck. Shaking her head mournfully, Lainey followed, not quite succeeding in quashing the lascivious thoughts inspired by an eye-level view of Scotch's ass.

It wasn't much warmer in the mudroom, but they quickly shed their outerwear, using a broom to knock excess snow from their boots before tugging them off. Lainey finished first and stepped into the kitchen. The warm blast of air burned her cheeks, and she shivered in pleasure. The smell of apple tarts warred with those of meatloaf and fried potatoes. The counter groaned under an avalanche of food, far more than was needed for their afternoon meal. Beyond the counter, in the dining room, most denizens of the kennel were already seated around the large table. A rumble in her stomach urged Lainey forward, and she sat down to lunch, Scotch beside her.

Two seats remained empty. Rye was on a long distance run in preparation for his first adult race. The Yukon 300 was open to seventeen-year-olds, and he was eager to get out on the trail and prove himself. He planned to enter the Iditarod next year.

"Where's Thom?" Howry buttered a roll.

Helen dished gravy over mashed potatoes for Bon. "In town. Scotch wanted more batteries for the headlamps. He's going to pick up the pizza too."

"Pizza!" Bon yelled, getting a laugh in response.

"Not for you, little man." Scotch waved a fork at him. "It's for the race."

"Idit'od!"

Miguel tousled Bon's blond hair. "That's right. The Iditarod."

"Well, I think you two can give up one pizza," Helen drawled.

"How are things going in here?" Scotch asked.

"Not bad," Irish said. "But if I see another dog bootie after March, I'm going to throw it into the fire."

Scotch grinned. "You say that every year."

Her sister glared at her. "I can't wait until I'm old enough to saw meat with you instead. Then Bon can get sick of booties."

Still feeling a phantom vibration in her hands, Lainey held up them up. "You'll change your mind after a couple of hours at it."

"Will not." Helen raised an eyebrow at her daughter and Irish blushed. "Sorry."

"No problem." Lainey smiled. Irish had taken to treating her and Howry as extended members of the family. It was kind of nice in an offhanded way. Lainey hadn't been involved in a home life like this since she was a teenager. She had always wondered what it would be like to have siblings, and the last few months had been a real eye-opener.

As she ate, she glanced over at the living room. It looked like a dump. Here the eighteen checkpoints were represented by colorful paper taped to the walls. At each place stood piles of dog booties, dog blankets, socks, gloves and all other manner of tools and comforts from home that Lainey and Scotch would need to survive the race.

Lainey nodded at the mess. "You guys do this every year?" Dismay colored her voice. "It's a lot of work for only a couple of weeks of racing."

"This year it's twice the work."

Helen tsked at Scotch. "Don't listen to her, Lainey. You're actually forcing us to practice what we'll be doing next year anyway. I seriously doubt we'll be able to talk Rye out of running. He's already drumming up sponsors for his rookie year."

"I don't think you'll be cooking so much meatloaf next year." Scotch was referring to her brother's distaste for the meal.

"No, but if he can figure out how to pack my turkey vegetable stew, he'll be in heaven."

Lainey reached for a second helping of meatloaf. "Freeze it in an ice tray."

"There's an idea—stewsicles." Scotch winked at Irish's laughter.

The dogs barked a rowdy greeting to an oncoming vehicle, and Bon cried, "Daddy!"

"Pizza," Howry reminded the toddler.

"Pizza!" Bon agreed, waving his hands in the air.

Lainey scowled at her colleague. "You know that's my dinner you're talking about, the one I'm going to be missing a month from now because you're eating it today."

Howry snickered. "You can afford to skip a meal or two. Less weight for the dogs to haul."

Before she could respond to his jibe, Helen gave Howry a stern look. With amazement, Lainey watched him redden just as Irish had moments before.

"Sorry." His eyes twinkled despite the apology.

Thom stomped into the kitchen from the back deck, carrying a paper sack. "Here's your batteries." He paused to kiss his wife in greeting before handing the bag to his daughter. "Got a couple of bags of Jolly Ranchers and chocolate kisses too."

"What about the pizza?" Irish asked.

Thom shrugged and sat down. "It's in the truck. Figured you wouldn't need it yet. Mom's got to get all this stuff packed and ready to go first." He gestured toward the food-laden counter and then began dishing up his lunch.

"First one there gets his or her choice of pizza," Howry said.

They stared at one another for a split second before exploding from the table. When the dust settled and the yells fell away in the distance, Thom looked at his wife and son, the only ones remaining in the room. "Pass the potatoes, please."

CHAPTER THIRTY

As the dogs crossed the finish line of the Yukon 300, Scotch whooped with euphoria. She stepped forward with several others to halt the passing team. Once the canines were no longer in danger of racing on, she rushed for the musher. "Eighth place!" Lainey leapt into her arms and they danced around in the middle of the street, yelling at each other. "You beat Rye! He's thirty minutes behind you."

"I know! I passed him at the last checkpoint. Tundra's got a strained ankle. He had to pull her off the line."

Scotch winced in sympathy and released Lainey. Losing a dog hurt more than just the dogsledder's race; each vital team member became a second family after long days on the trail. "Did you eat snow this time?"

Back on her feet, Lainey gave Scotch another hug. "Nope. Stayed upright the entire way."

"Very good." Scotch turned to the team of dogs. "Let's get these guys bedded down. We're staying about a mile from here at the Bakers' place."

"Are you hitchhiking?"

Scotch grinned. "Depends. You going to offer me candy if I get in your sled?"

Lainey smiled. "Oh, I'll offer a lot more than candy, sweetheart."

Scotch licked her lips. But they both had much to work for first. *And who knows whether there'll be anything more after.* Pushing away the slow burn of arousal, she grinned. "Then what are we waiting for?" Scotch jumped into the bed of the sled. "Mush on, O Iditarod Qualifier."

Lainey laughed and called to the handlers holding her dogs. Tails wagging, the team trotted down the street. Scotch studied them with a practiced eye, noting no telltale signs of latent strains or injuries. She looked over her shoulder at Lainey. "You're doing great. The dogs look like they could go for days."

"Not all of them. Apollo's headed for home now. He strained his shoulder before the first checkpoint and I had to drop him."

"He probably took a turn wrong. The rest of them seem ready for bear, though." Scotch saw their turnoff coming up and returned her attention to the road.

"I hope so. These runs are too short. Just about the time I get into the swing of things, the race is over and it's time to stand down." On Scotch's direction, she ordered the team onto a side road. "On by," she called as a pickup truck came toward them.

"That won't be a problem next month." Scotch tensed slightly, seeing Chibee's interest in the oncoming vehicle. The youngest member on Lainey's team, he still had a tendency to pull away in a puppyish effort to chase things. Fortunately, the three hundred miles he had just completed had mellowed his playful nature. The truck went by without incident, and Scotch relaxed. "You stuck to the six-hour rule?"

"Yeah. Six on, six off. It wasn't easy when people were passing me, though."

Scotch laughed at her disgruntled tone. "Remember the rookie meeting. Just because they're passing doesn't mean you won't be gaining on them four days down the line. If a musher wears out his dogs too early, it's a blessing for you."

"I know." Lainey sniffed. "I still don't like it. And neither does my team."

"Good. Got to keep the competitive juices flowing. Sometimes that's the only thing keeping you slogging down the trail." Scotch guided them into the large yard of a cabin and directed them around to the back where a small barn sat. Lainey halted the team in front of it and Scotch clambered from the sled. Within the hour, they had all the dogs fed and bedded down on straw inside.

Lainey swayed with exhaustion as they trudged toward the cabin. Scotch wrapped her arm around Lainey's waist to steady her. "Margaret's fixed a turkey dinner for you. We'll get you fed, watered, showered and bedded down in no time."

Lainey mumbled a response, snuggling closer as they reached the back steps.

Smiling, Scotch gave her a squeeze. *Even if nothing lasts between us in the future, I'll treasure this.*

CHAPTER THIRTY-ONE

March

Lainey stared at the mound of gear on the hotel bed. "Do you always get this much stuff at the musher meeting?"

Scotch dumped a matching pile on her bed and Irish happily sorted through her sister's booty. "Yeah. Every year we get things from the sponsors. It's best not to count on it, though." She tried on a pair of leather work gloves marked with the name of a business.

Sitting, Lainey rooted through the goods. She also had work gloves, as well as a two-pound sample bag of dry dog food, heavy duty mittens from a sporting goods store, nearly one hundred dog booties in bright neon orange, a travel toothbrush courtesy of a local dentist, two medium-sized dog harnesses and a handy little toolkit in a plastic pouch. Everything was prominently marked with company logos.

Irish held up the toolkit. "Can I have this?"

"Sure. You can have the mittens too, if you want them." Pleased, Irish pulled out the mittens and checked their fit.

Lainey set the dog food, booties and work gloves with her gear, sweeping the rest of the items back into the bag she had used to transport the stuff from the mushers' meeting. "I wasn't expecting the turnout." She lay back on the bed, hands behind her head.

Scotch examined one of the booties with a critical eye. "It's easier for folks to get to the start than the finish. At least they know when the race starts. Depending on weather and dogs, the ending can happen anywhere from eight to twelve days from now. No one can guarantee being there to greet the winner." She collected the booties and put them in a travel bag. "If you don't want all of that, you can leave it in the lobby for someone else to pick up. A lot of mushers can't afford much—keeping the dogs fed and happy takes a lot of money. An extra set of booties or gloves can come in handy."

Still lying on the bed, Lainey nodded, her mind on the information-packed meeting in which they had spent the day. The trail condition report had been the most informative, the race manager warning that temperatures had warmed areas of the interior, causing overflows at rivers and creeks. The rest of the time had been spent with the other mushers—signing commemorative items, turning in the last of their paperwork, and hearing speeches from the executive director, three sponsors and several race officials. A knock interrupted her musings and Irish hastened to the door.

Rye stuck his head into the room. Behind him stood Miguel and Howry. "Come on. We're heading over to Sullivan Arena."

"Don't want to miss that!" Scotch grabbed her parka.

Lainey grinned. Time for dinner, more speeches and the drawing of numbers to see in what order the mushers would be starting.

* * *

The Fuller Kennel clan had its own table. One seat remained empty, but that was intentional. Not only were mushers and their families or supporters in attendance, but many avid racing buffs had paid their entrance fee, as had a multitude of reporters. The vacant seat was continuously occupied by roaming fans appearing at the table to meet Scotch and get autographs or have pictures taken. Lainey was startled to discover a rudimentary fame of her own. She took it in stride, following Scotch's example of treating each visitor with courtesy and humor.

Once the latest Iditarod enthusiast had left, Lainey leaned across the table and said in a lowered voice, "They must be hard up for material if they're asking me for autographs."

Thom laughed. "Who knows? You might be Rookie of the Year this race. That alone would make your autograph worth something."

"Yeah, and maybe I'll win the race too." Lainey chuckled at the unlikelihood of such an occurrence.

"Lainey?" someone said from behind her.

She rolled her eyes at the Fullers before putting on a pleasant face and turning to greet the new arrival. Her expression faltered as a rush of pleasure and shame washed through her. She gaped at the man standing there. "Ben?"

Benjamin Strauss, *Cognizance* editor, smiled, his teeth white against the tan of his skin. "Is this seat taken?"

Howry came around to shake Strauss' hand and make introductions to the rest of the table. Lainey remained flabbergasted at her friend's sudden appearance. She vaguely heard Thom insist that he join them for dinner, and then Ben sat beside her.

"What are you doing here?" Her voice was a little harsher than she had intended, and she reached over to give him a belated hug.

"Since we're covering the bills and training, of course we'd be here to cover the race itself. The magazine also bid on the Idita-Rider auction." He referred to the program that added extra weight to slow down excited dogs at the start of the race. He ordered coffee from a passing waiter and then smiled at her with pleasure. "Guess who's riding in your sled on Friday?"

"You?" She laughed at his nod. "I hope you didn't have to pay too much."

Strauss busied himself with rearranging his silverware, an air of self-satisfaction about him. "You'd be surprised. It's no secret that the impressive Scotch Fuller has been training you. We actually had a bit of competition to win the bid."

Rye leaned forward in interest. "Really? How much did it go for?"

"Sixteen hundred."

Scotch whistled. "Wow. That's not bad."

"Thanks to you." Strauss raised his cup in toast to the experienced musher.

Scotch blushed, while Lainey grinned and patted her thigh under the table.

Dinner was served not long after Strauss' arrival. Most of the race followers settled at their own tables to eat, leaving the mushers in peace. Conversation was stimulating, especially when the Fullers discovered that Strauss also had field experience under his belt. The tales grew taller as the three journalists attempted to outdo each other for the most exotic locations and bizarre situations in their careers.

When talk wasn't focused upon her, Lainey nibbled at her meal. She had spent many a day over the last two months ruminating on alcoholism and her place within its framework. Scotch's ultimatum had had a lasting effect. Rather than push away the craving without thought as was her wont on a gig, she had endured a lot of winter nights on the trail by examining her desires. Online research, coupled with candid soul searching, had led her to the conclusion that she did have a problem with alcohol. *But I can't even say the words.*

She watched Strauss as he laughed at someone's comment. He had engineered this entire gig to force her off the booze, she was sure of it. She didn't know whether she should be angry or thank him. The anger was worn and familiar, sickening in a comforting way, a well-run trail. Three months ago, she would have been furious with him. *Now…Now I feel kind of numb.* She held back a snort, envisioning herself admitting to Strauss that he had been right. *He's going to be insufferable.*

"What's so funny?"

Lainey turned to Scotch. "Nothing." At the raised eyebrow, she grinned. "I'll tell you after the race." She struggled to keep the smile in place, her heart suddenly thumping in fear. *Can I tell her? Am I strong enough for that?*

Appeased, Scotch reached over and brushed her knuckles along Lainey's cheek, the motion unseen by Strauss.

As dessert was served, the chief executive officer approached the stage. At the podium, he cleared his throat and tapped the microphone. "Well, ladies and gentlemen, it's about that time." He waggled an elaborate cowboy boot that contained the names of the racers.

The audience cheered and clapped. Names were called in order of sign-up. As each musher picked a number from the hat, indicating his or her starting position, he or she took the opportunity to thank sponsors and family. Some had a long list and the time dragged on, time during which Lainey became more and more panicked, her heart beating harder in her chest. She had never spoken to more than thirty or forty people at a time, and this venue held hundreds. A nervous glance around at the other tables raised the question, how many people were there?

"Scotch Fuller."

Lainey smothered her anxiety by loudly applauding as Scotch stood. She envied the quiet confidence the woman showed as she wove her way through the tables toward the stage, pausing to shake hands with friends and fans along the way.

At the podium, Scotch grinned and waved, receiving another round of approval. She reached into the boot, pulled out a number, and handed it to the race official.

"Number forty-eight, Scotch Fuller!" A collection of groans mixed with the clapping and whistling. There were seventy-six mushers this year. Scotch would start right in the middle of the pack.

Scotch stood at the podium, waiting for the applause to die down. "Looks like I'll have to work extra hard to take the lead this year."

Lainey laughed with everyone else, enjoying the friendly tone, forgetting her concerns as Scotch continued speaking.

"I'd like to take this opportunity to thank my parents, Thom and Helen Fuller. Without them I wouldn't be here, let alone be racing dogs. They put together our kennel and taught me everything I know about dogs and sledding. I want to also thank Rye and Irish, my brother and sister, for all the work they've done to keep the kennel running.

"My thanks to *Cognizance* magazine for being my main sponsor this year. By extension, that thanks also goes to Don Howry, Lainey Hughes and Ben Strauss, all sitting at that table over there." She pointed, smiling at them. "Don's the reporter writing articles about me for the magazine; Lainey's our rookie entry and trainee; and Mr. Strauss is the one who helped it all happen."

Lainey smiled back at Scotch as she continued listing her sponsors: all the individuals who had purchased booties or "adopted" dogs over the Internet, the school kids who had put on bake sales and fundraisers to help with expenses and the various local businesses who had funneled money into the kennel in support of Scotch.

"And finally, thanks to all of you. You're a great bunch of people and I'm glad you're here."

The crowd broke into applause and cheers again as Scotch left the stage. The racing committee executive returned to the microphone.

"Lainey Hughes."

Having temporarily forgotten she would be next in line, Lainey felt the blood drain from her face. Around the table everyone clapped and laughed, urging her to stand. Lainey couldn't hear their words through the roaring in her ears. It was all she could do not to grab and drain Helen's wine glass. Howry stood and took her hand, pulling her to her feet to push her in the general direction of the stage. Lainey stumbled only once before gaining a modicum of control over her rebellious limbs. Halfway to the stage, Scotch intercepted her. Their hands met, and Lainey felt a measure of strength flow through the touch.

Pale blue eyes twinkled in amusement and understanding. Scotch leaned close, her voice loud to be heard over the applause. "You've faced down a rampaging moose...and you're the one that's still here."

Jerking her head back, Lainey unconsciously straightened. She most certainly had. She had also come to grips with an addiction she'd never wanted to admit she had. *You still haven't admitted it, Hughes.* Regardless of the sarcastic thought, a slow grin crossed her face. She squeezed Scotch's hand. "Thanks." Scotch sketched a little bow and released her.

Shoulders squared, Lainey proceeded to the stage. She was no less scared of her predicament, but it didn't hold as much power over her. The frantic desire for a shot of whiskey abated. Climbing the steps, she reminded herself that in two days, she would be far away from this madness, heading into the quiet Alaskan wilderness with her team. The boot of numbers was offered to her and she reached inside, swirling the contents around before taking a slip of paper.

"Number four, Lainey Hughes!"

Four? *Four?* She stared out over the celebrating audience, unable to clearly see her table through the glare of the lights. She would lead the rookies out of the gate.

The audience quieted and her heart pounded in her throat. *Moose. Rampaging moose.* When she spoke, she was pleased her voice wasn't trembling as much as the rest of her.

"I think that everyone at Fuller Kennels deserves the biggest thanks—Thom and Helen Fuller; Rye, Irish and Bon; and Miguel Sanchez, their handler. But mostly, Scotch Fuller, for taking on someone from Outside with absolutely no knowledge of racing to train for the Iditarod. All of them showed professionalism and patience in dealing with not only a rookie racer, but a greenhorn to boot." She blushed at the laughter and fumbled in her pocket for the index card she had prepared the night before. "Um, I'd also like to thank *Cognizance* magazine, my primary sponsor...and employer. By extension, thanks go to Don Howry, my partner in crime, and Benjamin Strauss, editor and close friend. The former traveled to the wilds of Alaska for a story; the latter sold me on this gig and sent me out here." Lainey went down the list of supporters on her card. Through the kennel website, she had her own fan club of schoolchildren and Iditarod aficionados that had sent in money.

When she finished, she gave a brisk nod and stepped away from the podium. The flood of relief almost made her stumble at the bottom of the steps. She heard the next racer's name called and breathed a sigh as the clapping and whistling were directed at someone other than her. Several attendees reached out to pat her back or shake her hand as she passed. Back at the table, she gratefully sank into her chair, surrounded by smiling faces. The musher on the stage began his speech, but no one at the Fuller table paid him any attention.

Scotch took Lainey's hand. "You did great."

"Yeah, you didn't faint." Howry raised his glass to toast her fortitude. Lainey stuck her tongue out at him, eliciting a laugh.

"It was an easy sell," Strauss said.

She shrugged one shoulder. "Thanks anyway." She saw his curious expression and realized Scotch was still holding her hand in plain view on the table. She raised an apologetic eyebrow, knowing that part of the truth was out. He now had a good idea why she had chosen Scotch for this article. Lainey supposed she should feel guilty for lying to him all those months ago, but she didn't. Shoulds and shouldn'ts were what had gotten her drinking in the first place. He, of all people, knew that. She smiled at him and squeezed Scotch's hand.

CHAPTER THIRTY-TWO

Lainey paced up and down alongside the dog truck. She had checked her sled for the sixth time, satisfied everything was in place, yet still feeling as if she had forgotten something. Her nerves jangled with the yipping of excited dogs, including the eight on her team that she had tapped to run the ceremonial start. They were tethered to the sides of a truck, which was parked on a side street because of the hundreds of people roaming about.

The circus atmosphere was contagious. Vendors worked the crowds, hawking everything from reindeer sausages to T-shirts to fuzzy moose antler hats. The people along the route were as colorful as the well-sponsored mushers. Lainey had seen working class Joes in conservative winter jackets, people wearing the latest styles from the Alpine ski circuit crowd and a few bona fide mountain men and natives dressed in outfits made entirely of leather and fur.

Fortunately Lainey was able to focus on things other than the race as her starting time inched closer. Her distractions weren't limited to the tourist crowd. Pulling the number four starting slot, she had suddenly become a minor celebrity and was approached by a number of folks wanting pictures or autographs and to talk dogs. Lainey eagerly welcomed the conversations, glad to get her mind off her nervousness.

Of her original twenty dogs, three more hadn't made the cut. Helen had doubted Apollo's shoulder strain would be healed well enough for him to finish the race. At the mandatory vet check, it became official. Lainey's slacker, Dablo, was also set aside. She couldn't spare the energy to deal with his negligent pulling. The toughest loss was Bast. He had done well through the training but had developed a cough. As kennel cough was a major concern, highly contagious and able to decimate entire teams during a race, Bast was removed at the vet check and sent home with Miguel to a warm dog barn and antibiotics. Glad to see none of the other dogs exhibiting symptoms two days later, Lainey hoped they had caught the illness in time.

Several volunteer handlers idled around the immediate area, those in front helping the second musher in line keep his dogs from launching onto Fourth Avenue, which crossed a half block away. The animals were jumping, all four feet off the ground in their enthusiastic desire to get on the trail. Lainey's team wasn't as boisterous, but she expected that to change once she began hooking them to the gang line. The thought giving rise to action, she went down the line again, making certain it was laid out neatly and all connections were tight. Only eight of her dogs would run this morning; the rest would join her team tomorrow at the actual start of the race.

Strauss watched her fussing with amusement. "You did that already."

"Shut up." She ignored his laughter. Her insides twisted with disquietude. It felt almost as bad as her short walk up to the stage at the banquet.

"Miss Hughes?"

Lainey looked up to see a youth on the verge of adolescence holding a camera. Two other kids were with him, all starry eyed as they smiled at her.

"Can we get a picture? Of you and your lead dogs?"

She forced her edginess aside and smiled. "Sure. Come on." Leading the way to Sholo and Trace, she knelt between them, pulling them into a hug. "How's this?"

"Great!" The boy snapped a couple of pictures. "You're Lainey Hughes the photographer, right?"

"That's me." She stood and brushed the snow from her knees.

He looked at his companions. "I told you!" Unzipping his jacket, he pulled a folded magazine from inside. "Can I get you to autograph one of your pictures?"

"You bet." Lainey's pleasant tone hid her uneasiness. Her previous career as a war correspondent still brought occasional nightmares, usually when she was sober. She didn't want a grisly photo to remind her of those years, not today.

The boy eagerly whipped open the magazine. One of his friends fumbled a pen from a pocket, and he handed both to Lainey.

Bracing herself, she looked down at a panoramic shot of the Serengeti covering the full two pages. In the foreground on the right page was a pack of spotted hyena worrying their latest meal, the carcass of an antelope. A real smile crossed her face. "Do you want me to make this out to you?"

"Yes!" He gave his name and she signed the magazine. "Thanks!

Feeling better, she watched them leave, peering at the autograph in excitement.

"Guess your reputation precedes you more than you thought."

"I guess so." She grinned at Strauss. "It's kind of nice to be remembered for something other than warfare."

"Amen to that."

"Lainey!" Thom trotted up with Rye and Irish. "Let's get ready! You're up in fifteen minutes."

She glanced up the line and saw that the second musher had finished hooking up his dogs. Her heart leapt into her throat, and she felt nauseous and jubilant at the same time. With difficulty she got her elated dogs into position. Several Iditarod volunteers helped keep them from taking off without her. Everyone was ready to go with four minutes to spare. Strauss climbed into the bed of her sled and bundled inside a sleeping bag. As her Idita-Rider, he would ride with her from the ceremonial start of the Iditarod until she reached the Campbell Airstrip. She almost didn't recognize her sled. It sported a new, bright yellow bag, the *Cognizance* logo prominently displayed on the sides. She wore a similarly colored parka with a badger fur ruff, gifts from her official sponsor.

For even more weight, another sled had been attached to hers, and Rye now climbed aboard the runners. Thom was going to ride behind Scotch's sled to add additional weight, since her Idita-Rider was a petite elementary school teacher. With all the noise and people, the dogs were more than eager to get going. The extra pounds would keep them from overdoing things or going too fast. Jonah, her wheel dog, deliriously bounced about like a seventy-five-pound puppy, the rest of her team doing the same.

The dog team in front was guided to Fourth Avenue and the starting line. A volunteer with a clipboard neared, waving her forward, and she swallowed hard. "Ready! Let's go!" she yelled over the din.

With a jerk, her team tried to take off at a full run. The ten volunteers pulled, holding them back, forcing them to trot toward the beginning of the race.

At the starting line, two other teams awaited the go-ahead. The sound of the dogs was drowned out by the cheers of the audience, who stood five deep on either side of the street. Lainey waved as the team stopped, vaguely noting that her hand was shaking. The volunteers held onto her team, as the dogs were in no mood to stand around.

Officially, she was the fourth musher to head out, but in reality she was third. Number One was an honorary position, the racing bib given to someone who had made an impact on dog racing. Hoping her breakfast would stay down, Lainey watched as the honored musher for this year was presented with the gear.

The second musher was introduced, and Lainey heard a woman counting down the seconds over large speakers. It was amazing she could hear anything at all with the cacophony around her. Then the team at the line took off, the crowd cheering as they started. The volunteers urged her team closer. Glancing back, she saw another team getting into place behind her. Somewhere back there was Scotch, and Lainey had a bone-deep yearning to see her.

"Number Four, Lainey Hughes!"

The crowd applauded again, and Lainey spun around. Number three was already away. She took a few breaths, trying not to hyperventilate as her team was maneuvered into the starting position.

"You ready for this?"

Lainey nodded at the volunteer and surprised herself by smiling. What was it Scotch had said? "Loaded for bear!"

He patted her on the shoulder and stepped back as the final seconds were called out.

"Ready!" Lainey hollered to her team. She heard the signal. "Let's go!"

The ten burly handlers released the dogs and her team shot off down the trail, snapping her head back. As they raced down Fourth Avenue, her only regret was not being able to say good-bye to Scotch, who'd had as busy a morning as she'd had.

Strauss whooped in excitement as they barreled down the street, the wind scouring their cheeks. Lainey estimated they were going about fifteen miles an hour, despite the added sled and men weighing the team down. She was glad for the company; there was no way she could have maintained control on her own. They whisked past the crowds, and she barely noted the colorful clothing blurring by or the sounds of their cheering.

Up ahead, a truck drove across the street. Several workers wearing Iditarod patches dashed into the intersection, shoveling snow into the tire tracks before she arrived. Police officers stopped traffic to give her right of way, and Lainey laughed at the absurdity of the situation. Where else but in Alaska would cops stop traffic for a dog sled? The team ripped by, Rye calling a "thanks" to the workers.

The trail took a turn, the people lining the street a better marker than any trail ribbon. She called the command and her team went into the turn. A bubble of pride swelled in her heart at their professionalism and she began to enjoy the ride, her nervousness taking a back seat. The crowds thinned and she spotted a trail marker ahead, remembering from stories she'd heard that this was a tough turn. "Gee!" Like a well-oiled machine, the team began the turn. Sholo and Trace found a secondary trail off the road and took it instead of completing the turn. Off they went, down the side and onto the new path.

"Crap!" she cursed. "Whoa! Sholo, Trace, whoa!"

Both she and Rye applied the brakes. Still eager, the dogs were reluctant to stop. The trail dipped into a patch of alder trees, and she used a nearby tree to attach a snub line while she set her snow hook and then jumped off the sled. Despite knowing a delay now meant absolutely nothing in the grand scheme of the race, she felt a tingle of irritation along the back of her neck. She sensed the teams passing by her position as she stopped to deal with this snag. Oblivious, the dogs wagged their tails and grinned at her as she went to the front of the line. It took a concerted effort to not take her annoyance out on them.

She gave each a pat and a good word, the pressure mounting on her as she imagined being out there so long that Scotch, in forty-eighth place, would soon go by. When she reached her lead dogs, she gave them heaps of praise and grabbed their collars. She physically pulled the dogs around, Rye and Strauss standing nearby. Now that the race was on, they were forbidden to help, lest they disqualify her. Rye kept a close watch, ready to jump on his sled brake if necessary.

When they were turned around and her passengers back in their proper places, she pulled the snub line and gave the command to go. A musher went by as they pulled back onto the street, and she grumbled. "Haw!" The dogs smoothly followed instruction. A few fans peppering the area had seen her snafu and applauded as she got back on the right path. She blushed furiously but forced herself to wave, breathing a sigh of relief. Her team poured on the speed, still frisky, and she caught up to the musher wearing bib number eleven. *Damn. Seven teams passed while I took a powder.* She reminded herself that the real race didn't begin until the following day in Wasilla. No matter how slowly she arrived at Eagle River today, she would still be third out of the chute tomorrow.

"Passing!" she called, warning the man she was coming up on his side. As her team began to overtake his, three of her dogs began barking at the competition. She grinned at her trash talkers. Her dogs yelled happily as they passed, probably making comments about the parentage and skills of their rivals. Montana and Chibee were the worst, watching the opposing team as they passed easily, smiling and shining as they went. The surprising one was Himitsu, a three-year-old male with yellow-brown fur. He was always so polite and quiet that his sudden voice was unexpected.

Lainey waved to number eleven as they passed, her trash talkers jostling each other and sneaking looks backwards. They acted like teenaged boys who had just pulled off a prank against the high school principal. She laughed with them, fully relaxing for the first time in days. Her team eased into a steady pace, ears pricking back to hear her chuckles. All along the path people were gathered, standing in front of their homes to cheer the mushers on. She followed a power line, seeing the next musher ahead. With little urging, her dogs picked up speed. As they neared, she saw a group clustered on the side of the trail handing something to the musher.

Strauss looked up at her from the sled bed. "What are they doing?"

"No idea."

The crowd held a few signs—"Go Iditarod Mushers!"—and called encouragement as she closed with them. A woman reached out with something in her hand and Lainey automatically stretched to take what was offered. She grinned at the large homemade muffin and turned to wave her thanks before putting it into her snack bag.

Her three recalcitrants bellowed insults again, and she warned musher number ten of her passing. If her team maintained this enthusiasm for the next two weeks, she would be well set for the race. Granted, the chances of that were slight, even with the high level of care the dogs received, but it would make for a great article if the rookie came in second or third. The path passed a park and followed bicycle trails for a bit. They skirted the Campbell Airstrip and Lainey saw a group of race officials ahead.

"This is where you get off."

"All right," Strauss said. "I'll see you at Eagle River. I may fly with Don along the race, but if I don't I'll definitely be in Nome when you get there."

When, not if. Lainey laughed. "I'd welcome the company." She called the dogs to a halt. They obeyed the command, their initial gusto mellowed with the miles they had run.

Strauss climbed out of the sled and took her hands. "Thanks for the ride. It was exhilarating."

"Any time." She took her foot off the brake and ordered the dogs onward, Rye still on his sled trailing behind her.

The rest of the trip was calm and easy. Her team didn't overtake any others, but she no longer minded the delay caused by their early detour. Eventually she came to a long hill, the trail thronged with cheering people. The VFW was ahead, and it looked like another circus in the making. It was just past noon and she looked forward to an afternoon of celebrating with the Fullers. Tomorrow she would be alone with her dogs on the last great race.

CHAPTER THIRTY-THREE

If Lainey thought she would be leaving civilization after the restart of the race, she was immediately disabused of the notion. Large crowds mobbed Wasilla. Scotch had told her that people would be up and down the trail all the way to Knik and beyond. According to Howry, who kept his ear to the ground as a good newsman should, there were anywhere from fifteen to seventeen thousand Iditarod fans crowding the narrow chute out of town.

Through the worst of her attack of nerves, Lainey ignored what she could. She concentrated on her dogs and on the fans who showed up looking for photos and autographs. When claustrophobia set in, the desire for a stiff drink predominant in her mind, she distracted herself with the memory of Scotch's good-bye kiss. Scotch had pulled out all the stops, a harbinger of the passion to come when they both arrived in Nome, and Lainey briefly touched her lips at the recollection.

Like the day before, several handlers stood on hand to keep her dogs from bolting. Her team yelped and shouted in excitement, all sixteen of them more than ready to get on the trail. The twenty-mile run the day before had done little to dampen their enthusiasm.

A checker came to her sled and Lainey opened the bright yellow sled bag to show her mandatory gear. The usual items were in place, along with a packet of mail and promotional materials she had to deliver to Nome. If she lost any of it, she would be disqualified from the race. Other than those items, she had little else on board. She and Scotch had sent their primary racing sleds to Knik with the dog trucks. There she would transfer her belongings before heading into the wilderness. Those sleds were more rugged and packed to the ribs with everything they would need.

"Everything's there." The checker marked her clipboard. "Have a good race."

"Thanks!"

Howry approached, a wide grin on his face. "Lainey." He gave her a hug. "Ready to go?"

"You know it." She gestured at the antics of her team. "I'm not the only one."

He held out an envelope. "Scotch wanted me to give this to you. She said not to read it until you reach your first long break."

Lainey had a powerful urge to rip it open right then but restrained herself. *If I can get through months on end without a drink, I can wait a few days for this.* She gazed at Scotch's neat handwriting and smiled softly. "Thanks." She tucked it securely into her personal bag.

Howry shuffled his feet. "Ben's been hinting around, asking me questions about you two. What do you want me to tell him?"

Lainey sighed, having known the questions would be inevitable after what Ben had seen at the musher banquet. "Go ahead and tell him the truth. It's not like he hasn't figured it out; he just wants verification."

Howry's brow furrowed. "You sure?"

"I'm sure. He's my friend. He might not like that I led him on in the beginning, but he'll get used to the idea."

He blew out a breath. "If you say so."

She gave him another hug. "I say so." A loudspeaker announced the upcoming official start of the race, and Lainey pulled away from the embrace. "I think that's me."

He laughed. "I'd say so. We're going to take your sled to Knik, and then fly to Finger Lake, so we'll see you there."

"Ben too?" Lainey saw a volunteer trotting toward her.

"Yeah. Ben too."

"I'll see you then." She stepped onto the runners of her sled. Her last sight of Howry was his wave as the handlers guided her dogs into position.

A large, prismatic crowd gathered along the barriers on either side of the trail, many calling her name and holding signs of encouragement. Her dogs, sixteen strong, were just as lively. Jonah, her wild man, hardly touched the ground as he reared up off all four paws. Even Bonaparte, regal snout in the air, wagged his tail and trotted with a swagger at all the attention.

Lainey watched the two teams in front of her take off, each time feeling an impatience to get out on the trail as she was forced to wait. Her team echoed her sentiment, voicing their disapproval with yips and howls. Then she heard her name and number and was ushered into position. When the announcer called "Go!" she didn't command the dogs. Trace and Sholo shot down the chute, glad to be free as they raced away.

Once beyond the designated chute, Lainey pulled onto a snow-covered highway. Her dogs sped along, the way smooth and easy. She knew they wouldn't keep this pace, but it would hold her competition at bay for the moment. She half expected Scotch to catch and pass her before the day was through. Along the way, Iditarod fans idled beside the trail. Several had fires or grills going, and Lainey smelled burgers and steaks cooking as she rushed past. She had never thought to see hard-core enthusiasts sitting on the side of a road in plastic lawn chairs, ten-foot snowdrifts as backdrop to the surreal scene. Several called to her, and she waved. It reminded her of parades she had seen in bigger cities, where the locals camped out on the sidewalks the night before to ensure a decent view of passing floats.

Up ahead, the road lifted. A yellow railroad sign stood on the crest. A few volunteers loitered about the tracks with shovels, ready to pack snow between the rails should a train cut through the race. She grinned at the oddity. The crowd didn't thin as the miles went by. Her team slowed to a more normal pace, and she relaxed into the familiar sensation of mushing. She watched the dogs run, checking them for odd gaits that would indicate potential injury. Doing so was second nature these days. None of the dogs nursed a shoulder or paw. As it neared noon, the day warmed. With some care, she pulled her parka off, leaning over the handles to tuck it into the sled bag. She wore bib overall snow pants and several layers of shirts and sweaters, more than enough to keep her comfortable.

"Passing!"

Lainey craned her neck to see a team coming up behind her. As much as it galled her, she didn't attempt to increase speed. The term "race" was a misnomer. The Iditarod was an endurance test more than anything. If she pushed her team to their limits now, they would scratch halfway through the course. "Whoa," she said, as the musher began to overtake her. "Trace, Sholo, gee. Whoa."

The dogs pulled to the side of the road and she set her snow hook. Now was as good a time as any to snack them. Her three trash talkers cussed out the passing team, but they remained in place rather than take chase. She grabbed a bag of frozen fish from her bag and went up the line, encouraging and praising each dog as she fed them. They reciprocated with licks and wags, letting her know they were ready for anything.

"Looking good!" A man sat in an old rocking chair a few feet away, nursing a cup of coffee. His family sat around him in beach chairs, echoing his sentiment, though none came forward to interfere.

"Thanks." Lainey smiled. Another team passed her as she double checked the gang line on her way back to the sled, and Chibee barked at them, shaking himself indignantly as they went on. She gave him a good scratching and finished her quick inspection.

The man raised his travel cup in salute. "To Nome or bust!"

Lainey laughed, stepping onto the runners and retrieving her snow hook. "To Nome." To the dogs she called, "Ready? Let's go!"

It wasn't long before she reached Knik. A couple thousand fans surrounded the frozen lake. Barbecues and icy picnics seemed the order of the day, and voices rose in welcome as her team closed in on the checkpoint. The exuberant nature of the crowd reminded her of tailgate parties at the Super Bowl. She directed the team to the official checkpoint, where she stopped. Her time in was noted, and she opened her sled bag to show her mandatory items.

"How long you staying?"

Lainey saw Howry and Strauss waving at her from near the checkers' station. "Just long enough to swap sleds."

"Remember to check out when you go."

"I will." Lainey trotted to the front of the line and led her leaders toward her friends, not trusting them to respond to voice commands with so much excitement in the atmosphere.

Howry waved her ahead, and she saw her sled waiting to one side. Strauss had a camera about his neck and waggled it at her. "Since Don's covering Scotch, I figured I'd help you with your article."

She grinned, stopping the dogs in front of her replacement sled. "Good! I expect I'll get some photos once things settle down, but right now it's just too hectic." Lainey walked up the line. At the sled, she disconnected the gang line and shock cord, transferring her team to the new sled. With swift motions, she moved her gear over and verified that everything she needed for the next fifty plus miles was in place. She removed her racing bib, packing it in with the promotional package she carried. She wouldn't need to wear it again until she left the second-to-last checkpoint heading for Nome.

The trail left civilization from here. In preparation, she stuffed dog booties in her pockets and went back up the line. She thoroughly examined each dog, checking paws for damage and replacing lost booties on each. Each received a moose liver treat as reward.

"Time to go."

"Good luck," Howry said, and Ben nodded.

Lainey waved and hopped onto the sled runners. Pulling the snow hook, she paused only long enough to officially check out of Knik, having been there for twelve minutes.

The trail climbed into a forested area, and trees soon hid the festivities at the lake. She felt her tension ease at the solitude, only now becoming aware of how edgy the crowds had made her. She laughed aloud, the dogs' ears flicking back to listen to her. Of course she had been worried. *Nothing like the rookie eating snow on the national news, huh?* She had already blown off the trail the day before, something probably noted on every website covering the race. She hoped her team would vindicate themselves from that little wrong turn by keeping to the trail for the next thousand miles.

Winding through trees, dropping onto frozen marshland and ponds, it was smooth sailing. Several teams passed, but she consoled herself with the possibility that they would burn themselves out. She would see them again when they ate her powder. Her dogs badmouthed the passing teams, receiving like sentiments from their competition. She dropped down onto the Susitna River. Here she saw the occasional marks of dog teams that had pulled aside. Taking their cue, she did the same. As soon as they stopped, her dogs enjoyed a brisk roll in the snow, snapping up mouthfuls to cool themselves down.

"Snack time, guys." She shook the bag of fish. "We'll have supper in a couple of hours." She made a cursory inspection as she went, talking to the dogs. They eagerly showed their appreciation for the break and for her kind words. Many had lost their booties on the trail, and she replaced those that needed them.

The sun lowered on the horizon. Lainey took the opportunity to get out her headlamp. She checked the batteries and bulb before fitting it over her musher cap, then made certain extra batteries were handy. It was starting to cool down as well, so she put her parka back on. As they proceeded, she took the opportunity to have a snack break of her own. She pulled a small thermos of Gatorade from her personal bag, eagerly downing the lukewarm contents. Trail mix and Scotch's special recipe pemmican filled her stomach. The food disappeared quickly. She hadn't realized how hungry she was, despite the awareness that she had been on the sled through lunch.

They wove along the trail—first on the river, then climbing into forest, dropping along a swamp, and back to the river. Three more mushers passed before the trail got too narrow to allow the action. Breaking through the trees, she saw the upcoming checkpoint. Her dogs picked up their pace as they neared, and she slid into Yentna laughing.

"Four fifty-eight p.m." The checker handed her the clipboard.

Lainey signed in, noting she had fallen to eleventh place. "Any news on Scotch Fuller?"

"Not on me. You'll have to check up at the tent. How long you staying?"

"Six hours." She leaned over her handlebars to open the sled bag for the gear check.

"Everything's good." He initialed next to her signature. "Head on over there. The vets need to do their check."

Lainey urged her dogs toward the tent. A woman waved her toward a pair of veterinarians waiting for her. One watched the team with a critical eye as they came to a halt.

"How're they doing?"

"Great! I haven't noticed any limps or problems. They've mostly been wearing booties through new snow." She handed him her vet book, a small notebook with all the paperwork on each dog.

"Good." The two proceeded to give each of her dogs an exam, prodding wrists and shoulders, removing booties to check paws.

"Everything checks out." The second veterinarian wrote something in her notebook and handed it back. "If you're staying, park over there. We've got straw, but you'll have to get water from a hole in the river."

"Thanks."

Lainey spent the next half hour doing a full inspection of her dogs, bedding them down in straw and covering a couple of them with blankets. As soon as they were resting, she retrieved a flimsy child's sled from her bag and went to the river to get water. The jagged hole revealed chucks of ice floating in the water below. Lainey carefully used the bucket dangling from a tripod over the opening to fill her pots. She had no concern about falling through the ice as the sides indicated a good two feet of thickness beneath the foot of snow on the river. She didn't want to splash herself, however, and took extra care to keep dry.

She lugged the water back to her dogs, her method of transport receiving an envious look from a fellow rookie from Minnesota who carried his pots by hand. She gave a silent thanks to Scotch and her detailed notebook, a carbon copy of which nestled in Lainey's coverall pocket. Lainey had the benefit of experience to rely upon.

Back at the sled, she set up her two cookers and started water boiling. Some mushers only carried one, not wanting the extra weight, but Scotch was of the opinion that weight ultimately counted for nothing if you weren't able to care for your dogs. By using two cookers, Lainey cut her cooking time in half and would be able to eat with her dogs and get through her checkpoint chores faster, thereby allowing her more time to rest. The dogs were the athletes, the ones coddled through the race. The mushers, on the other hand, rarely slept more than a couple of hours in a day as they worked to keep their teams happy and healthy.

She dumped a measure of meat and fat into one pot and tossed a boil bag of meatloaf and fried potatoes in the other. While she waited for the food, she dug out her notebook and skimmed through the information. According to Scotch's notes, Lainey was a bit slower than Scotch's previous runs to Yentna. That was to be expected since Lainey's team was officially second string. Since Scotch maintained a professional racing team, she had kept the kennel's better dogs for her string. Lainey noted the travel time between Yentna and Finger Lake, her next scheduled downtime, committing it to memory before turning pages. A shiver crawled up her spine as she saw the words "HEAVY MOOSE POPULATION" in capital letters. She didn't want a repeat of what had happened in November. She couldn't help a quick glance at her personal bag, almost seeing the holstered .44 through the nylon material. Swallowing hard, she returned to the notebook and read up on what to expect on the trail.

When dinner had finished heating, she added dry chow to the mixture and went up the line, dropping plastic Frisbees as food dishes. Her team roused from their nap to lap up the offering. Lainey returned to the cookers, plucked her dinner from the second pot and added the boiling water to the leftovers in the dog pot. She gave the dogs a meaty watering, talking to them and treating each to rough affection as she went.

With a sigh, she found clean snow nearby, not wanting to trek all the way back to the hole in the river. She piled it onto her small sled and started another pot of water for the dogs. Only then did she sit in the bed of her sled and eat her food, washing it down with the last of her Gatorade.

Lainey checked her watch. It had been an hour since her arrival. Scotch would be there soon. As much as Lainey wanted to enjoy a nap like her team, she still had things to do. Pleasantly full and warm from her meal, she forced herself to her feet and retrieved the now empty dog dishes. Another bag of meat and a quarter pound of fat went into dog cooker, and she started an additional pot of water on the second. When both were ready, she took the finished products and poured them into two coolers on the sled. To one she added the dry chow and vitamin supplements, a meal ready for a pit stop on the road. In the other, she deposited five of her juice packets, now frozen from the cold. When she got out on the trail, they would be thawed enough for her to hydrate herself.

Chores finally finished, she debated where to sleep. Her dogs curled up together, still on their tug lines, though she had released the neck lines from their harnesses to make them comfortable. Taking a cue from them, she settled into her sled bag. Scotch would arrive soon. Lainey would just wait here for her to arrive.

She never knew exactly what time she fell asleep.

CHAPTER THIRTY-FOUR

Lainey grumbled as someone nudged her sled. She dragged herself to consciousness and peered into the dark. Scotch grinned down at her. Still groggy, Lainey returned the smile and forced herself to sit up. After a wide yawn, she looked around the cordoned off area. "What time is it? When did you get in?"

"I got here about six fifteen. It's almost ten o'clock now." Scotch squatted in the snow beside her. "I saw your time in when I got here. You're due to leave in an hour or so, aren't you?"

Lainey rubbed the sleep from her eyes, amazed she'd been out of it for so long considering the cold weather. "Yes, coach." She threw her legs over the edge of the sled. "I've got to get more water."

"So do I." Scotch stood and took Lainey's hand, helping her rise. "I'll go with you."

Upending the child's sled to knock the snow from it, Lainey grabbed her pots and walked with Scotch. They stopped at Scotch's team so she could grab the same gear before trudging toward the river. Now fully awake, Lainey looked around the checkpoint. A lot of mushers had decided to take a rest break there. Not everyone, however. She speculated about who had left early. Were they driving their dogs harder than she? Or was it just the forerunners, those who had arrived before her, that had left?

"So, how'd it go?"

"Not bad. I can't keep Heldig in booties. I don't know what she does, but they fly off as soon as we're on the trail." She grinned at Scotch's laughter.

"That's nothing new. Just make certain to keep ointment on her paws."

"I will." Lainey took Scotch's hand and pulled her closer until they bumped up against one another as they walked. "I've missed you."

Scotch squeezed her hand. "I've missed you too." She craned her neck around, checking for witnesses before giving Lainey a quick kiss.

They continued to the river and Scotch drew water, waiting for Lainey while she did the same. As they made the return trip, Lainey asked, "How did your trip go?"

"Not bad. Ran into a mama moose about ten miles from here, but she was more concerned for her safety than into challenging the dogs."

Lainey grimaced. "I'm glad you didn't have trouble with her."

"Me too. I certainly don't want to run into an incident like Susan Butcher's." Scotch was referring to the 1985 race when a musher had to scratch early because an enraged moose had attacked her team. At the time, she had been considered a possible winner for that year's race. As it was, another woman had won instead—Libby Riddles, the first woman to win the Iditarod.

"No one does."

Back at the musher area, Scotch stopped at her team. "This is where I get off."

"Oh, I think you'll be getting off somewhere else. In Nome, if things go as planned." Lainey chuckled at Scotch's blush. "I'll see you on the other side of Finger Lake?"

"Yup. Three miles past. I'll be there."

Unable to help herself, Lainey gave Scotch a long hug, not caring whether anyone saw them. Scotch returned the embrace. Lainey reluctantly took her pots of water down to her sled.

Once more she set water to boil. Another meal for her and another for her team soon bubbled away. Her dogs slept on, trained to take rest when they could get it. She watched them fondly.

When the dog stew was ready, she distributed their plates, gently waking each animal with words and caresses. She dished up the chow from the cooler and then refilled the cooler with the fresh batch. Lastly, she made two trips, using the lukewarm water from her cooler to water the dogs. She ate her midnight snack—chicken and rice with broccoli and carrots—and used some of the freshly boiled water to brew instant coffee in her thermos. The rest of the water she put into her cooler with the juice packs.

Her team fed and frisky—a good sign—Lainey donned a pair of surgical gloves with hand warmers nestled in her palms to help her brave the frigid weather. She applied ointment to dog paws, all sixty-four of them, massaging the pads and wrists, checking for cuts and abrasions, looking for soreness in shoulders and hips. She saw no indication of injury. Satisfied, she nodded to herself.

Sleeping in the cold had stiffened her, and she winced when she stood upright. Strauss had given her the parka at the mushers' banquet and that had given her plenty of time before the race began to adapt it for a hand warmer. She removed her surgical gloves and stuffed one into the pocket next to her sore ribs. She collected the dog dishes, packing everything into her sled or into a trash bag. Scooping the inevitable doggie doo into her trash bag, she packed up the remainder of her belongings and found a place to dispose of the garbage, taking a quick side trip to take care of her own call of nature. She sorted through her snacks and refilled her personal bag on the handlebars. All preparations completed, she dug a watch out of her pocket and noted the time. Her six hours were nearly up. It was time to get back on the trail.

Lainey made another pass down her team, putting booties on all the dogs, even Heldig the Notoriously Barefooted. The traditional husky licked her face, grinning at her as if to say, "Why bother?"

She gave the dog a hug. "Try, Heldig. Keep them on for half an hour, that's all I ask."

She climbed aboard the runners and gave the team their commands in a quiet voice, so as not to disturb the other mushers drowsing nearby. As they passed Scotch's position, she waved, and Scotch blew a kiss in her direction. Wearing a silly grin, Lainey arrived at the checkpoint.

"You're out of here then?"

"Yep. Lainey Hughes. I came in eleventh."

The checker, a bleary-eyed older woman, located her name and time in. "Okay. You're out at…exactly eleven p.m."

"When was the last departure?"

She scanned the times listed. "Looks like Dave Creavey blew through the checkpoint three hours ago."

"Thanks." To her dogs, Lainey called softly, "Ready? Let's go."

As they headed away from the checkpoint, darkness enveloped them. Lainey switched on her headlamp. Her team ran easily, the respite having done them good. Eerie silence shrouded them as they traveled; only the sounds of the sled swishing through snow and her dogs panting kept Lainey company. Overhead, scattered clouds blotted out the vivid stars that she had grown accustomed to seeing out in the bush.

A trail marker came into view ahead, and she ordered the dogs to the left to follow it. They climbed into a spruce forest, the path wide and smooth. Despite the apparent ease of the trail, Lainey kept her attention on the trees they passed, not wanting a branch to sweep her off the sled. The dogs were refreshed and lively. If she fell off, they could very well make it to the next checkpoint without her. She didn't relish a thirty-mile hike to Skwentna.

Lainey made the extra effort to get off the sled and run up the low hills. She needed the exercise to remain awake, and it eased the load for her team when they didn't have to pull her weight as well as that of the sled. Then they slid back down to the river, an easy run. It seemed no time had passed before she saw lights ahead. The Skwentna checkpoint loomed in the dark. She directed her team toward the welcome lights. After the obligatory sled and vet checks, she guided her team to the food drops. They would have to carry everything they needed for the next seventy-five miles, through Finger Lake checkpoint and on to Rainy Pass. Between Finger Lake and Rainy Pass, there was the treacherous Happy River Valley to traverse. She needed to be prepared to repair damage to the sled and have extra food and gear on hand for the team.

She found her three bags, color-coded and with her name on them. Lugging them from the storage area and onto the sled, she urged her team a little farther away. As soon as they stopped, she went down the line with a bag of whitefish.

With the dogs occupied with their treats, she returned to the bags and cut them open with her Leatherman. She took a quick inventory, carefully referring to her notes and confirming everything was present and in good shape. Comparing the amounts Scotch had suggested with what she still had, Lainey transferred gear and food into her sled. Noting she had extra dog food, she flagged down a passing volunteer. She would drop the extra at the checkpoint's donation pile for other mushers who might be in need due to accidents, poor planning or undelivered drops. If no one used her leftovers, they would be donated to locals.

Content, she returned to the checkpoint and signed out. Twenty-two minutes. Not as good as Scotch's time, but not bad for a rookie. Her notes warned for vigilance as she left Skwentna. It didn't take Lainey long to see why. The area had a heavy population of dog mushers, and dozens of trails crossed hers. Fortunately, once she got onto the river, the maze of befuddling paths disappeared and the team traveled easily, eating up the miles.

Lainey yawned. "Not good." The long, boring river went on forever. Forty miles from the checkpoint, the trail was supposed to head into the hills through spruce and alder trees. She would need to keep awake or risk passing the next change of trail. Opening her thermos, she drank straight from the ingenious pop top rather than attempting to pour a cup. The bitter taste of the hot instant coffee caused her eyes to widen. "Whoo! That ought to do it!" Her dogs continued gamely on, ears twitching backward. She capped the thermos and put it away, imagining the caffeine coursing through her bloodstream.

Overhead the clouds thickened. As the team glided effortlessly over the river, a gentle snow began to fall. Snowflakes hit the brilliant light of her headlamp, the speed of the dogs making the flurry seem stronger than it actually was. The sight distracted her, and she turned the lamp off to keep from flinching as the spicules darted toward her face. When her eyes adjusted, she realized how truly light it seemed with all the whiteness surrounding her. The snow reassumed a non-threatening appearance, her only indication of its existence the chill spots of flakes as they hit her nose and cheeks. As the snowfall failed to become heavier, Lainey realized that her fear of a blizzard was baseless. Besides, someone would have warned her at the last checkpoint if the weather were going to turn horrendously bad.

She stopped once on the river to snack the dogs, quickly going over their feet and replacing booties before setting off again. Too many interruptions for too long a time could disrupt their run/rest schedule. While some delays were to be expected, the closer Lainey could keep them to their planned agenda, the better. As they ran, she finished her coffee and ate a slice of banana bread she had put into an interior pocket to thaw with her body heat.

Thinking she saw a trail marker ahead, Lainey turned her headlamp on again. There it was—the trail leading into the hills. The snow continued its slow, relentless fall. She wondered how long it had been falling in this area.

"Sholo, Trace, haw."

Her leaders took the trail up off the river and into trees. They slowed a bit as they began the incline. Lainey had been hours standing on the runners. She could see why some mushers had attached folding stools to their sleds. They, at least, would be more comfortable through the race. She decided to get off the runners for a little exercise.

Lainey sank to her ankles in the powder. Up ahead, the well-marked trail gave the appearance of being solid. As she trotted behind the sled, she realized her error. It must have been snowing in this area for some time, leaving close to a foot of snow on the ground. It was no wonder her team had slowed. They continued forward, moving steadily upward. As they did, the unpacked snow grew deeper until Sholo and Trace walked more often than they ran. Lainey cursed and called a halt, making sure to anchor the sled so it wouldn't slide back the way they had come. There was nowhere to get off the trail here, so she knew she couldn't take a long break. She had no idea when the musher behind her had left the last checkpoint. For all she knew, he or she was right on her tail. It wasn't time to snack the dogs, but she decided to do so anyway. They needed the extra energy and encouragement to make it the next few miles to Finger Lake.

At her sled, she donned snowshoes before going up the gang line with treats. Each dog received lavish attention and thanks before she made it to her leaders. Sholo appeared a bit cowed. He had never been on the Iditarod and didn't know what to expect. His experiences were with the mid-range races. Lainey gave him lots of cuddles, wondering whether she should swap him out. Montana, whose experience was the same as Sholo's, appeared eager and willing.

"I think you need a break, boy. You've done a great job. Good dog, good boy." She gave him an extra piece of fish and detached him from the gang line. "What do you say, huh? Give you a break?" Lainey pulled Sholo back one spot. After a few moments, she led Montana to the front. She gave Sholo another affectionate rub so he knew his displacement hadn't been because of something he had done. She wasn't sure whether the dogs understood that sort of thing. *But if they do…*

She tromped back to her sled but didn't climb onto the runners. Popping the snow hook, she ordered the dogs forward. The new blood at the front of the line sped things up a bit, but they still were moving at a slow walk. Calling encouragement, Lainey passed the dogs until she reached the front. There she grabbed the line and began breaking trail herself. It was arduous work, and she had to stop and remove her parka or risk sweating too profusely. Sweat-soaked clothing rapidly froze in these temperatures, creating a constant threat of hypothermia. Shedding extra clothes had been drilled into her by the Fullers, the entire concept at odds with her tropical experience.

On they went, inching along it seemed. Eventually they broke through the trees and Lainey was looking out onto a frozen lake. The snow had stopped falling, but it still remained deep and loose.

"Passing."

Startled, Lainey looked around to see a headlamp shining about a hundred feet away. Her team, tired from their exertions, hardly made a fuss as she directed them to one side now that the trail had widened. When there was room, the musher moved past, his dogs a bit more alert than hers. She wondered how long he had been back there benefiting from her struggles and couldn't help the slight resentment she felt.

The musher passed and then pulled to a stop just in front of her team. He stepped off his sled and walked back toward her. She recognized him: Drew Owens, a veteran who had finished the Iditarod four times.

"How you doing?"

"Not bad. Tired."

"Yeah. The trail here can be pretty bad some days. Since you broke the trail coming through there, I thought I'd do the same for you across the lake to the checkpoint. It's only fair."

Surprise tinged her exhaustion. "That sounds great. Thanks."

He grinned, his frosted beard crackling. "You're welcome."

While he made his preparations to break trail, she took the opportunity to treat her dogs. Heldig's bare paws had developed little balls of snow and ice under the toes. Lainey carefully cleaned those off before applying ointment and another set of booties.

"Yo! Why are you blocking the trail?"

Lainey stood to see the irritated newcomer pulling up beside her. "We have to break trail to Finger Lake. Drew's going to take the lead."

The disgruntled musher appeared momentarily nonplused before shrugging her shoulders. "Oh. I guess coming up behind you I didn't realize how bad it was."

"It was bad." Lainey packed up her things. Although there would be two mushers breaking trail, she returned to the head of her team. The snow would still be loose. If necessary, she would walk the rest of the way to the next checkpoint. Ahead of her, Owens began the trek toward the lights visible in the distance, followed by the recent arrival. Lainey pulled her dogs back onto the trail.

CHAPTER THIRTY-FIVE

The going was fair. Snow hadn't fallen so thickly here, a mixed blessing considering what she had gone through in the hills. Scotch could only imagine what it had been like for Lainey. At least riding in the middle of the pack had some benefits—like not having to break major trails in the beginning.

The lights grew brighter. Scotch grinned as she recognized the massive bonfire party near Shell Lake Lodge. Every time she came through here, the reality exceeded anything she believed possible. The noise carrying across frozen Finger Lake sounded like the shindig was in full swing. Despite enjoying the silence and solitude of the wilderness, her heart welcomed the sight and sound of the celebrants. The partygoers had been at it since the first musher arrived, and now it was six or seven in the morning.

Someone spotted her approaching headlamp on the lake, and a cheer rang through the wee hours. Checkers and volunteers spilled out of a tent, and several of the well-wishers moved closer as Scotch mounted the embankment leading to the checkpoint.

"Six forty-three a.m." The checker marked his board. "Number thirty-seven. Staying?"

"No. Blowing through."

"Got it." He waved the vet volunteers forward while Scotch produced her dogs' medical notes. After a thorough check, she was released.

"Scotch!"

She looked up in time to have a photo taken. Blinking against the flash, she barely made out Howry grinning apologetically.

He trotted forward. "How's it going?"

"Great. Pretty easy trail through the hills outside Skwentna." She glanced over her team, all the dogs looking over their shoulders at her. "I've got to get going. I'm supposed to meet Lainey three miles out. If I stay much longer, these guys are going to expect to be fed here, and when they're not, they may riot."

"She's about an hour ahead of you, maybe less. She's got a good team, according to Ben."

Scotch briefly wondered how Strauss would know, since he hadn't been a fan of the Iditarod before the magazine became involved with it. "Where is Ben?" She looked over his shoulder at the revelers.

"Snoozing. He stayed up all night waiting for Lainey to get here."

"Tell him hi. I've got to get going."

Howry stepped back. "We're flying to Nikolai."

"I'm taking a sixer in Nikolai." She referred to a six-hour rest break. "I'll see you there." Scotch officially checked out, leaving the party at Finger Lake behind. Small bush planes outfitted with skis peppered one side of the airstrip, testament to how everyone but the mushers had arrived. The party atmosphere combined with the comings and goings of reporters and race fans made rest there impossible. The trail out of Finger Lake wound along as it followed Skwentna River. The next leg would make or break her team.

They were well out of sight and sound of the party, when she saw the brilliant yellow sled bag ahead. Her heart leapt into her throat, and she pulled off the trail behind Lainey.

"Hey, you're early."

Scotch set her snow hook and wrapped Lainey in an embrace. "Had to catch up to you. I needed a hug."

Lainey returned the squeeze. "Always glad to oblige."

Eyes closed, she sighed, enjoying the closeness. Sometime over the next couple of days, she would pass Lainey's position. For now, Scotch welcomed what intimacy she could get. "I'd better snack these guys," Scotch murmured into Lainey's hair, not wanting to release her.

Turning in Scotch's arms, Lainey looked at the expectant team. "Yeah, you'd better." She chuckled and forced herself away.

They spent the next half hour discussing the trail that was behind them. Scotch gave her dogs a quick snack as she removed booties, rubbed ointment into paws and did the rest of her chores. She fired up the cookers, using melted snow to prepare the next meal. She fed the team from their cooler and used her cooler for their second watering. Ben had been awake for Lainey's arrival and had sent greetings to Scotch. He had told Lainey that several reporters wanted to interview her in Nikolai.

"I'm supposed to do the interviews, not be the interviews."

"That's the price you pay for fame." Scotch ducked a snowball thrown in her direction. "Ah, ah, ah, none of that. We need to conserve our energy for Rainy Pass."

Lainey saluted. "Yes, ma'am."

With no straw available, Scotch dug into her sled bag and produced blankets for her dogs. By the time she collected their plates, they were snuggled into their blankets and drifting to sleep. Scotch yawned, a wave of drowsiness flowing over her, but she forced herself back to her chores. By the time she finished eating her breakfast—two slices of pizza, wrapped in tin foil and heated on the lid of her cook pot—another dog meal was stored in their cooler. She drained two juice packs to rehydrate and then dropped frozen bottles of Gatorade into her cooler. Looking over at Lainey, she caught her nodding off. "Best get some sleep while you can. You'll need it."

"I know." Lainey stood with her and gave her another hug. "I'm glad you're out here with me."

Scotch smiled, soaking in the simple sensation. "Ditto that."

* * *

Lainey heard an irritating beeping in the silence. She forced herself awake to shut off the damned watch alarm. At some point, daylight had arrived. She dragged herself into it with a lurch. Muscles and joints creaked in protest, and she quickly donned her gloves and boots to retain her sleep warmth. Her bladder demanded release, annoying in its urgency. She grabbed a roll of toilet paper and trudged away from the trail and sleds for a bit of privacy. Baring her butt to the cold woke her completely. She grumped in complaint, wondering if any woman had ever tried to use a catheter during the race. She wasn't sure the discomfort would outweigh the sharp bite of frost on her ass.

Her private call answered, she returned to the sled, pausing a moment to see Scotch's knit cap poking out the top of her sleeping bag. A fond smile curved her lips, her mind's eye supplying the vision of Scotch in her sleep shorts last summer, thighs and belly bare to her searching gaze. The thought of arriving in Nome to finally surrender to Scotch's touch caused her chest to ache and her blood to rush to points south.

Lainey shook herself as a team appeared from around a bend in the path. She waved as the musher passed, hearing only the gentle tinkle of gear and the panting of dogs as they slid along. It was time to get things together.

Since she and Scotch planned to go through the pass at the same time, she had another hour before waking her dogs. Lainey would extend her time-out to allow them to travel together for the worst of the next thirty miles. She returned to her sled and began the process of packing up the gear she wouldn't need for the rest of the break.

Eventually another watch beeped in command. Lainey smiled when she heard the muttered curses from the sled behind her. It was good to know she wasn't the only one beginning to tire on the second day of the race. She started the cookers in considerably better humor as Scotch stumbled away to heed nature's call. By the time she returned, coffee brewed in Lainey's thermos and she had begun to wake her dogs.

They worked independently, their silence punctuated by praise voiced to their teams and the occasional bark or snort from a dog. When another team passed by, half of Lainey's dogs gave voice, not just her usual trash talkers, all seemingly eager to get back on the trail. Scotch's team echoed the sentiment.

Once they were both prepared, Scotch approached Lainey. Her eyes were a bit bloodshot, but she looked as enthusiastic as the dogs. "You about ready?"

"Yep." Lainey closed her sled bag. "You?"

"As ever."

Lainey wiggled her eyebrows suggestively. "I've heard that about you."

She feigned indignation. "Who's been talking?"

"Your dogs."

Scotch laughed. "Well, at least I'm not the only one."

Lainey grimaced as she looked down her gang line. "Traitors."

Returning to business, Scotch said, "All right. You remember what was said at the mushers' meeting about Rainy Pass?"

"Steep descent, two switchbacks."

"Yeah. There'll be no stopping until you get to the bottom, so hang on tight. Pay close attention to trail markers so you don't miss the switchbacks."

Lainey felt a shiver of dread. Once she got through the next day or so, the rest of the race would become a cakewalk. She wondered whether her dogs were rested enough. The potential for injury during this next leg would double with tired dogs. Scotch was still speaking and Lainey forced herself back to the lecture.

"...switchbacks back home, only a steeper incline. Half of your team has already been through here; the others are at least used to the sudden turns. Remember to stand on one runner or the other to distribute the weight on the turns." Scotch broke off with a smile. "And don't worry. You've got a great team, and you're a great musher. I'll wait at the bottom for you."

Spirits somewhat buoyed, Lainey squared her shoulders. "Just get off of the trail when you do, okay?"

Scotch chuckled as she stepped forward for another hug. "For luck."

Lainey held her tight, suddenly wondering whether she had made a mistake in going into this sled dog race. *Can't change anything now.*

"Nome or bust."

Scotch's confidence seeped through her trepidation. They had a date in Nome, and Lainey intended to get there under her own steam rather than in a plane. "Nome or bust."

* * *

The trail twisted back and forth upon itself as it climbed. Despite heavy snows in the area and many mushers having gone before them, the path was rough, with tree roots and beaver dams threatening to upset the sleds. Crowded by timber and brush, Lainey ducked a number of times to avoid sweepers. Yellow caution tape fluttered everywhere, flagging various dangers. Regardless of the racing committee's attempt to carve a decent trail through the mess, Lainey's sled bucked and rattled as it went, the unpleasant vibrations causing her palms to tingle.

Her team held good speed as they followed Scotch's sled up and up and up. They broke through the trees for a bit, following a five-thousand-foot ridge. Lainey stared in awe at the spectacular wilderness scene until forest blocked her view. She forced her attention back to the trail. No time to gawk, not if she wanted to get through this leg of the journey in one piece. Up ahead, Scotch stopped her dogs, raising her hand to signal Lainey to do the same. Swallowing hard, Lainey called her team to a halt. Her eyes widened when a stranger appeared out of the trees to talk to Scotch. *Who the hell is that?* They were ten miles from Finger Lake, and the man's jacket looked too new and pristine for him to be a musher.

Scotch spoke a few words with him and shook his hand. He bowed a couple of times as they talked. She tied off her snub line and walked back down the trail toward Lainey as the man went back into the trees.

"Who was that?"

"A Japanese reporter. Said his name was Tatsuya something. A few of his colleagues on the other side of the canyon are filming mushers as they go down this side."

"Fantastic." Lainey couldn't hide the sarcastic tone. "So, when I roll down the canyon, everyone in Japan will have a laugh on 'Japan's Funniest Videos.'"

Scotch smiled. "You won't roll. He said there've been a couple of close calls, but the cliff edges are well marked. You ready?"

Not liking the thought of cliff edges, Lainey nevertheless nodded. "Yeah. Let's get this over with before I faint."

"You'll be fine." Scotch squeezed her shoulder, her eyes staring intently into Lainey's. "We're going to fly down that canyon and hit the bottom in less than three minutes. You won't have time to be scared."

Lainey blew out a breath. "Let's do it."

Scotch stared a moment longer, gauging Lainey's emotions. Lainey raised her chin and leveled a calm gaze back at her. Scotch smiled and released her, then returned to her team.

When Scotch turned, Lainey tried not to hyperventilate. She gnawed her lower lip, nervously eyeing the dogs. They appeared oblivious of their mistress' anguish, tails wagging as they awaited their commands. Lainey reached down and prepared to pull her snow hook, knowing she had to stow it securely. If the trail down was as rough as the trail up, she didn't need a sharp pointed instrument bouncing around in her vicinity.

Up ahead, Scotch released her snub line and hook. Lainey clearly heard her voice as she ordered the dogs forward. They traveled no more than thirty feet before disappearing over the ridge.

Hands shaking, Lainey pulled out her watch, wanting to give Scotch a full minute head start. When the second hand clicked past the point of no return, she forced herself to release the snow hook. "Ready.

Let's go!" she called with more bravado than she thought possible. Sholo and Trace surged forward.

When they reached the place where Scotch had vanished, the dogs dropped down onto the trail. Lainey's stomach swooped with the sudden altitude change, and she grasped her handlebars with a death grip. Her team ran full tilt, Jonah and Samson looking more like woolly bears attempting to evade the sled than pulling wheel dogs. Lainey's feet left the runners, at first standing on the drag mat between them. When that didn't slow the sled enough, she stomped on the brake bar, the metal digging ruts into the trail. The sled no longer threatened to overrun her team but still rushed down the trail.

Yellow caution tape looked like a spider web, though she hardly registered it as she flew along. Ahead of her it looked as if the trail simply stopped, a makeshift fence of logs and tape pretending to be a dead end. Lainey's mind was numb, her eyes wide as they careened toward the barrier.

"Haw!" she bellowed, and her leaders took the first switchback.

Standing on the brakes seemed to help. At least her first wheel dogs didn't appear to be in imminent danger of being crushed. It didn't slow her enough. She screwed her eyes almost closed as she approached the jerry-rigged barrier at breakneck speed. At the proper moment, she leapt to her left runner, pulling with all her might to compensate for the whiplash effect. Then she was on the next section of trail. She felt a fleeting moment of relief before jumping back onto the brake bar. Fifty yards ahead, another dead end appeared. This one seemed a little less dangerous if the sparser amount of caution tape was any indication. Lainey knew from her notes that the cliff on the other side was still a fifty-foot drop. Her leaders arrived at the turn.

"Gee!"

They took the turn with smooth precision, and she felt a burble of pleasure at their elegance before preparing for her part. She hopped onto the right runner and pulled. The sled tipped left, despite her counterbalance, and she felt a moment of sheer terror as the runner on which she stood lifted off the trail. The sled thumped back to the ground. Heart in her throat, she swore a blue streak for the next fifty yards. The last bend came and she ordered the turn, easily negotiating it until she came onto a somewhat level surface.

"Whoa!" She saw Scotch ahead, waiting for her as promised. As soon as her dogs came to a halt, Lainey gratefully set the snow hook. She took two steps away from her sled, knees trembling from exertion and adrenaline, and flopped into a snowbank.

Scotch laughed and whooped. She trotted up to Lainey and grabbed her hands, pulling her back to her feet. "You did it! I told you!"

Lainey's fear faded, replaced by a flush of pride and exhilaration as Scotch hugged her. "I almost lost it on the second turn." She looked back up the side of the canyon, awed by the height she'd just traversed at breakneck speeds. "My runner left the trail completely. I thought for sure I was going to tip over."

Cuffing Lainey's shoulder, Scotch released her. "You didn't balance the load when you packed it, did you?"

No matter how hard she tried, Lainey couldn't feel chagrin at her mistake. She had taken on the Happy River descent and survived. She gave Scotch a cheeky grin. "I thought I did. But it's a lesson learned!"

"Yeah. I'll bet." Scotch stepped back. "Let's snack the dogs and get out of here. Someone could be right behind us, and there's no room to get off the trail until Puntilla Lake."

"Yes, coach."

The dogs were still rested from their six-hour break. As Lainey fed them moose liver, they frisked in the snow, picking up her excitement as she showered them with praise. She paused only long enough to get out her camera and snap some pictures of the canyon wall. They left, following the Yentna River. The river hadn't frozen solid here. Lainey saw standing water on the ice and running water through occasional gaps. She wondered if anyone had fallen through but saw no sled tracks near the holes. She supposed it happened sometimes, though so far not today. She shivered in sympathy for anyone suffering such a fate.

The trail began to climb, the hill to her right steepening until they traversed a narrow ridge. Ahead she saw Scotch leaning on her right runner as they went around a corner, and she followed suit. The path tilted down to Lainey's left, rising above open water on the river, and she compensated for the angle. Regardless, she felt a faint tremor of sideways movement. She called frantically to her team, "Let's go! Let's go!"

Her team put on a burst of speed, loping across what Lainey now realized was a twenty-foot ridge of ice. Before her sled could slide off the path, the dogs had her past the danger. For second time in an hour, she gripped her handlebars in an effort to remain standing. *Good God, what will the Farewell Burn be like?*

Lainey drew her focus back to the task at hand, assessing the trail's sharp incline. In reaction to the extreme climb, her team slowed. She forced her shaking legs from the runners. The exercise helped burn off the excess adrenaline. Soon her legs steadied as she pushed the sled up Happy Hill. It was with great relief that they reached the peak and came onto a level path. She breathed a sigh as the trail broke into a meadow for a short while. It seemed she had been going forever, but this trail between checkpoints was a mere thirty miles. Before Lainey could become complacent, she watched Scotch disappear into another steep descent. More caution signs met her gaze as she dipped down. The trail twisted back and forth, but nowhere as sharply as the switchbacks she had already traversed. She effortlessly held the sled on the sharp slope, her dogs running easily and heeding her commands as they went. At the bottom of the descent, she came out along Puntilla Lake. The wide expanse of level ground elated her. The worst of this leg completed, she had smooth sailing to Rainy Pass Lodge. To celebrate, Scotch pulled off the well-marked trail to snack her dogs.

When Lainey stopped, Scotch walked back to her, a wide grin on her face. "Take off your cap."

"What?" Lainey removed her musher's cap. "Why?"

"This is from Mom." Scotch held up a knit stocking hat of bright green. On it, a huge yellow smiley face wore its own musher's cap, the flaps dangling on either side. The words written beside the face proudly proclaimed "I Survived Happy River." Scotch pulled it down onto Lainey's head until it covered her ears.

Lainey laughed, dragging it off her head to get a better look. "That's priceless! Where did she get it?"

Scotch shrugged. "Don't know. But she wanted me to put it in my food drop so I could give it to you after you made it through."

She put the new hat back on and stuck her musher cap into her personal bag. "Thanks."

This time they snacked themselves as well as the dogs, filling up on trail mix, crackers and buttered pumpkin bread. Lainey finished the last of her now lukewarm coffee and then drank a thawed Gatorade. She grimaced as she watched Scotch eat a half stick of butter right from the package. "Yuck."

Scotch wrapped the second half in its paper. "Says you. At least I won't be freezing my butt off."

Lainey grimaced in answer. She heard noises and looked back at the trail behind them. "Sounds like somebody else is coming."

Standing, Scotch squinted up the hillside looking for the trail. "They're coming mighty fast. Wonder if it's a rookie."

In answer, a team of dogs burst through onto the level trail. It took a few moments for Lainey to realize that there was no musher standing on the sled. She rose, mouth open, not certain what she should do as the team swept toward their position.

"Whoa!" Scotch stepped out into the trail. "Whoa! Lainey! See if you can jump onto the sled as it passes."

Lainey dropped the detritus of her snacks onto her sled bag, adrenaline once again pumping through her system.

The new team heeded Scotch's command as they neared; they slowed down but didn't stop. Frisky and excited, they trotted toward Scotch, making the sled an easy target for Lainey to board. She ordered them to halt, firmly stepping onto the brake to further impede their progress. By the time Scotch got hold of the leaders' collars, they had come to a full stop and were rolling in the snow to cool off.

"Now what?"

Scotch looked around their immediate area. "Let's get them over there." She pointed at a stand of sturdy trees. "We can tie them there until their musher shows up."

Lainey glanced back up the perilous trail. "What if he's injured?" She saw the same concern in Scotch's eyes.

"We don't know where he lost the team. If it was as far back as the first descent, it could take us hours to get there by sled. Chances are good that someone coming from the other direction has already found him." She led the dogs toward the trees. "If he's closer to this end, it would still be better for us to get to the checkpoint and notify someone. They can get to him faster with a snow machine."

Lainey helped get the sled into position and tied the snub line to a tree. She set the snow hook as firmly as possible. "Isn't this considered outside assistance? Won't we be disqualified?"

Scotch opened the sled bag and located the Iditarod promotional package. "No, this is a legal action. If he's near enough to walk, great. Or he can hitch a ride with another team. It's one thing to assist someone to keep them going when they should scratch; it's another to leave somebody out here in the bush to die." She found the bib number so she could notify the committee. She put things back, and she and Lainey returned to their sleds, their dogs eager to get going.

"This ever happen to you?"

Scotch's face reddened, but she smiled. "Yeah. Once. My first Yukon Quest. A sweeper got me while I was dozing on the sled. Knocked me flat." She chuckled. "I walked for an hour or more before I found the team tied off the trail, waiting for me."

Lainey grinned. "Just returning the favor, huh?"

"Yup."

As they urged their teams forward, Lainey spared one glance back at the runaway dogs. They were curling up to take a nap as they awaited their lost owner.

CHAPTER THIRTY-SIX

Skirting Rainy Pass Lodge, the Iditarod utilized a small cabin as a checkpoint. Lainey kept pace with Scotch until they reached the small crowd of volunteers gathered there. It was fortuitous that Scotch's team was leading the way, for when young Chibee noticed a herd of horses near the lodge, he howled, attempting to break ranks and give chase. The rest of Lainey's team chose to follow the familiar scent of Scotch's dogs, and Chibee was forced to abort his pursuit.

"Hughes—five fifty-six p.m. Welcome to Rainy Pass." The checker marked down her time, grinning as he looked at her head. "Nice hat."

"Thanks!" Lainey tugged on it. "I think I deserve about a dozen more of them."

"I hear you," the checker agreed. "Maybe you'll earn a hundred hats for conquering the Farewell Burn."

"Man, don't remind me!" Lainey glanced at his clipboard, pleased to note she hadn't dropped behind the mid-thirties in placement. "Scotch and I found a team with no musher just on the edge of Puntilla Lake. We tied them down there."

"All right." He wrote something on his paperwork. "We'll get somebody out there to check on the situation." He waved her on to the veterinarians waiting nearby.

She quickly fell into the checkpoint routine—assisting the vets with her dogs, picking up her food drop and going over her team with a critical eye. All the animals seemed in good spirits, though Heldig's paws appeared a little worse for wear. Lainey used a different salve for the pads of Heldig's feet, telling her in no uncertain terms that she was going to staple her booties on if she continued shedding them. Less than impressed, the dog impudently kissed Lainey's nose.

As Lainey proceeded with her camp chores, a handful of reporters surrounded her, Ben Strauss among them. Her friend hung back, allowing the others to ask questions about the trail through Happy River Valley. Several took pictures of her new headgear. When she mentioned her trainer had a lot to do with her successful arrival, they drifted away to get an interview with Scotch. Relieved by the shift of attention, she finished cooking the dog food and loaded it into the cooler.

"That sounds as if it was pretty exciting."

She grinned at Strauss. "I'll say. I think you'd get a kick out of doing this. You should consider a leave of absence sometime and give it a go. You're always into the dangerous survival stuff."

"Maybe I will." He gestured toward the lodge. "Come on. I'll buy you dinner. The moose stew is good."

Not wanting to get on the wrong side of the "no assistance" rule, Lainey said, "Better yet, I'll buy." Strauss shrugged agreement, so Lainey turned toward the lodge. It felt a little odd to be leaving her team. She glanced over at the sleeping dogs; they would be oblivious to her departure.

"They'll be fine. A lot of the mushers grab a bite here rather than eat what they're carrying. It'll do you good to see people."

She laughed. "All right! I'm convinced."

They left the sled parking area and walked to the lodge. Even with the promise of a freshly prepared meal before her, Lainey stifled a yawn. It was the end of the second day, and she'd had about six hours total sleep. Still, she was doing better than most rookies, having had the experience of Scotch to draw upon. She couldn't fathom doing this without the extensive training she had put herself through since June.

The lodge had a stereotypical look: walls of thick logs, roughly hewn bannisters on the large covered porch and the requisite old dog drowsing by the door. Lainey saw Drew Owens sitting on a bench, hands in his parka pockets, feet stretched out and crossed at the ankles. He appeared to be sleeping, and she briefly wondered why he'd be napping out here rather than inside.

Strauss opened the door, and Lainey stepped into a fairly busy establishment. A large dining room stood off to the side, where quite a number of reporters, volunteers and mushers were enjoying each other's company. Her arrival sparked a round of welcome and toasts, and Lainey waved at the diners as Strauss preceded her to a table. Acclimated as she was to the frigid temperatures outside, the warmth was overwhelming. Sweat popped out on her forehead, and she hastily removed her outer clothes. The wind-burned skin of her face stung, and her sinuses clogged as the tissue swelled. By the time she reached Strauss' table, she felt as if her head was full of cotton. No wonder Owens was sleeping outside. If she hadn't offered to buy dinner, she would have turned around and gone back out to her dogs.

"Ugh." She sat down. Other mushers who were braving the indoors sat around half-clad. She followed suit, removing mukluks and liners, until only socks covered her feet. Next time she would bring spare liners and fresh socks to don inside.

"What can I get you?" a waiter asked. "The moose stew is hot and ready, or we can grill you up a sandwich, but that'll take more than a few minutes."

Lainey smiled despite her discomfort. "Served a lot of Iditarod mushers, have you?"

"Oh, yeah. We're happy to keep our doors open twenty-four hours a day during the race."

"The stew will be fine. And about three gallons of coffee."

The waiter took Strauss' order and left the table.

"You okay?"

Lainey rubbed her face. "Kind of fuzzy from the heat. It feels like I've got a sinus infection."

"Interesting. I suppose it makes sense. You've literally been out in the weather for over forty-eight hours."

"Yeah." Lainey tried to breathe through her nose and failed. "Ugh." Her order arrived and she dug into the hot meal. Despite her physical discomfort from the heat, the tasty stew triggered massive hunger. She ate as if starved.

"So. You and Scotch?"

Lainey sighed. Howry had warned her, and here it was. "Yeah, looks that way."

His brow furrowed. "You're not sure?"

"Well, it's not like we've followed through on things. We've been concentrating on getting through this race before we explore any... options."

"I thought you told me she was straight."

Lainey stopped eating. "Yeah. I did." She looked at Strauss. "At the time, it was only wishful thinking on my part. I really doubted she was gay. I had no idea she'd be amenable to a— " She paused, searching for the right word. *Liaison? Dalliance? Affair?* "A relationship," she finished.

His eyebrows shot up at the term. "A relationship?"

She was sure she was blushing, though how he could see it through her weather-reddened skin she didn't know. "Yeah. I don't think this is going to be just a fling."

"Wow." He sat back in his chair and stared at her. "Are you sure you...Are you ready for something like this?"

The ever-lurking anger and shame washed through her. "What?"

He sighed, scrubbing at his handsome face. "You know how I feel. I just don't think you're..." He waved his hand in the air, trying to come up with the words. "You need to focus on you first, you know?"

Booze. He means the booze. Fear trickled into the mix, taking her breath away. She inhaled deeply, pushing away the emotions, knowing from her research that they had no basis in reality no matter how much she thought they did. "I have to get through this race first. We'll talk in Nome." When he cocked his head in speculation, she placed her hand on his. "I promise." Strauss studied her, then nodded.

She squeezed and released his hand. Tamping down her reservations, she returned to her meal. Several seconds passed before she noted him staring, an amused expression on his face.

"What?"

He smiled. "I just never thought I'd see the day you'd be off the market."

Lainey grunted in mock aggravation, pleased to let the conversation flow beyond her possible addiction. "I don't know about that. We'll see how it goes after the race." She had admitted to herself she loved Scotch but had no idea whether Scotch felt the same. There was still a chance that her hope for more than a one-night stand would be crushed, that Scotch had no desire for more. *Not that I could blame her after last November.*

Seeming to understand the dangerous emotional trail she was riding, Strauss wisely refrained from further comment. "Don seemed to be worried I'd fire you over the issue."

Lainey pointed her spoon at him. "Well, I did mislead you about my real reasons for suggesting Scotch as the subject of the article."

"True, but the pitch was solid, or I wouldn't have bought it. The fact that you dove into the challenge after my bosses made their changes only sweetened the pot. You could have said no to the gig."

Lainey didn't disabuse him of the notion that she'd have put a stop to the entire deal. He had no idea how driven she had been to bask in everything that was Scotch Fuller. "I guess."

Another round of greetings informed her of new arrivals. Howry slid into the chair next to Strauss, and Scotch draped her parka over the one beside Lainey before sitting down.

"Moose stew at Rainy Pass Lodge." She happily tucked a napkin at her throat. "Best thing since sliced bread."

"I agree." Lainey returned to her food.

"Here you go, Scotch." The waiter set a bowl of stew and a plate of bread and butter before her. "You want hot chocolate?"

"You bet!"

"Come here often?" Howry asked after the waiter delivered Scotch's beverage.

"Once or twice," she said in an off-handed way, smiling when he laughed.

Strauss eyed Scotch. "You've moved up a few places since the start of the race. Think you'll win?"

She chuckled through a mouthful of stew, swallowing before answering. "We've got a long way to go before we think about that. The key is to gradually pull forward, not make a run for it in the first couple of days. Exhaust the dogs now, and they'll have nothing to offer down the trail."

"Still, you're considered a contender this year," Howry persisted.

"Doesn't mean I'll make it."

"Is that modesty talking?" Strauss asked.

Scotch shook her head. "No, reality. I can have the best team, the best times and the best weather, but anything can happen out there. Hell, if I bust my sled in the Farewell Burn and can't find a fix or alternative on the other side, I scratch. If the weather takes a turn for the worse and blizzard conditions make visibility zero, I could easily lose the trail. Lots of things can happen that I have no control over."

"Why do you do it, if not to win?" Ben asked.

Curious to know the answer, Lainey gave Strauss an intent look. Was he putting Scotch through her paces for Lainey's sake? Trying to draw Scotch out to measure her character and integrity, to make sure she was good enough for Lainey? Strauss ignored her, though he no doubt knew what she was thinking. Lainey puzzled over a combined sense of pleasure at his paternal actions and annoyance with the behavior. *Who does he think he is, my father? He has no right to judge.*

The conversation had continued without her, and Lainey hastened to catch up.

"Why climb Mount Everest? Why go on safari to hunt lions or rhinos? Why get up every morning?" Scotch had forgotten her food. "It's a challenge. Out here, my survival depends on me and my actions. It's difficult sometimes, yes, but satisfying on levels you can't even imagine."

Strauss considered for a long moment. "So, winning doesn't matter?"

Scotch's serious demeanor faded. "Didn't say that." She winked at him.

Howry held up his beer. "To survival."

"And winning." Strauss lifted an iced tea.

Scotch and Lainey chimed in. "To winning."

The indoor heat lulled her and Lainey placed a hand over a wide yawn. "Sorry."

"No. You've got every reason to be tired." Strauss put his glass down. "And there's still a long way to go."

"If I'm going to get any sleep, now is the time to do it." Lainey forced her feet back into damp liners and mukluks. She definitely needed to change them before catching a nap.

"Want company?"

Lainey smiled at Strauss, letting him know she understood his earlier ploy and bore him no ill will. "Naw. You'd just have to turn around and come right back here."

He nodded. "We're staying here another night and then flying into McGrath the next day."

"See you there." Lainey gathered up her outer clothing and headed out of the lodge. Her exit was met with a chorus from the people lounging around inside, wishing her luck. She waved as she closed the door against the chill, feeling immensely better now that she wasn't overheated.

Drew Owens still drowsed on the bench. Chuckling at him, Lainey stepped into the snow.

CHAPTER THIRTY-SEVEN

Reluctance in every bone, Lainey dragged herself from her sleeping bag. Though the heat and food in the lodge had made her drowsy, once back at her sled she'd had difficulty falling asleep. A couple of teams were still frisky after their foray through Happy Valley. Their constant barking whenever a musher arrived or left roused her between fits of slumber. Sleeping out in the wilderness definitely had its benefits. She now regretted not blowing through the checkpoint.

She put on fresh socks and boot liners, shivering in the night chill as she stomped into her mukluks. On her way to the privy, she entertained herself with thoughts of featherbeds, thick quilts and roaring fires. By the time she returned, the exercise had warmed and woken her enough for her to get to work. The moose stew stuck with her, so she didn't cook herself a meal. Instead, as the dogs' food heated, she doubled up on snack items. The extra banana bread, trail mix, jerky and pemmican would keep her going until the other side of Dalzell Gorge. Some people said that the trail to Rohn was as rough as the Happy River Valley one and took longer to travel. The next fifty miles wouldn't be easy.

Lainey quietly went through her team with their late night supper, waking each of them in turn with soft words and petting. All of them ate well, a sure sign of continued good health. The dreaded kennel cough hadn't been talked about among the other mushers; perhaps this would be a sickness-free race. After another watering, she began the heating process all over again, drinking freshly brewed instant coffee from her thermos.

A familiar voice spoke nearby, and Lainey looked over and saw Scotch mirroring her tasks. As the woman worked through her team, the dogs gave her love and devotion, and Scotch gave the same back to them. Scotch had been wrong in the lodge. It wasn't just her abilities that she relied upon to survive; the dogs had everything to do with it. Scotch might be the alpha dog in the pack, but it was still a team effort.

Lainey hurriedly grabbed her camera and snapped a couple of photos, catching Scotch in the act of bestowing attention on one of her dogs. The flashes attracted Scotch, who looked up at her. Lainey waggled her camera with a not-so-apologetic grin for the intrusion. Scotch merely smiled and returned to her chores.

The second round of dog stew prepared, Lainey stored it in the cooler. She shucked her heavy mittens for two layers of rubber gloves over silk liners. Stuffing hand warmers into the palms, she started down the line with ointment and booties.

"You ready to go?"

"Just about. You?"

"Yup." Scotch looked over Lainey's lively team. "You're doing a great job with them."

Lainey's skin reddened, a grin plastering itself across her face. "Thanks."

Scotch looked out over the dog parking area, scanning the surrounding darkness. Lights were visible from the lodge and from around the checkpoint, and stars sparkled overhead. "Remember, we're going to be crossing a few ice bridges this leg. Don't stop on one; it might not be able to hold the weight. The temperatures have stayed pretty low, but that doesn't mean a lot."

She nodded, not liking the idea of taking a midnight swim in the dead of an Alaskan winter. "What if someone else has already broken through one? How will we follow the trail?"

"We'll figure that out if we need to. It's only a creek, not a river, so that'll make things a bit easier."

Lainey's concerns weren't allayed, but she didn't argue. She didn't think they would be penalized for going off the trail in search of a different crossing. "Okay," she said, placing her confidence in Scotch's experience. "Let's do it."

They finished breaking camp and then urged their dogs toward the checkpoint. Seeing Scotch make her move, a couple of other mushers decided to get going as well. They began rousing their dogs, glancing over their shoulders at Scotch or at their watches.

Were those the ones who would give Scotch a run for her money? Would they be able to keep up? Lainey scanned her memory, putting grizzled faces to press release names and realized that these two were longtime veterans. She felt a swell of pride that Scotch, with her comparatively limited experience, was causing such a stir among men who had been racing almost as long as she had been alive.

"Midnight, straight up," the checker told her as Lainey initialed his paperwork. "Good luck. There's some mean winds blowing, so visibility may be shoddy."

"Thanks. That's good to know."

Again Scotch led the way. The trail immediately climbed toward the top of Rainy Pass. Once they passed this ridge, they would be travelling the interior of Alaska, through frozen tundra bracketed by mountain ranges. Lainey shivered in anticipation. Overhead, eerie wisps of greens and blues sheeted across the sky, a colorful backdrop behind grand Denali, which rose above them. She had a fleeting desire to see the view in daylight, but her thoughts focused back on the trail as Scotch began the descent. Solid and well-packed, the path twisted and contorted. Lainey barely kept up with the commands as the trail switched back and forth through hairpin turns then abruptly plunged into narrow ravines. Her headlamp picked up sheer walls of snow and ice, boulders rushing toward her from murky darkness, and the wagging tails of her dogs as they surged forward. She barely had time to force her heart out of her throat before the next danger whizzed toward her, her belated reflex to duck useless when the peril was quickly put behind her.

They hit the bottom of the gorge, the trail leveling out though it didn't become less twisting. Lainey used the less demanding moment to unclench her fingers from her handlebars. That descent had definitely lasted longer than the Happy Valley run. Despite her earlier apprehension, she took pleasure in the fact that they had taken the run at night. The trail had been scary enough with just a headlamp. Taking the descent in daylight would have caused her heart failure. Before she relaxed completely, the trail began a steep climb, slowing her team's pace. She hopped off the sled and helped push the cumbersome weight up the hill until they broke out of the gorge onto tundra.

Wind whipping about her lower legs and brushing her face, Lainey stepped back onto the runners. Powdered snow apparently covered the ground, but she couldn't see it for the windswept blizzard. Lainey saw only the tails and ears of her wheel dogs in the gloom, yet she was thankful to easily locate a six-foot tripod trail marker coming up in the distance. Her visibility obscured below her waist, she took in the sight of Scotch ahead, gliding through a cloud, pulled by unseen forces. She marveled at the eeriness, the sky illuminated by the Aurora Borealis, starlight flickering bright in the crisp, cold sky and shadowy lumps of hills bordering the shallow valley.

They continued to climb, moving from one valley into a narrower one. The wind died down and visibility improved. The trail crossed a river with standing water. As the team splashed through it, Lainey frowned. Heldig was bare-pawed again, as were a couple of other dogs. She would have to stop soon and take care of their feet before ice formed between their toes. The climb steepened, the trail weaving between foliage and a frozen creek as it went. It opened up onto an icebound lake. Lainey whistled to get Scotch's attention.

Calling the dogs to a halt, Lainey had a difficult moment stomping the snow hook into the icy surface. She grabbed a bag of frozen fish and snacked her team as she moved along the line.

Scotch met her halfway between their teams. "We need to go over their paws."

"That's what I was thinking. Heldig kicked off her booties miles ago."

"Let's get to it then. We don't have much farther to go, but it's still a rough road ahead."

Lainey returned to her team. The bitter cold nipped at her fingers when she removed her arctic mittens. She fumbled with the rubber gloves and then stuffed her pockets with dog booties. Even those dogs who still wore theirs would need replacements. She spent the next several minutes changing out wet booties, digging ice balls out from between canine toes, slathering ointment on pads and re-covering her dogs' feet with cordova booties. It took longer than she had expected, because even those with booties had ice developing on their paws from the water they had run through.

"Passing!"

Startled, she looked up to see a musher's headlamp coming toward her. She gave the musher a wave, noting he was one of the pair who had hastily prepared to follow Scotch when they had left the Rainy Pass checkpoint. She grinned and returned to her task, wondering if the man felt smug at catching Scotch so early in the race. Once finished with the dogs, she gathered the wet booties and put them in a bag with all the used ones not lost on the trail. There was a laundromat in McGrath. She planned on running a couple of loads through a dryer.

"You ready?" Lainey called out.

"Yeah." Scotch zipped up her sled bag and climbed onto the runners.

Not wanting to be left behind, Lainey's team hastened forward.

The trail fell into a steep decline that leveled out after a couple hundred feet. From there it traversed a timberline, following a creek as it zigzagged along. The winding path was a horror, worse than the one leaving Rainy Pass checkpoint. The path tipping left then right, Lainey fought to remain upright as she hit patches of bare rock, uneven ruts and sharp turns. Not wanting to run over Scotch ahead of her and fighting hard to not spill her sled, she kept a lot of weight on her drag mat. The ride was a cross between a roller coaster and a bucking bronco, and Lainey white-knuckled her way along, praying she wouldn't lose control. Eventually the path evened out, became narrower and climbed higher. Huge trees flanked her team. Though she couldn't see in the darkness, she had a sense that the ground was opening up to her right. Lainey balanced on the left runner to compensate, not certain whether the trail would remain level or tilt downhill. Her headlamp picked up an approaching sign, and she narrowed her eyes to catch a glimpse.

"Watch Your Ass."

Lainey blinked. She saw Scotch disappear in front of her, her only warning of the coming drop. When she hit the descent, her stomach swooped in response. After a moment, she frowned. The well-packed trail felt smoother than what she'd already traversed. *It's steep, yeah, but why the sign?* Her sled dragged on the left, but she couldn't see a cause, leading her to believe there was damage caused by the rough patches she had gone through rather than there being a problem with the current terrain. Was this part supposed to be tougher? Was there something at the end of the downslope she should worry about? She racked her brain for anything she had heard at the mushers' meeting but came up empty. Her befuddlement thickened at the bottom of the drop when the trail only wound back and forth over a creek bed.

With an exasperated shake of her head, she put the sign and its senseless warning out of her mind. Her adrenaline level at an all-time high, it inversely dulled her senses to experiencing the intermittent alarming and relaxing of her nervous system. She caught sight of

Scotch on the trail ahead, watched her sweep down and across the trail, water rushing beneath. Lainey held her breath and followed, crossing the first ice bridge with ease. On either side, the ground slanted upward again, huge trees creating vortexes as the trail twisted around them—onto the creek, across more ice bridges and onto narrow spits of land. She began to tire of feeling scared all the time, and a bubble of laughter welled up in her chest. This was a far better ride than anything at Six Flags.

The gorge opened up onto river ice. Her joy grew as they broke out of the claustrophobic section of trail. She heeded markers and ignored rough ice as she and her team bumped along. Her team skied through standing water and kept on, the lure of food and rest drawing them forward. More markers guided them off the river and into spruce trees. Soon lights flickered among the branches, and she felt a measure of shock as they pulled into the checkpoint that suddenly appeared.

"Lainey Hughes." she said as she halted her dogs.

"Four thirty-eight a.m., number thirty-one." The checker marked her time. "Welcome to Rohn Roadhouse."

CHAPTER THIRTY-EIGHT

After three days on the trail, Lainey's team had settled into their six-hour run/rest schedule. As soon as they pulled the sled into the parking area, they dropped to the ground and curled up to catch a nap. She disrupted their sleep to deliver straw and blankets, disconnecting the tug lines from their harnesses at the same time.

The area she and Scotch parked in was sheltered from the returning wind by spruce trees. A landing strip stretched adjacent to them, but there were no planes occupying the runway. Another team came in not long after them, the second of the veterans clinging to Scotch's tail. Lainey, still high on adrenaline and a touch of hysteria, chuckled to herself as she ladled out dog food to her hungry team, the dogs rousing themselves for a warm meal. She hoped Scotch would win this race, justifying the fears of the old timers who worried at her heels.

Once the entire team, both human and canine, had eaten, Lainey grabbed her child's sled, trudged to the food drop area and collected her bags, meeting Scotch in the process of doing the same. They grinned at one another, walking close enough to jostle shoulders. Lainey wondered whether she looked as goofy as she felt. If she had been a cartoon, there would have been little stars and hearts floating around her head. She blushed.

Back at her sled, she tilted it onto its right side to have a good look at the left runner. As she had surmised, the trip from Rainy Pass had done damage. The chewed and mangled plastic had almost completely separated in some places. Lainey used her toolkit to remove the bolts holding the runner in place. She slid off the mutilated plastic and took a fresh runner from her drop bag to replace it. After she had tightened the bolts, she pushed and pulled the rest of the fittings on that side of the sled, checking for loose joints. Everything else seemed to work as it should. To be thorough, she turned her sled onto the other side and replaced the less damaged right runner. Better to have fresh runners than have one totally shred midway through the Farewell Burn.

By the time she had finished, the dogs were deep asleep. Lainey checked her watch and winced. She had been working for almost two hours. That left her maybe three hours of sleep before getting ready to go again. The reason for the mandatory eight- and twenty-four-hour breaks became clear. Dogs weren't the ones to exhaust themselves on this race; it was the human contingent that needed the layovers in order to survive.

She glanced over at Scotch, who had also taken the time to go over her sled after the beating administered by the trail.

"Get your sleeping bag and some of the stuff you really need to dry. There's usually room in the cabin to spread out a bit. Lots of lines near the stove to hang stuff on."

Lainey looked over her gear. There was nothing she really needed dry except her boot liners. With her food drop, she had plenty of booties to get her to Nikolai, which boasted a municipal building with a boiler room for drying things. She grabbed up two spare boot and glove liners to take with her. Just in case, she stuffed her pockets with a handful of wet booties. Scotch joined her, carrying a similar pile of wet items, and they walked to the small cabin in silence. Lainey's eyes felt baggy from lack of sleep, even in the bracing chill of early morning. They passed others who had elected to remain with their dogs, as well as volunteers out and about for a number of reasons.

Lainey experienced a moment's dread at the cabin door. Staying with the dogs would be preferable to her sinuses clogging up like they had done at Rainy Pass Lodge. At least she would be able to breathe. Nevertheless, she followed Scotch indoors. The small cabin was crammed with mushers, volunteers and even a few intrepid reporters. A wood stove stood in the center of the room, giving off enough heat to make things comfortable but not overly warm. Lainey felt her sinuses begin to throb, but they didn't swell as before, making the interior temperature tolerable.

Scotch murmured greetings to those seated around a table nursing hot coffee and eating breakfast. A dry-erase board hung from one wall, listing the mushers and their times in and out of the checkpoint. Lainey snorted as she checked her placement by her bib number, then scanned through to see how others were doing. It seemed that all the previous champions were either there or had just left. Lainey knew better than to put herself in that category, but Scotch still had a good shot at winning. Scotch was holding her team back to get Lainey through the worst of the first part of the race. After that, Lainey would be on her own with some decent experience under her belt to her get the rest of the way to Nome.

"Lainey."

Turning away from the board, she saw Scotch waving her toward the stove.

They found empty space for their wet things on several cords draped across the room. Lainey used the Velcro straps on the dog booties as clothespins.

Several bunks lined the room, but none were unoccupied. Napping mushers also littered the floor. Lainey discovered an available corner and dropped her sleeping bag there. Scotch joined her. They used Lainey's bag to make a nest, and Scotch's to cover them. Before long, they were snuggled together. Lainey's sleep-fogged mind wandered as she drifted off. Would anybody notice her and Scotch sleeping together under the noses of the Iditarod committee and fellow mushers? *Does anybody but us care?* She turned on her side, cuddling closer. *Just my luck. I finally get to sleep with Scotch and I'm too damned exhausted to do anything about it.*

* * *

Scotch pulled out of the checkpoint at precisely twelve thirty-seven p.m. She was second in a convoy of six mushers, a rather different experience considering the solitary nature of running dogs. The next twenty miles of trail was considered reason enough to set aside competitive differences. They could use all the help they could get to slog through it.

Drew Owens had delayed his departure to lead the procession, with Scotch tailing him. Lainey came next, followed by Georgio

Spencer, one of the veterans who had been playing catch-up with Scotch. Behind him came his youngest son, Roman, the young man Lainey had met at the mandatory rookie meeting in December. Bringing up the rear was the second veteran chasing after Scotch, Jon Waters, a three-time Iditarod champion.

They left the checkpoint to find themselves mushing into a brisk wind. It hadn't seemed so brutal in the protection of the spruce trees where the dogs had slept. Despite the warmer temperatures of the afternoon, gusts now chilled Scotch's face and caused her eyes to tear. She fumbled for the goggles in her personal bag, relieved as the biting sting dissipated. She pulled her scarf up to cover the lower half of her face.

The wind had scrubbed the snow from the trail, baring patches of gravel and sand as they traveled along the bank of the Kuskokwim River. Driftwood piles dotted the landscape haphazardly, some coming perilously close to the trail. In other spots, the heat of the day—below thirty degrees but still rather warm for the animals—had resulted in overflow from the river. When not on dry land, they slipped over ice covered with a sheet of water. More than once dogs lost their footing as they trotted, stumbling as their feet slipped out from under them. Trail markers were few and far between. They would cross the river at some point, but Scotch couldn't see anything on the other side to indicate the location of the trail. Owens, who was a good fifty yards ahead, veered southwest across the wet ice. Scotch followed, squinting into the distance. Halfway across the river, she spotted the reflective markers. She wondered how Owens had seen them. He had twenty years of Iditarod experience. She would bet he could run this race blind. There were going to be some bewildered rookies getting lost at this point. Even she would have missed the signs if she had been traveling alone.

Her spirits rose as they headed into a stand of trees that protected them from the wind. Her team picked up a little speed now that they had better purchase on the trail. She felt the belated tingle of blood warming her cheeks, though a breeze still teased the ruffles of her badger fur hood. The trail remained smooth and relatively straight, clear of debris and far away from potential sweepers. It was nice to let the dogs run without a care in the world. She frowned, knowing this placid little section would end soon. The Farewell Burn loomed somewhere out there, and she wasn't traveling in a pack of mushers to enjoy the day. Sunlight sparkled off snow, crisp and clean, a contrast to her somber thoughts.

They broke onto another river. Taking a left, the trail climbed a steep bank. Before Scotch could become complacent, they trotted back onto another creek. This section of trail held irregular driftwood piles, slippery surfaces and bared gravel. When this creek thawed, she imagined it would boast whitewater, given the amount of rock sticking up to mar the ice. Her sled bucked and writhed under her as she fought just to stay aboard. Getting off the creek did little to improve the way. Owens crested the hill ahead and dipped over the other side. That was Scotch's only warning before she arrived at the apex of a small hill. Beneath her, she saw a ravine, the path a short one. It wasn't as difficult as the switchbacks at Happy Valley. Her trip down was fast and smooth compared to the trail leading up. At the bottom, she called the command to the dogs for a sharp right turn.

Scotch stared up at the upcoming hill. The climb appeared nearly vertical, and she watched Owens urge his dogs up, pushing his sled behind. She hoped the trail was solid enough for the dogs to gain purchase. She didn't have strength enough to push a five-hundred-pound sled up that incline by herself. She had no time to worry about being crushed by a backsliding sled. She knew she had to get up that hill before Lainey crashed into her from behind. "Let's go! Let's go!" she called to her team, getting off the runners to help muscle the sled to the top. The dogs put their backs into it and, though they slowed considerably, slogged steadily to the top of the hill. There was a short jog left through some trees, and Scotch came out onto an upper section of the ravine she had just climbed. Tracks on the trail there indicated that others hadn't been so lucky. Rather than remain on the marked trail, their dogs had continued the left turn, rushing them to the bottom of the ravine to climb that vertical hill all over again. Scotch silently thanked the experienced lead dogs, both on her team and Owens'. Her dogs followed the teams before them rather than the scent of those who had erred in the recent past.

Another ascent leveled out at a rock outcropping, which she easily avoided. Rocks studded the trail ahead, bereft of snow and easy to see. She gritted her teeth as she went, hoping not to hit anything that would irrevocably damage her sled. It had to last her to McGrath, where she had another waiting for her. Until she arrived there, this one had to remain in one piece. The convoy sailed out of the ravine, bumping across frozen and bare tundra. As they reached another tree line, Owens came to a stop, the rest following his lead. He called back to the line of mushers, each taking the message and passing it on like the elementary school game of Telephone.

"We're taking a break here," Scotch yelled to Lainey.

Lainey gave a thumbs up and called to Georgio Spencer behind her.

Scotch blew out a breath, unkinking her shoulders as she reached for the bag of frozen whitefish. So far, so good. They were about halfway through the worst of it. She went down the line, giving her team a snack and extra attention.

CHAPTER THIRTY-NINE

The convoy left bare tundra for thin forest and a gentle rise in altitude. Through the trees, Lainey spotted marshes and frozen ponds dotted with large shaggy bushes. She thought nothing of it until one of the bushes moved. Gasping, she narrowed her eyes and stared through passing branches and trunks. *Wild buffalo!* Her hands itched to grab her camera, but she knew the shot would be worthless with the woods in the way. Had she been alone, she might have stopped to get a decent picture. Grunting, she frowned back at the trail.

They reached the peak of the saddle and dropped onto the other side with little trouble. For the next several miles, the trail narrowed, more rocks and dirt showing through sparse snow cover. Changing her sled runners had been a good decision, as was the idea to have another set in her sled bag ready to replace these at the end of the run. Well-marked in most places, the trail disappeared upon occasion as creek overflows had frozen into icy ponds. Egypt Mountain passed slowly to the right, and the sky darkened. The light edged into that in-between stage where nothing stood out, so she donned her headlamp. The ground leveled out and widened. Trail markers, posted few and far between, seemed pretty much useless in light of the wide expanse of ice to cover. She tsked under her breath as her dogs swept through a puddle of standing water. Heldig had no booties again. They would have to stop soon to take care of their animals.

Twilight faded to evening as the group made their way from swamp to lake. Lainey saw a red beacon flashing in the distance and wondered what it indicated. It seemed close, but out here that meant little. She lost sight of the beacon as she moved off the lake and into more forest.

Lake followed forest, forest followed lake, for several miles. The night was far from silent, however. Lainey grinned at the singing she heard behind her. It sounded like Georgio or Roman belting out *Witchy Woman* at top volume. Her dogs' ears kept pricking back in curiosity, and she giggled. *Maybe I should join in on the chorus.*

She barely noted the "Dangerous Trail Conditions" sign before taking a sharp drop onto another lake. Other than that slight hiccup, there seemed no other risk. *Have we passed the Burn already?* From everything she had read about the place, it was supposed to be worse than Dalzell Gorge and Happy Valley combined. Surely they hadn't gone through it yet. The woods and forests they traversed showed no indication of fire damage. She was under the impression that even after two decades, the area hadn't grown back much from the horrendous fire that had destroyed the forest.

Ahead of her, she saw a headlamp closing in on her position. Odd. Why was someone coming this way? She squinted until she realized it was Scotch, standing beside her stopped sled. "Whoa!" Lainey called abruptly. She eased onto the brake, and her leaders automatically pulled off the trail to one side. Once they had stopped, she put in her snow hook. "Snack time?"

"Yeah. The Burn is just ahead, then we'll take a full rest break."

Smiling in anticipation, Lainey passed the message on. As she fed her dogs chunks of frozen moose liver, she was amazed at her lack of dread for the upcoming ordeal. Up until the gorge, Lainey had felt incredible apprehension over the physical challenges of the trail. Now she was almost eager to get to the confrontation, to accept the dangerous test of her abilities and win. It was reminiscent of stalking wild carnivores to get that one elusive photograph, not caring about the peril she put herself in to achieve the shot.

She did a careful examination of her dogs. Heldig's paws had gotten worse, though she acted as if they didn't pain her. If she kept this up, Lainey would be forced to drop her at the next checkpoint or the one after that. She wasn't looking forward to that. Realistically speaking, Lainey's chances of going the entire thousand miles without dropping a single dog were minimal, but it was a goal for which to aim. She admonished Heldig again and rubbed liniment into her pads before rebooting her.

They slid into more woods on a slow rise. Lainey gasped in surprise as her team broke out onto a stark and barren landscape. *Finally, the Farewell Burn.* The trail weaved this way and that through clumps of brush, snow-covered stumps and a few spindly tree husks spiking into the sky. It reminded Lainey of a movie, *The Nightmare Before Christmas.* The Burn would be an apt place to film a live-action version. All it needed was an eerie old castle in the background and bats flitting about the night sky. For all the hype, however, the Burn was mild in comparison to the obstacles Lainey had already faced. She felt a sense of disappointment as her team easily avoided a snag, wondering if this was all there was to the trail. As the miles went by, she began to think so. Disgruntled, she spent the time convincing herself that this was a good thing, that twenty-plus years had gone a long way toward making the trail accessible. She resolved to throw out all the Iditarod books she had accumulated during her research, at least all of them not published in the last five years.

The trail moved from one ridge to another. With no trees to block her view, Lainey suspected she could see ten or twenty miles in any direction. A dark shadow against the starry night sky indicated a far-away mountain, a single light shining from its top. Looking behind her, she saw the three headlamps of the rest of her party. Miles back, she saw two other lights twinkling along—other mushers on the trail. Eventually the convoy dropped into a gulch, sheltered from the unavoidable wind. Lainey saw structures to her left, her headlamp illuminating what looked like a camp of some sort. There didn't appear to be anyone occupying it, but fresh snow machine tracks indicated recent use. Depending on when it had last snowed, someone could have been out there in the last couple of days or so. They came to a stop, those in the back pulling forward to fill the narrow gulch. After the wide-open spaces of The Burn, the number of dogs and people gathered gave a claustrophobic feel to the clearing. After Lainey got her dogs braked, she joined the mushers forming a group nearby. Owens spoke as she approached.

"I'm thinking about heading over to the BLM cabin before calling it a night."

"That's what…ten more miles?" Roman Spencer asked as he joined the palaver.

"Yup." Scotch stifled a yawn and looked at Lainey. "I believe I'll bed down here."

"Sounds like a plan," Lainey agreed.

Roman looked from one woman to the other, then to his father, uncertain which way to jump. Georgio gave Scotch a calculated glance as he fiddled with his icy beard. Lainey saw the gears turning as he gauged whether or not to stay with Scotch, thereby keeping the competition close, or move ahead in hopes of beating her to the finish.

Waters, the last one in line trotted up. "What's up? Why are we stopping?"

"Looks like we're splitting up." Georgio slapped his son on the shoulder. "I'm heading to the cabin. These ladies are electing to remain here for a spell."

"Let's snack the dogs, and get going then," Waters said.

The men broke away to tend their teams. Scotch grinned at Lainey. "Let's get the dogs closer to the tent camp before bedding them down, give them a bit more shelter."

"Okay."

Scotch had them park close, sleds together. It meant struggling with Lainey's team to get them turned back down the trail, but it was worth the effort. By the time Lainey had her team situated and the cookers heating, she and Scotch were alone in the tiny gorge. She worked through her chores on automatic, her dogs soon sated with food and water, bedded down on their blankets and on their way to sleep.

Within easy speaking distance, they chatted to one another as they worked. When Lainey had her meal cooked, she went to Scotch's sled to eat.

"What do you have?"

"Meatloaf and potatoes." Lainey showed her bag. "What about you?"

"Moose stew."

"Hey! I didn't get any moose stew!"

Scotch's chuckle drew a forceful nudge that only made her laugh harder. "I have friends in low places."

Lainey eyed her suspiciously. "And what does that mean?"

"It means that the cook at Rainy Pass Lodge passed me a couple of packages before I left."

Lainey cursed, more for show than from any real heat. "Doesn't that violate the 'no help' rule?"

"It wasn't help, it was a gift. Besides, I won't tell if you won't. And I know he won't." Scotch's smile faded into suspicion. "What are you thinking?"

Lainey wiggled her eyebrows. "I'm thinking you said he gave you a couple of packages. My silence has a price."

Scotch groaned and rolled her eyes. "You've got to be kidding! I only have one left." Lainey gave her an angelic smile and Scotch cursed, though a smile teased the corners of her mouth. With a great show of petulance, she located the frozen meal and handed it over. Squealing in mock joy, Lainey gave her a hug.

They returned to their meal, Lainey feeling warm and tingly inside. A flash of her cartoon self surrounded by little throbbing hearts crossed her mind, and she grinned into her meatloaf. "How much farther to Nikolai?"

"About forty miles. We'll get there in the morning, take another break."

Lainey's good humor drifted away. "You'll be moving on now, right?"

Scotch glanced sideways at her. "Yeah. I've been holding the dogs back from the speed they want to run. If the wind stays down, we'll make good time to the next checkpoint. Most of the trail is straight and easy to see. It's got some bad spots, but we're through the worst."

Lainey forced herself to be businesslike. "Well, don't wait for me, okay? Get out there and kick Spencer's butt." She grinned at Scotch's laugh.

"Only if you kick Spencer Junior's butt."

Lainey held out her hand, clasping Scotch's. "Deal."

"I expect we'll have company soon." Scotch balled up the remains of her meal. "Did you notice the lights behind us?"

"Yup. Other mushers, right?"

"Uh huh. About ten miles back. I want to be sacked out before they get here, give them less reason to stop and talk. Don't want to interrupt my beauty sleep."

Lainey took her cue. "Honey, you could go without sleep for months and not need to worry about your beauty." Realizing what she had said, she froze, eyes wide and a mittened hand covering her mouth. *Good God, why did I just blurt that out?*

Scotch rose, laughing. "Thank you. And welcome to sleeplessness." She pulled Lainey's hand down, holding it in hers. "Better watch what you think, Lainey Hughes. In the coming days, you might say a whole lot of things that you don't mean to."

Her skin hot from pleased embarrassment, Lainey felt glad that it was dark and Scotch's headlamp was turned off. A stab of fear cooled her blush, as she wondered what other things might spill unbidden from her mouth. *I'm strong. I can do anything.* "Sorry."

"I'm not." Scotch closed the distance between them and held her close.

Lainey's self-consciousness faded in Scotch's arms. With some effort she said goodnight and forced herself to her sled for a nap. As she settled into her sleeping bag, she grumbled under her breath, "Damn, why can't this race be over already?"

CHAPTER FORTY

At one in the morning, they prepared to leave the tent camp for the trail. The air crisp with cold, Lainey dug her facemask out of the sled. The brisk chill penetrated even that protective barrier. Her eyes were gummy and she couldn't stop yawning. The lack of sleep was beginning to get to her. She had to get to McGrath, the checkpoint after this one, to reach her scheduled twenty-four-hour layover. Wearily stepping aboard the runners of her sled, she wondered if she would make it that far. "Remember," she called ahead to Scotch, "don't hold back for me, okay?"

Scotch waved acknowledgment. "See you in Nikolai." Lainey returned the wave, and they were off.

The trail remained smooth and easy, though spooky with the inescapable fire damage around her. Lainey heard her dogs panting, the swish of snow beneath the runners, the jingle of metal bits on the tow line and her own heartbeat.

Scotch drew farther ahead. For a while, Lainey's team tenaciously attempted to keep up, but they soon slowed their pace to a more comfortable one. This disparity between the teams was expected. Scotch had the champions of the kennel and Lainey, the second string. Some of her dogs could have mustered for Scotch's team, but not all of them. She felt no resentment at having second best. Winning had never been her intention. Lainey looked fondly over her dogs. She wouldn't part with any of them, not even Bonaparte, who trotted along as if he was the only one on the line.

By the time she saw the sign for the Bureau of Land Mangagment cabin, Scotch had vanished from view. Lainey passed the turnoff without stopping, wondering whether the mushers they had traveled with were still sleeping there or had gone on. Her dogs ran and her thoughts drifted. Daydreams of reaching Nome to the sound of cheers were interspersed with visions of warming Scotch in her bed at the cabin. Or a private session at the hot springs. Lainey could almost taste her.

She was drawn from her pleasant musings when bits of fiber from her facemask touched her tongue. "Blech!" She pulled the mask down to dislodge the lint from her lips. Bending over the sled bag, she retrieved a warm juice pack from her cooler, draining it in a minute. Feeling slightly more awake, she stuffed the empty package into her sled and covered her face again.

The trail began a gradual turn. Here and there, trees that hadn't met their demise in the Farewell Burn began to appear. Soon they flickered around her as the trail led through them. Her thoughts began to float again. As she enjoyed a particularly heated interlude with Scotch in front of the fireplace, the sled jerked, jolting her into the moment as she grabbed the handlebars. Trace and Sholo had easily brought the team through a blind turn. Lainey's lack of preparation for the abrupt twist had almost caused the sled to roll. Jonah, her wheel dog, spared her a single glance as if to ask what the hell she was doing before focusing back on his part of the job. Adrenaline kicking in, Lainey's heart pounded at the unexpected obstacle, even though she was already past it. Her reflexes slowed by lack of sleep, she watched her dogs take another sharp turn, unable to understand where they were going. By the time she arrived at the bend, she comprehended the problem and attempted to compensate by leaning into the turn.

Too late!

The sled toppled, and she hung on for dear life as her dogs kept going. "Whoa!" she called before plowing into a snowdrift. She shook snow from her face, glad she had the mask on to save her from getting a mouthful. "*Whoa!*" The sled began to slow, then there was a sudden mighty tug. Everything stopped so quickly that Lainey slid hard into the back of the sled.

She lay there a moment, catching her breath. With slow, careful movements she peeled her hand from the handlebar and sat up. The sled was half on the trail, teetering on the snowbank she had just cut through. Snow covered her entire left side, and she began brushing it off, checking for damage to herself and her parka. Some had gotten into her sleeve and when she pulled off her hood, she felt the chill of it on her ear and neck. Grumbling, she cleaned herself up and attempted to stand. Her knees shook and her ribs ached, but other than that she was in one piece. She looked at her team, seeing why they had stopped so unexpectedly. When the sled had cut its furrow in the side of the trail, it continued in a straight line. The brush bow was lodged in a stand of young trees. It looked like the dogs had tried to remain on the trail, but those on the left of the tug line were now in the timber.

Lainey hastened forward to check the team, wincing as her muscles complained at the abuse. She first gave the dogs a cursory examination to ensure they had not suffered any life-threatening issues like tangled neck lines or stabbing tree branches. Breathing a sigh of relief at the absence of trauma, she took a closer look, treating each to an in-depth scrutiny as she massaged muscles and searched for bruising or bone damage. Tecumseh, one of her team dogs, whimpered as she checked him, and she hissed in concern. It looked like his harness had caused bruising, and one of his wrists was sore. His was the only injury, however, and she counted herself lucky.

The sled wasn't going anywhere soon; the brush bow was thoroughly entangled with trees and branches. First she had to get her dogs out of the mess. She snacked them and then took each animal off the back half of the string and attached them to a nearby tree. The first half of the team still partially blocked the trail. Lainey pulled Sholo and Trace to one side, the rest of the line following so that Montana, Meshindi, Bonaparte and Kaara stood off the path. She tied Himitsu and Tecumseh to a tree on the other side. Chibee wriggled so much in excitement, Lainey worried he'd pick a fight with one of the others to expend his excess energy. He got a tree all to himself, while his running mate, Heldig, ended up with the previous two. Six dogs later, the sled had been divested of most of its dog power.

Her trash talkers bellowed, Lainey's early warning that someone was coming up on them. She grumbled to herself as she retrieved her axe. *Perfect time for a gawker. Do people at car wrecks feel this way as traffic slows to pass?*

Other dogs answered, and a team pulled around the corner. The musher stopped his dogs, who playfully rolled in the snow to show off their superiority to her team. Drew Owens took off his goggles. She thought she detected a bit of concern in him at seeing her in front of him.

"You all right?"

"Yeah, though one of the dogs might have gotten bruised."

He grimaced in commiseration. "Where's Scotch?"

"Up ahead. I lost sight of her before the BLM cabin." She felt a burble of amusement as his expression soured. "Where are the others?"

His lips twitched in a grin. "Probably just waking up."

"You skipped out on them." She smiled. "Impressive."

Owens lifted one shoulder in a slight shrug. "They'll probably be along soon. You need any help?"

"No. I'm good." She gestured at the branches around the front of her sled. "I'll probably be back on the trail in twenty minutes."

"All right. See you at the next checkpoint." He put his goggles back on and ordered his dogs onward.

Lainey watched him go and then turned back to the mess. Damned if she'd still be out there when the rest of the convoy came through. She began cutting her sled free with a purpose. Once she had muscled the sled back onto the trail and had her dogs hooked up, she felt better. Tecumseh seemed to know his time was limited. When she released him from the tree, he immediately pulled her to his spot on the tug line, as if to say, "This is where I belong." Lainey chewed her lip in debate, giving him another thorough massage. His shoulder was still an issue, but he put his full weight on his paws. Perhaps the damage wasn't as bad as she had initially surmised. She decided to leave him in position for the time being and keep a close eye on him.

Within minutes of getting started again, she arrived at Sullivan Creek. Open water rushed beneath a bridge, and she urged the dogs across. From there the trail was easily marked by Scotch and Owens going before her. As she went, her headlamp picked up few markers, and she felt a guilty relief that she wasn't leading this traveling party. She would have gotten lost a number of times on this stretch of trail alone. *What'll happen when I'm truly alone?*

Tecumseh did well enough. He didn't pull with his usual alacrity, but at least he showed no limp. Considering how Lainey felt after the crash, she hoped he would work through his injuries. After the exercise of chopping wood, her stiffness had eased, though her ribs still ached. She twisted a bit, wincing at the pain. A full ten minutes later, her lethargic brain remembered hand warmers for her side and ibuprofen in her bag. Cursing at her stupidity, she got another juice pack and downed some tablets.

Leaving the river, the trail led up through a small cluster of buildings. To keep herself awake, she fumbled through her notes, squinting at the writing in the beam of her headlamp. By the time she located the name of the place, she was past it. Salmon River fish camp. Twelve miles of smooth sailing to go. From there the trail was readily apparent. Despite her resolve to remain vigilant and not have a recurrence of her crack up, her thoughts drifted again. Featherbeds, steak dinners, romantic candlelight and roaring fires teased the edges of her mind as she went.

A passing branch snagged at her parka, startling her back to awareness. "Ugh!" she yelled, frustrated with not being able to stop and sleep, reinforcing her desperate need to remain awake. "What the hell am I doing out here?"

Loping along with ease, the dogs barely gave her a glance. Tecumseh's line was slack, but he continued to run with his mates. Her headlamp illuminated the beauty of the wilderness around her. The sky held a brilliant panoply of silent stars, occasionally interspersed with sheets of greens and blues and reds of the Aurora. She soaked in her surroundings, drawing the solitude and beauty into her soul. At first she had come to Alaska to understand Scotch, to discover the root of that confidence, to unearth the reason for her inexplicable draw to the woman. She had remained because of friendship and family—both human and canine—and a growing love for her surroundings and activities. She had come to the Iditarod as a rookie, a reporter doing a story, nothing more. But her time at the kennel, the presence of Scotch and the dogs, had taught her more than how to mush. It taught her about herself, illuminated what was broken inside her and offered a potential fix.

Lainey was there for herself and no one else. The magazine would never get as much out of the articles as she was getting by experiencing and defeating the challenges before her—not just the Iditarod, but the alcohol addiction as well. She wanted to have Scotch's self-assurance for herself. Loving Scotch was easy, though she didn't know whether the feelings were returned. Should their relationship escalate beyond a bit of slap and tickle, Lainey wanted it to be on equal footing.

The trail slid off the straight and narrow onto the Kuskokwim River. Markers were more difficult to locate, but Lainey pleased herself by keeping on track. In a few short miles, she pulled into the village of Nikolai.

CHAPTER FORTY-ONE

The vet checking Lainey's dogs agreed with her assessment of Tecumseh's status. As much as Lainey wanted to let him stay with his teammates, she chose to drop him for his own good. The bruising of his shoulders bothered him more than his wrist, and the constant pulling would eventually do serious damage. With a heavy heart, she removed her wounded comrade from the tug line and escorted him to the dog drop area. He would wait there until a volunteer bush pilot came through to pick him up and deliver him to Anchorage. By the time Lainey returned to her dogs and finished the remaining chores, Scotch was catching a nap. She had arrived a full hour and a half earlier. Lainey didn't want to disturb her, so she bedded down with her dogs outside the school that served as a checkpoint. A quick search for Drew Owens turned up nothing.

Oddly enough, sleep wouldn't come, though Lainey was mentally exhausted. Her mind kept turning over the day's events—the crash and how she could have avoided it. She wondered whether Owens had blown through. *Or is he somewhere near and I just haven't seen him? If he checked in and out again, is he asleep a couple of miles away, psyching out the competition?* Whatever he had done, it seemed to have worked. She had seen Waters come through while she completed her tasks. He stopped long enough to get his food drops and see who was there, and then he immediately left.

Was Scotch being overly confident by remaining there?

Mixed with all those concerns were the sensual daydreams that had almost cost her the sled: warmth, good food, a scotch on the rocks and Scotch on a bearskin rug. She didn't bother banishing the alcohol from her mind. It seemed like a glass of water just out of reach while she died of thirst. She had been sober for months, but that didn't lessen the visceral yearning. The other Scotch, however, *that* she enjoyed daydreaming about. There was no bearskin rug in the cabin; they would have to make do with the braided rug in front of the fireplace. Or the comfortably overstuffed couch. Or maybe the rickety kitchen table.

Lainey's consciousness faded as she toyed with Scotch in her fantasies.

* * *

Scotch left before Lainey woke. Unhappy that she had missed telling her good-bye, Lainey went about waking and feeding the dogs. She signed autographs for a group of village children and talked to them about her dogs and how long she had been mushing. At least three of the children had far more experience than she, and they laughed at the disparity. Then a pair of reporters approached her for an interview. She groaned when they asked about her wreck but answered honestly. Along the trail, word traveled faster than dogs.

She checked out at twelve twenty-seven in the afternoon. The sun was high in the sky, but cloud cover kept the worst of the heat at bay. She chuckled to herself as her team headed across the Kuskokwim River. A year ago she froze her ass off in twenty-degree weather; now she worried about overheating at the same temperature. What had the world come to? Alone, she dug out her iPod. No reason why Georgio Spencer should have all the fun. As the dogs took her along the easy trail and wide-open spaces, she sang with Peter Gabriel as he shook the tree.

This part of the trail had heavy snow machine traffic between the two checkpoints, both of which were populated villages. McGrath was the bigger of the two and boasted laundromats and grocery stores, not to mention an unending supply of hot water. Lainey looked forward to not having to boil water for the dogs and getting an opportunity to get properly clean. She planned on taking her twenty-four-hour layover there to catch up on some vitally necessary sleep. Scotch would be doing the same, so they would have a little time to spend together before they separated again.

Even with the diversion of music, the trail seemed to go on and on. Bored to tears, Lainey kept switching between playlists, looking for music to keep her mood up and her eyes open. There was no danger of sweepers to knock her off the runners or sudden twists to overturn the sled. Instead she worried about falling asleep at the handlebars and waking in the snow, her team disappearing into the distance. She pulled out her camera for the occasional photo, but one section of trail looked like any other. One shot befouled her mood—her running dogs with the empty spot where Tecumseh should have been. She put the camera away.

Finally the landscape changed. The ground fell away in the distance, dropping back onto the Kuskokwim River. It told her that she was at the halfway mark. She felt an irrational urge to cry, despite the pleasure she felt at her progress. She still had twenty plus miles to go to McGrath. Twenty more miles to stay awake. Before they arrived at the river, Lainey halted her dogs for a snack break. They joyfully rolled in the snow, cooling off after their run. A few had lost booties and, as always, Heldig's were gone. Lainey used her fingers to break up ice balls and clean off paws, then rubbed salve into their pads. More booties followed. She didn't even bother begging Heldig to keep them on this time, though she considered picking up a roll of duct tape in McGrath. Maybe that would keep her paws covered.

Chibee, Himitsu and Montana began barking, looking behind them. Lainey stood up to see who was riding the approaching sled. She recognized Roman Spencer's team and smiled as he neared.

"Looks like it's just us," he said when he was within hearing distance.

"Your dad already ahead?"

"Yeah. He left a couple of hours ago." His team pulled past. "See you in McGrath."

Lainey waved and watched his team flow into the descent ahead of her. So, Georgio, Waters and Owens were all ahead now and hoping to pass Scotch. Lainey sent encouraging thoughts to her friend. Roman disappeared from view and her trash talkers became silent. She realized her dogs were staring at her, tails wagging. "You want to catch him?"

Chibee yipped in excitement and Jonah jerked the sled as he tried to dislodge the snow hook on his own. Lainey laughed and gathered her things. Minutes later her team was rushing forward to show Roman's team who was better.

* * *

She arrived in McGrath two minutes before Roman, a smug grin on her face. They had leapfrogged the last twenty miles, breaking the boredom, though Lainey had kept her dogs from going full tilt. Even though she was headed for a twenty-four-hour break, she didn't want to give her team the idea they were there to race other dogs. They would exhaust themselves long before they ever reached Nome. Instead, she ran them hard enough to overtake Roman and then kept at a steady pace until he returned the favor.

"Six oh four p.m.," the checker said. "You staying?"

"Yeah, I'm taking my twenty-four here."

"Okay." The checker called a volunteer over. "She's taking a twenty-four. Put her in the back forty."

Lainey grinned. "The back forty?"

The checker winked. "It's the rear of the parking area. Less excitement there. Gives the dogs a chance to rest without all the interruptions of comings and goings."

She nodded. "Oh, good. Thanks." Lainey let the volunteer guide her team to their resting spot for the night. It was farther away from the checkpoint building, which housed the diesel-powered boiler for hot water, but Lainey was willing to make the trek if it meant getting decent sleep. She thanked her guide and barely got down to the business of getting her dogs comfortable when a pair of veterinarians arrived for the mandatory exams.

"Helen!"

The Fuller matriarch gave Lainey a hug. "Welcome to McGrath."

Lainey produced her dog notes, and Helen passed them to her companion. "I'll stay out of this one, since the dogs belong to our kennel." She turned her full attention on Lainey. "Well? Have you officially caught the Iditarod bug, or are you still slogging through for the magazine?"

"At this point, I would love to do this every year."

254 D Jordan Redhawk

"Completely smitten, I see." Helen laughed, her arm over Lainey's shoulders. "You're missing a dog. I know you dropped one, but not why."

As they spoke, the other vet finished his inspection and handed Lainey's notes back to her. "All is good. You're going a great job with dog care, though one has abrasions on her paws."

Lainey rolled her eyes. "Heldig. I'm considering super gluing her booties on."

He grinned. "You know about it, then. Good. If it gets much worse, she'll have to be dropped, but I think she's got some miles to go before that point."

"Thanks."

Helen gave her another hug. "You take care of these guys. When you're done, head over to the checkpoint. Don will take you to a place you can get some decent rest and a shower."

Lainey raised an eyebrow but agreed. As they left, she glanced around the teams parked near her, presumably all on their mandatory twenty-four-hour layover. Only one musher was with his dogs; all the others were absent. *Where is everybody?*

Roman pulled up nearby, disrupting her thoughts. She grinned impudently at him, and he shook his head in amusement before turning to the vets waiting for his paperwork.

In high spirits, Lainey went through the line, distributing straw and releasing harnesses. She fed her dogs with the chow from their cooler, gave them a second watering from hers and made certain they were comfortably ensconced in their blanket nests. Once finished, she got out her child's sled and trekked to the checkpoint. It took two trips to gather her food drops and more hot water. The water was a blessing; all she needed to do was toss the ingredients into the cooler and close it. By the time she returned for another feeding, the chow would be ready to go. While getting her drops, she also located her new sled. It was the same as the one she had now, without the wear and tear of the trail. Not needing it until she was ready to leave, she left it where it was.

With nothing else to keep her going, her energy faltered. She stared at her sled for a full minute before gathering some fresh socks and underwear. Helen had mentioned a shower, so she also retrieved another T-shirt and sweater. It occurred to her that she hadn't been properly clean in days, and a whole set of itches and discomfort settled onto her. Lips curled in distaste at her grunginess, Lainey collected her sleeping bag. She had no idea where Howry was going to take her, so she wanted to be prepared. Back at the checkpoint, she found him waiting beside a snow machine.

"Hey, stranger, how goes it?"

"Great." Lainey yawned, her jaw creaking with the effort.

Howry laughed. "Come on, let's get you into a shower and bed."

Clutching her belongings, Lainey climbed onto the back of the vehicle. "Where are we going, anyway?"

"A friend of the Fullers. The villagers open their doors to mushers every year, giving them someplace other than their sleds to catch some shuteye." He started the machine and pulled away from the checkpoint.

She looked over her shoulder at her dogs, a pang of dread arcing through her chest. *Maybe I should stay with them.* Before she could make the decision, Howry drove away, and her team was lost from view. A few moments later, they pulled into the yard of a modest home. Dogs barked a welcome, a small kennel of six animals. A couple of trucks and two more snow machines sat in the yard.

Howry shut off the engine. "Come on." He escorted Lainey up the steps to the front door.

The warmth of the interior did exactly what she expected: her nose suddenly clogged as if she had a head cold. Her cheeks and forehead burned with the heat, and her eyes felt hot and dry. A crowd in the living room came forward to welcome her. It was a colorful mass of people, and Lainey's dazed mind plodded along at a lethargic rate as she was invited inside. She barely caught the names of the three people who lived there, hardly noted Thom and Rye grinning or Strauss pushing a plate of food at her.

Lainey stumbled through on automatic pilot. She was divested of her outer clothes and seated on a couch with a TV tray of caribou venison and pasta. Her responses to their comments and questions were somnambulate, and somewhere deep inside she was embarrassed at her inability to concentrate or at least be polite. When it appeared she would topple into her plate, she was packed up and marched off to a dark bedroom, deposited inside and the door closed behind her.

She wavered in the center of the room, squinting as her eyes adjusted. A clock near the bed indicated it wasn't even eight at night. She blinked. Someone else was in the room; she could hear them breathing. Lainey shuffled forward, peering at the bed. Her expression relaxed as she saw a familiar mop of tawny hair. *Scotch.* She shucked off her clothes, retaining her underwear and bra.

Feeling immensely better without the extra apparel, she climbed gingerly into the bed. Scotch sensed her presence but didn't wake, rolling over to drape her arm over Lainey's waist.

With a deep sigh, Lainey relaxed fully for the first time in days. As much as she wanted to enjoy this intimacy, her mind shut down and sleep overtook her.

CHAPTER FORTY-TWO

In Lainey's dreams, Scotch was massaging her breasts with firm strokes, her lips and teeth creating a fiery path from Lainey's collarbone to her jawline. Their legs entwined, Lainey's belly twisted in arousal as they moved against one another, a constant shifting as they enjoyed the sheer beauty of skin upon skin. She groaned at a particularly vicious bite at her throat and clutched the woman in her arms. Her hands roamed along a muscular back to a tight ass, and she squeezed.

The gasp in her ear drifted into a moan as she squirmed, her thigh coming into contact with Scotch's panty-covered clit. Despite her enjoyment, she frowned to herself. For a dream, this felt realistic, especially when her dream Scotch rolled onto her to grind their hips together. The weight was delicious, and Lainey's hands went to those nicely rounded hips and butt, caressing what she had only seen from a distance.

Scotch continued a languid rocking, her warm breath coming in pants as she returned to tasting Lainey's ear. Groggy, Lainey thought it amazing that she felt hot dampness against her thigh where Scotch was rubbing. *God, when was the last time I had a dream this detailed?* She arched when Scotch pinched her nipple through her bra.

Bra?

As Scotch's lips left her ear, moving unerringly across Lainey's sweaty brow and toward her lips, Lainey startled fully awake. This was no dream. Her eyes popped open in surprise.

Scotch's body undulated over hers and a rush of lust assailed Lainey, making her weak. Had she been standing, she would have fallen down. A long neck arched just within reach. Looking beyond that, she had an excellent view of breasts begging for attention. Her nose twitched with the smell of their combined excitement and another, more earthy odor. It was vaguely familiar, and her dazed mind sputtered along in an attempt to name it. Scotch's lips edged closer, kissing the bridge of her nose, angling down. Lainey licked her lips in anticipation—and tasted what could only be described as a cat litterbox in her mouth.

Reality slammed into her. That odd aroma was her—unwashed for days on end. Her mouth was a sewer. She hadn't done more than pop breath mints since Sunday's restart in Wasilla.

"Ugh!" Lainey turned her face away, pushing Scotch aside so she could sit up.

"What?"

Lainey swung her legs from the bed and shook her head, her body demanding to return to its previous activity, hygiene be damned. She glanced over her shoulder and saw Scotch's concern. "I need a shower. I need to brush my teeth for a week." A confused and slightly hurt expression crossed Scotch's face, and Lainey turned abruptly toward her. "No! I meant I'm a mess! Not that you're a turn-off." Her eyes ran across more of Scotch's skin than she had ever been allowed to see before. Her body demanded satisfaction. "You're definitely not a turn-off."

Scotch's smile was slow and sexy, doing nothing for Lainey's restraint. "You're no slouch in that department either, Miss Hughes." She ran her fingers from Lainey's shoulder to her hand.

The featherlight touch caused Lainey to shiver, though she felt overly warm from desire and from being indoors after days on the trail. "You're a cruel woman."

"I hear it's one of my redeeming qualities."

Lainey laughed and took her hand. "Not right now."

Scotch shrugged. "You win some, you lose some." She squeezed Lainey's hand. "There's a bathroom right across the hall, with a shower kit for you to use. Why don't you catch a shower, then we'll have some breakfast and go check on the dogs."

She sighed at the return to business as usual. "I can't wait to get you in Nome."

"We'll see who gets who." Scotch's grin turned mischievous. She released Lainey's hand. "Go on, get cleaned up. Molly said she has the fixings for French toast in the kitchen. I'll get breakfast started."

Lainey realized it was still quite dark. The house held a pervasive stillness she associated with the wee hours. The digital clock said three a.m., which meant she had slept seven hours straight. "Okay." She stood and stretched, groaning at the pleasurable pain in her muscles.

"And you call me cruel."

With a coy smile Lainey located the clothes she was wearing when she arrived, as well as her clean things. "Paybacks, you know."

Scotch murmured wry agreement as they dressed. Before they left the room, she kissed Lainey's forehead. "When your teeth are brushed, I'm going to get that kiss. That's a promise."

Lainey hugged her. "I'm glad you have a reputation for keeping your promises."

They broke apart and Scotch led her to the bathroom, leaving her at the door with a regretful air. Resigned to their parting, Lainey sighed and stepped inside. She switched on the light and stared wide-eyed at her reflection. Her dark hair, always unruly, stuck up in clumps of greasy tangles. The skin of her face and hands was wind burned and red, in stark contrast to her forearms, which retained little of her summer tan.

She blushed. Scotch had seen her like this. *How totally…disgusting!* This physical manifestation of her grubby feeling was worse than the fetid odor of her breath. "Ugh."

Lainey set her clothes on the counter. A bath towel and washcloth lay folded there, along with a toothbrush still in its plastic wrap. Sticking out of a glass jar were a variety of combs, brushes and odds and ends, and another held cotton swabs. Lainey gave herself another distasteful once over and stepped into the shower. Turning the knob to what she thought would be a normal warmth resulted in blistering heat. She fiddled for some time before she found a tepid temperature her cold-acclimated skin could tolerate.

Lainey felt days of strain and grime sluice down the drain. Her hair, which was particularly nasty, she washed three times before she was satisfied. Her body still throbbed with want, and she wished Scotch would forget breakfast and join her. Regretfully, she did not. Not one to deny herself, Lainey leaned against the wall under the spray of warm water and brought herself to quick climax. She gasped at the strength of her orgasm, almost losing her balance as the sensation rolled over her. *God, what will it be like with the real thing?*

With the edge taken off her arousal, she finished washing and then stepped out of the shower. Her mirror image was clear and crisp, no steam fog clouding her view, and she nodded to her reflection. The water had been cooler than she normally enjoyed. She stepped forward for a closer examination. There were bruises on her left side from the sled crash, though none looked too threatening. Her hands and face were red, chapped from constant exposure. Her feet looked to be in good condition; she regularly changed socks and liners to combat trench foot. All in all, she was in decent shape to keep going. She combed out her hair and brushed her teeth in blissful relief before dressing in clean clothes.

Gathering her belongings, Lainey eased the bathroom door open onto a dark hallway. Across the way was the bedroom she and Scotch had shared. To her left, the hall glowed with distant light, and she made out the end of a couch. The kitchen was that way. She turned off the bathroom light, dropped her things in the bedroom, and eased down the hall. Her nose twitched at the smell of coffee and the promised French toast. Her stomach rumbled.

The small, tidy living room had a cozy feel. A quilt-wrapped body lay on the sagging couch. She remembered sitting there a few hours earlier with a delicious dinner, though she barely recalled eating. Hearing a muttering snore emitting from the depths, Lainey identified the individual as her colleague, Howry. She almost tripped over another bundle curled up on the floor by the fireplace—Strauss. Lainey wondered where the others were sleeping. She hadn't hallucinated seeing Thom and Rye after seeing Helen at the checkpoint, had she? Soft voices beckoned her, and she continued past Strauss, through a tiny dining room, and into the brightly lit kitchen.

Scotch sat at a wooden table, nursing a cup of coffee. A woman stood at the stove, spatula in hand, poking at a slice of bread in a frying pan. Lainey recognized her as their host. A sudden sharp stab of hunger overcoming her, she struggled with her body's natural instincts, leaning against the door as she forced her mind to work. "You must be Molly," she finally said, attaching a name to the woman's face.

The woman smiled. "Yes, I am. I'm surprised you remember."

Lainey blushed. "So am I."

Molly laughed. "Have a seat. Breakfast is almost ready. Scotch, get her a cup of coffee."

"Yes, ma'am." Scotch grinned and winked at Lainey, waving her to a seat at the table before following orders. Lainey sat down, her stomach growling.

"Sounds like you're hungry," Molly observed. "Good thing. I've made enough to feed an army, but half the troops are still asleep." She gestured toward the living room with her spatula.

Lainey was glad her face was already reddened from weather. It took an effort, but she slipped into professional mode, giving Scotch a smile of thanks when she delivered a steaming cup of coffee. "I'm not sure I said this last night, but thank you for putting me up and feeding me."

Molly waved her gratitude away. "I volunteer every year. Having you folks come through McGrath is a celebration. Thom and Helen have bunked here every year for the last ten." She flipped the toast in the pan. "And I've watched this scamp since she first entered the Junior Iditarod."

Scotch sat down beside Lainey, still smiling.

"Scamp, huh?"

Scotch shrugged, eyes twinkling.

"Scamp," Molly intoned. She removed the pan from the burner and put the toast onto a plate already piled high. Transferring the plate to the table, she set it before Lainey. A motherly hand reached out to rub Lainey's shoulder. "Eat up. There's plenty more where that came from."

"Thank you!" Lainey tucked into her breakfast, moaning as the French toast and maple syrup hit her tongue. It was a far cry from her lustful daydreams but just as satisfying.

As they ate, Molly kept up a running chatter about other mushers who had come through her home. She never let their coffee run low, constantly topping off their cups as she puttered around the kitchen. Lainey heard all about the mushers who had spent time in the spare bedroom on their way to winning the race. Some tales were humorous and some acerbic, but Molly seemed proud to be involved with the Iditarod in this way.

Lainey ate until she was ready to burst. Finally she stared mournfully at her plate, a half-eaten slice of toast soaking in syrup.

"Finished?"

Her taste buds screamed no, but Lainey nodded. "Unfortunately."

Molly grinned and took their plates.

"That was wonderful, as usual." Scotch leaned back into a luxurious stretch.

"Yes, it was." Lainey startled herself by yawning.

Molly chuckled, wiping the table before them. "Needing a nap already?"

"Appears so."

Lainey stuck her tongue out at Scotch, receiving an eyebrow wiggle in response. She ignored the sudden flush of desire through her body. "I've got too much to do. I really need to get to my dogs."

"Me too."

As they both stood, Molly retrieved keys from a pegboard by the kitchen phone. "Here. Take the snow machine." She bustled to the sink. "Since you're checking out around five, Scotch, I'll have a decent dinner ready by three, okay?"

Scotch came up behind the shorter woman and hugged her, kissing her temple. "That'd be great. You're fantastic, Molly."

Molly clucked and shooed them away, though Lainey saw the attention pleased her. She added her thanks before trailing Scotch to the bedroom.

Her eyes needed to adjust to the darkness, so she crept along the hall until she located the correct door. Stepping in, she quietly closed it behind her. Before she moved into the room, Scotch grabbed her and pressed her against the door.

"I said I was going to get that kiss from you after you brushed your teeth," she whispered.

Their lips met and Lainey moaned. Scotch tasted of coffee and syrup, and Lainey opened her mouth in invitation. Their hands roamed each other's bodies, their tongues pursuing one another back and forth. Despite the relief Lainey had achieved during her shower, her desire resurged under the fresh wave of arousal. Their intimacy lasted forever, it lasted years, yet it ended far too soon. Scotch was breathing hard as she rested her forehead on Lainey's. She licked her lips, and Lainey so wanted to reach forward with her own to help.

"That was nice."

Lainey chuckled breathlessly. "You have a magnificent ability for understatement." She squirmed a little to feel Scotch's body against hers.

"Thank you. I've cultivated it for years." She gasped as Lainey's hand slid beneath her sweater. "Unfortunately, we have chores to do and a race to run."

Pouting, Lainey caressed Scotch's belly, not reaching upward to take rounded breasts into her palms. "Nome."

"Nome," Scotch promised.

Lainey pushed away from the door, forcing herself to disengage from the luscious body that had her pinned. "You're driving me insane."

"At least you have company for the trip." Scotch stepped back.

"Well, let's go get the dogs fed before I change my mind."

"Yes, ma'am."

CHAPTER FORTY-THREE

Scotch smiled when she saw her team. Most still slept, but Idduna rolled over at her approach, offering Scotch her belly. Her sleepingmate barely acknowledged the loss of her warmth.

"Hey, sweet girl." Scotch squatted down and gave Idduna some undivided attention. "Did you have a nice nap?"

A couple of others shook themselves from their slumber at the sound of her voice. She proceeded to scratch and rub anyone awake enough to want petting. She pulled a bag of moose liver from the sled and snacked her team. Even her morning sourpuss, Skaldi, gave up his grumbling when she offered him his favorite treat. Once everyone was awake, she doled out the dog chow from the cooler. Her team wolfed down their breakfast in much the same way Lainey had eaten her French toast at Molly's. While they ate, she fetched water from the checkpoint boiler to start their next meal. She sorted through her clothing, separating dirty socks, wet booties and damp work gloves from the much smaller pile of clean and dry items. When the dogs finished, Scotch went down the line and collected plates. She scooped up excrement, freshened their straw beds and swapped out wet blankets and dog coats for fresh.

She spent the next hour tending each dog, starting with her leaders, Ayla and Sukita. She petted and massaged each one, giving them bonding time with her at the same time she was examining them for latent injuries. Paws were carefully examined and salve applied. When she got to Jacob, she gave the yellow-brown dog a little more loving than the rest. His partner on the line had been Mu Tan. With his buddy dropped due to strained wrists, he now ran alone, and Scotch wanted him to know how much she depended on his quiet, well-mannered ways.

Spartacus wriggled in pleasure. Being the youngest, he still exhibited a lot of puppy appeal and energy. Scotch appeased his adolescent urges by wrestling with him until he was on his back and then gave him a thorough tummy scratching. He grinned at her, tongue lolling from the side of his mouth.

Farther down the line, shaggy Savasci tugged on one of the disconnected tow lines with his teeth in a broad hint, his desire to get going obvious. Scotch laughed. "Not yet, big fella. We've still got," she looked at her watch, "about ten hours before we can blow this joint." She shook her head. *Ten hours. What a wealth of time.* She could squeeze so much into ten hours, even a lengthy nap.

"You ready to go?"

Scotch looked at Lainey, smiling. "Yeah." She gave Savasci a final scratch before gathering up the laundry she had piled in a dog blanket.

"I want to stop at the laundromat too."

Scotch walked beside Lainey, her bundle thrown over her shoulder. "Why? There's plenty of time for both of us to get our stuff done at Molly's." She waved distractedly at a volunteer who had called her name in greeting but continued to speak to Lainey. "You can grab another nap while I do my wash."

"I don't want to mess up her machines with the dog blankets. She seemed pretty proud of them."

In fact, having just bought the washer and dryer new last summer, Molly was very pleased with her facilities. They were the first new appliances she had ever had, and she had bragged for ten minutes when she offered their use to the mushers.

"Well, we could go to the laundromat," Scotch shrugged, "but we'd insult her for sure. She wouldn't have extended the invitation if she didn't mean for us to take her up on it. And she sure as hell knows what all's involved with the offer."

"You sure?" Lainey frowned, peering at her. "I don't want to break something."

"I'm sure. Besides, it'll take more time if you do loads in two different places. Trust me, it seems like you've got forever, but the minutes and hours will race by." Scotch climbed aboard the snow machine and balanced her load in her lap.

Despite the awkwardness of extra baggage, the ride back to Molly's was quick and smooth. In no time Lainey was back at the kitchen table, drinking coffee and watching Scotch sort through her things. Howry and Strauss were still sacked out in the living room, and Molly had gone back to bed.

Lainey yawned large, her jaw creaking. Before she could stop it, another yawn burst out of her. "God, I'm sorry."

"Go to bed. You can use the rest." Scotch placed a glass of water in front of her. "But drink this first. Part of the reason you're so tired is that you're not getting enough fluids."

"Yeah?" Lainey picked up the glass.

"Yeah. You need to drink at least six of your juice packs or Gatorades a day. Have you?" Her fingers strayed to the lightly salted black curls, brushing them away from Lainey's temples.

Lainey, swallowing water, merely rolled her eyes.

"Thought so. If you don't take care of yourself—"

"You can't take care of your dogs," Lainey finished. She lifted her glass and emptied it. "Yes, ma'am. Point taken."

When she stood, Scotch intercepted her and held her close. "Get some sleep. I'll wake you when I'm done. Three or four hours, not much more." Her eyes slipped shut as she savored the feel of Lainey's body against hers.

"Okay," Lainey whispered. She lifted her head, searching blindly for a kiss.

Always willing to oblige a lady, Scotch dipped her head and received the sweetest kiss imaginable. Not knowing when the next one would come, she wanted to draw it out, make it last. Someone coughed politely at the door, and they broke apart.

Howry leaned against the door jamb, arms crossed and an unrepentant grin on his face. His hair stuck up at an odd angle, which ruined his attempt at a knowing and devilish appearance. Scotch almost laughed but bit the inside of her cheek to control herself.

"So this is what happens on the trail." His voice was rough from sleep.

"No, this is what happens in kitchens," Lainey said. "You can't imagine what happens on the trail."

Howry's grin widened as he wiggled his eyebrows. "Oh, I think I can." He pushed away from the jamb and walked over to the coffeemaker, which was near them. "All that snow and ice...A girl's got to keep warm, right?"

Scotch hugged Lainey closer but leaned slightly toward Howry. Her voice lowered so no one else could possibly overhear, she bragged, "And I do a remarkable job."

Lainey snickered. "I can attest to that."

He barked a laugh, taking a cup from the dish drainer. "I'll just bet!" He poured a cup of coffee and held it to his nose, inhaling deeply of its aroma. "So, what are your plans today, ladies? Other than the obvious." He lifted his chin to indicate their embrace.

"She is going to bed."

Howry's eyes sparkled, and he plastered a determinedly innocent expression on his face. "Do tell?"

Lainey laughed. "And she is going to do laundry."

He shook his head and tsked at them. "That's certainly not how to keep Lainey warm," he said to Scotch conversationally. "If you'd like, I have some pointers you can use. Not that I've had the fortunate experience with her myself, but I've heard some stories." He winked lewdly. "I know exactly what trips her trigger."

"Really?" Scotch said, intrigue in her tone.

Lainey's mouth hung open in horror. "You wouldn't." Howry smiled. "Don," she growled, moving away from Scotch to glare at him.

"Sí, mi amiga?"

"Someday you'll find the woman of your dreams. And when you do, I'm going to be there to tell her all about that Egyptian villager you 'liberated' from her husband."

He blinked at her, his expression unreadable. "You wouldn't."

It was Lainey's turn to smile. "Or maybe that little chica in Rio. What was her name? Consuelo?"

"Well, Scotch," he said without missing a beat, "you might not know this, but I have extensive experience with a variety of laundry soaps. Perhaps we can talk about liquid softeners versus those ugly dryer sheets instead."

Scotch laughed. "That'll be fine."

Smug, Lainey tweaked Howry's bearded chin and turned away. She collected another kiss from Scotch before sauntering out of the kitchen.

Waiting until she heard the soft snick of the bedroom door closing, Scotch turned to Howry. "About that fabric softener..."

"Yeah, about that—"

* * *

The nap did her good. Or maybe it was the extra water. In either case, when Scotch gently woke her, Lainey felt refreshed for the first time in days.

She tucked Scotch in for her nap and then left the bedroom with great reluctance. She might not be wiped out any longer, but that didn't lessen her desire to spend time cuddling. Regretful, Lainey forced herself to focus on her errands. Only seven hours to go before she got back on the trail.

By this time everyone had awakened. Strauss and Howry sat on the couch, chatting with a small native man. Lainey's sluggish memory provided a name—Frank, Molly's husband. Rye and Irish ate brunch in the kitchen, their mother frying them eggs, while Molly carefully folded Scotch's laundry. Despite having had a huge breakfast, Lainey's stomach rumbled loud enough to be heard. Helen peered at her and added another pan to the stove. "Get your laundry started and grab a plate."

Lainey grinned. "Thanks, Helen."

Four hours later, the last of her items tumbling in the dryer, her stomach obscenely full with her second breakfast, Lainey eased back into the bedroom with a cup of fresh coffee. She set it on the nightstand and then slipped under the blankets. With gentle strokes, she woke Scotch, enjoying the sleepy warmth under her palms. It took great restraint to not escalate things as the woman beside her moaned and stretched in appreciation. Scotch had no more time to dally. She needed to get some lunch into her and then get back out to her dogs.

"Come on, sexy. Time to get up."

"Mmmm. I'm up," Scotch mumbled, her eyes still closed.

"Liar." Lainey eased her hand along Scotch's torso, fingers lightly pressing along her ribs.

Scotch's eyes jerked open. "No tickling!"

"Are you going to get up?"

"Yes!"

Lainey grinned. She dug into Scotch's ribs once and was nearly bucked off the bed by the exuberant response.

"That was mean." Scotch pouted, half sitting up in the bed.

"You'll thank me, later. It's after two, and you need to eat before you start out."

Scotch rubbed her face and stared at the alarm clock. "Yeah, you're right." She scratched her head. "Coffee?"

"Yup." Lainey leaned across her to retrieve the cup. She froze as Scotch caressed her back and butt. "This isn't getting out of bed." Her heart thumped in her chest as the hand eased down her thigh.

"Maybe not, but it's certainly waking me up."

Lainey chuckled, forcing herself away from Scotch's touch and handing her the coffee. "Me too. And I didn't need waking up, thank you."

Scotch sipped from her cup. "That's a matter of opinion."

Amused, Lainey shook her head and got out of bed. "Come on, Fuller. You have a race to win. A little slap and tickle will interrupt your rest/run schedule."

"Yes, ma'am," Scotch said mournfully.

"Molly said to tell you she has a bowl of ham and beans waiting for you in the kitchen."

Scotch's frown cleared, and she licked her lips. "Well, why didn't you say so? Let's get going."

CHAPTER FORTY-FOUR

As much as Lainey wanted to see Scotch off, she had tasks to complete. Howry drove Scotch to the checkpoint, leaving Lainey to wave after them as they departed. Her last sight of Scotch was the woman's profile as they turned off the street and went around a corner. They would only see each other for an hour or two over the next few checkpoints. Scotch would then be too far ahead for Lainey to catch up to her.

Lainey spent the next hour at Molly's, getting the laundry finished and pulling the last of her things together. Over Lainey's misgivings, Molly insisted on stuffing her washer to the brim with dog coats, and Lainey had to admit that the new appliance was sturdy enough for the task. Strauss sat at the kitchen table, officially interviewing her for the *Cognizance* article as she worked, accompanied by Molly's husband, who contributed his own mushing wisdom. Then Molly insisted on grilling up cheese and tuna sandwiches for a quick lunch, wrapping several in tin foil and pushing them into Lainey's already laden arms as she headed out the door.

"Thank you so much for putting me up." Lainey climbed onto the snow machine, clutching her bundle of gear and food.

Molly smiled. "You just get to Nome, honey. That'll be thanks enough. I'll be listening to the reports." She remained on her porch, mukluks on her feet and a shawl wrapped around her housedress, hardly noticing the two-degree temperature. She waved as Strauss drove the snow machine out of the yard.

At the checkpoint, Lainey climbed off the snow machine. "Will I see you again?"

"Yeah. Don and I have been talking about flying into Ruby and then Unalakleet, weather permitting."

"Great!" She turned away.

"Lainey?" She looked over her shoulder at him. "Take it easy, okay? I don't want to lose my star photojournalist to an avalanche or anything."

Lainey grinned at him. "The worst is over, Ben. It might not be smooth sailing all the way to Nome, but it's way better than what I've already been through."

"I'm just saying."

She returned to him, bussing his scruffy cheek. "Thanks. I will." They said their good-byes, and she watched him go before striding toward her sled.

The dogs were eager to see her, all of them awake and bright-eyed. She walked among them, talking to and petting them for a few moments. Grabbing a dog harness, she headed over to the drop point to pick up her new sled. She hooked the harness to the sled and put her arm through one of the loops, dragging the new conveyance back to her parking area. As the team ate lunch, she transferred everything—sled bag and all—from one sled to the other, carefully making certain to center the weight of the load. She didn't want a repeat of her crash. Soon the sled was packed to the ribs with the gear she had carried in and the food drop she had distributed among her belongings. She placed the mandatory items and promotional packet in an easily accessible spot, grabbed the child's sled and went on another water run.

With dog chow steeping in one cooler and too many Gatorade packets for her taste thawing in the other, she checked her watch. *Damn, only twenty-five minutes. Where did the time go?* It seemed only an hour ago she had marveled at having twelve hours of time to work with. She ruefully shook her head.

Rather than manually dragging her old sled back to the drop point, Lainey connected it to the back of her new one. She went down the line of frisky and eager dogs, cleaning up their messes and booting their feet. Their excitement ratcheted up a level as she worked. They recognized the signs that they were getting back on the trail and frolicked accordingly. As impatient as her team was, Lainey knew better than to simply mush them toward the checkpoint. Just her luck, they would take off out of town, forcing her to turn them around so she could check out properly. Instead she hooked a harness to the tug line in front of Sholo and Trace and led the team herself. *Who's the lead dog? I am!*

Leaving the parking area, she waved at Roman Spencer who was in the final stages of preparation himself. Despite coming into McGrath behind her, he was leaving before her. A musher's twenty-four-hour break was where the Iditarod committee evened out the playing field. Lainey's break had, in actuality, lasted twenty-five plus hours because she had left Anchorage well over an hour and a half before the last musher. The only people staying longer than she on their twenty-four were the second and third mushers out of the gate. When all the mushers had taken their twenty-four, her standing would reflect her true position in the race.

Lainey guided her team to the drop point where she unhooked the old sled, labeled it for shipment back to the kennel and dumped her trash and extra dog food. By the time she arrived at the checkpoint, she had three minutes to wait. Roman had already gone, and her dogs picked up his team's scent, barking and surging forward in an attempt to catch them. Laughing at their anticipation, a couple of volunteers stepped forward to hold them back.

"Looks like they're full of beans." The checker handed her his clipboard to sign out.

"They certainly are."

"You're due to depart at seven fifty-eight," he said. He counted the time on his watch. "Which would be...five...four...three...two... one...now."

"Ready!" Lainey warned the volunteers and got her dogs' attention. "Let's go!"

The team took off at a full lope, rushing forward in an attempt to catch up with Roman's team.

* * *

The trip to Takotna was an easy twenty miles. Lainey's dogs took the trail down to the river smoothly. Less than a mile later, they climbed up the left bank and headed across frozen swamps amid scattered tree lines. The solid, well-marked trail had just enough fresh snow to make it interesting. The sun had set, leaving the air crisp with cold. She snugged her hood closer to compensate, her headlamp illuminating wagging dog tails. With the team burning off their excess energy, had it been any warmer, it would have been disastrous for them. As it was, they availed themselves of the fresh snow, biting at it as they ran.

The ground rose at a gentle angle as they mushed along. Soon the ascent became a bit more extreme, though nowhere near as drastic as previous climbs she had experienced. Still, Lainey jumped off the runners to give the dogs less weight to pull. Running helped keep her warm. At the top, they ran along a forested ridge for a few miles before the trail veered to the right and down the side. As they came off the ridge and onto the river, she saw Roman's sled perhaps a quarter mile ahead of her. Her team saw them as well, and Chibee yipped in glee. The dogs surged forward and she gave them their heads. By the end of this run/rest leg, they would have burned off the extra get up and go. Until then, it wouldn't hurt to allow them a little more exercise.

She heard barking ahead as her team neared his, Roman's trash talkers beginning to swear at the approaching competition. Montana answered back, echoed by Chibee and quiet Himitsu. Lainey snorted as Montana somehow made his run more of a swagger, an arrogant gait apparently designed to show off his lowly opinion of the dogs they were overtaking. Roman's team put on a burst of speed, and Lainey grinned. *So that's the way he wants to play it, huh?* "Let's go!"

She chased him down the river and up an embankment. Suddenly they were on a street, and she saw markers indicating the next checkpoint. "Whoa!" She stood on the drag mat between her runners. As much as she wanted to pass Roman, a five-second lead meant nothing at this stage of the game. Her adamant team wouldn't stop until they bypassed Roman at the checkpoint.

Lainey laughed as volunteers jumped forward to stop the dogs. She shed her gloves and officially signed in.

"Staying?"

"Nope. Just came off our twenty-four." She reached into her sled bag to snack her dogs. Roman had opted to blow through, and he waved at her with a grin as he pulled out of Takotna.

The checker nodded. "There's a steak dinner in it if you stay."

"Really?" Lainey returned the bag to her sled and grabbed booties and ointment. "I ate a pretty hefty dinner when I left McGrath."

He shrugged. "Oh well. The villagers like to roll out the red carpet. A few of the mushers take their big break here for the steak dinner."

Finished with her chore, she repacked her gear and climbed aboard the runners. "If I do this again, you can bet I'll stay here on my twenty-four." She adjusted her headlamp and signed out at nine thirty p.m.

"If I do this again," she muttered to herself, amused. "What the hell am I thinking?"

This stretch of trail stayed on a road, an easy section since it appeared well-maintained during the summer months. For the next eight or nine miles, she played tag with Roman as they climbed gradual inclines. Eventually their dogs settled into a rhythm with less yelling. It looked like she and Roman were evenly matched, and she started seriously considering strategies to beat him to Nome. They left the road, sweeping up to the right and overland for a bit, then dropped back onto it, heading downhill. In some areas, it seemed the trail was more ice than snow. Lainey saw sheets of ice frozen across the road from creeks alongside. Once or twice, the trail avoided the ice altogether by slipping into a ditch on the other side. Where bridges were built to span water, the path sometimes led off the road and passed the bridge rather than crossing it.

Roman Spencer pulled off the trail and Lainey slowed to pass him. "You okay?"

"Yeah. I'm just going to snack the dogs," he called back. "I'll catch up."

Lainey nodded and urged her team forward. Despite being in the lead, she wondered whether there was something ahead that he knew about and she didn't. She frowned as her sled whipped along the road at an easy pace, trying to remember anything from the trail reports she had received. Nothing came to mind, and she finally decided he actually did only want to give his dogs a break rather than tricking her into an unenviable position.

She crossed several different creeks, some with signs and some without, and they followed the Innoko River for a spell. Her light picked up dark structures to the side of the road, evidence of old mining camps and cabins. Then a sign loomed closer.

"State Maintenance Ends"

The checkpoint was coming up fast. In the distance she saw lantern light, a warm glow shining from a cabin window. She smiled as she neared. The place looked like a Kinkade Christmas card, with snow on the roof and yellow light emanating from within, promising a grand welcome home to the weary traveler. Barking dogs behind her broke her concentration, and she glanced back to see Roman's headlamp closing. Lainey laughed aloud and urged her team to hurry along.

She pulled into the Ophir checkpoint a little after midnight, a full minute and a half before Roman Spencer. It was time for another rest.

CHAPTER FORTY-FIVE

The couple who owned the Ophir checkpoint cabin filled Lainey with hot stew. Volunteers, mushers and drying gear filled most of the available space. There wasn't room for mushers to sleep inside, but Lainey wanted to be with her dogs after her extensive rest break in McGrath. She easily slipped back into the rhythm of the race, making sure her dogs were fed, watered and healthy before caring for herself. It took a little doing, but she forced herself to drink two of her fruit juices instead of one, as Scotch had recommended.

After a three-hour nap, her alarm woke her with soft beeping in her ear. She quickly looked around to see if Roman had ditched her. He snoozed on his sled a few yards away. Four other mushers had taken their breaks there, but they didn't concern her. With careful movements, Lainey got up and began her parting chores. She didn't want to wake Roman if she could help it, though she figured he would be up on his own soon enough. *No reason to give him an edge, is there?*

Not wanting her voice to carry to Roman's sled, she didn't talk to her dogs, though she still gave them all the affection they were accustomed to as she fed them. She stepped lightly, trying to make as little noise as possible. Halfway through her tasks, Roman jerked awake, probably due to his alarm. Seeing her in the middle of her preparations, he shook his finger at her and dragged himself from his sleeping bag.

Lainey grinned, moving faster since she no longer had a need for stealth. Before he had time to finish feeding his team, she had booted dog paws and cleaned up their parking area. She waved cheerily at him as her team swept past, heading for the checkpoint. She thought she heard him grumbling; it made her chuckle.

It was about six thirty in the morning as her team left the Christmas cabin. The sky was still dark, though the sun would be rising soon. Lainey waited until they got away before drinking more juice, mindful of Scotch's warning. She couldn't allow herself to get as physically fatigued as before. There were no more twenty-four-hour breaks ahead, and still two-thirds of the race to go.

The trail was both a gift and a curse. Cold weather and easy trails let her get farther in less time but gave the same advantage to Roman and anyone else coming up behind her. Within the first few miles, the team crossed the Innoko River twice before going into trees and onto tundra, paralleling the river as they went. The dogs trotted along, still energetic after their layover, and Lainey watched with pride. She had trained them, and they worked together scamlessly, as if they had been doing this for years. Granted, some of them had been, but not in this particular working arrangement. As the miles passed, she kept an eye out for Roman. She estimated he was half an hour behind her in leaving the checkpoint. The question was whether or not he would catch up before she reached Cripple. The sun rose, and she turned off her headlamp, putting on sunglasses to combat the glare of daylight on snow. Her heart ached at the sheer beauty. If the Iditarod didn't pass through here, no one would travel along these hills and river at all. This section of trail was too remote for anyone other than summer backpackers.

She stopped and snacked her dogs, keeping an eye behind her for evidence of Roman's approach. She still saw nothing.

The trees thinned and disappeared. Blackened stumps thrust up through the snow. Even in the dead of winter she smelled a hint of ash. A fire had come through there recently, and the trail led right through the damaged terrain. Lainey prepared herself for a rough ride, but it never materialized. This burn was far less dangerous than Farewell Burn. Her team ate up the miles, rolling in snow to cool off when she stopped to snack them. The trail crossed the river again. Burnt trees faded, replaced by healthy ones.

Lainey's bladder began to remind her of all the liquids she had drunk, and she fought with it for a while. Sooner or later they would come to the next checkpoint. She dug out her copy of Scotch's notes, flipping through the pages. Scotch said it normally took four to six hours. Lainey checked her watch. She had been on the trail for close to four. *Should I stop and find a shrub or keep on a little longer?* Deciding to tough it out, she fantasized about being in the middle of the desert, trying to convince her body that she hadn't had anything to drink for days, that she was parched with thirst. It worked for a few more miles, but as the sled jounced over ruts and bumps, her bladder twinged, more and more insistent. She considered how long it would take her to drop her drawers to pee and move on. Her worries grew by leaps and bounds as she traveled, becoming so waterlogged that she almost missed the checkpoint when it came up.

"Whoa!" She stomped on the brake and then cursed as the liquid in her bladder shifted dangerously. Just what she needed was to pee her pants out in the middle of an Alaskan winter. She checked in, breathlessly requesting the location of the latrine.

The checker, a thin woman with a bright orange parka, chuckled. "It's over there. Go ahead. I'll have the vet wait until you're done."

"*Thank* you!"

When she had finished, she ambled out of the outhouse wearing a relieved smile. Her dogs watched her, grinning and laughing as if to say they had it far easier than she. They had been trained to relieve themselves as they ran. A couple of men stood with them, already checking each animal's health.

"Feel better?"

Lainey chuckled. "You can't imagine." She found her vet notes and handed them over.

"Looking good." The other completed his examination. He made some notes on one of the pages. "That one has some cumulative abrasions on her paws, though."

She gave Heldig a concerned look. "I don't want to run her into the ground. Do you think I should drop her now?"

The veterinarian considered a moment, even going back to Heldig to go over her feet again. "Not yet. I think she's good for a few more miles. She's definitely healthy enough to get you to Ruby, maybe even Galena."

Lainey nodded. Ruby was the next checkpoint, seventy miles away. Galena was the one after, about sixty miles farther. "Okay. Thanks."

She turned away from the vets just in time to see Roman arrive. She debated snacking the dogs and then getting out of the checkpoint to camp in the wild. Just her luck, he would decide to do the same and pass her up somewhere along the trail. Then he would know it for the ruse it was. There was still plenty of time for friendly competition when they neared the end of the race.

She directed her dogs to the holding area and began the process of feeding them and putting them to bed: melted snow for water, two Gatorades drained, dog chow distributed and straw laid out for them. It pleased her to see Roman also remaining at the checkpoint. She heated a couple of Molly's sandwiches on the lid of her boiling pot, following them with warmed pumpkin bread slathered with butter. The butter tasted better than the bread, and she remembered Scotch eating a stick of the stuff. While the thought of doing the same still made her lip curl, her mouth watered. Maybe one of the upcoming villages would have a store or something. Not having planned for the craving, she didn't have any extra butter in her food drops like Scotch did.

Lainey yawned and put aside her considerations. She heard Scotch's voice in her head. "If you don't take care of yourself, you can't take care of your dogs." Smiling, Lainey prepared her sled and sleeping bag for a nap.

* * *

When she woke, it was still daylight, though the sun hung low enough to play hide and seek among the treetops. It was cold but not terribly so. She had a small thermometer attached to her sled. It indicated the temperature was hovering somewhere above zero. Lainey felt a mental burble of laughter. That wasn't how she had felt last year about the weather.

A few mushers were also utilizing this checkpoint for a break. As before, she kept her activities concealed, making as little noise as possible. Roman had learned his lesson, though. He had parked as close to her as possible and woke when she started up her cookers. Lainey sighed in resignation as he rolled out of his sleeping bag with a knowing grin.

"Fool me once..." He began his own preparations.

Lainey smiled. "Didn't anybody teach you that the female is the more devious of the species?"

He barked a laugh. "Is that my warning?"

Giving him a complacent look, she didn't answer. He laughed again, and she turned her attention to her team.

Lainey donned her latex gloves and hand warmers and slathered Heldig's pads with ointment. "Duct tape is still an option," she told her. Heldig's response was a snuffling kiss on the cheek.

Chibee whined in excitement as dinner was dished out. "You act like I never feed you." He ignored her chiding, falling to his chow with single-minded purpose.

Nearby, Roman chuckled. "It's never enough." He glanced up from his cookers. "You might want to up their fat intake a little. How much are you running?"

"About a half pound." Lainey went back down the line with the extra water.

"Maybe make it three-quarters, at least through the interior. They'll burn it up."

She murmured a non-committal response and continued her tasks. Would Roman endanger her dogs by giving her poor advice, all to beat her? From what she had read and heard of the Spencers, they seemed to be decent kennel owners. Georgio Spencer had won three Iditarods and two Yukon Quests. Roman had the experience of being raised at a kennel, just like Scotch had. There was also her craving for butter. Were the dogs feeling the same?

Lainey decided that he wouldn't give advice designed to affect her dogs, even if that changed her standing in the race. Besides, what would be the point? So he could arrive in Nome a few places before her? He'd still be in the upper middle of the pack, just like Lainey. The major contenders for the championship were already jockeying for position in a race neither she nor Roman could possibly win.

Regardless, she resolved to not take his advice until she had talked to Scotch. Chances were they would see each other in Ruby. She would ask then. The only reason Scotch hadn't been at the Cripple checkpoint was because she normally blew through to camp in the woods nearby. Lainey still held a little trepidation about being alone so far from civilization. Even the miniscule population at a checkpoint in the wild felt safer. There would be no choice between here and Ruby. The next checkpoint was too far away for the dogs to run all in one round. Lainey would have to camp in the wilderness at her next break.

She gathered doggie dishes and blankets, cleaned her area and booted her team. It had become second nature; she finished the tasks in less than fifteen minutes. By the end of the race, she would be doing it in five. She grabbed a bale of straw and lashed it to her sled. The dogs would need warm bedding out on the trail.

"See you out there," she told Roman, who was in the final stages of preparation himself.

"I'm right behind you."

Lainey grinned at the inherent threat in his words. Rather than take the bait, she ordered her dogs toward the checkout point. It was time to put some distance between them, at least for a little while.

CHAPTER FORTY-SIX

The straw lashed to her sled made the ride a bit ungainly, but the good weather compensated for the extra weight. Cool temperatures and the setting sun made for decent trail. Anything softening up during the day would freeze over at night. Lainey's team trotted along in the footsteps of thirty mushers with little difficulty. She joined the dogs, stripping off her parka to combat overheating as she ran alongside the sled.

They passed through an abandoned mining town with old, deteriorating cabins perched on either side of the trail. This was Poorman, once a boomtown in the early 1900s when the siren's song of gold had plucked the strings of many a man's heart. After they left Poorman behind them, occasional mining camps sat desolate and forgotten off in the distance. Lainey wished she could stop and explore them. If it weren't for the threat of Roman overtaking her, she might have. Instead, she sighed and continued to run with her dogs.

The team climbed to high ground. When they dropped to the Sulatna River, Lainey hopped back onto the runners. Iditarod markers were easy to see. Along this stretch there were many trails—evidence of wildlife, trappers and trail breakers. Even with the well-marked paths, it was easy to be tempted onto a different one. Lainey kept her attention on the trail instead of sightseeing. She went over her notes while riding the easy sections, though she still watched for sweepers. Once they hit the road, she expected the difficulty to increase. Chuckling, she said, "What the hell is a road doing out here?"

The road in question loomed up before her and the team ran along it. Up ahead was the Sulatna Crossing, a steel bridge spanning a creek. According to trail markers, Lainey was supposed to go over the bridge, but she halted the dogs. In the light of her headlamp, the bridge looked pitted and worn, just as dilapidated as Poorman had. Was it safe to cross? She snacked her dogs and checked Heldig's paws. She had one bootie on, and Lainey added three more. She walked back to the bridge and peered down a fifteen-foot drop, no worse than falling off the roof of the cabin. *At the cabin I wouldn't have a heavy sled and fifteen dogs to tangle in if I slid off.* She reached out and thumped the steel. It seemed solid enough, and there were no tracks around the area indicating that mushers ahead of her had taken a different route. She had not gotten lost; the bridge bore an official Iditarod marker.

She heard barking behind her and ran to her sled. *Damn. Roman's coming. I'll be damned if I let him catch me waffling.* "Let's go!"

Her dogs, eager to keep ahead of the approaching team, bustled across with ease. Lainey glanced back to see Roman coming up to the bridge. She envied his assurance as he never wavered, letting his team pull him across without a second thought. Was she more cautious than he was? Or did he simply have the benefit of hearing Iditarod tales as he grew up? In any case, he was there now, and she could either urge her dogs forward or let them run at their own pace. Lainey reminded herself that she still had days to go before reaching the finish line. Risking her dogs now would do nothing but force her to scratch before Nome after they exhausted themselves. Keeping that firmly in mind, she refused to become too disgruntled as Roman passed, a grin on his handsome face. Her trash talkers had other ideas. They bitched and kvetched at Roman's dogs, who returned the favor with lots of swagger and tail wagging. She laughed at her team, proud of their attitude. "That's right, you tell 'em!"

The trail continued on the road for several miles. They followed it between two lakes and across a creek. There was overflow there, but nothing too dangerous. A decent breeze pushed through the area, causing small drifts that smoothed into the trail, but even that hardly slowed them. Passing Roman while he was snacking his dogs, Lainey tried not to grin too impudently. He would pass her when she stopped to do the same.

Apparently the road followed switchbacks that the trail did not. Her team went off the road for a time, only to return to it for a while longer, then repeat the procedure. In the dark it was a rude surprise to find herself suddenly crossing into a ditch, due to glacier-like runoff crossing the trail. A couple of times she balanced on one runner to keep upright. A spiteful little voice hoped Roman was having the same difficulties. They passed a highway maintenance shed, though there was no way this road could be termed a highway, even without snow and ice covering the pavement, providing there was pavement under the snow. The breeze grew stronger, but the tree line kept its effect to a minimum. It wasn't long before the trail climbed out of the meager protection.

Here the wind strengthened, scrubbing parts of the trail clean. Lainey learned firsthand that the road wasn't paved as her teeth rattled from travelling over bare gravel. Rather than worry about Roman overtaking her, she now ran along with her team to lighten the weight of the sled, hoping the runners would survive the rough ride. She had spare plastic runners to replace the shredding ones, but if the metal hardware was damaged…Lainey had only one other sled waiting at a checkpoint—her sprint sled, which was at Unalakleet two hundred miles or more away. The occasional patch of remaining snow gave a smooth contrast to the grating of the road and the wind pulling at her parka. When the trail dipped back into the protected tree line and snow once more carpeted the ground, she breathed a sigh of relief.

Lainey passed a sign, *Mile Point 30*. She would have to stop soon. Not wanting Roman to see her in the darkness, she turned off her headlamp and looked behind her. His lamp was nowhere in sight. Either he had dropped back, or he had turned his lamp off for the same reason. Lainey grinned. More signs indicated where the trail ran through a summer village called Long. The buildings seemed well cared for, though everything was boarded up for winter, not like the aging Poorman she had passed earlier. According to her notes, she was at the halfway point between Cripple and Ruby. If she went much farther, she would be back in exposed wind and weather. Again she glanced back. *Has he stopped for a rest break? Should I?*

Outside of Long, Lainey pulled her team to the side of the trail. She turned on her headlamp to read her watch, surprised to see she had only been out for four hours. She still had two more to go before reaching her recommended run/rest schedule. Two more hours would put her almost to Ruby. It would be ridiculous to rest then, knowing she only had twenty miles to the checkpoint.

Lainey snacked the dogs, giving them moose liver chunks, which they snapped up as if starved, then returning to her sled to grab a bite for herself and to think.

Scotch was at Ruby already. Lainey really needed to talk to her about increasing the fat intake of her dogs. Besides, she missed her. They hadn't been separated for this long since Lainey's arrival in June. It had been over twenty-four hours since Lainey had seen her. If she were to follow her original plan and camp out, she might miss seeing Scotch in Ruby. On the other hand, running the dogs on through might be a hardship on them. She had confidence they could handle the extra mileage but worried that it would upset her carefully planned schedule. Why had she put a rest break here?

Lainey flipped through her notes. They were a combination of Scotch's trail notes, Thom's retellings of his Iditarod days, and Lainey's personal research. She sipped at a juice pack, absently nibbling at a frozen Twinkie in between pages. It took a few minutes, but she finally located the reason she had originally planned a full rest break. When Thom had run the race, the trail between Cripple and Ruby had been over a hundred miles long. For various reasons Lainey wasn't privy to, the trail had been altered a few years ago, cutting that mileage to just over seventy. Scotch's notes showed a good place to camp out near Long, but Scotch also tended to blow through checkpoints and park away from people. Lainey had combined the older trail information with Scotch's camping spot and assumed she would need to park before reaching Ruby.

She frowned at the bale of straw lashed to her sled. Damned if she'd drop it out here for no reason; it would be the same as littering. She would look like ten kinds of fool bringing it into Ruby. Lainey blew out a breath. *Oh well, nothing to be done for it.* At least she could take the time to go over her sled runners and change them out if necessary.

It was too early to feed the dogs, so Lainey gave them a second snacking instead. Then she began the process of unloading her sled in order to turn it on its side. A few minutes later, she was pleased to note that the sharp gravel hadn't done as much damage as she had feared. She chewed her lip, wondering whether she should give the runners a good waxing before packing up again. Her team sprawled on the snow, some catching a quick nap and others watching her as if to ask, "Are we staying or going?"

If she stayed much longer, her dogs would go to sleep. She'd play hell waking them. An interruption like that might cause them to give her trouble for disturbing their slumber. She set her sled upright and quickly repacked it, talking loudly to her team to keep them awake. By the time she tied the straw back on, most of them were at least sitting up. Lainey went down the line, scratching, petting and wrestling with them until even Bonaparte was ready to go. She returned to her sled and popped the snow hook.

Back on the trail, she thought of Roman. *Where is he? Surely he'd have come up on us by now.* Lainey turned to look behind her, seeing nothing. Maybe he'd had more difficulties than she had on that stretch of gravel. Either that, or he had the same outdated information she had and was holed up for a nap.

The dogs took her through a quiet little valley. With no sign of pursuit to keep her alert, Lainey's eyelids drooped. She yawned and forced herself to stand up straight. Now wasn't the time to snooze. Rummaging in her personal bag, she pulled out a fresh battery pack for her iPod. Soon she was "dreaming on" with Aerosmith. After hitting Mile Post 18, she climbed a high ridge, maybe thirteen hundred feet in altitude. On the other side was a gradual downgrade. She traveled on the road, so overflow and ice remained a problem, making what should have been an easy run hazardous. The trail bottomed out and crossed a bridge before rising again. She went up and down hills with some regularity, always on the road. In some cases, her headlamp illuminated nothing to her right, indicating a steep drop off. She kept a wary eye on the trail at those points. An overflow heading downhill could force her toward the edge before she knew what was happening.

At the top of the last hill, she realized she had come to an intersection. Grinning, she saw lights in the distance. Ruby was just ahead. As the sled battled the icy road, she made out large square shapes along the sides. At first she thought they were small buildings or tree trunks, but one was near enough that her headlamp lit it well. It was a sign, a crudely drawn picture of a dog team with a childish scrawl over the top—"Welcome to Ruby Checkpoint, Iditarod Musher!"

Lainey laughed. Six hundred fifteen miles done and only four hundred ninety-seven to go!

CHAPTER FORTY-SEVEN

Lainey pulled to a stop beside the log community center of Ruby in the wee hours of morning. The check-in procedure was quick and painless, though one of the volunteers wondered aloud why she had a straw bale with her.

"Weight training." She was glad for the chapped skin of her face. At least her blush didn't show too much. "Is Scotch Fuller here?"

The checker, an amused expression on his face, looked over his clipboard. "Yeah, she is. She'll probably be getting ready to leave soon, though."

"Thanks."

Lainey directed her dogs to the parking area and got them fed and bedded down on the straw from Cripple. After the longer run on this stretch, she planned on taking a full eight-hour break here. Though two mandatory eight-hour breaks were required on the trail, she decided it was too early to claim it here. Not doing so would give her the freedom to leave earlier if the team looked rested enough. Her schedule called for taking her first mandatory at Kaltag. The next would be on the other side of the Yukon at White Mountain. She hadn't planned on taking her mandatory here, though, so she hadn't notified the checker of her intent to stay a little longer than was typical. Her team comfortable, she grabbed up wet dog booties and gear and headed into the community center. Hopefully there would be some place to dry some of this stuff before she had to head out. Inside, her sinuses promptly clogged from the change of temperature but not before she caught a whiff of delicious moose stew.

"Hey, hey! The prodigal rookie arrives!"

Lainey grinned and waved at Howry, but it was the sight of Scotch sitting beside him that caused her heart to beat faster.

Strauss returned to the table with a cup of coffee and stopped to give her a one-armed hug. "You can put your stuff in the back there." He nodded toward a mass of makeshift laundry lines dangling over a large stove. "Grab a bowl of stew and join us."

"Yes, boss."

He chuckled. "Wow! You must be exhausted to be calling me 'boss.'"

Lainey stuck her tongue out at him and slipped from under his arm. After arranging her stuff to dry and getting food, she sank into the chair beside Scotch. Before applying herself to the stew, she took the time to kick off her boots and liners, giving her feet a chance to air out.

"So, how's it going?" Strauss asked. "Any problems out there?"

"Not really. Bare ground's a bitch, but my runners are in better condition than I thought they'd be. I'm not so sure about Roman Spencer though."

Scotch frowned at her. "Why?"

"He was right behind me, but after we got out of the timber and onto the bald patches, I lost him." She looked at the door as it opened, but it was one of the veterinarians. "I took a pretty extended stop to go over the sled. By all rights, he should have passed me and been here by now."

"Maybe he cracked his sled?" Howry suggested.

"Or his dogs balked," another musher suggested from farther down the table. "I've had a team quit on me when the wind got too bad."

"It's possible." Scotch nursed her coffee. "How are the dogs?"

"Good." Lainey was surprised to realize her bowl was empty. She hadn't expected to be that hungry. "I might leave Heldig here, though. She's been tiptoeing through the snow, and it's messing with her pads."

Scotch nodded. "Yeah, that sounds like Heldig. Has Bonaparte been giving you any trouble?"

"Nope. Not a lick."

A slight grin crossed Scotch's face. "There's still time."

Lainey pursed her lips and raised her chin. "You know, just because he's given you trouble on the trail doesn't mean he'll do the same for me."

"Ah, yes. I remember how well he performed for you last month." Scotch grinned, and Lainey smacked her on the leg with a scowl. If anything, Scotch's grin widened.

She frowned at the reminder. During a training run, Bonaparte had decided it was time for a snack break. He simply sat down between one step and the next, allowing the team to drag him a few feet before Lainey halted them. She had been horrified at the sight of his limp body plowing through the snow, positive he had been killed in some freak accident. Closer examination showed him to be hale, healthy and alive, but he refused to run another step. Nothing Lainey tried forced him to budge, and she finally resorted to loading him into the sled to be towed home. Only upon her arrival, fearfully handing him over to Helen for an exam, did she discover that it was a regular trick of his when His Majesty had decided he had run enough for one day.

Scotch checked her watch. "It's about time for me to get ready."

As she rose, Lainey stood as well. "I'll walk with you. It's too warm in here." She pulled her boots back on and donned her parka, while Scotch did the same. Soon they were back outdoors and she sighed in relief. *Who would have imagined I'd be more comfortable in five degrees than in a warm community center?*

"This'll probably be the last time I see you before Nome." Scotch crunched over snow.

"I know. I guess I'll just have to run a little faster to shorten the time we're apart."

Scotch chuckled. "Yeah. You do that."

"There was something I wanted to ask you about the dogs." At Scotch's nod, Lainey said, "Roman said he was feeding his team three-quarters of a pound of fat now and suggested I do the same. Is that something I should do?"

"Yeah, you can do that without harming them. As cold as it is this year, it might be beneficial. They'll burn it off keeping warm."

"Okay. I just wanted to double check before changing their diet."

"You didn't pack any extra in your food drops, did you?"

Lainey shook her head. "Nope. I hadn't planned on it. I took your list and cut it down by the amount you take for yourself, so I don't even have that."

"Well, the next checkpoint is Galena. They have a cafe there. If it's open when you arrive, you might be able to buy something from them. A few checkpoints after that is Unalakleet; they have a couple of stores."

"I'll check into them when I get there." Lainey looked over the parking area as they got to Scotch's team. A few mushers curled on their sleds or with their dogs. It looked like two more had arrived while she was inside, and they were in the final stages of settling their dogs. Neither of them was Roman. What had happened to him?

Scotch brought her back to the here and now by pulling her into an embrace. "Remember, it'll be easy running for the next few legs until you reach the coast. After that, be careful."

"Only if you'll be careful too." Lainey snuggled close. "I have big plans for you in Nome."

"And I have plans for you."

Scotch's voice was rough from the weather, but the huskiness in her tone struck a chord in Lainey's heart. With reluctance, Lainey released Scotch and stepped back. "Happy trails."

"Same to you."

Lainey dawdled a bit, watching Scotch wake her dogs and prepare them for the trail. A yawn big enough to swallow the Grand Canyon reminded her she needed to sleep. She regretfully shuffled away to her team. On her way there, she saw Roman had finally arrived. He looked none the worse for wear, but he had his sled on its side as he closely examined the runners. It looked like the bare gravel had done quite a number on them.

She yawned again as she reached her team. Her dogs nestled in straw, bright green and yellow blankets draped over their motionless forms. Lainey walked down the line to check them, returning to her sled satisfied. As she pulled out her sleeping bag, she looked up to wave at Scotch leaving the parking area. She doubted she would see Scotch again until she arrived in Nome. *Best to not think about it.* With any luck, she would get a good five hours sleep. She climbed into her sleeping bag and got comfortable. In no time, she was fast asleep.

* * *

Despite her extra hour of rest, Lainey's eyes felt grainy when she left Ruby. Daylight dawned on the horizon, but she kept her headlamp on. This was supposed to be another easy stretch. She regretted having to take it during the heat of the day, but it was either leave now or give

Roman a chance to jump ahead. He was already getting his team ready to leave, only staying six hours despite the extra time he had taken to get there.

The trail followed the road out of town, but at the bottom of a hill it took a right turn. From there, it dropped onto the Yukon River, a mile-wide expanse of snow and ice. With all that room to maneuver in, the trail breakers had made the way a straight shot as far as her eye could see. She yawned. Her dogs trotted along happily, tails wagging. Heldig had remained at Ruby, her paws too abraded to continue without causing potentially permanent damage. She had barked and pulled on her chain as they left the checkpoint, wanting to stay with them. Because she had no other injuries, Lainey felt bad about leaving her behind. With two dogs missing, she had shortened the line, placing Chibee next to Himitsu. *Maybe Himitsu will calm Chibee down.* She snorted at the idea, doubting anything could mellow her youngest pup.

Lainey drank a juice pack, her mood worsening in direct contrast to the rising sun. She felt tired, cranky and still stiff and sore from her tumble a couple of days earlier. Her ribs ached from cold, exertion and sleeping in contorted positions on her sled. She felt grimy and knew she stank something fierce, despite the shower she had taken in McGrath. *Ugh. Who am I fooling? Sure, I'm past the halfway mark, but I still have over four hundred miles to go to reach the finish line. What's the point? All this for a stupid magazine article? Ben isn't paying me nearly enough to take this abuse.*

She considered scratching from the race at Galena, just pulling in and ending it there. There had already been mushers who had scratched; she wouldn't be in the ignominious position of being the first to bail out of the race. Lots of rookies didn't make it to the finish line. *Hell, lots of mushers try every year and never make it to Nome. What makes me so special? I've got plenty of material for the next article and hundreds of photographs. Would it really be so bad to pull the plug?*

The miles cranked by slowly, and Lainey removed her headlamp in favor of her sunglasses. Cloud cover obscured the direct light of the sun, but it was still bright. Her team trundled along with little direction, but she took care to keep an eye open for trail markers. It was best not to get too complacent. She could end up in Fairbanks by mistake.

God, the trail just keeps going and going. She imagined flying into Nome and being at the finish line to see Scotch's arrival. Lainey smiled, knowing that after a decent nap and a shower, she would have

Scotch all to herself. While the resulting lascivious daydreams would have been fun, her mind insisted on following its depressing line.

What's going to happen when it's over—the Iditarod finished for another year, the Cognizance *article filed and published…What then? Another job, another article, more travel, that's what.*

Lainey had to follow the money. That was the joy and the curse of freelance work. Strauss would possibly have an idea for an article, or Lainey could check in with a number of other magazines to find something interesting to pick up or pitch. Off she'd go to grab photos of exotic wildlife far from here.

The dogs were Scotch's life. Alaska was Scotch's life.

Where does that leave us then?

Grumbling, Lainey stopped the dogs to snack them. They all had healthy, positive attitudes, and she didn't know if she should snarl at them or let them jolly her out of her plummeting mood. Chibee wriggled and licked her face as she checked him, his breath foul with the frozen whitefish he had just finished gulping. Unable to help herself, Lainey laughed, and he grinned at her.

"Thanks, boy. Nothing like a doggie kiss to wake me up to reality."

Whatever she decided between here and Nome, she would survive. Scotch would survive. They were both tough and confident, able to handle anything the world sent against them. If they were destined to be together, fine. If not, at least it had been a wonderful, entertaining and unforgettable year.

She finished checking the dogs and climbed onto her sled. "Let's go!"

CHAPTER FORTY-EIGHT

Lainey arrived at the Galena checkpoint at nine fifty-seven on Saturday morning. She had been on the trail for a full eight days. Working on autopilot, she parked the team, fed and watered them, and settled them for their nap. She completed the entire process in less than an hour. Earlier in the race, she would have been impressed with her increased efficiency. Now, her mind, numb from lack of sleep and boredom, flitted between morose thoughts about Scotch and the waking dreams of the sleep deprived. Fortunately the team hadn't been too affected by her temperament. They frisked a bit before settling into their straw beds for some sleep.

Once they were cared for, Lainey got out her small sled and went to locate her food drops. She lugged them back to the sled but didn't bother to open and sort through them. There was something more important she had to take care of, and the sooner she did, the sooner she would join the dogs in slumber.

As in Ruby, the Galena checkpoint was the village community center. Lainey stepped inside with an armload of gear. She was in luck, finding room to hang the things to dry. That task done, she cornered one of the volunteers, a thin native woman. "Hey, is the cafe open yet?"

The volunteer smiled. "It should be. But there's lots of food right here to choose from. And our moose stew is the best in the Yukon."

Lainey tried to inhale through stuffed sinuses, but she couldn't smell a thing. A buffet was set up along one wall, laden with food—even a roasted turkey that had been picked nearly clean. "I don't doubt that." She grinned. "But I'm looking to buy cooking oil or butter for my dogs. At least enough to get me to Unalakleet." She chuckled to herself. *Man, that sounds odd.* Even in her wildest imagination, she would never have conjured up asking for lard for dogs.

Despite the strangeness of the request, the woman—who had introduced herself as Suzy—didn't bat an eye. Instead, she scooped up her parka and put it on. "I'll take you. I've got a snow machine right outside."

Lainey blinked. "Oh, You don't have to do—"

"Don't be silly! You've been on the trail for days and need your rest as much as your dogs do. The sooner we get this done, the sooner you get food and sleep."

Lainey was hustled out the door and onto a snow machine. Moments later, Suzy ushered her into a tiny cafe. Four booths lined the wall to the left, and a breakfast counter stood to the right. A double swinging door led back to the kitchen. Lainey saw a cook through the serving window behind the counter, leaning on one hip and reading a book. The air smelled of bacon, eggs and coffee.

"Wait here." Suzy waved her to a stool at the counter and then disappeared, presumably into the kitchen.

Bemused, Lainey sat. A young couple in one of the booths nodded greeting to her, which she returned. Lounging at the counter a few seats down, a grizzled old man returned her stare.

"Musher?" he asked before she became embarrassed at her rudeness.

"Yeah."

He sucked his teeth and looked her over. "Rookie, huh?"

Lainey looked down at herself for a sign. Maybe it hung above her head, blinking in garish neon. She grinned. "That obvious?"

The man chuckled. "Sometimes. I seen them all come, every year since the first one through here. Haven't seen you before; I'd remember."

She laughed. "Yeah, this is my first Iditarod."

"Suzy said you need cooking oil or something?"

Lainey turned to the waitress, another native woman, who had appeared from the back room with Suzy at her side. "Yes. It's been colder than I expected, and I wondered if you have any oil or butter to spare that I could buy. I need to increase the dogs' fat intake." She felt a wave of absurdity as the words came out of her mouth. The thought of walking into a restaurant in Queens and asking the same thing almost made her snort.

The waitress took the request in stride, which made the entire situation even more ridiculous. "I think we can help. I could give you two pounds of butter and a gallon of cooking oil."

"Really? That'd be great. How much do you want for it?" She reached under her parka in search of an inner pocket where she kept her money.

The waitress dithered a bit, looking at the other patrons with a frown as she figured out monetary values. She finally quoted a price that was well below what Lainey expected. The village stood in the middle of wilderness, and everything had to be trucked in through fair weather and foul. That made the costs she took for granted in the lower states double or even triple in some places here. She sensed that arguing the point would only insult the woman, so Lainey paid what was asked and the waitress went back into the kitchen area to get the goods. As soon as she was out of sight, Lainey folded a twenty dollar bill in half and slipped it under a sugar container, leaving just the corner sticking out. She blushed as she realized both the old man's and Suzy's sharp eyes had seen her furtive movement. A smile on his face, he nodded and sipped his coffee. Suzy acted like she hadn't seen a thing.

"Here you go," the waitress said. "Would you like any coffee or anything? I've a fresh pot. We could whip you up a great breakfast too."

Lainey took the brown paper bag and rose from the stool. "I'd love that, but I've only got a few hours to sleep before I head out. Thank you so much for this. You're a lifesaver."

The waitress reddened. She brushed at her apron but appeared pleased. "You're welcome. Maybe some time you can come back for a good meal."

"I'd like that."

"What's your name?" the old man asked as Lainey edged toward the door with Suzy.

"Lainey Hughes."

He lifted his cup in salute. "Good luck, Lainey Hughes."

The others in the cafe murmured their good wishes, and Lainey thanked them before stepping outside. Soon she was back at her sled, stomach full from a meal of moose stew and fresh buttered rolls. Her team slept deeply, and she joined them. She was unconscious almost before her head hit the rolled-up clothing she was using as a pillow.

* * *

When Lainey woke, she grabbed her thermos and returned to the community center. The rolls had been wonderful, and she hoped there were more. At the very least, a thermos of coffee or even warm Tang would taste better than the juice packs and Gatorade she was carrying. She had tried to get an assortment of flavors in her food drops, but the taste was getting old. Maybe next time, she would substitute a couple of other items to drink. *Next time? Where did that come from?* Lainey snorted and shook her head.

Inside the community center, the faces of the mushers had changed, new ones having arrived in the afternoon while she slept, others having left. Roman Spencer was there, looking groggy as he spooned stew into his mouth. Lainey was pleased to see him, wondering whether he had just arrived and if he planned to stay long. It looked like she might have set herself up to evade him for the rest of the race. She could only hope.

Lainey went to the drying racks and scooped up her things. Most everything was dry, though the boot liners were still slightly damp. She ruefully wondered if there would be a place in Kaltag to dry things. That was her next layover. She could really use those liners before reaching Unalakleet. She fumbled for her notebook and checked her food drop inventory for Kaltag. Seeing that two pairs of liners were included in that drop, she blew out a sigh of relief.

"Lainey?"

She turned to see Suzy. "Hey, how are you holding up?" She grinned, putting away her notebook and juggling her belongings.

"Better than you guys." Suzy indicated the unshaven, exhausted mushers peppering the center. "While you were asleep there were a few deliveries for you. I've got them over here."

Puzzled, Lainey followed her to where the volunteers had set up their office, a row of tables covered in paperwork, radios and all manner of odds and ends. "Deliveries? I didn't ask for anything to be delivered here. Other than my food drop, of course." She looked at the large chalkboard on the wall, searching for Scotch's name. It looked like she had left Kaltag several hours earlier. Roman had only just arrived, giving Lainey the potential for a five- or six-hour lead.

"Well, old Harris spread the word after we left the cafe this morning." Suzy pulled a large cardboard box out from under a table and hefted it to the top.

"Harris?" Lainey lifted the flap of the box and blinked at the contents. A lump swelled in her throat, making swallowing difficult.

"Yeah, the man at the cafe counter. He let some folks know about your need. We've had five or six people show up to give you these."

Lainey pulled a plastic gallon jug of cooking oil from inside the box. There was another just like it, as well as several sticks of butter and margarine of different brands, obviously from someone's home refrigerator. A large plastic bag held chunks of meaty bones, still mostly frozen, enough for sixteen dogs. In a smaller paper sack, there was a canning jar filled with a thick yellow fluid. "What's this?"

Suzy whistled. "That's seal oil. It has a very high fat content. That was probably meant for you, not the dogs. You can either drink it straight or dip bread or something into it. Ever have it before?"

"No." Lainey didn't know whether to laugh or cry. Unable to make the emotional decision, she smiled as tears stung her eyes.

"Well, if you like fish, you should like this. It's got a fishy aftertaste, anyway."

Sniffling, Lainey found cards from a couple of children and seven notes from well-wishers. "Harris, you said?"

"Yep, Harris." Suzy poked through the cards and messages. "Everybody who brought something left a note for you."

Lainey read each one. The children had drawn crude pictures of a sled and dogs. One even showed her bright yellow sled bag, so the kid had to have seen her while she napped. The others held scribbled messages for good trails and encouragement to reach the finish line. She made certain she had the names of the people who had contributed, asking Suzy to translate those signatures she couldn't read. Though it took precious time, Lainey wouldn't leave until she had written a thank-you note to every one of them, including Harris and the waitress at the cafe. When she finished, she gave them to Suzy, who promised to deliver them.

Before Lainey left the community center, Suzy pulled her over to the buffet table, insisting she grab a snack to take with her. She chuckled as the volunteer buttered four rolls and wrapped them in tin foil for the trail.

Still a bit weepy, Lainey took the box—now piled with donations, rolls and her dry gear—out to her sled. It was a little after three in the afternoon, and the sky was darkening. Her six-hour break would soon

298 D Jordan Redhawk

be at an end. Still, she stopped and gazed at the village around her, memorizing its appearance. She dug out her camera and took a few photos, more for herself than any magazine article. What an amazing group of people lived in Galena, Alaska!

She put away her camera and forced herself back to the business of dog sledding. After firing up the cookers, she moved down the line to rouse her dogs. The lump remained in her throat, but she forced it down. There was only one way to repay the villagers—she had to finish the race.

CHAPTER FORTY-NINE

Scotch didn't know whether it was the constant howling through the cracks of the cabin door or her watch alarm that woke her. In either case, it was time she got up and hit the trail. Scrubbing at her face, she forced herself out of her warm sleeping bag, shivering at the draft whirling around her. The original Old Woman Cabin was nothing but a plywood structure suffering the deterioration of time and coastal winds coming up the Unalakleet River. Despite its dilapidated appearance, it offered welcome shelter to those in need and boasted a working stove that still felt warm to the touch.

Mushers rarely stayed there, preferring the sturdier Tripod Flats Cabin fifteen miles back or the new Old Woman Cabin a ways farther on, which was why Scotch had decided to break there. There were five of them vying for the Iditarod lead—Owens, Waters, Scotch, Georgio Spencer and Dave Creavey. When Scotch blew past Tripod Flats a few hours earlier, three of the competition had been stopped there. She hadn't yet seen Owens, and she wondered if he had made it into Unalakleet before her.

She rolled up her sleeping bag and gathered her things. The cabin rattled from a rough gust, and she looked up to the rafters. "Hang on, now. I'm not leaving yet. I won't forget." Her words seemed to appease the unseen spirit, and the wind eased. It was common practice for anyone using the cabin to leave food behind for the Old Woman. Those who didn't invariably suffered ill luck. Superstitious drivel perhaps, but after days on the trail, every little bit of positive energy helped. Out here in the bush, folklore had a way of coming to life and biting disbelievers in the butt.

Scotch stepped out into a brisk wind, sun glistening on the nearby hilltops. She trudged to her sled and dumped her belongings in the bag. Her team lay partially sheltered from the wind along one side of the rickety cabin, a few pricking up their ears at her activity. She set up her cookers and gathered snow to melt.

An hour later, an offering of a hot meatloaf meal left behind on the Old Woman's stove, Scotch drove the dogs out of the small clearing and back onto the trail. It wound along Old Woman River and out onto the tundra. Windswept ice hid any indication of the passing of other sleds. She couldn't tell if her competition had come up from behind to pass her while she'd slept. A BLM sign indicated the new Old Woman Cabin to the right. She saw it from the trail, grinning as she noted the team of dogs sleeping there. *At least I know where Owens went.*

Her pleasure faded as the wind hit her full force. A couple of her dogs shook their heads at getting a snout full, but they gamely kept running. She pulled up her facemask and placed goggles over her eyes. Hunkering down on the sled as best as she could, she suffered the wind battering her as they crossed the tundra. Between here and Unalakleet, she had two rivers and a number of wooded areas to traverse. The heavy wind kicked up ground swirls, making visibility all but impossible despite it being daylight. Fortunately, she had put Sukita in the lead next to Cleatis. He had a sixth sense when it came to finding trails, something she hoped her other leaders could learn from.

Exhausted from days on the trail, the monochrome unable to keep her engaged in the present, Scotch's mind drifted to her favorite topic—Lainey Hughes. Rather than pursue her daydreams of their reunion in Nome, her unsteady emotions took her mind on a downturn.

What the hell is going to happen when this is over? Scotch had several ideas, most of which she didn't care for. The one she really liked—that Lainey would decide to stay with her in Talkeetna, that they would live together in her cabin and race the dogs every year—didn't have a chance. Lainey had a lucrative career; it required her to travel the world over. Even if she decided to use Scotch's home as her base of operations, she would be gone several months out of the year. She had talked about her job often enough at dinner with the Fullers. Scotch knew that each gig took at least a month, sometimes longer, to get the right photo.

Then there was the elephant in the room. Scotch's thoughts returned to Lainey's weeklong drunk after the moose attack. Aside from their initial discussion after Lainey sobered up, neither of them had spoken of the incident. The last thing Scotch wanted was to become intimately involved with an alcoholic in denial. She snorted at herself, rubbing her nose as lint from her face cover tickled her nostrils. *Idiot. You're already intimately involved, even if you haven't gone to bed with her.* Even in the unlikely event that Lainey decided to stay in Alaska, Scotch would insist she got herself into Alcoholics Anonymous. There was no other way Scotch could live with her.

The thought of that battle generated acid in Scotch's stomach. Forcing someone to admit an addiction was impossible unless they had bottomed out. *Is Lainey at that point? What if she's not? I can't deal with her problem. I don't deserve to.*

Light flickered and dappled across her vision, drawing her out of her uncharitable thoughts. She looked around, a little startled that they had already made it to the Chiroskey River. The wooded section cut some of the wind but not a lot. Scotch barely saw her dogs through the fog of wind-driven, loose snow. They had a mile or so to go before pulling back out onto tundra. Chewing her bottom lip, she encountered a bit of lint and spent the next few minutes trying to spit it out.

There was a sharp yelp, and the sled dragged to left. Belatedly, Scotch jumped on the brake and drag pad, cursing. After setting the snow hook and tying a line to a nearby tree, Scotch moved up the line. Each dog became visible when she was within a few feet, all panting and happy from their run. Someone whimpered up ahead and Scotch's adrenaline soared.

The first three dogs on the left were in the trees. At first it looked like the trail narrowed in this section, but closer examination showed that a recent deadfall had encroached on the prepared trail. Snow covered much of it, and it was all but undetectable. Cleatis whined, ears back, a mournful expression on his canine face. Scotch saw spots of red on the snow. Her heart in her throat, she approached calmly, knowing even well-socialized dogs could lash out in pain.

"Hey, boy. It's okay. Let me have a look at you, okay? We'll make it better."

Cleatis stood still, accepting her light caress with another whimper. He had run straight into a branch, the sharp tipped wood piercing his left shoulder. Whining, he tried to pull away from the pain, but Scotch held him in place.

"Not yet, Cleatis. Let me have a look."

The natural spear hadn't gone completely through, but it was buried beneath his fur. Scotch counted him lucky that he hadn't jammed the thing into the joint itself or worse, his chest. The injury looked only a couple of inches deep. She would have to stop the bleeding until they arrived at the next checkpoint.

She disconnected him from the tug line and neck line, keeping a firm grip on his harness. "Okay, boy. Here we go." Crouched down behind him, she took his muzzle in one hand to keep him from snapping. Wrapping her other arm around his chest, she braced herself and winced, pulling sharply backward. Cleatis bucked his head and yelped as the branch came out.

With a shaky breath, Scotch picked him up and carried him back to the sled. His wound bled sluggishly, a good sign. At least he hadn't hit an artery. Using her first aid kit, Scotch applied a blood-stopping bandage to the injury, wrapping a roll of gauze around his shoulder and over his chest to keep it in place. Taking a dog leash and doubling it to shorten its length, she hooked Cleatis to her sled. She wrapped him in a dog blanket and gave him a bit of frozen fish as a treat. "You're a good boy, Cleatis. We'll get you to the next checkpoint and fixed up in no time."

Taking her bag of fish, Scotch went up the line and snacked the dogs. On her way back, she thoroughly examined each one. Senshi, who had been behind Cleatis when the accident happened, whined as Scotch massaged his left shoulder. There were no surface injuries, but his tug line had hooked onto scrub around the trees, giving him a good twist. Scotch rubbed some homemade liniment into the injury, talking gently to him, letting him know he was going to be okay.

She made another trip to her sled and back, this time returning with her hand axe. Though it wasn't her job to clear trails, something had to be done before others came behind her. The tree had probably come down a day or two ago, after the Iditarod trail breakers had been through. Angry at the loss of Cleatis and the probable loss of Senshi, Scotch made short work of the snag. Half an hour later, Cleatis comfortably ensconced in the sled bag, Scotch drove her team out of the wooded stretch and back into tundra, her thoughts as dark as her depression.

* * *

Lainey spent the night on the trail, stopping at the Nulato checkpoint only long enough to treat her dogs. She pulled into Kaltag a little after three in the morning and took a break. The dogs enjoyed their Galena bones, gnawing and cracking them before they fell asleep.

Her notes indicated the next stretch of trail to Unalakleet had the potential for problems. A straight shot through wasn't unheard of, despite the fact that it was ninety miles. As she woke her dogs from their mandatory eight-hour break, she gauged their strengths and weaknesses for a possible twelve-hour run. They had been fortunate enough not to pick up any of the illnesses floating through the race. It was inevitable for dogs to get ill, what with hundreds of them on the trail. It only took one with a cold or canine version of the flu to infect a dozen others parked in the same area on the route. Her team ate heartily, especially now that she had the extra fat to include in their diet and appeared no worse for wear.

Physically, they pulled with abandon though even her monster wheel dog, Jonah, had curbed his overbearing enthusiasm. He remained eager to get on the trail after every stop, but his boundless energy had mellowed with the many miles that had passed beneath his paws. None of them appeared to be straining anything. The veterinarians gave them good marks at every checkpoint. In fact, Lainey was one of the few remaining mushers with fourteen dogs. By this point, most had dropped to thirteen, some to as few as nine. According to the recent postings, even Scotch was down to fourteen dogs, and she was renowned for taking excellent care of her team.

If anyone on the team was fading, it was Lainey. She was the weak link. Her emotions were shooting all over the place, and the easy trails left her plenty of time to moan and grumble over everything from the idea of scratching in favor of a long drink of alcohol to avoiding the complications of her feelings for Scotch by taking the first plane out of Nome. The desire for a drink grew stronger, her perpetual thermos of coffee and many juice packs not quenching the need. She hadn't quite started hallucinating, but she knew from other mushers that sleep deprivation and not taking care of her health could cause her to see things that weren't there. Snorting, she packed her sled bag. Maybe she would finally see pink elephants. She never had when she was drunk, so at least the possibilities were entertaining.

One thing helped keep her on the trail, an acronym she had learned in her alcoholism research: H.A.L.T. It stood for Hungry, Angry, Lonely, Tired. Her entire being throbbed with those conditions, but she tried not to jump to the wrong conclusions, giving herself breathing space to think first, act later. She chuckled grimly as she prepared the team to leave Kaltag. As long as she refused to make a decision, she remained in the race. If she made it to Nome, it would be due to avoidance tactics. *What a way to finish—too morose and exhausted to quit.* She wondered if anyone else felt the same.

Returning to the assessment of her dogs, she questioned one of the vets about their fitness to cover an extended distance. He graciously went over her team again and returned with a verdict that they could make it to Unalakleet in one hump, providing she watched them closely for any signs of injury. None appeared on the verge of injury, but she well knew the things that happened on the trail.

She thanked him and readied the team. One of her reasons for pushing through was her distaste for camping in the middle of nowhere. According to the standings, unless someone behind her blew through Kaltag and tailed her, she would be in the wilderness, hours away from anyone. If she forced the team to keep going, at least they would take another eight-hour break in Unalakleet, a town of several hundred people. Civilization was preferable to the bush, and after a ten- or twelve-hour run, the extra rest would be beneficial before they started their run along the Alaskan coast.

Murky gray clouds obscured the rising sun. Weather reports said a bit of a storm loomed on the horizon. This stretch of trail was notorious for sudden and extreme squalls. *H.A.L.T.* She laughed to herself again. *No hasty decisions.* If a situation came up, she would stop and camp out. *If not, look out, Unalakleet; here we come.* She finished the chores and signed out, mentioning that she was attempting a straight shot. Better to alert the officials. If she took too long to get to the next layover, at least someone would have an idea when to start the search for her.

She didn't need to yell to be heard anymore. The dogs had calmed down considerably with their time on the trail and easily picked out her voice. "Ready." Her team, ears pricked in eagerness, awaited her order. Trace and Sholo pulled them straight, their eyes only for the trail leading out of the checkpoint. "Let's go."

Over the next hour and a half, the team climbed a gradual ascent through woods and tundra along the Kaltag River Valley. There were a couple of places where the sled tilted with the grade. It remained on track, following the well-delineated path of previous mushers and trail breakers. By the time she reached the summit, about eight hundred feet above sea level, the sun had fully risen behind its veil of cloud cover. The sky was gray and heavy, the ground white with a dry, powdery snow. Trees in varying achromatic shades broke the landscape but not the dreariness. The view wasn't as stark as Farewell Burn, but Lainey's already dismal mood seemed to descend with the trail down into another valley. The drop was as gradual as the rise and the path easy. No snow had fallen recently, and the trail was packed solid and smooth. It was bitterly cold. When Lainey forced herself to eat something, she finished by putting on her facemask and tightening the ruff of her parka hood.

What the hell am I going to do about Scotch, other than the obvious, when I get to Nome? Am I really entertaining the notion of retiring from freelance work to settle down? Introducing Lainey Hughes, Alaskan housewife! Ludicrous!

The reason she had become a photojournalist in the first place was because she loved cameras and had itchy feet. Sooner or later, the urge would hit her and she would be on the next plane out of Anchorage, guaranteed. It was a rare gig that kept her attention for longer than six months. She ignored the little voice reminding her she had yet to feel that itch in the nine months she had been cooling her heels at the Fullers' kennel.

Besides, that domestic daydream rested largely on Scotch's shoulders. Who said she wanted more than a brief liaison? They had never discussed a relationship, only the need to hold off from jumping into the sack until after they finished the race. Lainey had played the field for years. Women as attractive and confident as Scotch were players. Granted, she didn't have as much opportunity to sow wild oats out here in the bush, pun not intended, but the potential was there. Had Scotch grown up in New York, she would have been the toast of the town, sleeping her way through a multitude of warm and willing partners. Lainey grinned. Taking Scotch to New York would be fun. It would be a blast to visit her old neighborhood, take Scotch to Broadway, go dancing and show her off. Her pleasant thoughts disintegrated at a vision of some hussy cutting into their dance, smiling with sharp teeth and an eye toward seduction.

"Ugh!"

The dogs heard her yell but did nothing more than flick their ears in response, not having heard a useful command.

Lainey took stock of her surroundings, surprised they were no longer moving downhill. Instead, they had wandered around many small lakes—she had a vague recollection of passing several—and now traversed a wide, flat land. She checked her watch and realized two hours had passed while she'd wallowed in her pit of gloom. A quick look at her notebook told her she was deep in the Tripod Flats area. It was long past time to snack and check the dogs. She called them to a halt. In less than fifteen minutes, they were moving again.

Okay, so maybe taking Scotch to New York isn't such a hot idea. Lainey couldn't imagine asking her to give up dog sledding. It would be fun to bring her on photo shoots during the summer, though, when she wasn't in training. Egypt, Africa, Australia—Scotch would love to see those places. She liked to grill Lainey on where she had been, what the people were like and what she had seen. Scotch had a deep curiosity about different cultures and foods. Maybe Lainey could take her on as an assistant for a couple of months out of the year.

Eventually, though, Scotch would want to return home to drum up sponsors and begin the next season's training. Running a kennel was expensive, not only due to the care and feeding of the dogs, but also to the costs associated with the Iditarod and any number of other races each year. With Rye turning eighteen soon, the family's cost of racing would double. Lainey had sat in on a few of their "board meetings." Rye and Scotch might have to switch off running the Iditarod each year; Fuller Kennels could only afford to send one of them at a time. As it was, this was Scotch's fourth Iditarod, and she had been eligible to run it for seven years. The reason she hadn't had to skip this year was because of the magazine's involvement and sponsorship. Lainey frowned in thought. If it were a foregone conclusion that Rye would enter next year's Iditarod, Scotch would be free for an extensive "vacation." Lainey could hire her as an assistant for the next few months, maybe even a year. The money Scotch made could be funneled to the kennel to help cover Rye's entry fees. Living in the bush in Third World countries meant saving a lot of money, as Lainey well knew. Since Scotch had a home in Alaska, rent-free, she wouldn't have the money drain that Lainey had with her sublet in New York. It was something to consider.

On the other hand, if she wins this year, that'll guarantee her entry fee next. And if I can beat Roman in as Rookie of the Year, Scotch could be buried in training requests. This could be her ticket.

Hell, if Scotch were amenable to a long-term relationship, Lainey could give up her apartment and move into the cabin. Would that make her eligible for the Fuller Kennels board? If that were the case, she would gladly invest in the kennel, especially if she were able to enjoy the occasional racing season herself. Lainey felt her mood improving. *Is it so easy, having the best of both worlds?* She and Scotch could be together for a lion's share of the time. She would continue traveling and following her career and still spend every other winter in Alaska following the races. Scotch would get a steady income, a break from the constant need to search for donations and sponsors, an opportunity to travel and experience all the things of which she dreamed.

This could work. Lainey frowned, remembering Scotch's expression as she laid down the law regarding her drinking. *Providing she'll have me. When I tell her what I have to tell her, she might want to run in the opposite direction.*

A BLM sign brought her attention back to her surroundings. The Tripod Flats Cabin was just ahead, the sign indicating where to pull off the trail. They were thirty-five miles from Kaltag. Old Woman Cabin was another fifteen miles farther on. Lainey looked at her watch, pleased to note that they had been on the trail for about five hours. At this rate, they would pull into Unalakleet in eleven hours.

Rather than take the turnoff, she guided the dogs past and then pulled off for a rest break. Even if they weren't taking a full rest break, the dogs needed more food than the occasional snack. Not wanting the dogs to get the idea it was nap time, Lainey didn't break out the cookers or release their neck lines. Instead, she set out their plates and dished out the prepared food in the cooler. When they got to Unalakleet, they would take another eight-hour break. She would use the time to cook a fresh meal for them upon arrival.

CHAPTER FIFTY

As Lainey's mood lightened, her appetite grew. While the dogs ate, she scavenged through her own snacks to find edibles that didn't require heating. The pickings were slim, and she was relegated to pemmican, trail mix and various breakfast breads slathered in butter. She debated firing up a cooker to boil one of her meatloaf meals but decided against it. The dogs needed to be ready to go. If there was going to be a mutiny for whatever reason, it would happen somewhere between here and White Mountain. She took a slice of pizza in tin foil, wrapped a couple of activated hand warmers around it, and shoved it into her bib pocket under her parka. It formed a hot and icy lump against her chest. Maybe the pizza would thaw enough to eat. In the meantime, she still had a number of banana and pumpkin breads from which to choose.

As she packed away the dogs' plates, she unearthed the brown paper sack from Galena. The rolls were frozen, but the jar of seal oil wasn't. Lainey eyed the sluggish liquid speculatively as she tilted the jar. Suzy had told her it had a fishy aftertaste, but was good. It was part of the cultural diet of the natives. Quite possibly Lainey would find the whole thing revolting. Still, she wasn't one to back down from a challenge. With a shrug, she unscrewed the lid and took a sip.

Her initial response was to cringe away from it, the texture of a straight shot of oil insulting to her bland American palate, but she forced herself to swallow. It didn't taste bad, per se, but she was unfamiliar with the flavor. Her face screwed up in automatic distaste, but her body responded to its desire for more fat by demanding another sample. Once past the split second shock, she found herself drinking deeply of the thick fluid, barely managing to stop before draining a good portion of the jar.

Lainey smacked her lips. "That wasn't half bad." She glanced at her immediate wheel dogs, Jonah and Aziz, who were content to wag their tails at her. Pleased with herself, she sealed the jar and put it back in her sled. There was definitely a fishy aftertaste, not surprising considering the natural diet of seals. She felt a rush of heat as her body stoked itself on the extra fuel. Had Scotch ever had this stuff? She would have to ask when she saw her next. In any event, Lainey decided she liked it and wondered where she could get more in Unalakleet.

Darkness settled in. She changed batteries in her headlamp and put it on. Sealing her sled bag, she climbed aboard the runners and stowed the ice hook. "All right."

Most of the dogs stood up in response to her warning. Trace and Sholo shook themselves and pulled the line tight, forcing the few recalcitrants to rise and get to their places. Bonaparte gave her a long, calculating look before taking his position.

Lainey didn't push them. There was no hurry, and she didn't want any of them to be stubborn about things, especially His Majesty. "Let's go."

The team moved forward and she sighed in relief. Scotch had intimated that Bonaparte would eventually bollix things up. Lainey was actually surprised he had gone on as long as he had. Barring any unforeseen accidents, she had long ago accepted the fact that he would be one of the dogs she would have to drop. Bonaparte hadn't run the Iditarod before, though he had plenty of mid-range race experience. He had been nine days on the trail and was surely beginning to feel the need for the more regal treatment that suited his station. Kaara would be heartbroken to continue without him, but she had run without him before and would do so again.

Almost immediately after passing the BLM sign, they approached a bridge with no side rails. Before Lainey had time to worry about its stability, they were across the deep ditch with little fanfare. As they continued through rolling hills, she wondered if she would have been scared of the previous bridge had she been well-fed and rested. After over a week on the trail dealing with all sorts of physical challenges, she was a lot more confident in her abilities in both survival and endurance. Either that, or her hormones were all out of whack and the proper flight-or-fight response was buried beneath exhaustion and dehydration. She supposed the proof would be in the pudding after she had a week of pampering. Maybe she would join Strauss' next bungee jumping excursion to test the theory. Lainey smirked. His interest in death-defying vacations baffled her. She would never be caught jumping out of a perfectly good airplane.

It was getting too dark to see, so Lainey turned on her headlamp. Despite her best intentions, she drifted in and out of consciousness, drowsing as she slumped over the sled. She knew she should be alert and ready for any trouble, but she had no energy reserves on which to draw. The dogs kept plodding along while her mind drifted from the trail to split-second daydreams of Scotch and back again, with little to delineate where reality ended and fantasy began.

The snow became a road in Australia, heat beating down on them as they drove through the interior hunting for a rare bird. When she saw the dogs take a turn, she roused herself enough to see the trail marker. Heat on her chest became Scotch's head, resting after an extensive lovemaking session in a hammock. She remembered the hand warmers and the frozen pizza with sluggish interest, more tired than hungry. Scotch smiled at her in wonder as they followed their guides in the Amazon, sweat slicking her skin and a smudge of dirt on her cheek. Lainey reached in for a kiss…and jolted back to reality as she nearly toppled.

Before she completely gathered herself, a dark shape loomed out of the night and she recoiled with a yell. For an instant she transposed a memory of the Jeep in Kosovo as her fire team rode up to an abandoned house—the house where the ambush occurred and she had been shot. Lainey's ribs twinged in sympathy, and she felt a flash of hot and cold until she realized that the hulk was the BLM sign for Old Woman Cabin.

"Christ, I need a drink." Lainey removed her facemask in hopes that the icy wind would keep her lucid. "I guess this is what they mean by hallucinations," she told her dogs.

Their response was lukewarm at best. Only Chibee and Meshindi glanced over their shoulders; everyone else continued to pull, flicking ears behind them to listen for further commands.

They moved at a decent clip, but Lainey forced herself from the runners to trot with them. Every time they looked to get too far ahead, she jumped back aboard to catch her breath. The on again/off again weight probably didn't help the dogs, but it kept her going a few more miles without falling apart. The trail moved into open tundra broken by the occasional stretch of ragged trees. Here the wind blew harder, and Lainey was forced to put her facemask back on or risk frostbite. At least the exercise had succeeded in waking her. Eventually she remained on the sled long enough to dig out her warm pizza and eat. The added fuel forced her drowsiness away. The trail meandered along, crossing overflows and glaciers from the creek beds and river she paralleled.

Though the way appeared easier, her team began to slow. Lainey checked her watch. They were coming up on the nine-hour mark, a good time to stop and take a breather. She called the dogs to a halt and went up the line with snacks, booties and ointment.

Once stopped, she realized how hard the wind was blowing. It was something they would have to get used to, unfortunately. Coming out of the interior and onto the coast meant a lot more of the same. As she reached the front of her team, she noticed the trail had been blown over in some places, drifts of snow impeding her leaders. No wonder they had slowed down. If things continued this way, she would have to lead them herself and break the trail. Her dogs were tired, as evidenced by several of them settling down for a nap. Even with hand warmers in her latex gloves, her fingers were numb with cold. She worked quickly and efficiently, rubbing ointment into their paws, checking for snow balls and replacing wet booties with dry ones. Speaking to each animal, she teased and loved them, urging them to stay awake until they reached Unalakleet, which was only a couple of hours away.

"Ready." Trace stood and shook himself off, looking back at her in weariness.

"Ready, boy," Lainey repeated. "We're almost there."

He yawned and took his place, tugging the other dogs into line. All but one followed his lead.

Grimacing, Lainey strode up the line. Taking Sholo's collar, she pulled him to his feet and forced him into position next to Trace. He sat down, ears back and an expression of sorrow on his canine face. A gust of wind pushed past them and he winced away from it, closing his liquid brown eyes.

"Come on, Sholo. Ready," she urged. "Only a little longer and you can take a nap."

Her leader was having none of it, ducking his head in shame. Whatever reserves of strength he had tapped to get this far were gone.

Lainey could tell he wanted to obey, wanted to continue, but the wind and cold and exhaustion had taken their toll on his confidence. She sighed in frustration and looked back down the line at the rest of the team. They sat or stood in place, watching to see what she would do. Bonaparte seemed to smile at her, his mocking grin indicating his thoughts of joining the mutiny. She petted Sholo, reminding herself that this was his first Iditarod. Regardless of how well he had done up to this point, he had never been on the trail for such an extended time. Being in the lead put special pressures on an animal, much more stress than for the other dogs on her team. If she didn't handle this correctly, she would break Sholo's spirit, and that was unthinkable.

He looked so forlorn. She scratched his head. "It's okay, Sholo. Good boy." She quickly released him from the tug line, pausing only long enough to bring Montana up beside Trace. Then she walked Sholo back to the sled.

Soon he was wrapped in blankets, his neck line attached to one of the ribs of the sled, and Lainey tried again. "Ready."

Montana took his place with Trace, the other dogs rising from their resting places. Bonaparte stared speculatively at Lainey before standing as well, and she breathed a sigh of relief. She didn't know whether there would be room for two dogs in the sled.

"Let's go."

The team started forward. They made slower time than she had hoped. Wind blew snowdrifts onto the trail at various intervals, forcing her dogs to slog through the mess. In a couple of places, Lainey strapped on her snowshoes and broke the trail for them. She had hoped for a ten-hour run with the good weather, but it took more than twelve to arrive at the Covenant School gymnasium where the checkpoint was located. The last couple of miles were spent skating over glare ice, and she could see her dogs' collective relief as they arrived at civilization.

Covered in frost from the weather, she peeled off her facemask to speak to the checker. "I'm taking an eight-hour break here."

He frowned, looking at her race statistics. "You've already taken your mandatory?"

"Yeah, but we didn't stop between here and Kaltag. We'll need the extra rest."

Marking her time in on his sheet, he glanced at her listless team. "Looks like it. But don't worry; they'll bounce back pretty quick." He grinned at her. "Quicker than you, most likely."

Her chuckle was more hysteria than amusement. "You're probably right."

The checker was replaced by the vets. While two examined the dogs on her tug line, one cornered her at her sled to check Sholo for injuries. The team was tired and Aegis, one of Lainey's wheel dogs, appeared to have a slight strain in her left shoulder. She was told to double check Aegis before leaving.

"Nothing a nap won't fix," the vet said of Sholo. "And a good meal."

"Are you sure? I've never had a dog balk on me like that." At least not from exhaustion. Bonaparte's foibles were a known hurdle.

"Yeah. He's not hurt, just tired. Maybe the wind messed with him too." The vet glanced over Sholo's paperwork. "Some dogs can't make the transition from mountains and trees to the coast. Has he ever been over here before?"

"Not that I'm aware of, and he's only run mid-level races."

The vet nodded and handed the paperwork back to Lainey. "It'll be your call then. If he's the type to spook at his surroundings, you might want to drop him here."

"Thanks."

Lainey followed her guides toward the parking area behind the school. She had been told that the checkpoint supplied hot water. Rather than break out the cookers, she gave her dogs a double dose of whitefish, knowing they probably wouldn't remain awake long enough for her to cook them a proper meal. After their snack, she distributed straw and blankets and removed booties, massaging tired paws. Once they were asleep, she grabbed her pots and her small sled. Time to locate hot water and her food drops.

Though it was past midnight, several people were loitering at the tables inside the checkpoint, nursing coffee and eyeing the statistics board near the volunteer tables. Signs indicated the location of the boiler room, showers and sleeping room. The idea of a shower captivated Lainey almost as much as the thought of Scotch lying naked in her bed. Snorting at how far she had fallen, she fetched hot water for her dogs.

Back outside, her face no longer burning from the heat of the gym, she trudged back to her team. The brisk wind guaranteed she would have to break out the cookers. Her hot water had already cooled, making it too cold to thaw the meat for her team. Grumbling, she forced herself through the process. Her dogs didn't even move an ear at the familiar sounds and smells of dinner. She grinned ruefully at them, wishing she could simply drop into their straw and sleep as well.

The first batch went into their cooler and she started another. Opening her own cooler, Lainey saw her last two thawed juice packs. As much as she wanted to chuck them into a snowbank, she forced herself to drink them. *Why did I ever think these juices tasted good?* After days and days of nothing else, she vowed to never drink the stuff again. When the second batch of food had finished cooking, she fed her team. She was reluctant to disturb their sleep, but they needed the nourishment to stay warm. At each one, she prodded and petted until they were awake enough to eat. Only Samson and Aegis refused, giving her bleary looks. As much as she wanted to, Lainey didn't push the issue. Both of them were wheel dogs and had extra work to do during a run. Hopefully they would eat when they woke.

She collected their bowls and then ate her delicious meal of meatloaf and fried potatoes. It was the first decent meal she'd had since the last checkpoint, and it was heavenly. She polished off a slice of pizza and three banana breads, as well. Sated, and becoming more groggy as time ticked by, she trudged back to the checkpoint with her wet gear and sleeping bag. Soon her things were hanging in the overly warm boiler room, and she bedded down in the sleeping area.

CHAPTER FIFTY-ONE

Lainey's alarm beeped in her ear, and she groaned in frustration. *I only just got to sleep! It can't be time to get up yet!* She shut the damned thing off and peered closely at the numerals. *Crap. It is time to get up.* It took a monstrous effort of will to drag herself out of the sleeping bag. Gathering her things and collecting two more pots of water, she staggered out into the cold morning, toward her dogs.

Just as the veterinarian had predicted, the break had done the team a world of good. Only Aegis remained sluggish and distant. Samson eagerly demolished his breakfast, as did the rest of them, and he inhaled his second watering. Sholo was somewhat subdued, but he seemed to have gotten over whatever moodiness had overtaken him on the trail. Their lifted spirits eased Lainey's concern, and she gave them all extra loving.

According to the ratings inside the checkpoint, she ranked well. In nineteenth place, she was leading the rookies, an almost unheard of lead for someone with so little training and experience. She knew the only reason Roman Spencer wasn't in the lead was because of whatever had befallen him on the trail to Ruby. And she still had two hundred seventy-five miles to go to get to Nome. Anything could happen between here and there.

In sixth place, Scotch was en route to White Mountain. It looked as if she was riding in a pack of five mushers, veterans all, with barely five or ten minutes' difference between their times out of Golovin. At White Mountain, she would take her second mandatory eight-hour break and then make the push for Nome. Lainey sent a silent cheer to her favorite musher.

Revived by food and caffeine, she unloaded her food drop into her sled. Discarded items went into shipping envelopes for return to the kennel, perishables to the donations pile near the checkpoint and trash to its designated section of the parking area. Lainey frisked with the dogs, getting them excited for the next leg of the journey. If they could keep up this pace, she would be in Nome in as little as two days' time.

Aegis refused to be cheered from her inactivity. While even Sholo wagged his tail, Aegis sprawled on her share of straw. Lainey fussed over the dog, her mood rapidly sinking. With much coaxing, she finally got Aegis to stand, but the dog grunted with the effort and sat as soon as Lainey stepped away. A careful massage of her shoulder caused a slight whimper, and Lainey understood the problem. Whatever damage had been done to the muscle, the cold wind had made it worse. With a sigh, she disconnected Aegis from the tug line and attached a drop cable to her collar. They would all miss her sweet disposition, but running her into the ground wouldn't get them any closer to Nome. With a heavy heart, Lainey turned the dog and the necessary paperwork over to the checkpoint volunteers and mushed her team to the trail to check out.

The checker offered Lainey his clipboard to sign. "Watch out. The winds are pretty bad."

"Yeah?" She glanced at Sholo, whom she had placed back in the lead. His ears were back, but he remained on his feet, pulling the team into line with Trace.

"Yup. Wind chill's pretty low too. It was minus twelve at midnight."

Lainey had gotten in just before midnight, and she shivered in memory. "Thanks for the heads-up."

"You bet! Hang in there; you're almost done."

"Ready? Let's go."

The team started at a walk but made it less than twenty feet before Sholo sat down.

Lainey sighed. "Sholo, ready." He stood. "Let's go."

Another twenty feet, and then he stopped again.

She slumped. Obviously he hadn't gotten over his aversion to the wind blowing up his snout. She set her snow hook and walked up the trail to her leader. He sensed her disappointment, lowering to his belly by the time she reached him. "It's okay, boy. It's not your fault. You've done a great job." She scratched behind his ears and released him from the tug line. On her way back to the checkpoint, she stopped at the sled for a dropped dog cable.

As the sun began to brighten the gray skies, she and her team followed the trail to Shaktoolik, minus two dogs instead of one.

* * *

Scotch sat at a table at the Elim checkpoint. The large state maintenance garage had been converted into a decent enough place to rest and gave good shelter from the northern wind. She had already had her break and would be leaving within the hour, but she had one thing left to do.

The rest had helped ease the doubts and confusion she had suffered on the trail regarding her relationship with Lainey. Scotch would rather spend whatever time they had together by celebrating their attraction than get caught up in the drama of their different life choices. If she never saw Lainey again, she didn't want to spend the rest of her life regretting the "what if" factor. She had been through pain before and would undoubtedly suffer it again in the future. Better to live than to hide away in her cabin any longer.

Lainey had inadvertently shown Scotch the error of her thinking in regard to her past. Lainey's drunken binge had forced Scotch to shine a light on her own negative behaviors and thought patterns, patterns that had mired Scotch in depression for far too long. She owed Lainey a deep debt of gratitude for her part in the resultant revelations.

Scotch looked down at the blank piece of paper. A smile graced her face, her mind on their layover in McGrath. "Lainey, remember our twenty-four in McGrath?" she wrote.

* * *

The next few miles of trail paralleled the coastal road but did not ride on top of it. Snowplows kept its gravel surface clear of snow and ice. It looked to Lainey as if the ride across those rocks would slice up her runners far worse than the bald spots that had messed up Roman Spencer.

With a fresh leader in front, the team picked up speed again. They traveled at an easy pace— not too fast and not tediously slow. Montana swaggered next to Trace, occasionally looking over his shoulder at his teammates as if to say, "Look at me! I'm running this show now!" Lainey thought Trace was showing remarkable restraint regarding his new partner's expanding ego. She hoped Montana could make it the rest of the way in that position. These two were her last leaders, and Montana had never been in front for longer than a few hours. None of the other dogs had the aptitude, that special talent needed to keep the team on the proper trail.

Markers guided the team farther inland on an ascent. She dug out her notes for this section, swearing as she realized she hadn't done so before leaving Unalakleet. Not mentally preparing for what lay ahead of them was as stupid as falling asleep on the trail. Muttering under her breath, she found the proper passage and read along. Three hills to climb before they passed over the Blueberry Hills, and the third was one of the most difficult in the second half of the race. She wondered what the most difficult one was. Had she already passed it without knowing? Would this be as anticlimactic as the Farewell Burn?

They rose to about three hundred feet before following an easy descent back to sea level. Knowing Scotch's idea of trail issues to be reckoned with, Lainey doubted that had been one of the three hills mentioned. The trail took them closer to the coast and through a fishing camp huddled against the brisk wind. There they crossed a creek with some overflow and turned back inland. A steep incline loomed before them and Lainey decided this was the true first of the three hills. Despite the sheer slope, it stood a mere three hundred feet in height. Her dogs took it at a run, easily reaching the top with her pushing from behind. The wind buffeted them as they remained on the ridge for a mile or more. Then they dropped back onto the coastal side, past another creek. A little farther on, the trail turned into a sheltered valley boasting stunted trees. Protected from the wind, Lainey sighed in relief, not having realized how tense she had been until she relaxed. Her face tingled with false warmth, but she didn't remove her mask. Being out of the wind chill was nice, but the temperature still sat at or just below zero.

They were almost to the halfway point of this leg. It was only about forty miles long, a vacation compared to the trip to Unalakleet. She called her team to a halt and snacked them. Better to do it now while they were leeward. The next climb was as steep as the last and twice the distance. Her dogs did her proud, clambering to the top with little trouble. Again they dropped down the other side, losing all the altitude they had gained and skating past another frozen creek. Lainey felt irritation. It would be easier to deal with the wind on the coast than with this constant up and down. If that was the second hill, she still had the mother of all hills ahead of her.

The third loomed before her and they began the ascent. The climb was steady but uneven. At some points of the lower half, it seemed near vertical; in others, the gradual slant gave her and the team a breather. Trees were scattered here and there where the wind was less, but the higher they went, the fewer pockets of calm were available. In a spot bare of vegetation, the incline dramatically steepened. When Lainey's feet hit the trail to help get the sled up, she sank ankle-deep in drifted snow.

"Crap!" She urged the dogs on while they slogged through, realizing that Montana and Trace were chest-deep in some places. Once they were through the worst of it and had found a somewhat level place to halt, Lainey put on her snowshoes and worked her way up the line. She gave each dog attention, encouragement and a chunk of moose liver before finally taking the lead. Since drifts only threatened the trail in the bald spots, it meant going slower over the protected snow pack, but she'd rather be in the lead than have to run up and down the line the next couple of hours. She had to break trail to the summit of this damned hill.

There were two more steep climbs, both badly drifted. Lainey was glad she had made the decision to be in front. In some instances, the snow might have buried her smaller dogs. For every step they took, she took three, stomping back and forth across the trail to make it firm. Despite the wind chill, she felt sweat beading on her forehead from the exertion. Not wanting to court hypothermia on top of her fatigue, she shed her parka and tied the arms of it around her waist. When they crested what appeared to be the summit, Lainey's elation quickly crashed. The trail dropped into a steep ravine and then rose again beyond.

"God damn it!" she yelled. "Does this thing never end?" She turned to look at her dogs, Trace and Montana flinching away from her anger, and she slumped. "Sorry, guys," she apologized, easing forward to calm them. "It's not you I'm mad at." She petted and scratched, studying the rest of the team. They all sat where they had stopped, conserving energy. At least they didn't appear demoralized like Sholo had been before she dropped him.

"All right. Ready?"

Pleased with her attention, her leaders stood and chivvied their mates into position. The others stood up and shook themselves off.

"Let's go."

Lainey led them down into the short ravine. She had to run to keep ahead of the dogs, an awkward shuffle since she wore snowshoes. Her wheel dogs had a sled riding their asses, and the team needed to stay far enough ahead to keep from being run over. On the other side, the last bit of trail shot skyward, and she tried to retain their speed as they climbed. That was impossible, but they got several feet along before being forced to slow again.

At the summit, Lainey laughed aloud. *We made it!* The constant wind plucked at her clothes, forcing her parka to billow from her waist. As much as she wanted to stop to congratulate her team and get a photograph of the spectacular view, she knew they needed to get to shelter.

"The worst is over, guys." She walked back toward the sled. "A little farther along and you'll be chowing down on lunch." She put her parka back on and stashed her snowshoes. There would still be bits of trail that the snow had blown over, but it was all downhill from here.

"Let's go!"

CHAPTER FIFTY-TWO

The descent was a dangerous combination of fast and icy. Trees lined the trail in several places, and Lainey had to stand on the brake and pad to keep from overrunning her dogs or losing control of the sled. The trail curved back and forth, creating the constant threat of tipping or running into the sparse tree coverage. They hit the bottom hard and then climbed a hundred-foot ridge before they lost any speed.

On the other side of the ridge stretched the coast, the trail paralleling snow-covered dunes. On somewhat level ground and with a fresh leader, her team picked up speed. In a few places Lainey saw where other mushers had climbed out of the slough to ride on top of the dunes. The marked trail was visibly blown over in places, and she decided to follow her predecessors' more experienced lead, directing Trace and Montana to climb onto the crest of the dune. Here the ride smoothed, but the wind remained a constant irritant. According to her notes, it had less force than it would have in a few hours. The wind had a tendency to die down just after dawn and pick up in the late afternoons. Lainey dug out her watch. It was coming up on noon now. Without even trying, she had lucked into the perfect time to travel this section. She certainly hoped the wind wouldn't pick up too much.

Sometimes the gusts were so bad that mushers could not leave out of the next checkpoint.

In the distance, she could see buildings. *Almost there!* As her team neared the abandoned town of Shaktoolik, she sluggishly estimated her time on the trail. It had been four, maybe four and a half hours since they had left Unalakleet. The next section of trail was to Koyuk, about sixty miles away. After the exhausting twelve-hour stretch she had run the day before, she didn't think it would be a good idea to forge on past this next checkpoint, regardless of the possibility of being forced to remain longer than planned. At the very least, the dogs needed a full meal in their bellies and a short nap. Lainey hoped the winds wouldn't gust too strongly in the late afternoon.

She studied her team, searching for moodiness or failing energy levels. They all were running steady and strong. Montana still swaggered and Chibee loped along, snatching mouthfuls of snow to quench his thirst. All in all, they looked damned good, and tears stung Lainey's eyes as her fatigue sapped her control of her emotions. She laughed aloud at her maudlin feelings. *Who needs booze? Exhaustion gives the same sensations, hallucinations included. It's cheaper too.* Past the old town, more buildings became visible ahead. New Shaktoolik beckoned.

* * *

Lainey checked in at the National Guard Armory. Her team was guided around to the south side of the building, where the wind was less bothersome. She immediately fed the dogs and prepared them for sleep. She planned on remaining about four hours, hardly time for her to get any sleep at all. Cold water was available, and she set about cooking up the next batch of food for her team and herself. She thawed the buttered rolls from Galena, fondly remembering Harris and the others who had donated butter and oil. It had lasted a lot longer than she had expected, a welcome additive to help combat the frigid wind. She had wanted to get more, but she had left Unalakleet before the stores opened. With some regret, she cut the last stick of donated butter into the dog chow along with the additives she had in her food drop. She still had a half gallon of cooking oil, but that would only last her another couple of stops.

As much as she yearned for sleep, Lainey forced herself to stand and move around. Sleeping now might mean the difference of three or four places, maybe even Rookie of the Year. She might not hear her alarm when it was time to move on. With nothing constructive to do while the dogs rested, she stepped into the armory checkpoint to look over the standings.

Scotch was still out on the trail with a number of the top veterans. Georgio Spencer was already in White Mountain, and it was anybody's guess who would arrive next. Jon Waters, Drew Owens and Dave Creavey were all in the same pack. Scotch wasn't the only woman in the sweet spot, either. Alice Westin, a ten-year veteran, was right up there with the rest. Lainey wondered whether any of them were getting nervous at Scotch's current position in first place. As it stood, even if she came in behind all of them, she would still place higher than her personal best.

"Lainey Hughes?"

She turned with a smile. "Yeah?"

A volunteer smiled at her. "Thought that was you. I saw you had checked in." She nodded at the board. "I've got something for you."

Certainly Harris and his cronies can't send butter and oil all the way over here, can they?

The volunteer pulled a crinkled envelope out of her pocket. "Scotch told me to give this to you when you came in. I'm glad you decided to lay over, or I'd have missed you."

Lainey took the envelope with a grin. "Thanks." She paused long enough to grab a cup of coffee from an urn and then sat at a rickety table to open her treasure.

Lainey,
You've made it this far! You can finish, I know it!
The trip to Koyuk is going to be the worst—flat, straight and boring as hell. Don't let it get you down. Don't stop. It's less than fifty miles but I guarantee it'll feel like a hundred and fifty. Put on your iPod and keep yourself entertained, but don't get complacent. Keep alert, and watch for the trail signs.
I dare you to make it to Nome. Double dog dare you.
I'll be waiting,
Scotch

"Double dog dare, huh?" Lainey doubted either of their teams would be pleased by Scotch's slander, if they could understand the words. Her eyes watered as she held the note to her chest. That was one thing she wouldn't miss when this race was over—these overly emotional reactions. Sniffling, she glanced around self-consciously, but no one appeared to have noticed her minor outburst. She reread the note three times before putting it back into its envelope and tucking it into her bib pocket. Had Scotch written it after arriving here, or before she even started the race? There was that note that Howry had given her at the starting line—

Lainey blinked.

She was supposed to have read that one at her first eight-hour break and had completely forgotten it. Word from Scotch, even old and outdated word, was better than none. Lainey grabbed her parka and hastened outside to her sled. The dogs slept on, hardly rousing at her arrival. She opened her personal bag and rooted through the munchies and camera gear to find the crumpled, smudged envelope. Grinning, Lainey sank down to the sled and opened her letter.

Lainey,

If you waited to read this like Don told you, you've reached the Yukon. Congratulations! You've made it past the worst obstacles the first part of the race has thrown at you.

The next bit gets tricky. The trail isn't the danger now, you are. It's so easy to fall into the traps here. You can exhaust your dogs as you try to beat other mushers, getting caught up in the "race." Or you can allow the lack of sleep and the poor diet to bring you down until you wallow in emotional trauma or even make yourself sick.

Be aware of the reality of the situation. As much fun as it is to kick some musher's ass on a sprint, it isn't worth exhausting the dogs. The Iditarod started as a medical emergency run, but it's all about the dogs now.

As for the depression, I want you to know that no matter what you think or feel about yourself, I love you…

Lainey gasped aloud and reread that sentence. Swallowing against a lump in her throat, her heart thumping, she read on.

As for the depression, I want you to know that no matter what you think or feel about yourself, I love you. I know I could have chosen a better way to tell you, but we've been busy getting everything prepared for the race, and there's been no time to really talk about our situation. I had planned on telling you when you got to Nome, but watching you sleep has inspired me to get out of bed and write this.

We need to talk. I have no idea what our future holds, Lainey, but I do know I want one with you. Maybe I'm putting too much pressure on you; I mean, you've traveled the world. Surely that's more fun than hanging out in Alaska with a bunch of smelly dogs. But no matter what you decide, I'll support you, okay?

Well, now I'm getting emotional. I think it's time to close.

Keep going, Lainey. I know you can make it to Nome. You've survived so much before you ever came to Alaska...what's a thousand-mile dog sled race, huh?

Love,
Scotch

Lainey sniffled and sobbed, not entirely certain which emotion was the strongest. Surprise, of course. The last thing she had expected was a love letter. Not that Scotch was unromantic, but her primary focus was on the kennel and its operations. She and Lainey had spent many nights at the cabin, curled in front of the fireplace, talking about all sorts of things, but never this. A warm, fuzzy blanket of relief rolled over her, relaxing a tension she hadn't known she was carrying. Since Howry's discovery of her feelings for Scotch, Lainey had unsuccessfully fought it off. She had never loved anyone before, but she had seen friends and acquaintances fall and fall hard. Not many made it out the other side of a relationship intact, especially when the object of their affections didn't share them. Lainey's biggest worry was that Scotch would want a fling, nothing more, and urge her to leave for the next gig with nary a thought beyond a fun lay. Now Lainey had discovered that Scotch felt the same way as she did.

The contingency plans Lainey had dreamed up on the trail suddenly loomed in her mind. Even as she had schemed, there was always the consideration that Scotch would laugh in her face. But now? Now it seemed that her idea of having Scotch along with her for future freelance gigs seemed plausible. Maybe they could have the best of both worlds. Her tears ice upon her cheeks, she wiped them away, forcing herself to stand. The note went back into its envelope and was tucked beside the one already in her bib coverall pocket. Snuffling, she dug out her toilet paper and blew her nose, depositing the wadded mess into a small trash bag in her sled.

"You okay?"

Lainey turned to see a musher hovering over his sled. She couldn't remember his name but knew he was a rookie like herself. He had started far back in the pack. He must be good to have made it so far, so fast.

"Bad news?"

"Good news." She smiled tremulously.

"Good for you." He nodded. "How long you staying?"

Her competitive edge shot to the fore, and she tried to recall whether he had been there when she checked in earlier. Glancing casually at her watch, she realized he'd just come in. It had been two and a half hours, and she had less than two to go before she wanted to leave. "I'm thinking of staying for a full seven hours," she lied. "We took the Kaltag to Unalakleet in one jump, and the dogs still really need the rest."

He nodded again, eyeing her in speculation. "Sounds like a plan. I hear the next stretch is boring as hell."

"Me too." Lainey said her good-byes and headed back toward the checkpoint. She needed to stay awake long enough for him to fall asleep. From here on out, every musher would begin to think of the Iditarod as a race, not an endurance run. No more working or running together, the goal was getting to Nome before everyone else.

Smiling, she stepped into the armory, pressing the letters against her chest.

Getting to Nome is definitely the goal.

CHAPTER FIFTY-THREE

The unnamed rookie decided to weather his break inside the armory rather than in the elements. While he slumped at a table, head on folded arms, Lainey yawned and made a production of going out to her sled for some shuteye. Her ruse didn't completely work. Once she began the process of waking her dogs and cooking a quick meal for all of them, another musher appeared from the checkpoint building. The woman grinned and winked at her before beginning her own chores. Lainey sighed. At least the rookie hadn't gotten suspicious.

By the time everything was ready to go, the veteran musher had already left. Lainey kept a close eye on the front door of the armory, half expecting the rookie to come bursting out as she signed the checkout sheet. He didn't, and she urged her dogs to get a move on. They obliged, hardly showing the effects of their recent twelve-hour run. It wasn't until Shaktoolik was out of sight that Lainey breathed a sigh of relief at stealing a lead on her competition.

As Scotch had said, the trail was easy. Too easy. It shot straight as an arrow, with little variation of scenery. It was flat, bland and boring, the only excitement provided by the occasional swell of ice that roughened the ride. Even the blowing wind did little to make things interesting. Lainey saw the veteran about a mile ahead but knew better than to try to catch up. She still had two hundred miles to go. Instead, she followed Scotch's suggestion and put her headphones on, listening to music as her team ate up the miles.

Distances were deceptive, as was the rushing of the wind on her face. The two combined made her feel as if they were speeding along at a good clip of fifteen or twenty miles an hour, an impossibility for her team—which had been clocked at fourteen for a short sprint on an excellent day back at the kennels. They couldn't actually be maintaining that pace for this long. The view rarely changed, giving credence to the sensation of speed. It seemed that they ran, ran, ran on a huge hamster wheel—no matter how long or hard the dogs trotted, nothing changed. To keep her spirits up, she frequently pulled out Scotch's letters, especially the first one she'd written.

The sun went down and she stopped to snack the dogs and check them over. Everyone appeared strong and vigorous, and she gave them each an extra chunk of moose liver for their efforts. She put on her headlamp and changed the battery pack for her iPod. Riding on sea ice, far from shore, she jumped at a deep resounding boom somewhere to her left, yanking the plugs from her ears. That had been sea ice cracking. She stared, suddenly wondering if she was too far out. She had been vigilant so far, always finding the next trail marker. The dogs glanced in the direction of the sound but didn't seem anxious. *The trail breakers wouldn't send us too far out onto the sea, would they? Has it been warm enough to melt sea ice?* She recalled a book she had read on the first woman winner of the Iditarod, something about the sea ice breaking and sending the trail marker several hundred feet out to sea. The ice had then re-formed, and her team had led her straight out to sea to get to that marker.

"You know what you're doing?" she asked Trace.

He glanced back at her as if to say, "Well, duh. I am the one with the experience here."

Lainey decided to leave the iPod off for the time being. Several times through the course of the evening, she heard ice cracking again but saw nothing that indicated any danger for her team. Eventually she turned the music back on and ignored the sounds, though it was difficult. Her ears strained to listen beyond the tunes, and she whispered along with the lyrics in a further effort to distract herself.

After what seemed like a full night of mushing, she saw lights ahead and felt a thrill of relief. Her initial pleasure faded as the lights sat off in the distance forever, a shining beacon that they were almost to their destination, but never seemed to get closer. It was another hour or more before she actually arrived at the checkpoint.

"That sucked."

The volunteer chuckled. "Yeah. We hear that a lot. Almost makes you wish you were back at the Burn?"

"Almost!"

The race officials had rented a nearby building where mushers and volunteers could rest, but it was a couple of blocks from where the dogs were parked. As she fed and watered her team, Lainey considered her options. While it would be nice to dry some of her gear, providing there was room, she would lose whatever edge she might be able to cultivate. Anyone staying in the building would know when she left to prepare for departure. If she slept with her dogs, she had a shot at sneaking out when no one was looking. Decided, she devoured her dinner.

* * *

Scotch blew into the Safety checkpoint, glancing over her shoulder for her competition. When she had left her mandatory eight-hour break in White Mountain, Owens was due to leave twenty-seven minutes later. She had since seen him closing in on the trail, his dogs looming closer and closer as the miles went by.

"First place!" The checker offered his clipboard for her to sign.

"Any word on how far back Owens is?" Scotch dug through her pack for her vet check paperwork and dog booties.

"Reports on the radio say about fifteen minutes." The checker waved the veterinarians over. "He's making good time."

Scotch swore under her breath, handing off the paperwork and grabbing a bag of frozen meat for the dogs. "That's too close." She went down the line, giving treats to her team as the vets went over them. Working her way back, she booted the dogs who needed it and confirmed everyone was still in good health.

"What do you think, Scotch? Think you'll be the winner this year?"

She glanced up at a cluster of reporters standing alongside her sled, careful not to impede her activities. "I think Owens has a hell of a team—strong and fast." She found the packet of promotional materials, locating her racing bib along with them. Slipping the bib over her head, Scotch took off her gloves in order to tie it at her waist.

"But I'm still fifteen minutes in the lead." She grinned rakishly at the reporters' laughter, ignoring the flashes of photography.

The lead vet returned her paperwork. "All good. You're clear to leave."

Scotch put the papers away, double checked her required gear and closed up her sled bag. Clambering back onto the sled, she motioned the checker to her. "I'm out." After she signed his paper, she called her team to order and gave the word. They pulled out of Safety amid calls of encouragement and congratulations.

They had twenty-two miles to traverse, maybe an hour and a half of time, to get to Nome first. With Owens breathing down her neck, Scotch felt a strong urge to push her team for all they were worth. She forced her eagerness down, knowing it was too early to pour on the extra speed. She had pampered her dogs as much as she could to maintain a reserve of energy. That type of all-out running couldn't be initiated until she was on Front Street.

She sped along the Nome-to-Council road, enjoying the wide, packed surface. Unable to help herself, she constantly looked back over her shoulder. The road was an easy run for ten miles, a negative for her with Owens closing in. Word had gotten out about her approach. Unlike the Anchorage or Wasilla starts, the roadside wasn't packed with people. However, the occasional hardy soul ventured out to catch sight of a passing Iditarod racer, especially one this close to winning. Over the next several miles, Scotch waved and called to a handful of people who had come out to pay their respects.

Dropping off the road, they sledded along the tidal flats, then up a four-hundred-foot saddle. The dogs barked, pulling a little more speedily as they neared the top of the saddle. Scotch grinned, pleased with their enthusiasm as they told off the small musk oxen herd that invariably wintered on Cape Nome. She saw two or three dark heads lift to stare at them, but none of the beasts wandered over for a closer look.

A few minutes later, Scotch frowned as she heard other dogs barking. She looked back to see Owens coming over the saddle, maybe a mile away and closing. "Shit." Spinning back around, she gauged how far she had to go, knowing she couldn't call her team to top speed yet. The trail followed along the Nome River. "Three miles," she muttered to herself, checking on Owens' progress. He had to be within a half mile of her now. She searched the way ahead, finding the tall radio towers ahead on the right. As soon as she arrived at that point, she could let the dogs have their heads. Any sooner than that would be too risky.

As soon as they drew abreast of the radio towers, Scotch yelled out to her team, "Let's go! Let's go *home!*" The added word propelled her dogs' efforts as they pushed forward, knowing they were nearly done for the day.

Owens' team talked trash to hers as they got closer, putting forth their own concerted effort to reach the finish line. Past the bridge and along the embankment, the two teams sped, urged on by the few fans who had ventured out to catch sight of the first finishers. As Scotch's team took the sharp turn leading up to Front Street and the waiting police escort, she caught sight of Owens' lead dog almost even with her.

"Home, boys! Let's go home! We're almost there!"

The weather here had made for good sledding. Snow covered the street, and a growing crowd filled the sidewalk on either side. The excitement spurred her dogs onward, too stirred up to trade attitude with the dog team closing in on their right. Scotch couldn't hear Owens' team or the man himself, though a quick peek behind showed he was hollering for all he was worth.

The trail ahead narrowed, and there were barriers on either side to discourage racing fans from getting in the way. The police escort pulled aside to let them pass. Owens' team inched forward, and Scotch hoped they didn't have what it took to reach that beautiful burled arch before she did. Deafened by the roar of the watchers, she nevertheless screamed at her dogs, not caring that they probably couldn't hear a single word. The bow of Owens' sled pulled into her peripheral vision.

Then they were past the arch, and a horde of volunteers leaped out to catch the dogs as they pelted past. Scotch stood on the brake and drag pad until the sled ground to a halt. She stepped off the runners into a mass of friends and family, all yelling and slapping her on the back. Turning back to the race officials at her sled, she unearthed the mandatory items from her bag and officially signed in on the checker's clipboard. Despite the pandemonium around her, she distinctly heard the loudspeaker as the announcer said, "First Place, Scotch Fuller of Fuller Kennels! Second Place, Drew Owens. Congratulations!"

Clutching her brother and father to her, Scotch burst into tears, wishing Lainey was there to celebrate her very first championship.

* * *

Six hours after her break started, Lainey was at the checkpoint with her team, ready to go. She grinned to herself when she saw the rookie she had ditched in Shaktoolik snoozing a couple of sleds over. He had yet to wake by the time she pulled out of the parking area. This guy was good, but Roman Spencer had been harder to trick. She wondered how Roman was doing and vowed to check his statistics at the next checkpoint.

"This is for you."

Lainey smiled as she took the envelope from the young woman. She recognized Scotch's handwriting and tucked the letter into her pocket. "Thanks." She signed the clipboard and headed out of Koyuk at three in the morning. Keeping tabs on the trail ahead, she quickly opened the envelope.

Lainey,

Forty-eight more miles down, forty-eight to go to the next checkpoint. You've mushed for over nine hundred miles! You have less than two hundred to go!

When you get to Nome, I'll introduce you to a friend of mine. Her name's Beth. She and her girlfriend have offered us their spare room while we're in town. They live on the outskirts of Nome. Lots of hot water for showering and clean clothes, privacy, a large fluffy bed to catch up on your rest. And Beth is a fantastic cook.

You'd better not take too long or I'll use up all the hot water.

Love you,

Scotch

She knew the grin on her face was wide and foolish but couldn't help it. Those cartoon hearts and fireworks twirled about her head again. She laughed aloud. Thank God she was the only one who could see those hallucinations.

Soon boredom set in as they continued along sea ice. It was ten miles or more before the trail cut inland and across low ground. She felt a modicum of relief at the knowledge that those forlorn-sounding cracks from the ice would no longer indicate a potential danger. The trail climbed a series of small hills and ridges, working its way back into a stand of trees. The added protection from the wind cut the bite. It felt almost balmy after hours of riding in wind chill. This was hardly the tropical gig she had planned on getting from Strauss all those months ago.

At the final height of the last summit, she saw a red light in the distance. Switching on her headlamp, she dug out her trail notes. It was a radio beacon at Moses Point, about twenty miles away from her. She wondered whether she would get closer to it before Elim or if the trail would turn away. Putting her notes away, she checked her watch as they headed back into a valley. Two hours had passed. Conceivably she was nearing the halfway point of this stretch. Her dogs looked healthy and strong as they loped down the trail. She had planned to take another six-hour break at Elim, but she began to wonder if she could push through to Golovin instead, only another twenty-six miles beyond. She took her notes back out to study.

The wind picked up as they descended, becoming fiercer. Weather reports hadn't indicated gusts of this strength. She realized they were running into a small river valley, which created a natural wind tunnel. The trail ahead had blown out in some places, and her dogs began to slow as they forged their way through. Her visibility remained good, despite the wind plucking at her parka and gear. Strong enough in some places to make the sled shudder, the wind was coming from her right rather than behind her. Stopping wasn't suggested in her notes. She had no idea whether or not the wind would die down. She might be waiting quite some time before it diminished enough to make her run easy. There was a cabin indicated on the other side of the river she was crossing, and she considered stopping. No. They were nearly at the halfway point, and any delay would take a notch out of her standings. That rookie was still back there, and she knew a couple of other mushers had gotten the jump on her at the last checkpoint. Another scan of her dogs showed them strong and solid. They would push on through.

The Kwik River lay before them and the team crossed with ease. Within a mile or two, the trail turned so that the wind blew more at their backs than crossways. Lainey breathed a sigh. Even her dogs seemed happier, their tails wagging as they no longer had to fight every step of the way. They dropped back onto sea ice. The Moses Point beacon blinked ahead of her, and her team pressed forward on the smooth, straight trail. Even the false menace of cracking sea ice didn't faze her now. Soon even that potential threat vanished as they climbed back onto shore.

Old Elim was ahead, abandoned for whatever reasons and converted into a fishing camp. They passed old buildings boarded up for winter. In the darkness before dawn, Lainey thought she saw a light shining in one of the cabins. Did people come out here for the race?

The wind nipping at her heels, her team ran on, leaving the ghost village to whatever brave soul preferred the solitude. More buildings loomed ahead—the Moses Point station, also abandoned. As the sky lightened toward dawn, Lainey made out towers in the distance. The solitary beacon blinked on and on. Once she passed the last of the towers, the trail turned onto a road.

The wind had blown the road bare in spots. The gravel here didn't devastate her runners as badly as the patch they had hit just before the Unalakleet checkpoint. The rough ride made her direct the dogs to the shoulder where some snow remained. Flat lands gave way to a steady climb. The snow here was packed, and she jumped off the runners to run along with the dogs until they reached the summit. It wasn't as difficult as the three-step series of the Blueberry Hills to Shaktoolik, but it was a tough climb nonetheless. As they struggled, Lainey realized that coming through before dawn was the perfect time. She shed her parka to keep from sweating. She didn't envy others coming behind her arriving in the heat of the afternoon; their dogs would suffer from overheating.

At the summit, she hopped back aboard the sled, and they began a leisurely descent. She could see the lights of Elim. It was after eight in the morning; they had been on this stretch of trail for just over five hours. The leg to Golovin was only twenty-eight miles. *Should I snack the dogs and blow through or take the six-hour break I scheduled?* Had she come through in the afternoon, waiting for nightfall would have been the plan to give the dogs a chance to cool down. Such wasn't the case, and her team looked ready for bear.

The checkpoint was at a state-run maintenance garage. Lainey pulled up and signed in.

"Staying?"

"Nope. Blowing through."

The checker nodded and made a notation. "Had a good run then?"

"Better than some." Once the vet had checked her dogs, she picked up her food drop. That would see her through to White Mountain. It seemed silly to have a food drop at the Golovin checkpoint, which was such a short distance away. Between Elim and White Mountain was the one small checkpoint and only fifty miles, so she hadn't sent anything to Golovin.

After the drop was packed, she went up the line with treats, booties and ointment, moving on autopilot as she greeted each animal with affection and food. She ascertained the health of each dog, heaping praise upon their furry heads. Bonaparte surprised the hell out of her by licking her face. Lainey blinked at him in shock but didn't pursue the issue, not wanting to get his back up. *He must be as tired as I am to allow his regal manner to slip.*

She brought the team back to the checkpoint.

"Lainey Hughes!"

A volunteer skidded forward, holding a white envelope, and Lainey smiled.

CHAPTER FIFTY-FOUR

Lainey,
Remember our twenty-four in McGrath? When I woke up, I was wrapped around you. I couldn't help myself. I've dreamed of holding you like that for months. I can't wait for you to meet me in Nome.
Our room is tucked into the back of Beth's house. I'm looking forward to sharing the bed with you. No parents, no little brothers or sisters, no dogs, no race to prepare for. Just you and me in our private hideaway.
I don't plan on stopping next time.
Hurry!
Scotch

Swallowing hard, Lainey gripped the handlebars of her sled. Her knees felt weak from the rush of arousal pulsing through her body. No matter how tired she was when she arrived, she vowed to get a shower and brush her teeth before going to bed. There was no way she would have the willpower to interrupt Scotch's waking her again. She carefully put Scotch's latest note with the others, stomping on her rampaging libido. Now wasn't the time to get sidetracked. She forced herself to pay attention to the trail.

They promptly headed back out onto sea ice. Even when she heard a deep booming crack, she didn't falter. She had more important things to consider—like getting to Nome and jumping Scotch Fuller's bones. "Stop that!" she said aloud, a smug smile on her lips. Used to her occasional outbursts after so long on the trail, Samson grinned at her from his position. She returned it.

After only a couple of miles, the trail pushed inland and upward. The gradual climb brought them near forest that cut the wind. As they mushed along, Lainey almost imagined they were back on one of the familiar trails of home. Protected from wind, the trail wasn't drifted over. Two miles farther they pulled out of the tree line, reaching the top of a ridge.

Lainey's notes specified *"Great View,"* underlined in bold. Since they were traveling on level ground, she called the dogs to a halt. Granted, they hadn't gone very far, but she gave them a small snack anyway. She was considering blowing through Golovin too, pushing through to White Mountain. Better to give the team frequent rest breaks now than exhaust them before the end of this run.

As they snapped up the whitefish, she took in the scenery, glad it was daylight with good visibility. There was a hefty cloud cover but also occasional bald spots of blue sky. Scotch had underestimated; it was an awesome view. In fact, Lainey thought she could see a musher on the ice in the distance. She got out her camera and took photographs, then snapped one of the dogs as they rested, watching her. The camera safely stowed away, she pulled the snow hook.

They remained on the ridge for about a mile and then dropped down into a valley. There were no trees here. Lainey missed them. Another incline towered before her and she urged the dogs onward and upward. This climb was shorter in length than the last but steeper. The trail had been used recently, the only indication that someone had left Elim before her. At least she wouldn't have to pack it down for her dogs. It topped out on a saddle called Little McKinley. From there she could see the next checkpoint on a rocky peninsula. Lainey stopped her team long enough to accommodate her obsession by taking another photo.

The downslope turned out to be more difficult than the climb. As they began the run, she only braked enough to keep the sled from running up her wheel dogs' butts. At the first turn, however, she realized how fast she was going when the sled nearly tipped over. Shades of the Dalzell Gorge came to mind, and she stomped on the brakes and brake pad to force the dogs to a crawl. It was a good thing that she did. The next three or four miles proved precarious as she fought twisting trails, glare ice, side hills and even bare ground. Eventually the trail leveled out, and they continued on a gentle decline into a creek valley and toward the sea. Again they dropped onto the ice, this time in full view of Golovin. The solid trail helped them make excellent time along the bay and up onto the peninsula.

There appeared to be no official checkpoint, at least none Lainey could see. She mushed the team right into the center of town, stopping at an Iditarod sign. An old fellow came out of a building, zipping up his parka, a clipboard under his arm.

"Welcome to Golovin," he said. "I've got your time in at ten fifty-three a.m. and thirty-two seconds."

Just under two hours. And White Mountain was only eighteen miles farther on. Lainey signed in.

"If you want to stay, I can guide you to Semko's backyard. He's down the street a bit, on the left."

Smiling, Lainey looked at her team. None had lain down, letting her know that she could probably push them a little further with no repercussions. "What do you think, guys—take a nap or go home?"

All the dogs had learned "go home" in the course of their training. It indicated they were almost finished and heading for the kennel for food and rest. Scotch had told her to use the command sparingly on the race trail. Ultimately, it was a fake-out to keep the dogs moving that extra little bit toward their destination. If used too often, the team would know it for a lie and would not give her the added effort necessary to reach her goal.

Chibee and Montana yipped and the others shook themselves, tails wagging.

"I think that answers that question. Let me snack them and then I'll check out."

She gave them each a chunk of frozen salmon and a quick examination of their paws and wrists. It was somewhat underhanded to trick them like that, but it would be foolish to take a break here and then the mandatory eight-hour break just a couple of hours down the trail. Lainey knew anyone coming behind her would do the same. In ten minutes, she was mushing out of Golovin.

Even with it nearing noon and the temperature heating up, the dogs had an easy run along a straight and well-established path. The trail was so even, it took some time for her to realize they had left the sea ice behind and were working up a river valley. They soon began a gentle series of climbs and drops, edging farther along the river as they went. Eventually the trail swung to the right, and Lainey could see the town of White Mountain on the river bank. Trail markers guided her to the checkpoint right on the bank of the Fish River beneath the town. She checked in a little after one in the afternoon. Her team had run for a full eight-hour stretch and still seemed in good spirits. At least they weren't as tired as they had been on their last monster crossing. After a good lunch, they promptly snuggled into their straw beds.

Lainey was as tired as they were, though the tantalizing promise of seeing the end of her journey kept her energized. She gathered wet gear and her sleeping bag. The checkpoint building was a couple of blocks away, just like in Koyuk. There she had slept outdoors to avoid other mushers divining her plans. Here, it made no difference; everyone checking in at White Mountain was required to cool their heels for eight hours. Times in and out were publicly posted. No one could cut their time short to get a jump on the competition.

The building was a combination city hall and library that also boasted a kitchen. Several people lounged about, some sleeping in corners as they awaited their departure time. As much as Lainey wanted to join them, she went directly toward an area draped with clothesline, where she hung dog booties and a pair of boot liners to dry.

"I'm whipping up fried egg sandwiches," a familiar voice said. "You want one?"

Lainey spun around. "Ben?"

Strauss grinned at her, a spatula in one hand. "Does that mean yes?"

"Yes!" She gave him a hug, not surprised at the tears in her eyes. *God, I need sleep.* Hastily wiping her nose with some tissue she pulled from her pocket, she released him. "I'm glad to see you."

"Ditto that." He waved her toward the kitchen.

Lainey tossed her sleeping bag under a table and sat down. "How long have you been here?"

"Came in yesterday afternoon once we figured out about when you were going to be arriving."

His back to her, he cracked an egg into a frying pan. Another volunteer worked at a counter, slathering mayonnaise on slices of bread. Besides Lainey, there were two other mushers waiting to eat. One drowsed in his chair and the other nursed a cup of coffee in silence. Neither looked any more alert than she felt.

"I haven't had time to check the standings. Has Scotch made it in yet?"

Strauss turned and beamed at her. "She sure did. Finished yesterday. She won! A damned close call too."

Lainey wanted to get up and dance but couldn't dredge up the energy. Instead she kicked off her boots with a sighed. "That's fantastic! How close a call are we talking about?"

The sound of sizzling egg turned Strauss back to his pan. "Well, Drew Owens pulled in seconds after Scotch. She had to make up some good time to pass him and Jon Waters."

He flipped an egg, and Lainey's good mood rapidly shifted to impatience. "And?" she urged.

Strauss shrugged. "Well," he repeated, "it was neck and neck between Owens and Scotch. You should have seen the excitement at the finish line! Man, they were screaming and yelling so loud that I couldn't even hear the dogs barking."

Lainey didn't have to imagine it; she had witnessed a similar finish the previous year. Considering this was for first place, it was easy for her to conceive how much of a hullabaloo there must have been. She remembered Drew Owens eyeballing Scotch back at the beginning of the race.

"Anyway, at the last minute, Scotch's dogs put on an extra burst of speed and gave her a near photo finish. She couldn't have been more than five feet ahead of Owens." Strauss slapped a fried egg onto one of the prepared bread slices.

"Knew she'd win one day," one of the mushers said. "Been sayin' it for years."

"I know." Lainey felt pleasure for her friend's success. "I hope I'm there to see it happen again."

Strauss delivered a plate to her, an alert expression on his face. "Think you will be?"

She gazed levelly at him. "Yeah, I think I will."

He nodded in acceptance. "Eat up." He turned to the stove and started another egg.

Lainey knew they would have a long talk in the near future but not until after the race was over and she'd had time to talk to Scotch. Not wanting to dwell on the impending discussion, she ate her lunch, following the conversation as the others continued to chat. When she was finished, she stood and stretched. "I'm going to catch some sleep."

"You might want to wait a little longer for that." Strauss pulled a piece of paper out of his pocket and handed it to her, then sat down to eat. "There's a phone in the other room. You're supposed to call that number."

She gave him a suspicious look. "Is this who I think it's from?"

He considered a moment, chewing. "Tall, blonde and tired?"

"Yeeeeess."

"Yup, that's who it's from."

Lainey smacked him on the shoulder. "You should have given this to me the minute I walked in the door!" She spun around and headed for the phone.

"Uh-uh. I was ordered to make sure you ate first."

A sign next to the phone said that each musher was allowed only fifteen minutes. This was the nerve center of the checkpoint. The statistics board hung on one wall and a white board beside it listed the finishers. Scotch's name was first on the list, her time three seconds different from Owens'. A ham radio set-up hulked on one of the tables, manned by a…woman. Lainey smiled at the word play as she gave the operator a nod. The woman nodded in return, not even pausing in her discussion over the airwaves.

Lainey's hand shook as she dialed the number. She felt ten kinds of fool for being so nervous. This was Scotch, for crissakes! They had been living together for months. There was no reason to be so edgy. As she listened to the line ringing on the other end, she drew in a deep, calming breath.

"Hello?"

Lainey frowned at the unfamiliar voice. *Ben did say this was the number for Scotch, right?* "I'm looking for Scotch Fuller?" She chewed her lower lip. *Did I dial the number wrong? I only have fifteen minutes!*

"Is this Lainey?" The woman on the other end sounded as if she were smiling. Before Lainey could answer, she said, "Hold on, I'll go get her."

It had to be Beth or the unnamed partner. At least Lainey knew she had the correct number. She sat on a folding chair and rested her elbows on her knees. Even with the promise of hearing Scotch's voice, her body had other ideas. Her feelings alternating between shaky nerves and fatigue, she yawned widely and scowled at the floor. A full eight hours here gave her plenty of time for a nap. Waiting a little longer to sleep wouldn't kill her.

"Hello?"

Lainey's petulance washed away at the sound. "Hi there. Congratulations on first place!"

"Thanks. How are you doing?"

"Right now? I'm doing fantastic." Lainey wiped tears from her eyes. "I miss you so much."

Scotch's tone was warm. "I miss you too. What time did you check in at White Mountain?"

Lainey took a deep breath, forcing herself to focus on the race rather than her seesawing emotions. "A quarter after one, give or take. Ben just fed me and gave me your number. When we're done, I'll take a nap."

"How are the dogs doing? I saw you've dropped a few. Anything serious?"

They discussed Lainey's experiences during the race, how her team had managed and which dogs were dropped for what reasons. Talking shop served to ground her flighty emotions, and Lainey soon lost the urge to cry.

"You've still got His Highness?" Scotch asked in surprise.

Lainey's allowed a smug tone to creep through. "Yup. Not only that, but he kissed me."

"Liar."

Her smile widened, knowing Scotch didn't really call the occurrence with Bonaparte into question. "Yeah, he did, and I've got thirteen furry witnesses."

"I bet Kaara was jealous."

"Oddly enough, she didn't seem to be."

"Well, I am. That mutt better steer clear once I get you here."

Lainey grinned and lowered her voice so the radio operator wouldn't overhear. "I think that can be arranged. Don't tell him, but I prefer your kisses to his any day." Scotch's laugh warmed her to her toes.

"That's not saying much, Lainey." Scotch chuckled. "Bon's kisses are better than a dog's."

"Yours are way better than a three-year-old's," Lainey assured her.

"Well, that's a load off my mind."

It was her turn to laugh. "I can't wait to see you again."

"I know. I feel the same." Pause. "If you're going to get any sleep, we need to hang up."

Lainey frowned, toeing the floor with her sock. "I know—" Her voice trailed off into a shared silence that Scotch finally broke.

"I love you, Lainey Hughes."

She felt as if she was going to burst. "I love you, Scotch Fuller."

"Now hang up the phone, and go get some sleep, baby. You'll be here by tomorrow morning."

"Yes, ma'am." Lainey wiped at her returning tears. "I'll see you tomorrow."

"Tomorrow."

She reluctantly hung the receiver on the cradle. Her hand remained on the phone for the longest time, not wanting to lose even that tenuous connection with Scotch.

"You all right?"

Lainey looked up to see Strauss standing in the doorway, his gentle smile a contrast to the concerned lines on his brow. The desire to weep overwhelmed her, and she stepped into his embrace and cried.

She had no idea how much time passed as she vented her exhaustion, worry and relief. There had been a vague sensation of movement, and when she became aware of her surroundings again, she found herself on a couch with Strauss holding her. Embarrassed, her chest feeling hollow and her outrageous mood swings alleviated, she pulled away from him. He offered her a tissue, which she accepted, wiping her face and blowing her nose. "Thanks. I really needed to do that."

"Anytime." His hand rubbed gentle circles on her back. "I know you don't think you have a problem, but what I've said in the past still stands...anytime, anywhere, Lainey, call me."

She smiled. "I might take you up on that." She patted his knee, squeezing the hand that covered hers.

"Are you going to be all right?" His words indicated the here and now, but she knew him well enough to understand the real question.

"She finally said it. She said she loves me, and I said I love her back. I think I just needed to let go of all the crap I've been riding with this week."

Strauss nodded in commiseration. "I know. It's been exhausting for me just following the trail. I can't imagine doing the real thing like you are. You've got a set of balls the size of Texas, girl."

She laughed out loud and blew her nose again. "Thanks. I'll take that in the spirit it was given."

"It was inevitable, you know."

"What was?"

"You and her. You've always loved scotch best."

Lainey burst into giggles. "Yeah, you've got that right."

"On the rocks."

"I suppose I had to come to Alaska to get the right ice for her."

Strauss joined her laughter.

CHAPTER FIFTY-FIVE

After a nap, Lainey felt more refreshed than she had in days. She was certain it had everything to do with her phone conversation and the crying jag. Refusing to be embarrassed by her outburst, she used the kitchen microwave to warm up a meal of chicken and dumplings. As a special treat, she had brought in two pieces of apple strudel that had thawed while she slept.

Six more mushers had arrived while she napped, but all were an hour or more behind her check-in time. The predominant discussion around the table was the weather on Topkok. As she ate, she learned that this was the most treacherous section of the race, surpassing even the Dalzell Gorge in its dangers. Lainey didn't know if it was an indication of her exhaustion or her newfound confidence, but she felt no fear at the scare stories being passed around the room. Nothing would stand between her and Scotch. She had a woman to kiss senseless at the other end of this race and meant to get there to do so.

"You're out of here soon, right?" a woman asked, her plain face rugged with windburn.

"Yeah. In less than two hours." She pried open the tin foil encasing her strudel.

An older man fingered his gray beard. "Bad time to be out there. Nighttime's never good on the mountain. You can't see what you're heading into."

Lainey stood to fetch herself a cup of coffee from a pot on the stove. "Think I should wait until a couple of hours before dawn?" That was the preferred time to depart White Mountain. If the wind was going to die down, it would be after dawn, making a musher's trip to Topkok a lot easier.

The man's expression became sly and a couple of the others smiled at her. "Would you do it if I said yes?"

"Nope." She sipped the strong brew and nibbled at her dessert.

They laughed as Lainey finished eating and dumped her trash. She took her mukluks and slipped them on.

Before she left the kitchen, one of the rookies tailing her said, "Good luck."

"Good luck to you too."

"I'll see you in a couple of hours."

The others guffawed at his boast, Lainey included. "No offense, but I hope not." She waved farewell to the others and left to collect her belongings.

Strauss met her at the door, his hair rumpled from a nap. "Wind isn't picking up any, but it's still going to be a bitch," he informed her. "Remember what Scotch said about visibility."

"I remember, *Dad*." Lainey stood on tiptoe and gave him a kiss on the cheek. "I'll probably be in Nome before you are."

"No doubt. And you'll likely be busy until the awards banquet."

"Very busy." She winked at him.

"Kick butt, Hughes."

"You know I will, Strauss."

When she arrived at her sled, Lainey was pleased to see her dogs rouse themselves. "Hi, guys! You ready to hit the finish line?"

Lainey worked her way up the line, talking to her team as she removed dog blankets and checked them over. Then she dished up dinner. While they ate, she cooked another batch. Chances were good that she would be in Nome for their breakfast, but if Topkok was as bad as everyone said, it would behoove her to have an extra meal or two prepared in case of emergency.

Some mushers went through their sleds and dropped as much weight as possible at this point. Scotch's notes didn't mention doing this until the Safety checkpoint. If something happened on the next stretch of trail, Lainey would rather be going more slowly and have the necessary survival gear. Even hardened veterans had come close to losing dogs, life and limb at this point in the race. As a rookie, Lainey knew to be extra-cautious. What little gear she could afford to lose was set aside for shipment to the kennel. This included extra socks, work gloves, boot liners, her mid-weight long underwear, leftover lithium batteries for the headlamp, extra dog booties and wrist wraps. She almost put the .44 revolver into the pouch but was uncertain whether it could be mailed legally. With a sigh, she eyed the ugly thing and put it back into her bag.

Lainey checked her watch. She still had half an hour to go. She walked down the line, picking up dog plates, then she donned hand warmers and latex gloves. Each dog received a thorough paw massage and ointment application and had booties put on. Bonaparte licked her face again, and she laughed at him. He wasn't acting quite like a puppy, but his regal manner was hovering on the edge of a desire to frisk.

"Who are you and what have you done with Bonaparte?" He yipped and wagged his tail, and her mouth dropped open.

"This is a day for miracles, that's for sure." She hugged him, surprised when he didn't protest the manhandling. "You've been hanging out too long with Chibee."

Her youngster, Chibee, whined in pleasure at hearing his name. Lainey finished her task in amusement, finally getting everything into the sled.

"Ready?" Trace and Montana hopped into position, the others following their lead. "Let's go."

* * *

It wasn't windy in the parking area, but once they had rounded the bend of Fish River, it blew harder. Lainey hunkered over her sled in determination. She had dealt with worse than this, but she also knew she was nowhere near the primary trouble spots on this leg. They followed the river for a short while before turning onto land and heading southwest. Here the ground was barren, the landscape dotted with scrub brush, and trail markers were few and far between. As her leaders followed the clearly visible path ahead of them, the sled jerked and shuddered with the wind, as if she were driving a small car being passed on the highway by speeding eighteen-wheelers. Lainey knew Sholo, had he remained with the team this long, would have never left White Mountain. As much as she regretted dropping him, she was glad she had Montana in the lead now. He seemed to take the weather in stride, slightly turned away from the onslaught of the wind but never faltering.

Their forward motion no longer a concern, Lainey worried about the scarcity of trail markers. She located maybe one reflective indicator every mile or so. Was the wind so strong it had knocked down the sturdy tripods the trail breakers used? As the dogs plodded on, she saw a flash from the ground downwind of her. Barely visible through a minor ground blizzard, a marker lay collapsed in the snow beside the trail. A gust shook her sled and she saw the depression where someone had fallen against the tripod and into the snow, knocking it down. No wonder markers were missing. She had half a mind to put them back up but doubted they would be stable. And stopping for each marker would invariably slow her down to worse than a crawl, giving her competition plenty of time to catch her.

The barren landscape faded into a tree line as they approached a creek valley. Open water gurgled in several places both up- and downstream, with an ice bridge spanning one section. Her dogs took her across the ice, standing water spraying to either side of the sled runners. Lainey winced, knowing her next stop would be to change wet booties. They cut into a river valley with less wind. The Klokerblok River was completely iced over with some overflow. There were two trails there, one on the river with the official markers and another, a private trail, along the right bank. Lainey figured that was the one the locals used when the river was not frozen. In any case, both trails eventually converged, the overland trail dropping down to cross the river and turn left onto the river bank.

The river continued on its own path while her team followed the trail southwest and into another river valley. Her headlamp illuminated a dilapidated building that might have been a cabin at one time. It hardly looked sturdy enough to shelter a mouse now. Overflow from the river surrounded its base, and she could well imagine the frigid interior. Starting a fire in whatever that structure used as a stove would cause the entire place to become a humid, dripping mess. Even so, it was time to give the dogs a break. They had run for several miles without a stop, and the worst was yet to come.

After the dogs were snacked and Lainey had changed wet booties for dry ones, the team followed the Topkok River Valley to the coast. Several miles later, they passed another cabin, this one in better repair. Scotch's notes indicated this was the last shelter between here and the other side of Topkok. Lainey stopped the dogs to test the wind. It was still blowing, though not with much force. From what the veterans had said at White Mountain, that didn't mean anything. The Topkok trail was literally a series of wind tunnels. There was no telling what she would mush into.

"Ready, guys?"

Bonaparte's tail wagged, his eyes carrying an unfamiliar light of devotion. Trace yawned and grinned; this was old hat to him. Montana wriggled in his halter, still pleased at being in front despite the battering the wind gave all of them. The others stood at their places, awaiting her order.

"Let's go."

Past the cabin, the trail took a sharp turn upward as it left the river. As level ground and the nominal protection of the valley dropped behind them, the wind picked up in strength, blowing across them from the right. It wasn't strong enough to knock Lainey over, but she had no doubt such a thing was conceivable. The trail climbed the four-hundred-foot height, following the side of a hill. To compensate for the angle, she balanced her weight on one runner of the sled. She didn't want to roll back down to the river. The wind plucked at her and the sled, maliciously taunting her with the possibility. They reached the ridge and dropped down the other side to cross a creek. Down in the hollow, the wind disappeared. Lainey remembered reading a story by a well-known horror author about a sentient storm that lashed out at an unwary township. She shivered. It almost felt as if something was watching her in the sudden calm. She shook off the sensation, glad her dogs were frisking in their harnesses. At least they weren't spooked.

Again the trail ascended a similar rise, the wind becoming stronger the farther along they went. She helped her team along by pushing the sled, using sheer willpower to keep it balanced on the hillside as they went. The pace slowed, and she peered over the handlebars to see her leaders struggling through chest-high snow. The trail had drifted badly here, and the last musher had gone through hours ago. Lainey was unable to move forward to help them; she needed to keep the sled on the trail. They eventually made the ridge and flew down the other side, the wind not quite dissipating this time. Lainey called a halt, which her team obligingly complied with. The tiny valley screened the worst of the wind, but that didn't mean it wouldn't blow through here. These blow holes were notorious for sudden hurricane-force winds rising and falling with little warning.

Lainey snacked her dogs again and gave them extra scratches and hugs as she checked harnesses and massaged muscles. Her team wasn't so eager now, but none of the dogs appeared on the verge of breaking.

She cheered the team, doting on the more morose ones until they all grinned and yipped at her. Looking up the next incline, she gauged the distance. It wasn't much farther than the two she had already completed. With no vegetation to see, however, she couldn't gauge how hard the wind was blowing there. The trail looked a little more level. She wondered whether her dogs could keep the sled on track while she packed down the drifts with snowshoes. Her dogs sat in their harnesses, watching. She had to get started now or lose whatever ground she had gained. She couldn't afford to let them to think it was a full rest break here.

Lainey climbed aboard the runners. "Let's go."

As soon as they climbed out of the protected valley, Lainey knew they were in trouble. The wind howled around the team, shaking her sled and shoving her dogs into the snow at the side of the trail. The drifts here were worse than the previous ones, something she wouldn't have believed possible, though the side hill slant wasn't as pronounced. Lainey couldn't see the next trail marker through the snow flurries rising to her chest, but she knew her team was cowering before the might of that wind. She had to do something or they would balk where they stood. That could kill them all.

She stopped the dogs, amazed that they heard her over the wind. With quick movements, she donned her snowshoes and slogged forward with dog coats. The slower pace and wicked wind raised a very real danger of frostbite for her and the dogs, and she spent the next few minutes securing the jackets onto her team to help combat their heat loss. When she reached the front of the team, she found her leaders chest deep in a snowdrift. Ahead of them she located one of the markers and breathed a sigh of relief. Her notes indicated there was some concern about losing the trail here; the easier path led toward cliffs, and that was the wrong way to go.

Lainey hooked a dog harness to the front of the tug line and put her arm through it. "Ready?" she called to Trace and Montana. "Let's go!"

She guided them to the trail marker, and from there she searched ahead for the next one. Unable to see it and unwilling to take the dogs farther until she did, she called, "Whoa!" She trudged farther up the ridge, pulling the ruff of her hood close as she peered forward. Several steps later, she saw the next marker and returned to her team to move them closer.

One blustery, freezing foot after another, they made their way to the summit of Topkok. In a couple of places Lainey lost sight of her dogs before she found the next marker. Clouds covered the sky and ground squalls obscured her view. Only a cool head and careful thought allowed her to find her way back to urge the team forward. She had gone a good twenty feet before realizing she was on the downgrade. The wind had lessened, though it was still strong, and it appeared that the trail was clearer. She whooped aloud, her voice lost as soon as it left her mouth, and removed the harness she was using. On her way back to the sled, she played with the dogs, allowing them some time to frolic after their hard work.

"Trace! Let's go!"

The trail wasn't steep, but it also wasn't a laid-back ride. Several sections held nothing but ice, and even her brakes didn't slow them appreciably. It was a relief when they leveled out, though the wind picked up again. At least there she wasn't forging a new trail or fighting to keep her sled upright on a slanted surface. They passed the Kennel Club Cabin, but Lainey wanted to get out of the next stretch of wind before snacking the dogs again. This was considered the worst blow hole of the entire race. She could ill-afford to rest there.

They went out onto a frozen lagoon, the wind having scrubbed the area bare of anything but ice. Her dogs slipped and slid along, their booties giving them little traction on the ice, and the wind pushed them along when they managed to remain upright. Lainey cursed when she stepped off the runners and almost fell flat on her butt. This wasn't going to work for any of them. She called the dogs to a halt and dug out her notes and map, using her body to shield them.

Scotch's handwriting suggested the dune line, though the notes remarked that the going was dangerous because of driftwood and scrub brush sticking out here and there. It would take Lainey a little longer to skirt the lagoon rather than cross it, but that was hardly a loss considering how long it would otherwise take to get her team across the bare ice. The notes also said that the trail on the other side of the lagoon would end up on those same dunes and to stick close to the trail markers when she got there. Decided, Lainey carefully put away the paperwork, mindful not to lose it to a gust and ordered her team toward shore. She still had a two-hour lead on the next musher out of White Mountain. If the winds kept up on Topkok, she doubted anyone would catch her anytime soon.

It took forever to return to the dunes. Going was slow as Lainey let Trace and Montana pick their way along. The wind mellowed, but she kept close tabs on its location. Experienced mushers had been known to get lost in this area, the wind and snow blinding their dogs until they found themselves on sea ice, heading toward open water.

Soon they picked up the Iditarod trail as the markers reappeared along their path. It was heavily marked here to keep the racers aware of the dangers and pitfalls of the uneven trail. A reflector or wildly fluttering caution tape appeared every three feet, and Lainey wished there had been that much care taken to point out the trail on the other side of Topkok. Visibility was much better down here than on the summit, and she was able to navigate the tangled mass of driftwood and brush with little difficulty.

They passed another cabin, this one called Tommy Johnson's in her notes, and the trail filed between the ocean beach on one side and another frozen lagoon on the other. Several miles later they crossed the Solomon River, Lainey carefully keeping to the marked trail. Visibility was decent enough, but the driftwood barrier between the beach and sea was breached by the mouth of the river. If she was going to get lost and head out onto sea ice, this would be the place it would happen.

Once safely past this stretch, they continued their trek. The wind eased even more, and Lainey took the opportunity to grab something to eat. She watched with satisfaction as they neared the Bonanza Ferry Bridge, where the Nome-to-Council road met the mainland from the spit she was traversing. Somewhere north of the bridge was the Last Train to Nowhere, a series of steam locomotives rusting away after their heyday in the early 1900s. In the darkness, her headlamp didn't shine far enough to illuminate them.

They surged up onto the road, which was bare gravel in places. She grinned, knowing they were close to Safety in more ways than one, and urged her team to stay on the shoulder and follow the tracks of other mushers. What wind there was flew up her back, relieving them from the constant cross breeze that had threatened to knock them down. The next ten miles were a cinch compared to the previous forty. Up ahead there was a bridge that lead into Safety, but the trail dropped down to the left. From there it rose to the other side and deposited Lainey and her team at what looked like a warehouse. They had made it to the Safety checkpoint.

CHAPTER FIFTY-SIX

"One zero four and forty-eight seconds." The checker marked the time on her clipboard. "You look like you've been sitting in a freezer for the last six hours. How's the trail?"

"Blown over in spots." Lainey signed in. She had to pull her facemask off to talk, and it crackled with frost. "And the wind's blowing fierce on the third ridge and on the trail between the cabins." She opened her sled bag for the mandatory inventory and grabbed a bag of treats for her team.

"Visibility bad?"

"Surprisingly, no." She waited for the veterinarians to finish checking her team. "On Topkok it was bad, but not on the coast."

The checker nodded. "Good. I'll radio that back to White Mountain. Maybe you won't be the only lucky one tonight. We had a couple of mushers pinned at the Kennel Club Cabin for a few hours yesterday."

Lainey followed her normal procedures—feeding, massaging, salving and putting on fresh booties. When she returned to her sled, she donned the racing bib with which she had started. The rest of her gear went into three piles: items to keep, items to discard and items to ship back to the kennel. Only twenty-two miles from Nome, the less weight she carried, the better. Once everything was divvied up, put into shipping bags or piled in the donations pile by the checkpoint entrance, Lainey carefully inventoried what remained. The packet of promotional materials and her mandatory gear stayed with her. She kept only one of the coolers, the one with the team's next meal soaking, and left both of the cookers and their pots to be returned home.

Again she checked the required gear. She had heard of mushers forgetting their axe or the promotional items and having to turn around and mush back to pick it up. No way was she going to give someone the opportunity to pass her because of an avoidable error. She was on the verge of taking the Rookie of the Year award, and any backtracking she had to do would handicap her. Finally satisfied, she checked out of Safety and headed for Nome.

And Scotch.

The trail stayed with the road for half of the stretch, and the wind remained at her back. A lot of snow machine traffic during the winter kept the snow packed here, making this one of the easiest sections Lainey had seen in a while. It wasn't as featureless as the path to Shaktoolik had been, for which she was grateful. An easy trail that didn't involve mind-numbing boredom was always a good thing. Occasional areas of construction spiced things up, and her team veered past berms and dipped into the infrequent ditch.

Ten miles passed quickly before the trail slipped off the road and onto the beach. For the first time in days, Lainey saw signs of civilization on the trail. Headlights from a car moved slowly on the road she had just left, pacing her run as she crossed snow-covered sand. She wondered if it was a press car or an avid fan. At this early hour, it couldn't be anyone else. The car followed the road for the next five miles of her trek, then it went over a bridge while she and her team dropped down to cross the Nome River. Three more miles to go. She could almost taste Scotch, and for a change it wasn't the burn of alcohol in her throat and abdomen. The woman's natural scent mingled with the taste of coffee, French toast and syrup overcame the bone-deep craving she'd had for...forever. The intensity of it washed through her. She breathed deeply. *Nearly there.*

Radio towers loomed to her right, their warning lights blinking, and the car on the road continued to pace her. She heard snow machines buzzing in the distance, coming closer as volunteers came out to check on her. A stupendous grin crossed her face and her dogs echoed her sentiment, tails wagging and a frisky edge bouncing in their steps. Her three trash talkers began yipping at their approaching company, and the team picked up speed.

"Almost there, guys!" Lainey called as she saw the lights of the first snow machine.

Two approached, each carrying two people who waved at Lainey. She waved back and they swung around to tail her. She was glad they were staying far enough back to not overexcite her dogs. Chibee looked like he was ready to make an escape attempt to run with the newcomers rather than his team. The car on the road slowed to a stop, and the trail took a sudden turn off the river and up a steep embankment. On the other side, she saw the familiar view of Front Street, the famous burled arch of the Iditarod finish line bracketing the road ahead. She hadn't ever seen it from this angle. She was so used to the darkness on the trail by now that the flashing police lights caused her to blink. She could tell by the radio logo on its door that the car that had followed her was press.

It felt surreal to travel down this stretch of road. A year ago, she had stood on the sidelines with the racing fans and news crews, taking photos of the half-crazed men and women as they pushed their dogs and themselves to the limit. And for what? A chance to torture themselves for ten to sixteen days over a thousand miles of deprivation? Ill-equipped for the cold, freezing her ass off, she had spent the entire time thinking that the people here were loony while she daydreamed of a Mexican Caribbean gig. Now the thought of an assignment on a tropical beach caused her to break out in a sweat.

She laughed to herself as she directed the team to the shoulder of the road. Here the snow barely covered the pavement, but there was enough on the sides to save her plastic runners, not that it mattered. There were only a couple of blocks remaining in the race. Shredded runners were the least of her concerns, but it was an automatic consideration after months of running dogs.

The lights of the police escort faded behind her as she entered the barricaded chute. Even with it being the wee hours of the morning, people crowded the sidelines, yelling and cheering her on. Flashbulbs went off from all along the route, concentrated around the area reserved for press. She wondered if Howry was there. *Is Scotch here? Did anyone tell her I'm coming in?*

"Trace! Montana!" She hoped they could hear her over the mass of humanity waving their arms and calling to her and her team. "Let's go home!"

* * *

Twelve hours after hanging up the phone with Lainey, Scotch was nursing a cup of coffee at the small Iditarod convention center. Open twenty-four hours a day while the race was on, it looked like an overgrown checkpoint more than anything else. The double statistic board hung against one wall, showing current times in and out of the checkpoints as well as the list of mushers who had completed their runs. Two large coffee urns squatted on a table beside a more svelte pot of hot water, surrounded by packets of creamer, sugar, tea, instant oatmeal and hot chocolate. Three tables had been crammed together in one corner, the nerve center of the Iditarod—two ham radios, three telephone lines and two volunteers. Several smaller tables and chairs were scattered around the rest of the room, occupied by volunteers, veterinarians and fans awaiting the next musher into Nome.

She shared her table with Howry and Miguel, who had left the running of the kennel in the hands of the neighboring Schrams while he awaited the Fuller mushers at the finish line. After a week and a half on the trail, Howry looked bedraggled and grizzled. In comparison, Miguel was more animated, his beard well-trimmed and minus extra baggage under his eyes. Even Scotch was more alert than Howry, who had just come in that afternoon. He and Strauss had split up to better cover both women. High winds and the threat of a blizzard had canceled Howry's bush flight back to Nome, and he had been forced to sit out the last few days as a volunteer at one of the checkpoints. Subsequently, Strauss had been able to catch Scotch's exciting finish before catching a ride to White Mountain. Scotch thought Howry was more angry at missing her winning run than anything else, since the *Cognizance* story was his assignment. She had consoled him with being able to catch Lainey's arrival on film. Strauss had called from White Mountain to say there wouldn't be a flight from there until morning due to high winds. Somewhat mollified, Howry dragged his butt out of his hotel and now drowsed at the table, a mug of hot chocolate at his elbow.

A battery-operated radio sat on the table between them, tuned to the Iditarod update frequency. Lainey had been spotted on the trail outside of Nome, moving at a good clip according to reports. In between mentions of her location and appearance, the reporters in the car chattered about her lack of history in mushing and what they knew of her training. Scotch's name was mentioned fairly often, which brought the conversation to her first place win scant seconds before

Drew Owens the day before. Then Lainey would navigate a pile of brush or move far enough ahead for another remark about her, and the entire cycle would start over again.

It had been days since she and Lainey had seen each other, and Scotch had suffered from withdrawal. After cleaning up and sleeping ten hours, she'd had a huge steak dinner. With those needs satisfied, she had spent the rest of the time feeling empty. Not being on the trail, there was nothing to distract her from the yearning. *How did Lainey get such a strong hold on me? What will become of us? What can become of us?* Lainey would recuperate from the race, pack up her things, and Scotch would be back to the silence and the ghosts. Funny how that seemed so lonely now. Less than a year ago she had had reservations about sharing her cabin with a stranger. Now she didn't want Lainey to leave her to the solitude, something Scotch had always treasured. Despite the heaviness weighing on her heart, she hoped Lainey would stick around for a couple of weeks. Maybe she could talk her into visiting sometime.

Scotch didn't know if she liked that idea any better. Being a part-time squeeze might appeal for the short term, but she doubted it would work in the long run. *Don't forget her alcohol problem. You can't afford to get involved with that instability.* Lainey had said she loved Scotch. Did she love Scotch enough to fight against her addiction? As much as Scotch wanted to do the right thing by insisting on a serious intervention discussion before things got too far between them, she knew it wouldn't happen. Her body and soul ached for Lainey in a way it hadn't for anyone else, not even Tanya.

The radio announced that Lainey was almost to Front Street, interrupting Scotch's brooding over a future that would never take place. She nudged Howry's shoulder to wake him. "Come on. She's almost here." She didn't wait to see if the men followed, pulling her parka over her head as she made her way to the door.

She pulled up her hood and snugged it tight against the cold of early morning, muscling her way toward the finish line. Even at the early hour, the sidewalk was filled with others who had been listening to the broadcast. This far after the early finishers in the race, many would have been asleep, but this was the first rookie arrival and merited more attention than most of the mushers finishing lower in the standings. By virtue of her celebrity—the trainer of the incoming musher, the owner of the dogs arriving, and this year's winner—Scotch was able to make it to the finish line and out onto the street to help stop the team. Just as she stepped out onto the trail, Lainey's team came up from the river and hit the street.

Scotch's heart beat triple-time at the sight, even though she could barely make out who was riding the sled from this distance. A smile lit up her face. The dogs were familiar, and she shook her head in amazement: Montana was in the lead and Bonaparte was still with the team. She would never have gotten that mutt to accept the harness for this long. It seemed like seconds flashed by, and then Lainey's dogs swept under the arch, crossing the finish line. Several volunteers reached out to stop the team before they could continue down the road. Scotch was supposed to do the same, but she completely forgot the animals as she made her way toward the musher.

"I made it!" Lainey yelled at her, to be heard over the applause and cheers. "I made it!"

"You made it!" Scotch picked her up in a hug. They were joined by Miguel and Howry, the four of them dancing next to the sled with everybody watching.

Over the sound system, a race official announced, "Arriving in twenty-fourth place, Number Four, rookie Lainey Hughes for Fuller Kennels, two fifty-five a.m. and twenty-three seconds." More cheers and applause drowned out the speaker, and he had to yell through the microphone to be heard. "Congratulations, Miss Hughes! You're no longer a rookie, you're a veteran, and you've just become the Rookie of the Year!"

Scotch ignored the words, ignored the slaps on Lainey's back from her well-wishers. She kept a tight hold on Lainey, basking in the contact, enjoying what could only be a brief and intense connection.

CHAPTER FIFTY-SEVEN

Once Lainey had finished checking in, she drove the team to the dog lot with Scotch and Miguel on the sled. Miguel took over handling the dogs, chasing Lainey away when she tried to assist. Scotch walked her back to the truck she had borrowed from Beth and whisked Lainey away. Lainey was introduced to her hostesses, stuffed to the gills with a good country breakfast, and sent to the showers. By the time she emerged from the bathroom, smelling of lavender, she could barely keep her eyes open.

Still tired from her time on the trail, Scotch happily joined Lainey in their bedroom. Cuddling with the smaller woman was a balm to her doubt and insecurity. Her worries about their future faded. In no time, the exhausted Lainey fell asleep, Scotch soon following.

Hunger drove Scotch out of the warm blankets a few hours later. After she had eaten, she forced herself out of the house, borrowing Beth's truck to get to the dog lot and check both teams. She had to admit, Lainey had done her proud. Not only had she won the Rookie of the Year award, but she had done a spectacular job with her dogs. All of them appeared happy and healthy and glad to see Scotch. Except Bonaparte. He gave Scotch the cold shoulder, scanning the handlers in the dog lot. She had the distinct impression he was looking for Lainey, as absurd as that seemed.

Her obligations met, Scotch returned to the house to torture herself while Lainey slept. As much as she wanted to wake her and show her exactly how much she had been missed, Scotch sat in the living room with Beth and Danna, rehashing the race with a few of their friends who had come over. After the hundredth time she'd stared wistfully down the hall, Beth plucked the coffee cup from her hand and shooed her off.

Scotch eased the bedroom door closed, glad she'd had the foresight to oil the creaking hinges before Lainey arrived. She waited for her eyes to adjust to the dark room. A dull light glowed around the edges of the curtains. The clock on the nightstand said it was mid-afternoon. Lainey made an enticing lump in the center of the mattress, and Scotch heard a gentle burr coming from the general direction of the pillows. Lainey never admitted to snoring. Scotch thought it was cute. It wasn't loud enough to be obnoxious.

She stripped down to her T-shirt and panties before crawling under the covers. Lainey was sleep-warm and cozy, and Scotch sighed as she fitted her body around the smaller woman. Lainey mumbled in her sleep and stirred, turning to snuggle closer. Smiling, Scotch adjusted herself to accommodate until they lay wrapped about each other. She wasn't tired but closed her eyes anyway to better enjoy the feel of Lainey's arms and legs entwined with hers. This was the place to be, the rightness of their proximity overriding the futility of their situation. Lainey wore only a camisole and panties, and Scotch ran her palm along the bare arm. A smile curled her lips when Lainey hummed in sleepy response.

The temptation was too great. Several months spent sleeping in separate beds took their toll. Scotch slipped past Lainey's arm, caressing her shoulders and neck with a firm hand. Lainey's mumble encouraged her, and she slid down to touch the bare skin where the camisole had ridden up. It was a simple matter to slide a hand beneath the waistband of Lainey's panties and explore what she'd only known in her fantasies. Well, not strictly fantasy. McGrath had given her the opportunity to roam where she hadn't been before. The memory fired her already smoldering desires.

"That feels good," Lainey murmured.

"You're awake," Scotch said needlessly. Her touch became a little more forceful as she cupped the rounded flesh and gave it a gentle tweak.

Lainey chuckled, her lips finding Scotch's pulse point. "Mm hmm." She brought her leg up to cross Scotch's torso. "In more ways than one."

Pleased, Scotch rolled onto her back, taking Lainey with her. One hand remained in place beneath Lainey's panties, the other crept up under the camisole. Her fingers brushed scar tissue. Not shying away, she examined the feel of the thick skin there. She loved everything about Lainey, even this, and she wanted to be sure that Lainey knew it.

Lainey shifted until she straddled Scotch's hips and pushed herself into a sitting position. The blankets fell away and she drew her camisole over her head, grinding herself once against Scotch's belly before tossing the silky material to the floor.

Mouth dry at the vision before her, Scotch brought both hands up to caress Lainey's belly, slipping along the firm muscles of the abdomen to reach the breasts above. The skin was soft and warm, the nipples taut with anticipation, and Scotch wanted so badly to taste them. She squeezed their heaviness, her fingers rolling Lainey's nipples as she enjoyed the soft weight.

Lainey moaned, and her hips moved again. She braced herself against the head of the bed as she rocked slowly, her eyes half closed in concentration. "You feel so good, Scotch."

"So do you." Scotch pushed partway up, leaning on one elbow as her mouth found what it desired. She sighed in pleasure, echoing Lainey's moan as her lips enveloped one of the inviting nipples. Surging upward, dislodging Lainey's grip on the bedstead, Scotch sat up, her hands cradling her lover as she suckled.

Lainey gasped aloud, caressing Scotch's back and shoulders, fingers digging into muscle with a particularly sharp grasp. Then Scotch felt her hair being pulled, dragging her from her conquest until Lainey's lips met hers in a hard, wet kiss that made her forget everything. The next several minutes were nothing but tongues and teeth, sighs and soft grunts of exertion, heated flesh and insistent touches.

The sound of rending cloth roused Scotch from her feelings of ecstasy. Lainey lay on her back, one hand buried in Scotch's hair, the other gripping the headboard again. Scotch was paying homage to Lainey's firm abdomen with one of Lainey's legs hiked over her shoulder as she moved steadily down the luscious body. The torn cloth was Lainey's panties, the two tattered ends gripped in Scotch's fists. The smell of Lainey's arousal was stronger with no underwear to diminish it, and Scotch hastened to get her fill, the ruined garment forgotten.

Her first taste was intoxicating as she tongued the swollen clit, Lainey's cry, the sweetest music she had ever heard. Scotch bent to her task with a purpose, exploring past the protective hood and outer lips to savor all of Lainey. Moaning, Lainey pressed against Scotch's mouth, her hips in constant motion. Scotch settled into place, Lainey's thighs cradling her head, Lainey's hand in her hair as she concentrated her attentions on the sensitive bundle of nerves. Her fingers slick with Lainey's essence, Scotch thrust deep within her lover, relishing how Lainey tasted, how she sounded, how her muscles contracted rhythmically around the fingers that stroked velvet skin. The bed rocked with their exertions, the thump of the headboard against the wall intertwined with Lainey's harsh panting and demands. *God! I'll never get enough of this! Of her!* Scotch thrust deeper, filling Lainey as she teased the tender clitoris with her mouth.

Lainey's orgasm swept over Scotch, and she drew it out as long as possible, not wanting it to end. Her efforts were rewarded by another hitch in Lainey's breathing as she came again, calling Scotch's name. Only when Scotch was certain Lainey couldn't stand another round did she slow her attentions, pulling her fingers from the warmth of her lover. She looked up Lainey's sweat-slicked body to see lazy, satisfied hazel eyes looking back.

"Come here," Lainey rasped, beckoning weakly.

Scotch scooted up the bed and pulled Lainey into her arms. They lay together in silence for several minutes as her lover caught her breath. She felt a fierce ache for Lainey's touch, her soul rejoicing in the afterglow. A part of her hoped that perhaps her lover would decide to remain with her in Alaska, but she knew that couldn't happen. Lainey had a life outside Alaska and dog sledding, a life so much larger than Scotch's.

Lainey drew her hand along the hem of Scotch's T-shirt. "That was magnificent."

"I'll say."

Lainey chuckled. "In a few minutes, I'm going to find out for myself."

"Take all the time you need; we've got three days before the awards banquet."

Scotch closed her eyes as she caressed Lainey's cheek. *When will Lainey leave? Will she only stop back at the cabin long enough to pack?* Her thoughts dumped ice into her blood, cooling her ardor. She must have stiffened because Lainey pushed up on one elbow to peer at her. Not wanting to see her lover's expression, Scotch kept her eyes closed.

* * *

It took a moment before Lainey registered Scotch's body language. What was once warm and pliant had suddenly become stone. Was it the mention of the awards banquet that had caused the retreat? That made no sense. Scotch had been to many an Iditarod banquet. The only difference with this one was that Scotch would be up there as champion. She sat up and studied Scotch. "What's wrong?"

Not looking at her, Scotch shrugged. "Nothing."

The unfamiliar expression on Scotch's face took Lainey several moments to decipher. When she did, her eyebrows rose to their zenith. Scotch's inborn confidence had first drawn Lainey down this trail. After a few months, she had figured out that it came from mushing dogs. By then, Lainey wanted that self-assurance for herself, which was why she had continued to train for the race even in the face of falling in love with her coach. After she had dealt with Lainey's drinking binge, Scotch's self-assurance had seemed stronger, as if the adversity of the situation had strengthened her will. Lainey realized she was witnessing the return of Scotch's uncertainty and diffidence, and it set her back on her proverbial heels. Scotch was afraid—deeply, thoroughly afraid.

Lainey's mind raced with this new information, trying to understand what could put such fear into a woman who regularly spat defiance into the teeth of the Alaskan wilderness. Lainey drew back a little, though not enough to lose physical contact. "Something's wrong." She lightly caressed Scotch's sternum through her T-shirt. "What is it?"

"It's stupid," Scotch mumbled.

"If it makes you feel like this, it isn't. Tell me."

Scotch reached up and captured Lainey's hand, gripping it tightly. With an obvious effort, she forced herself to look at Lainey. "What's going to happen to us?"

Lainey blinked. In her mind, her plans for her and Scotch were a foregone conclusion. The solution she had dreamed up on the trail seemed so right for both of them that she had forgotten she hadn't discussed it with Scotch. A relieved smile crossed her face as she dropped her head to rest it on Scotch's shoulder. "I've got some ideas."

"Yeah?"

"Yeah." Lainey's hand roamed Scotch's skin. "Want a permanent roommate?" Scotch's body tensed, alarming Lainey. Again she propped up on one elbow to peer at her lover. "What? What is it?" Terror shot through her heart. *She doesn't want me.*

"I've had one before. A 'permanent' roommate." Scotch kept her eyes squeezed shut, denying Lainey an opportunity to see inside. "Her name was Tanya."

Lainey frowned. In all the dinner table discussions of the previous nine months, she had never heard the name. Surely if this Tanya and Scotch had been involved, there'd have been some family talk. "How long was she at the cabin?"

Scotch sniffled. "About a year."

Apprehension trickled through her. *She said her name* "was" *Tanya.* She gently wiped a tear from Scotch's cheek. Her voice soft, she said, "Tell me?" The silence lasted so long that Lainey didn't think Scotch would answer.

"We met online. She found me through the Iditarod site after my first year. We spent a lot of time emailing back and forth and talking in chat rooms. She wanted to come out for my next race, be a handler, help with the dogs." A fresh stream of tears dampened Scotch's face, and she swiped at them with irritation. "I shouldn't have agreed to it. She'd never seen an Alaskan winter, didn't have a clue what to expect. She arrived just after spring thaw."

Lainey sat up, taking Scotch's hand and tugging. Scotch reluctantly opened her eyes and allowed herself to be pulled up from her reclining position. Knowing it would be easier for Scotch to speak without seeing her, Lainey scooted behind her and began to gently massage Scotch's shoulders.

Scotch cleared her throat. "It was a good summer. We had lots of fun getting to know each other. She liked the dogs well enough, got along with my family. When training started, she helped a lot, but her heart wasn't really in it." She took a deep breath; it hitched once. "Once the sun started going away, she did too. She didn't handle it well."

That sounded ominous. Lainey didn't prompt her to continue. Scotch had held this in for a very long time. Knowing she had her own confessions to make and recognizing the sheer terror and difficulty of getting the words out, Lainey remained silent, continuing to caress the strong shoulders.

"She started getting depressed, a lot. Sometimes I couldn't coax her to get out of bed in the morning. She'd just lie there for hours, buried under the blankets. When she did leave, she'd go into the village and spend hours at the tavern."

Lainey winced at the sharp memory of her own binge. She rested her forehead on Scotch's neck. *I couldn't have devised a more effective way to hurt her if I'd tried.*

"I didn't know what to do. I tried to tease her, joke with her, get her out of bed and into the world. It became so difficult that some days I stayed away from the cabin all day long." Scotch drew her knees up, wrapping her arms around them. "When the Iditarod came around, she perked up. She'd always wanted to see it. I hoped she'd finally worked her way through the depression, that things were going to improve." Hugging her knees, trembling, she stopped speaking.

Sensing the imminence of something important, Lainey leaned into Scotch's back, wrapping her arms around Scotch's knees. "Tell me."

"We had an incredible time for about three weeks after the race, and then one morning she didn't want to get out of bed. It was the first time she'd shown any depression since before the Iditarod. The sun was coming back soon, so I figured it'd be okay. She'd be okay. Once there was more light, her mood would improve." Scotch trembled, sighed, and leaned back into Lainey. "Rye and I brought breakfast back to the cabin for her. She'd..." A sob escaped her lips. "She'd hung herself on the loft bannister."

Lainey's arms tightened around Scotch in shock, for a brief moment unable to wrap her mind around the statement. *She hanged herself? In Scotch's beloved hand-built cabin? My God! And I thought I was thoughtless.*

Pushing aside the rush of anger for the dead woman who had wounded Scotch so badly, she cradled her weeping lover. As Lainey rocked her, caressed her and murmured words of support, she realized something important about her being drawn to Scotch. She might have been fascinated by Scotch's confidence in the beginning, but it had been Scotch's moments of self-doubt and hesitancy that had kept Lainey intrigued. Those moments of uncertainty and confusion had spurred her to find their cause, and here it stood between them—a stark reminder to Scotch that she couldn't control everything.

Am I any better? Tanya was screwed up for whatever reasons, and they both paid a price. What if I can't stay sober? How can I ask Scotch to put up with my baggage after all she's suffered? Lainey's heart dropped to the pit of her stomach as a wave of craving swept over her. She fought against the imagined smell, taste and burn of alcohol, clinging to her lover as much as supporting her. *I can live without the booze. I can't live without her.*

Scotch sniffled, shifting to climb out of bed. "Damn, I'm sorry. I shouldn't have...I wanted today to be so special and instead I've ruined things."

Lainey hugged her, not letting her flee. "You didn't ruin anything. You needed this." She tugged at Scotch, forcing her to remain beside her on the bed. "And I needed this." With gentle fingers, she tilted Scotch's chin until they were looking into one another's eyes. "I love you, Scotch Fuller, and that's not going to change. I'm so sorry about what happened to you, and I apologize for putting you through hell in November. It must have felt like Tanya happening all over again."

Scotch didn't answer, her eyes skittering away from Lainey's gaze.

Swallowing hard, Lainey gathered her courage. "My turn." Surprisingly, laughter bubbled up at Scotch's alarmed expression, and she grabbed on to the pleasant feeling to soothe her fearful soul. She leaned forward for a brief kiss. "You're not the only one hiding things here. I'm just not as good at hiding them as you are. You already know what I'm going to say—" Despite herself, Lainey's voice caught. She looked away, and stopped to clear her throat. "I've never said this before to anyone. It's not so easy."

"You don't have to say anything."

Lainey caught Scotch's eyes. "Yes, I do. It's the first step, and if I want to have a life with you, I have to take it." She caressed Scotch's tear-stained cheek. "And I so want a life with you." Scotch leaned into the caress.

Her hand dropped to Scotch's shoulder and she took a deep, bracing breath. She reminded herself that she had successfully completed a thousand-mile dog race. "I. Have. An alcohol. Problem." She winced and waited for the fallout. *After the shit she's been through, Scotch won't want me. I'm broken.*

"I know." Scotch smiled gently. "And I still love you. What's the next step?"

Lainey gaped at her. "That's it?"

Scotch sniffled through a light snort. "I told you back in November that there'd be no alcohol brought into the cabin, and you couldn't borrow the trucks to go out drinking. You stuck by that, even though you didn't have to." Her hand slid around to cup the base of Lainey's skull. "The rule still stands, but I think you should talk to Miguel. He goes to meetings twice a month."

Cringing away from the thought of a public declaration, Lainey leaned close, resting her forehead on Scotch's. "I'll...try. I know I need to get involved in some sort of program to get me through this." She closed her eyes, suddenly feeling exhausted. "God, I love you."

"And I love you."

The kiss chased away the emotional fatigue, reminding Lainey that she hadn't had the opportunity to explore previously uncharted territory.

CHAPTER FIFTY-EIGHT

Scotch and Lainey arrived at the massive dog yard near Front Street an hour before sunset. Half of the remaining racers had arrived already, and the impromptu lot rang with the voices of the several hundred dogs in residence. Scotch idly noted that this year's volunteers had done an excellent job with organization and dog care. Other than feeding her team, all other responsibilities for them were out of her hands—at least until they returned home.

Smiling softly, she looked at Lainey. When not engaged in other, more lascivious activities, they had spent the last few hours talking about a future together. *Maybe this can work.* The idea of joining Lainey on a photo shoot during the late spring and early summer months appealed to her. She had never been on a vacation, let alone a working one. In fact, she had never been out of the Alaskan/Yukon area. Lainey wanted to invest her earnings in the kennel and move her home from a little apartment in New Jersey to Scotch's cabin. It all seemed too good to be true.

A pang of anxiety caused Scotch's heart to stutter, a reminder that she had felt this way once before about someone, a situation that had ended in disaster. She felt the smile fade from her face, her brow furrowing as she compared what she had right this moment to what she'd had three years ago with Tanya. At the time, Scotch had been wild and free, in love and happy. Over the intervening years, she had come to realize there had been a level of intimacy missing between her and her former lover, one that she hadn't even realized existed. There had been secrets between them, a holding back of things deep inside. After Tanya's suicide, Scotch had taken the burden of that death upon herself, believing it had been something lacking in her that had caused Tanya to take such a drastic way out.

She felt a nudge and glanced at her lover. Lainey smiled at her, hazel eyes showing light concern at Scotch's expression. Scotch grinned reassurance, taking Lainey's hand in her own. Lainey winked coquettishly and squeezed Scotch's fingers before returning her attention to the path.

It had taken Howry's frank discussion last November to wake Scotch up to the fact that Tanya had been the one with the secrets, the one with a depressive disorder. Her inability to deal with whatever inner demons she carried, coupled with the lack of steady sunlight, had been the problem. If anything, Scotch's gut instinct that something wasn't right between them to begin with had caused her to keep something of herself apart from the woman she had loved.

The dog yard was peppered with volunteers and veterinarians, kennel owners and private handlers. Fans and press gathered along the outskirts, taking photographs and speaking with those mushers nearest the outside edge. She tightened her grip on Lainey's hand, not caring that they were walking hand-in-hand in public. It didn't matter if anyone noticed the love between them. There was nothing to hide and no one to hide from, least of all herself. The baring of souls they had shared had eased Scotch's fears. Even if she couldn't join Lainey on shoots or if Lainey needed to sign on for gigs through the Iditarod season, Scotch knew they would be together in their hearts.

Lainey called out to a familiar team. "Hey, guys! How are you feeling?" Her dogs jumped up from their blankets and straw, barking and frisking at her approach. Lainey laughed, releasing Scotch's hand to trot the final few feet.

Scotch grinned as she watched Lainey's exuberant welcome for her dogs. She frolicked with the best of them, rubbing exposed tummies and wrestling with the roughhousers. Crossing her arms over her chest, Scotch enjoyed the display, amazed at how in tune Lainey had become with her team. *Hard to believe she's never owned a dog.*

It was slow-going, but Lainey eventually made it up to the front of her line. When she reached His Highness, Scotch's mouth dropped open. Bonaparte jumped up, placing his front paws on Lainey's abdomen and stretching his neck to give her a kiss. Lainey shook her head with a chortle and gave him a hug, bending down to accept his licks. "What the hell, Hughes?"

Turning, Lainey laughed at Scotch. "I know! Isn't it weird? He's gotten more and more loving as the days go by. It took about a week for him to break through that holier-than-thou thing he had going." She turned to Bonaparte and rubbed his cheeks and ears as she said, "Isn't that right, young man?"

Scotch didn't know which was more shocking—Bonaparte breaking out of his regal persona or him accepting such…plebeian attention. And accept it he did. *Lapping it up, more like.*

"*Dios*, I never thought I'd see the day."

Scotch turned to see Miguel had appeared beside her, and he was gaping at Lainey. "Ain't that the truth?"

Lainey eventually got Bonaparte to settle down so she could finish greeting the rest of her team, but Scotch continued to stare as Bonaparte watched Lainey with adoration, tail gently swishing straw back and forth.

"I guess he's been waiting for Lainey to get here, huh?"

Scotch chuckled. "Yeah. I think we all were." She grinned at Miguel.

"Ah, so that's it, eh?" He gave a knowing nod. "It's about time for that too."

She felt the flush crawl up her neck. Bumping his shoulder with hers, she said, "Hush."

Miguel laughed as he slapped her on the shoulder. "Congratulations, *chica*. I hope you have a life full of happiness and love."

Eyes on Lainey as she played with Montana and Trace, Scotch nodded. "I think I will."

* * *

Lainey blew out a nervous breath, a puff of steam obscuring her view of the door.

"You'll be fine." Scotch squeezed her hand. "This is the next step. When you're done, we'll go back to Beth's if you want."

She looked at her lover for moral support. "Can we go back now?" As soon as the words had escaped, Lainey closed her eyes and shook her head. In that split second, she imagined the disappointment in

Scotch's expression. That hurt worse than the cloying fear filling her heart. *This was your idea, moron.* She sighed, bracing her shoulders as she reopened her eyes. "All right, let's do this." Taking the lead, she knocked on the door.

A few moments later, the door swung open to reveal a whirlwind in the form of a blonde woman. "Scotch! Congratulations! Come in! And you must be Lainey. I'm Susan. I used to work for Thom years ago." She gave them both a hug, then stepped back and gestured for them to enter. As they passed her, she closed the door behind them, continuing her chatter. "The only way I get to see the Fullers now is to insist they stay here during the race every year. Everyone is in the living room, Scotch. You know the way." To Lainey, Susan smiled. "Congratulations are in order for you, too. Rookie of the Year is a great accomplishment in these parts."

Lainey blinked at the sudden pause, realizing that was her cue to speak. She fumbled for her manners and professional demeanor. "Um, thank you. I couldn't have done it without Scotch's help."

Susan dismissed her comment with a wave, preceding them into the house. "Save it for the banquet, sweetie. You had to have some gumption in you to have made it this far, Scotch's excellent training notwithstanding."

Opening her mouth to dispute the demurral, Lainey saw Scotch smirking at her. "What?"

"Don't bother." Scotch jutted her chin at Susan, who continued to herd them toward the living room. "No one has won an argument with Susan in the twenty years I've known her."

Snorting with laughter, Susan didn't rebut the statement. "Look who's here, people—the stars of the hour!"

The next several minutes were spent in congratulatory hugs and kisses as the people gathered there paid tribute to Lainey and Scotch. The group included Ben Strauss and Don Howry. Miguel and Rye had brought Irish with them when they brought the dog trucks to Nome. Adding to the number were Susan's husband and three children, making it a rambunctious welcome. Both Thom and Helen Fuller were still on the trail as volunteers, though they would be back in time for the banquet.

When things settled down, Lainey found herself crammed onto a small couch with Scotch and Agnar, Susan's husband, a cup of hot chocolate warming her palm. For the next hour, she and Scotch entertained the folks with talk of the race and their experiences on the trail. Throughout the discussion, Lainey found it difficult to look at

Ben, her heart leaping into her throat each time she did. As the hour crept by, she could see he had noticed the disparity in her focus, and his expression had transformed into one of concern.

A knock on the door interrupted the pleasant interactions. The children had long since left the room, bored with adult conversation. As Susan went to answer the door and Agnar hustled to the kitchen to refill the beverages, Lainey felt a gentle hand on her thigh. She glanced at Scotch, getting a reminder that this was a good time to do that for which she had come. Lainey gave her a nod. Fighting off the sudden nausea, she stood.

"Ben, can I speak to you a moment? Alone?"

Startled from his silent thoughts, he blinked. "Sure. I'm sharing a room with Don at the end of the hall."

"That'll be fine." She followed her friend, half-feeling as if she was walking to her final reward. She looked back once, bolstered by Scotch's expression of sympathy and encouragement before Ben waved her into a room.

"Have a seat." Ben shut the door.

Lainey sat at the foot of a twin bed. "Thanks." She looked around at the various toys pushed into the corners sharing space with Strauss' and Howry's baggage. The room obviously belonged to the children.

He settled beside her. "Is everything okay between you two? Are you all right?"

Taking his hand in both of hers, she smiled. "Everything is fantastic between us, thank you." She leaned into him and his arm draped over her shoulders. He had always been her rock, whether in a war zone or the African Serengeti. In Bosnia, he had physically saved her life and had attempted to save it again multiple times in the last two years. She didn't know if he actually was an alcoholic as he claimed, but he believed he was. His offers to sponsor her into an AA program had never wavered, despite her caustic responses. If anyone deserved to know what she had learned about herself on this gig, it was him.

"What's this about, Lainey?"

Her throat swelled, making it difficult to swallow, let alone speak. *This is the next step. You're not doing it for Scotch, you're doing it for yourself...and for Ben.* "I wanted you to know that you're right about me. I'm an alcoholic." She silently waited for his reaction.

His breathing remained slow and easy, and he hugged her with one arm, letting her avoid eye contact as she stared at their joined hands. "You know, I was pretty proud when I got the report that you had made it to Nome, and you picked up Rookie of the Year on top of that. I have to say that this moment outshines that feeling by an order of magnitude." He kissed the top of her head. "It takes a lot of strength to admit an addiction. Thank you for telling me."

The tears pushed past the lump in her throat, and Lainey cried again as her best friend accepted her, warts and all. Intellectually, she knew that his approval of her admission was predetermined, but her emotions had prepared her for rejection, and relief caused her weeping. Having been through this once already with Scotch, she gained control of herself in a just few moments. She released his hand and embraced him. "Thank you for being here. Thank you for your patience. It couldn't have been easy."

"The best things never are." They sat that way for long moments. "So, what happens now?"

A smile broke out on Lainey's tear-stained face. She pulled back to look at him. "I'm moving in with Scotch, probably by next June." She sniffled, wiping at her face to remove the moisture.

"Here." He handed over a box of tissues he fished from a nearby shelf. As she mopped her tears, he said, "What about your career, your apartment?"

She gave a disdainful wave of one hand, tissue flailing. "I'll let the apartment go. I'm rarely at the flat anyway. Most of my stuff is already here." She blew her nose. "I can work out of Alaska just as well as Jersey. Though I might go part-time for a while."

Strauss inhaled, setting his jaw. "You can't give up the booze in a vacuum, you know. You'll need to find a group. I can't sponsor you into one if you're up here." He laid a hand on her shoulder to be sure he had her attention. "The alcohol isn't the only problem. It comes with a set of psychological issues that have to be dealt with. You can't do that alone, no matter how much you might want to."

Lainey pushed away the irrational annoyance. "I know. I'm going to talk to Miguel when we get back to the kennel. He meets with a group twice a month. He'll sponsor me in."

"You sure he'll do it?"

She grimaced at him, pulling away and removing his hand. "You know, it's not always 'your way or the highway,' pal. I may have an alcohol problem, and you may have addressed your addiction first, but I've got a damned good support group going here. I don't have that in Jersey, even with you nearby."

He sat back, brief surprise fading to wry humor. "Good point. I stand corrected." His grin widened at the sudden defusing of her temper. "Just know that I'm always here. If you can't find anyone to connect with here, you call me. I can at least lend an ear when you need one."

Chagrined, she ducked her head, a blush crawling across her face. "Thanks. I'm sorry. I'm just a little edgy."

"After spending the majority of the last ten days alone, you're surrounded by strangers, strangers who think you owe them something because you came in as Rookie of the Year." He shrugged, laughing. "I'd feel edgy in your position too."

Leave it to Ben to see to the heart of it. "Yeah, that's probably it." There was a knock on the door, and she heard Scotch's muffled voice. "Lainey?"

Strauss stood and opened the door. "To the rescue?"

Scotch opened her mouth but couldn't think what to say, gawping for a second.

Lainey laughed, rising to step into her lover's arms. "My knight in shining armor." She gave Scotch a hug. "Watch out, Ben. She'll kick your ass in a dog sled race."

He held up his hands in surrender as Howry called from the living area, "Hey! C'mon! Lunch is on the counter!"

"I trust you'll take good care of her?" Strauss asked.

Scotch smiled, holding Lainey close. "Always."

Lainey rolled her eyes. "Good God. Could you two be any more stereotypical?"

"I get to give her away at the wedding?"

Lainey stared at Ben in shock.

"Of course!" Scotch turned and escorted Lainey to lunch, Strauss' laughter following them.

CHAPTER FIFTY-NINE

The banquet hall looked the same as it had the year before, the only difference being Lainey's vantage point. Last year she had sat at one of the reporters' tables off to the side, relegated to the outskirts of the celebrants and fans. She smiled at the memory, touching her water glass to Scotch's at one of Howry's semi-ribald toasts. Now the Fullers surrounded her, just as rowdy and happy as they had been the year before. The only one missing was young Bon, who had remained in Talkeetna with Phyllis Schram. To Lainey's right, Miguel and Strauss joked with one another, the two having become fast friends since Lainey's revelation to both of them. Across from her, a shy teenaged girl sat beside Rye, slightly overwhelmed by it all.

Servers cleared the table of dinner plates, replacing them with dessert and coffee, or refilling beverages. The general hubbub of conversation ebbed and attention turned toward the stage. Lainey saw the president of the Iditarod committee climbing up to the podium, a woman and younger man following him. As the president cleared his throat, causing a slight whine of feedback, his companions moved to the long table behind him where the awards had been laid out.

"Looks like we're done for another year." A round of applause stopped him and he grinned, holding his hands up for silence. "And we had a bit of an upset for first place. That was one hell of a race, wasn't it?"

A cheer rose from the Fullers' table, echoed by the audience.

"Well, without further ado, I'd like to invite this year's champion up to the stage to get some well-deserved attention. Scotch Fuller! Get up here!"

Lainey gave her lover a quick hug, her smile wide as she watched Scotch approach the podium. Flashes popped as the journalists took photos. For a split second, Lainey was back to a year ago, watching from the dance floor as this gorgeous woman took the stage and wishing she could spend a single night with her. *Now I can spend every night with her.*

Scotch trotted up the steps, her smile vying with the stage lights for the most brilliance. She waved to the audience, getting another cheer, and reached out to shake the president's hand. With the help of his assistants, he handed her a large trophy and an oversized poster copy of the winning check. She already had been allowed to take possession of the new truck handed out every year.

Without thought, Lainey flew to her feet, yelling and applauding. Around her the rest of her table surged upward. It wasn't long before a third of the audience had risen to give Scotch a standing ovation. When the audience settled down and Lainey resumed her chair, tears of joy pricked at the back of her eyes.

Leaning into the podium, Scotch said, "Wow. I'm honored. Thank you. That was terrific."

"So are you, Scotch," a woman yelled from another table, causing a swell of laughter.

Scotch blushed but nodded in the woman's direction. "Thanks." She cleared her throat, set the award on the podium, and leaned the poster on edge against it. "Hold on a sec, I need my notes." She dug through her back pocket until she came up with a handful of index cards, grinning at the smattering of applause. "All right. Here we go. I don't want to forget anybody. Most of you know that it's not just us out there on the trail—there are a lot of volunteers and sponsors throughout the year and during the race itself that support us. Each and every one deserves as much recognition as I do, because I wouldn't be here without 'em."

Lainey listened, charmed as ever with Scotch's public persona as her lover went down the long list of sponsors and donations that had come in over the year.

"...and Bobby and Theresa Coletti from Bedford, Virginia. They and their family visited the kennel last summer, and they donated a year's worth of hard-earned allowances to buy dog booties for my lead dog, Sukita." Scotch nodded at the applause. "The most important thanks go to my family and friends. They started me on this path, helped me overcome the obstacles and put up with a lot of issues over the years. When I call your name, I want you to stand up, got it?" She peered through the lights at their table. "Helen and Thom Fuller, my parents. Rye and Irish Fuller, my siblings. Miguel Sanchez, the best dog handler in the great state of Alaska. Ben Strauss and Don Howry from *Cognizance* magazine."

A swell of applause rose for each person named. Blushing, Rye's girlfriend tried to remain seated, but he insisted on her sharing the limelight. When all but Lainey had been recognized, they sat back down.

"My deepest thanks go to the woman who approached me about doing a series of articles for *Cognizance*. She learned how to care for and run dogs, producing a lot of sweat in the process, and she offered me a glimpse of my future. If she hadn't advocated for me with the magazine, I wouldn't have been on the trail this year. If she hadn't shared the last nine months with me, I wouldn't be who I am. I might have taught her how to run dogs, but she taught me so much more. She taught me how to love." Scotch swallowed. "Lainey Hughes, stand up."

The joyous tears slipped down Lainey's cheeks as she rose. The audience clapped and yelled, drowning out Scotch's voice from the podium. Though she couldn't hear the words, she easily read Scotch's lips as she said, "Thank you."

Nodding, Lainey reached blindly for the back of her chair. Strauss helped her get back into her seat without stumbling and handed her a wad of tissues. Grateful, she blew her nose, once again annoyed at her constant need to cry these days. "Thanks."

"Former Boy Scout. I come prepared."

Lainey gave a watery snort. Clearing her sinuses and drying her face, she looked presentable by the time Scotch returned to the table. Drew Owens' voice droned over the crowd as he accepted his second-place award and began his speech.

Scotch slipped into her chair and took a large gulp of water. Wishing they were alone, Lainey leaned close. "That was mean, Fuller. You made me cry."

Grinning, Scotch took Lainey's hand. "Get used to it, Hughes. I love you. I can't keep that quiet."

"And Scotch—" came a voice over the sound system.

They turned to look at Owens on the stage.

"Next year, you're going down." Hoots and cheers erupted as he tromped good-naturedly down the stairs.

The president watched Owens' departure. "Well, if that ain't a grudge match, I don't know what is. Looks like we're going to have another good race next year, folks."

Once the cheering died down, the awards continued with the third-place winner. The awards ceremony continued for almost an hour as the committee worked down the list of veterans. Most mushers claimed their prizes with a few words of thanks, some a little more long-winded than others. Lainey's attention remained primarily on Scotch, basking in their closeness, listening to jokes and asides about several of the more colorful men and women called to the stage.

"Twenty-fourth place and Rookie of the Year winner, Lainey Hughes!"

Even knowing it was coming didn't keep Lainey's heart from going into overdrive as she froze, water glass halfway to her lips. She was shocked by the display of jubilation as the people at her table jumped up. Warm fingers touched hers as Scotch removed the glass from her hands and helped her to her unsteady feet.

She leaned close, the warmth of her breath brushing Lainey's ear. "Moose."

Lainey pulled back abruptly, staring at Scotch. Then she remembered the opening banquet two weeks ago and the encouragement she had needed to get up on the stage. She shook her head and laughed, taking her notes from the table and walking to the stage. En route, she received handshakes and calls of congratulations. On stage, the committee president shook her hand and passed her a decent-sized trophy cup and an envelope containing her check. She thanked him and started toward the podium.

The president blocked her way, waving to his two assistants. Leaning toward the microphone, he said, "And just to make things more interesting, I'm happy to award the Leonhard Seppala Heritage Grant award to Miss Hughes for the exemplary care she gave her dogs." He handed her a large plaque as a wave of sound welled up from the audience.

It took Lainey a moment to regain her bearings. She looked at the sea of elated people, unerringly locating the Fuller table. By winning this award, she had just cinched Scotch's reputation as a trainer. Even if Scotch never ran another race, people would come from miles away to pay for the privilege of being trained by her.

The applause died down and Lainey realized they were waiting for her speech. She juggled the two awards, receiving help from the president before he backed away. Staring for a moment, she forced her nervousness down and took her place at the podium. "As I was recently reminded, I've faced down a bull moose, so this should be a piece of cake." She grinned at the laughter and catcalls. "My list is much like Scotch's, though maybe not quite as extensive. Let's get on with it then, shall we?"

She ran through the list of people and businesses that had forked over money or equipment to support her bid for the Iditarod. After she finished with the smaller donations, she focused on her friends—and family. *Yeah. They're my family now.* "When Ben Strauss from *Cognizance* approached me about this gig, I laughed in his face. See, I don't do cold." That got another laugh. "I know, right? But I'd been here on a one-day shoot to take photos of this very banquet, I saw someone intriguing, someone with confidence and personality, who had just run her third race and came in at tenth place. Knowing Ben would shoot me down, I suggested Scotch Fuller as the subject of our magazine articles. And this is what I get for making that suggestion. Nine months in the cold." She gave a mock shiver, finding enjoyment at the attention.

"So, top of my list is Ben Strauss. He has saved my life a number of times over the years. Even this one, Ben." She saw him wave at her. "And thanks to my partner in crime, Don Howry, who joined me on this expedition. Little did he know how familiar he would become with a pooper scooper when he accepted the job." Another laugh. *Oh, I'm liking this! Why was I scared to come up here?* "The Fullers opened their hearts and home to me. At times I took it for granted, and for that I apologize, but please accept my sincere gratitude for putting up with me. I know it wasn't easy."

Lainey's gaze fell upon Scotch. "Most of all, I want to thank Scotch Fuller for taking the time to train me. She lent me the use of her dogs—not just second stringers but some of the cream of the crop. She singlehandedly corralled my inner demons and reminded me what true friendship and caring were about. When I first saw her last year, not even in my wildest dreams could I have imagined that I'd be right here, right now. Thank you, Scotch, for teaching me so much more about life and love than I ever knew existed." Lainey swallowed, knowing her eyes were bright with unshed tears. "Thank you."

She stepped back, retrieved her awards and left the stage to applause. The trip back to the table was just as crowded as her departure, until finally she sank into her chair and pseudo obscurity.

"And you call me mean." Scotch's face showed evidence of crying. She wrapped her arms around Lainey, hugging her tight. "I love you."

Lainey basked in the contact. "I love you too."

They embraced until Strauss poked Lainey in the ribs. "C'mon, guys. Get a room."

Grinning, Lainey released Scotch and poked him back. "Now that that's over, let's talk about my next gig."

EPILOGUE

Lainey took off her straw hat and used a kerchief to wipe the sweat from her face. Spending the better part of a year in Alaska had screwed up her internal thermostat. The mercury hadn't even reached eighty-five and she felt as if she was melting into a puddle. *What will it be like in the full heat of summer?*

Villagers with yellow skin and round faces gathered around her, chattering in their native language. One of her guides, Ngawang, stood nearby and interpreted. Visitors didn't often come here; the only ones they had ever seen were distant relations arriving for annual festivals or the military searching for bandits. That the strangers were searching for a rare plant was even more bizarre. The native women, dressed in layered skirts and scarves, smiled nervously as they studied her. Men, being men, snorted at the new arrivals as if to say nothing good could come of such craziness. All of them were much more interested in her companion than in Lainey, having rarely seen her coloring.

Listening to one of their guides with an intent frown, Scotch towered over the small people. Someone made a crude joke about her golden skin and blue eyes, not realizing until the last minute that his words were being translated to the foreigner. The gathering collectively held their breath. Would the woman be offended at the rash words? Instead, she looked across the villagers to Lainey and smiled.

Deciding these strange women were to be honored visitors, the headman urged his wife forward to invite them to a feast. Since the invitation was given to Scotch, she accepted for the both of them.

Lainey grinned at seeing her partner's confidence shining forth. In three months, they would return to Alaska to train for the Iditarod. Meanwhile, there was an entire world to show Scotch. Lainey was looking forward to escorting her anywhere her heart desired.

Bella Books, Inc.

Women. Books. Even Better Together.

P.O. Box 10543
Tallahassee, FL 32302

Phone: 800-729-4992
www.bellabooks.com